P9-DVQ-685
EX
LIBRIS

Romance
Treasury

THE ROMANCE TREASURY ASSOCIATION

TORONTO · NEW YORK · LONDON
AMSTERDAM · PARIS · SYDNEY · HAMBURG
STOCKHOLM · ATHENS · TOKYO · MILAN

These stories were originally published as follows:

ROMANCE TREASURY is published by
The Romance Treasury Association, Stratford, Ontario, Canada.

Story Illustrations by Wes Lowe
Book Design by Charles Kadin
Printed and bound by Kingsport Press Inc.

ISBN 0-373-04109-8

Printed in U.S.A. A109

CONTENTS

Tree of Paradise

Jane Arbor

Donna had been sent to her uncle's banana plantation in the Caribbean to see why a previously profitable portion of the family business had become such a liability of late.

Her uncle sourly blamed most of his misfortune on a neighboring competitor, Elyot Vane, but Donna couldn't agree. Elyot was a dynamo of a man whose dreams—for the estate at least—closely matched her own.

This was more than petty business rivalry—it was an intensely personal battle. And Donna was being forced to choose sides!

CHAPTER ONE

THE BUSTLE ATTENDANT upon the arrival of an aircraft was over. The knot of people behind a rustic trellis barrier had done their waving and shouting of their greetings to the straggle of incoming passengers, who in their turn had gone through Customs and Immigration before being collected or dispersing of their own, and now the modest inter-island, one-runway airport was left to what was probably its customary afternoon stupor.

Officials, quickly divested of linen uniform jackets, strolled and gossiped in their shirt-sleeves; the Bureau de Change closed down; the last of half-a-dozen taxis, disappointed of a fare, revved up and departed; the owners of the boutiques in the duty-free annexe came out to sit in front of their gift counters and fan themselves, and the air-conditioned restaurant-cum-bar had only three customers—Donna, sitting close under the counter with her back to it, and a yard or two away two men also turned from it, elbows rested backwards against it as they talked over their long drinks.

For the nth time since she had taken refuge from the sizzling heat coming off the tarmac outside, Donna glanced at her watch.

Four thousand miles of Atlantic flight behind her, and Bran hadn't had the common courtesy to be on time to meet her! Her plane had been punctual and he—or Uncle Wilmot—had been airmailed as to when it was due. Yet neither of them was here, and she was going to give them just another ten minutes, or as long as it took her to finish her iced grapefruit juice, before she telephoned the Louvet Estate to demand why!

Her order had itself taken twenty minutes to be served, at the hands of the single waiter who was now making a tour of the tables, wiping them clean of non-existent stains and furnishing them with cutlery or china by making individual slow journeys to the back quarters of the restaurant for each piece he required. He moved at the rate of a walker in a slow-motion film, and as she watched his leisurely, mobile-hipped progress, something clicked in Donna's memory, a phrase forgotten from childhood until now—"Larayan time."

Larayan time. At eight years old, she remembered asking what it meant, to be told it was the island's kindly tolerance of unpunctuality. Mere "time" was unexpectedly prompt time; Larayan time could be anything up to an hour of tardiness, and would still be forgiven. For who, on age-old, seasonless, tideless, all-summer Laraye, need hurry unduly? Except, perhaps, from an earthquake, a hurricane or a volcanic eruption, none of which had been more than unfulfilled threats for many years. To achieve Larayan time for any lesser urgency was, by the island's judgment, good enough.

Donna straightened her face to gravity as she saw that one of the two men had noticed the half-smile which the memory had brought to her lips. His brows had lifted, as if in question that the smile had been meant for him or his companion. So she looked away. Meanwhile she felt a little kindlier towards her cousin's or his father's delay of welcome to her. They had both lived in Laraye for so long that to all intents they *were* Larayans, with easy-going habits to match. Perhaps their car had had a puncture or they had been held up in traffic. She would give them a little longer than her threatened ten minutes.

She sipped her juice and found she was listening to the talk of the two men, having no scruples at doing so, and listening in to strangers was not eavesdropping, but mere idle interest in one's kind. Nor were they troubling to keep their voices down as they discussed local conditions and people and seemed to understand each other in unfinished sentences and meaningful shrugs or nods.

She studied them when they weren't looking her way; decided they were colleagues of a sort and that the more formally dressed of the two—wearing a jacket and collar and tie and owning a bulging briefcase—might be travelling by the next plane due, and that the other one was seeing him off.

The latter—the one who had met her smile—was the taller. His hair was reddish-brown, making a curved eave above his broad brow and a thick club-cut at his nape. His shoulders were wide and athletic-looking; his hips narrow by contrast. His clothes were those which she was to come to recognise as almost the Larayan male uniform known as the "shirtjak"—the tailored shirt, worn open-necked and over trousers, and of almost any hue or pattern under the sun. His eyes, Donna noticed, ranged through a whole gamut of expression as she watched the two talk—deep interest, amusement, emphatic agreement, casual acceptance, but no boredom.

A pretty vibrant type, was Donna's mental verdict on him—and she realized with a sharp stab of dismay that she was no longer merely listening in. She was eavesdropping.

For she had heard a name that was familiar to her—Louvet, the title of her uncle's banana plantations. And then his name—Torrence—which was also her own. The two were discussing him and the estate in no complimentary terms and, affronted by their criticism, Donna kept straight on with her eavesdropping, feeling it was justified in view of her involvement.

The taller man had said, "I doubt if Louvet has turned in a decent consignment these last two years. Not that Torrence could seem to care less."

The other man said, "Can't the Growers' Association do something about it? Discipline him, or at worst, expel him?"

"No affair of theirs, as long as he pays his whack and goes on nominally growing a crop. While it is a banana land and Torrences own it, he can let it down as he pleases."

"Well, if he has no success with bananas, why doesn't he switch? To aubergines or pineapples or avocadoes? Or even sell out?"

"If he cared, there's no reason why he shouldn't make a go of bananas. Louvet marches alongside Marquise, and there's nothing to choose between them as to land. Anyway, he's too hidebound to switch, and too dog-in-the-manger to sell. I know, for I'd willingly add it to Marquise, and have put out feelers for it. But—" a shrug.

"You're not popular, for your success with Marquise?"

The tall man laughed. "An understatement. I'm Ghenghis Khan. Attila the Hun and the original bloated plutocrat. Wilmot Torrence and I don't mix. Or not willingly."

"Well, there's a boy, isn't there? What about him?"

"Estate-wise, he's a non-starter too. A land rock that wants to be in the water, and yearns for the shore once it gets there. Can't settle. Currently he's working for Margot le Conte as a kind of gentleman tourist guide."

"Ah, Margot." The other man seemed to recognise the name. He returned to his questioning. "Why doesn't the parent company—Torrence and Son, isn't it—send out a trouble-shooter to put a bomb under the two of them, I wonder? 'And Son,' for instance?"

"Yes, well, they're only in import now. With Wilmot T. they still have an interest in Louvet, but after sugar failed here years ago, they sold out and went back to England to import sugar and rum, though bananas must now be their biggest deal. A sizeable slice of the land they used to own is now part of Marquise—the *best* slice, one hears, to the green in the eye of friend Wilmot Torrence! And anyway, there isn't an 'and Son' to that side of the family. Just—"

Simultaneously they both looked up and listened to a far-off but gradually nearing hum from the sky. They both set down their glasses. "That will be yours," said the tall man. "It's due."

"Yes. But don't wait for take-off, please."

"I won't either. Just see you to the departure gate." They went out together as the airport personnel, newly dynamised by the imminent arrival of another aircraft, put on its jackets, busied itself at counters, and drove luggage-carriers out towards the runway—the whole operation being as tranquilly conducted as at a country railway station on a branch line.

Donna stayed where she was. In a minute or two she *would* go and telephone. But first she needed to collect her poise, to make sense of a mental jigsaw and to nurse her righteous gall over that obliquely petty gossip. She had become aware of a counter-irritant too—a physical one. Under the thin mesh of her stocking her left ankle and calf were itching in several places; she could see and feel the telltale lumps which meant insect bites, and the impulse to scratch was almost irresistible. She compromised by rubbing her ankle with the toe of her other sandal, which made her look knock-kneed but afforded a little comfort while she pieced the jigsaw.

Marquise. Yes. The huge banana estate which neighboured small Louvet. From time to time it had figured—sourly—in her uncle's letters. As had also its owner's name—Vance, Elyot Vance—which made, didn't it, the taller one of her late companions Vance himself—the self-satisfied, opinionated cock of the walk, with his impertinent thumbnail sketches of Uncle Wilmot and her cousin Brandon, which she would bet he thought clever and dry and caustic! Well, if only he knew what *she* thought of them, uttered in public! And it didn't take much to guess that when he had broken off at the sound of the incoming plane, he had been about to say "Just a girl"—dismissing her, Donna Susan Torrence, as a considerably lesser mortal than the non-existent "And Son" they had seemed to find so droll.

She was almost sorry he had said that he and her uncle didn't mix. For she would have welcomed a chance to cut him down to size. How, she didn't know, but there should be ways... Meanwhile, remembering that at the moment she wasn't too pleased herself with her maligned relatives, she stood up, gathered her hand-luggage and was poised on one leg, giving her ankle a last savage massage, when Elyot Vance reappeared and came across to her, purpose in every stride.

"You're still here." He made a statement of it, then glanced down. "And suffering too, I see."

"Yes, I've been bitten by mosquitoes."

He laughed. "You haven't read the right travel brochures. We have no mosquitoes on Laraye."

"Well, I doubt if I'm being chewed by vampires," Donna retorted tartly. "Do you mind—?"

She meant the question to indicate that he was in her way. But he did not move. "I came back because, if you were still here, I was going to offer you my services," he said. "That is, if you aren't camping here for the night, may I give you a lift somewhere?"

Donna said, "Thank you. But I'm being met."

His brows went up. "Met? You came off the Antigua plane, didn't you? Your friends' timing isn't very good, is it?"

"I was just going to telephone to see if my uncle or my cousin have been held up." She fixed Elyot Vance with a cold eye. "My uncle is Mr. Wilmot Torrence of Louvet," she said.

"Louvet?" he echoed. "Well, well, how one's indiscretions do come home to roost! You—er—heard?"

"How could I help it? You and your friend weren't exactly whispering, were you?"

He shrugged. "Just chatting while waiting for his take-off for Grenada. He's in the spice business. And we weren't to know a recording angel was present. If I thought about you at all, I concluded you were a rather disorientated tourist. Whereas in fact you are—?"

"Donna Torrence. The 'And Son' of 'the other side of the family,'" she quoted.

His glance measured her slight feminine figure from head to toe. "Really? You surprise me. How come?" he asked.

"My father is a fan of Charles Dickens." She was gratified to puzzle him, and then wasn't so pleased when he understood what she meant. She had expected he would need to have the reference explained to him, and he didn't.

"Ah—Dombey And Son who were really Dombey And Daughter? I see. Good thinking, if your father wanted a son, got a daughter instead, and made the best of the situation, as old Dombey *père* did," he commented. "And so you are his 'And Son' partner, are you?"

"I work in the firm as his personal secretary. But I'm not a partner in it," Donna said, wishing he hadn't summed up so acutely her father's disappointment at his lack of a son. Most people, even when they recognised it, had the delicacy to refrain from spelling it out...

"Nor a militant trouble-shooter, one imagines?" she heard Elyot Vance asking.

After his caustic criticism of her Uncle Wilmot, she wasn't going to admit that that, in a sense, was what she was. If he "thought about" her at all, let him discover for himself the part-purpose of her coming out to Laraye! She said shortly, "Of course not. I've come to visit my uncle and my cousin Brandon. And now, if you'll let me pass, I'm going to telephone to them."

"There's a booth just round the corner. I'll wait to hear the result," he offered.

"Please don't."

But he was still there when she emerged from the kiosk to report that their housekeeper, Juno, had said that both Mister and Young Mister were out—Mister, she believed, gone to the library, Young Mister "out on the job." She seemed surprised that Donna should believe she was expected today.

"Then that settles it. I'll have to drive you," said Elyot Vance. "By the way, I don't have to introduce myself? You'll have heard of me, no doubt?"

"Yes. And *from* you," Donna added, "that you and my uncle don't get on. So do you think he would approve your offering me a lift to Louvet?"

"The alternative being your waiting around until they do choose to remember your existence?"

"I could get a taxi."

"Nonsense. There's no need, when our roads are the same and we're neighbours—or as near as makes for neighbourhood on Laraye. So don't quibble, and come along." He glanced again at her purpling ankle. "We'll stop off in the town and get you some repellent spray for any future attacks from our non-existent mosquitoes. Or no—on second thoughts, we won't. It's closing day for the shops in Calvigne. Sorry, no deal."

"That's all right." She went with him to his car, and he put her luggage in the boot.

"We need only skirt the town; then we climb," he said. "I hope you're not nervous of heights, for you'll have to get used to them here. Also to mile upon mile of potholed roads at which old Macadam, the surfacing chap, would turn in his Victorian grave." As the car took a new height he pointed. "Look—the harbour. There's a cruise liner in—there, at the dock, do you see?"

Donna sat forward and noticed that distance and height had made the busy harbour as much of a collection of toy sheds and toy shipping as it had appeared from her incoming aircraft. "We're driving inland and away from the sea all the time?" she asked.

"In a manner of speaking, yes. Though you'd be surprised how, owing to the turns of the coast and the long inlets and creeks, the sea is apt to turn up around the next corner, as it were. At Marquise I'm a fair distance from it, but at Louvet, being lower, you're not much more than a stone's throw from your private beach. You swim, I suppose?"

"Oh yes." Noticing the water-filled potholes in the track and the ridged slither of red mud ahead, "It must have rained quite a lot very recently," she remarked.

A nod. "And that"—the car bounced into and out of a pothole and was manoeuvred expertly through the mud—"that, like the complete extinction of our mosquitoes, is something else you shouldn't take as gospel straight from the brochures' mouth—namely that, year in, year out, it's eternal, sun-filled golden day in the East Caribbean—for it's not."

For a moment Donna was silent. Then she said, "I know."

"A tourist—and you're neither surprised nor affronted by the news?" he mocked.

"No. Because I remember how it used to rain. Suddenly, rather as a child cries, and stops as suddenly. And when it rains almost out of a clear sky or only from one or two clouds, there's a Larayan saying about it. I can't remember quite how it goes—"

It was his turn for silence. Meaning to surprise him, she evidently had. Then he said, "It goes: 'The Devil is beating his wife again.' That is, the Devil losing the fight when the sun continues to shine, and winning it when the rain persists. But how did you know?"

"I told you—I remembered. I was born on Laraye," she said.

He threw her a swift glance. "You were? When?" He paused. "All right, I know it's a question no gentleman asks, but you are young enough not to mind. So when?"

"Twenty-two years ago."

"Then I beat you to it by ten years. And so—?"

"My people went back to England when I was eight. My mother had always disliked the Caribbean, and none of us has been back since."

"Where did you live when you were here?"

"In Calvigne. But there was another house to which I used to be taken to spend the day, and sometimes, for a treat, to sleep there for a couple of nights. It was the original planter's house on the estate. It was all sugar then, of course."

"And it's still there, on Louvet land, though exactly on the border of Marquise." He paused. "Well, that puts a frame round you, so here's one for me. I was born here too. My father was French descended—'Vance' is a corruption of 'Voyance;' my mother was Scottish—hence Elyot. When the French owned Laraye, they were generous with their gifts of land, and my great-great-grandfather's share was Marquise, also under sugar until the trade failed. Both of my parents died in the Calvigne fire which destroyed a lot of the town. But meanwhile my father had gone into banana-growing early, and since I've inherited, I've expanded a lot."

Donna said, "So we've heard from my uncle."

"And if you were listening to all I was saying to my friend Grant just now, you'd have heard that I'd be willing to take over Louvet at the right price."

"The right price as it appears to you—or to Uncle Wilmot?"

"A good question. But I'm afraid the principals haven't got as far as discussing price, owing to the door of prejudice which your respected relative keeps firmly closed."

"Though if he doesn't want to sell, does that necessarily make him the dog in the manger you accused him of being to your friend?" Donna retorted.

"I declare, you *were* listening to future purpose,

weren't you?" his tone mocked her. "But as I understand the epithet, it means the refusal to give up, for stubbornness' sake, something you don't value yourself. So in the circumstances, I stand by 'dog in the manger.' What, for instance, do you know about the Louvet land?"

Donna drew a sharp breath. "I've only just arrived! How should I know anything for it or against it?"

"Sorry." He didn't sound particularly contrite. "What I really meant to ask was whether—news of its present condition having percolated through to Torrence And Son—you were on a mission of inspection perhaps. But that, I daresay, you could tell me is no affair of mine?"

"Yes, well—you're right," she said.

"Right? Then you are—?"

"Right—that it's no affair of yours," she snapped, and waited for the snub to take effect, which it did not.

He only laughed. "Door-slamming on purposeful discussion evidently runs in your family! However, let's not press the point," he offered. "How long, then, are you staying—on holiday?"

She was glad of the switch of subject. For, forced on to the defensive for her uncle's management of Louvet, she would have hated him to know how shrewd had been his guess as to the reason for her open-ended errand to Laraye. She answered him indifferently. "I don't know. It depends—" And before he could ask on what it depended, added, "How far have we to go now? Are we nearly there?"

"Just about. Presently you'll get a glimpse of the sea again—the Anse Louvet, that will be, and then we drop down to your uncle's house."

And drop they did—suddenly and precipitately at a V-fork off the road—down a badly ridged track leading to a wide stretch of crab grass on which Elyot Vance made a big U-turn with the car and backed it up to the side wall of the house, a long, over-verandahed bungalow which faced outward to the Anse Louvet, the tiny bay below from which it took its name.

Donna recognised the house from snapshots of it. On cold winter days in England she had often longed to experience the brooding heat from which that shadowed verandah would afford relief if you wanted it. She had pictured the grey-to-pink of tropical dawns, and sunsets over seas streaked green through blue to pure amethyst, and her imagination had heard the high chirrup of tree-frogs which, as a child, until she learned differently, she had supposed were eccentric birds which sang all night. Whenever she had thought about it, she had known an ache of memory of this island. And now she was here again. And the heat was indeed intense. And there was no one of her own to welcome her. And the verandah was shabby, with gaps in its balustrading and the paint of its woodwork cracked, and in contrast with the glare outside, the inner recesses of the house were dark as caves.

As Elyot Vance took her cases from the car and brought them to the verandah steps, a stout West Indian woman—Juno, no doubt—emerged from the shadowed interior. She wore a garish flowered overall, a jangle of bracelets on each bare forearm and a quiff of scarlet ribbon and feathers pinned to her topknot of black hair. She reached for the suitcases, but Elyot Vance eluded her and carried them into the house. As she and Donna followed him in, she stated with conviction, "You not come today, miss. You come tomorrow. Mister say so, so I know." And then, as if accepting the very real fact of Donna's presence, she bared magnificent teeth in a smile and adding, "But you here now. So I go, make room ready for you. Today or tomorrow—what matter?" She disappeared, humming off-key as she went.

As her sight adjusted from sunglare to ordinary light, Donna looked about her. There was no hall; the verandah gave directly into this room through a half wooden, half glass sliding wall. There was too much furniture of mediocre quality; the white distemper of the remaining three walls was yellowing to beige, and in an island which was rich in flowers, still nobody had troubled to arrange any here. It was obviously a room where people lived. But it had no air of being loved.

Watching her, Elyot Vance asked, "So far—up to expectation? Or worse than? Or better?"

She guessed he was testing her reaction to the house, but, on the defensive for it, she pretended to think he meant the impression of Laraye.

"How can I tell? I've hardly seen anything yet," she said, and knew she hadn't deceived him when, on a short laugh, he retorted, "And in the face of the enemy, loyalty is all, isn't it?"

"The enemy? What enemy?"

"The one that I assumed too hastily 'And Son' had come out to face, and got snubbed for my pains. Of course, you're on holiday merely. So may I wish you a good welcome and good swimming and realities which don't let your memories down?"

"Thank you," said Donna. "And thank you for coming to my rescue. How far away do you live yourself?"

"Through the plantations, not very far. By the road, a few more twists and climbs, and my house stands high enough to afford a view over almost the whole of Marquise. How good, by the way, is your memory of the plantations?"

"None. Or very few. I told you, we left Laraye before bananas became the main crop instead of sugar. At work I've filed data on bananas, and invoiced bananas, and hunted lost consignments of bananas, and typed hundreds of letters about them—"

"And slipped on the odd banana-skin, I daresay?"

"Yes, that too," she smiled.

"Without ever having traced a bullhead through its cycle from push-out to harvest and shipment and ripening? All that paperwork theory, and you haven't wanted to know?"

"But of course I have, and I do know the whole process in theory," she defended herself. "It's just that I haven't seen it in practice, and I'm sure that my uncle will rectify that while I'm here."

"Of course," her companion agreed blandly—too evenly altogether for Donna's recollection of his outspoken criticism of Louvet and Wilmot Torrence when he hadn't known she had overheard. But she couldn't very well pick a fresh quarrel over a mere tone of voice into which she may have read more irony than he had intended, and even surprised herself by realizing that she didn't really want to quarrel with him—as long as he didn't deliberately provoke her.

She watched him as he left her to go back to his car; liked his athletic stride, the carriage of his head, the purposeful way he moved—physically attracted to him, yet guardedly hostile at the same time. It was a curious contradiction, this—being halfway to liking someone, yet resenting both his effect on her and his casual indifference to what she thought of him!

He got into his car, turned it, but at the sound of another car coming down the steep slope where two couldn't meet abreast, he halted and waited until the other—a slightly battered estate car—lurched into view and was pulled inexpertly to a jolting stop by a driver who could only be Donna's uncle, a lean, narrow-shouldered figure, wearing spectacles and a flop-brimmed Panama hat. He would have known her as a baby, but they had never met since, and in the snapshots she had seen of him he had never appeared younger than he did now, nor had he ever been photographed in any but just such an ancient hat.

She stayed where she was, curious to see how the two men would greet each other. They did it with exchanged nods across the width of their cars; whatever the other man said briefly brought her uncle's glance sharply towards the house. Then Elyot Vance drove on, and Wilmot Torrence got out of his car. He was carrying a bundle of books in an ill-secured webbing strap, and as Donna ran down the verandah steps to meet him, the strap slipped and the books cascaded at their feet.

With an exasperated "Tchah!" he stopped to grope for them before he addressed Donna with a slightly aggrieved, "Well, so you've arrived. But you were staying over in Antigua tonight—how is it you have got here today?"

She retrieved a book he had missed and handed it to him. "That was *last* night in Antigua, Uncle. I arrived there by jet from London yesterday, and came down by the island plane today."

"I'm sure you were to stay two nights in Antigua," he grumbled. "That would mean you'd have been here tomorrow, and if you hadn't muddled things so, Bran or I would have met you, of course!"

"But of course I know you would," Donna soothed.

"Instead you had to accept a lift from that fellow, Vance. Why didn't you telephone from the airport to say you were there, and then wait for Bran or me to come down for you?"

"I did ring you, and spoke to Juno, who said you were both out. And when Mr. Vance offered—"

"Putting us under an obligation to him, which must have pleased him no end! I suppose he told you who he was—that he's that—that outsider from Marquise?"

To Donna, "outsider" was about as outdated an aspersion as "cad" or "bounder." If her father had used it of anyone she would have teased him, "Oh, Dad, don't be so *square*!" But as she dared not laugh at her uncle in this mood of grievance against both herself and Elyot Vance, she said quietly, "Yes, we exchanged names and case-histories of a sort, and when I knew he was your neighbour, and that I shouldn't be taking him out of his way, I saw no harm in—" She broke off to add impulsively, "Anyway, Uncle, does it matter very much? I'm here now, and *so* glad to be! And do you realise I don't remember ever seeing you in the flesh before? Nor Bran? And what do you think of me? Am I much as you expected—or not?"

They looked at each other in silence. Of him she noted how narrow-chested he was, how bony and old—though he could only be about fifty-five—were his hands; how parchment-tanned he was, how his brows beetled over his shortsighted eyes, and how vague was his scrutiny of her.

She doubted whether, put to the test even a minute or two hence, he could come anywhere near to describing her as she would assess herself. Reasonably slim and long-legged; brown hair, centre-parted and shoulder-length; complexion—fresh?, English?, natural?—she wasn't sure. Eyes, grey-green—she would have preferred them green, but except in certain lights, had to settle for grey; one dimple, and a nose which flattery would call retroussé or tip-tilted, but which honesty knew was merely upturned or even snub. There was nothing at all "rosebud" about her lips; her mouth was too wide; her father often teasingly warned her against stretching it further with laughter...

But in answer to her invitation of "Well?" all her uncle said was, "Well, I've seen your photograph, so I knew what to expect. You've a nice colour and there's a look of your father about you. But all you young girls are pretty much alike these days, with your figures as skinny as laths and your hair straight as rope. I suppose you've seen Juno, and she knows you're here?"

Donna told him yes, and carried some of the books for him into the house. Glancing at their titles, she saw they were botanical treatises and she remembered what she had heard about his hobby—the study of Caribbean flora. Some time she must ask him about it, for if she had ever known the names of the island flowers, she had long forgotten all but the bougainvillea and the poinsettia which everybody knew.

Her room was at the far end of the bungalow, with a little outside stairway of six steps to the lawn below. Juno showed her to it, demonstrated how the window-shutters worked—("But we only close them against the rain,"), turned down the bed, and to Donna's inquiry about a mosquito net, stated firmly, "No need. No mosquitoes on Laraye any more," making it a fact with which there was no dispute.

By the time Donna had unpacked and showered and changed the early dark of the tropics was falling. There had been a golden sunset over the sea, the day wind had dropped and the crickets and the tree-frogs had begun to rival each other's chorus, and hearing them again in reality, she thought, "I never knew how I missed them until now."

She returned to the living room to find the table laid for the evening meal and her uncle on the verandah, drinking a rum punch, with ice and passion-fruit juice, and she chose the same for herself. She had expected that by now her cousin Bran might be home, but when she asked about him, his father's tone made such a grievance of their never knowing when to expect him that she was discouraged from discussing Bran any further for the moment.

He had still not arrived when Juno served their dinner of minced beef and sweet potatoes with a cole-slaw salad, followed by a gateau which owed more to stodgy sponge than to cream or icing. Her uncle ate as if it were a chore which bored him, and Donna found herself wondering whether his obvious lack of interest in food had ever irked his wife, who had died while Bran was a schoolboy of twelve. But perhaps he had been different then. More—alive.

For two people with business interests more or less in common, their talk over the meal was rather laboured. Wilmot asked after his brother and sister-in-law, whether the former had a substitute secretary for Donna, and how the business was doing at the English end. But the answers she gave him led to no expansion of the subject, and her own careful questions to him evoked much the same lack-lustre response.

Poor, was his laconic verdict on the current banana harvesting. As had been the last; as would probably be the next. He couldn't afford the necessary labour force, and once laid off, it got snapped up by the big estates which could "carry" a few bad crops. A combination of sharp practice and inherited wealth could send the owners of thousand-acre estates, like Marquise, laughing all the way to the bank. It was poor, small plantations like Louvet which had no slack to take up when things went wrong.

Donna winced slightly at "sharp practice." Elyot Vance was too sure of himself and hypercritical of other people. But, reluctant to think of him as a cheat, she made no comment, and asked instead about Bran and his particular role on the estate.

"*Bran?*" Wilmot's tone dismissed Bran. "If ever I had to depend on *his* application to the job, I'd be out of luck. Growing bananas—or anything else—isn't his scene, he says, whereas the social one is, it seems. He wants to work for and with people of his own kind, he claims. And at the moment, that means getting on the tourist band-wagon, acting as a kind of freelance guide to the island, for one of the hotel owners—a woman—who runs a tours service on the side. On call by telephone at any hour, if you please—a common taxi-driver, no less!" Bran's father finished in distaste.

Donna suppressed a sigh and abandoned the subject of Bran as being unprofitable to any accord with her uncle. What could she say or ask him which wouldn't lead to yet another sour tirade? Ah, perhaps his hobby—But before she could frame a question, Juno came through from the adjoining room, Wilmot's estate office, where she had answered the telephone.

"Mister Brandon," she announced. "He ring to say he's on late drive with party into mountains. He'll not come home after. He sleep with Miss le Conte instead—"

"He's doing *what*?" exploded Wilmot with a violence of which Donna would have judged his dourness incapable. But Juno only beamed her innocence of an unforgivable *gaffe*.

"He stay at the hotel, like he did before—often. Miss le Conte find him spare room. Back to breakfast in morning, he say," she amended calmly.

"That's better," growled Wilmot. "All right." He let her go, then rose from the table. "Yes, well—it's early yet," he said awkwardly to Donna, "but I daresay you're tired after your journey, and I've got some work to do. So if you would like to make an early night of it, you needn't stay up for me."

Donna was not tired, but though too early as it was for bed, she was not unwilling to escape to her room. She had remembered her little private flight of steps to the outdoors; no one was going to know if she made a small foray into a night that was as warm as an English June day, before she wasted the rest of it—her very first night!—in sleep.

She had not even put on a coat when she tiptoed down the steps and picked her way across the rough grass in the direction of the sea. At the far edge of the grass there was a hedge of russet-leaved crotons; beyond the hedge the land dropped sharply down to the shore, a small crescent of sand, reached by a flight of uneven rock steps, on which the tideless sea lapped and curved, sometimes lazily, sometimes with a surging rush of foam, as if to show that mere wavelets were not all it could muster when it liked. For less sheltered coves than this, the foam warned, it had plenty of menace and rollers in reserve.

Donna went through a gap in the crotons, but did not venture down to the shore. Whenever she had been able to, she loved to swim after dark. But before she swam here she must ask about currents and underwater shelving; for now it was enough to stand and stare—out to sea between the two horns of land which made a bay of the Anse Louvet, up at the velvet of the sky, and at the dark silhouettes of the coconut palms, sturdily rooted in nothing but sand, their trunks aspiring straight to heaven, their fretting topknots of fronds umbrellas for outsized giraffes, no less!

She sighed for utter happiness in the moment. Behind her was an uninspiring house at odds with itself; problems which she had come to Laraye to look at and try to help to iron out if she could; a diplomatic road she would have to tread very warily—all this, with the addition of a neighbour who irked her too easily, yet intrigued her against her will. But probably, with what sounded like a no-man's-land of estrangement between him and her uncle, she would not have to see too much of *him*.

And anyway, she decided on a "high" of enchantment with the warmth and the lovely night and the promise of tomorrow's sun, nothing was going to spoil the magic of this island for her. Nothing at all!

CHAPTER TWO

DONNA WOKE EARLY to the beat of rain on the roof. But after it had stopped abruptly, as at the turning of a tap, she slept again, and when she had dressed and gone through to the verandah, her cousin was already at breakfast there. A used place showed that her uncle had already eaten and left.

Bran, two years her junior, was tall and loose-limbed, with a mop of fair curly hair and blue eyes, both features in sharp contrast to the deep tan of his skin. At sight of Donna he stood to greet her with a peck of a kiss on her cheek, then held her off and said, "Surprise, surprise! If we'd known you were coming yesterday we'd have baked a cake— Instead, I gather you stepped off on the wrong foot with Dad by accepting a lift from our friend and neighbour, Vance? How come?"

"Because," said Donna, "he was at the airport and you weren't, and he offered, after he'd seen me waiting around for nearly an hour."

"Yes, well—we seem to have got the dates mixed," said Bran easily. "Sorry about that. But let's have a look at you. Last picture I remember of you, you were in a swim suit on a beach—rather puddingy, with a moon-wide grin. But you've slimmed down a lot, haven't you? You're quite a gal, though my word, don't you need a tan? How long are you staying? What do you think of our pad? And how did Elyot Vance strike you, *before* Dad had his say? Anyway, come and eat. Rolls and coffee and fruit juice do you? Or do you want eggs?"

Donna declined eggs, took her place at the table and answered his questions in reverse order. Of Elyot Vance she said, "He rather put my back up when I overheard him criticising Uncle Wilmot to another man at the airport, and he was pretty high-handed about refusing to take no to his offer of a lift. Rather sure of himself, isn't he? Enjoys his success?"

"And *how*—and with reason, I daresay," Bran agreed. "More than a bit of the Midas golden touch to Elyot V. Seems he can't go wrong with Marquise, with his work force, with women—Sure you didn't fall flat yourself for the oomph he has for all the girls?"

"Far from it," Donna denied loftily. "He's got 'poisonality,' I'll give him that. But as I told you, he rubbed me up from the start, and I only let him drive me here because he said it was all on his way, and juggernauted me into accepting." She went on to answer Bran's other questions. "I've fallen in love with this place—the situation and the *view*, and swimming from your own private bit of beach—superb! As to staying, well, perhaps for as long as Uncle and you will have me. Or until—" She stopped, not quite sure how to word the truth which ought to come next.

"Until—" Bran supplied for her—"you've learned all you came to find out about Louvet and have enough grisly facts to report back? All right, all right," he soothed as Donna flushed and looked away. "Not so difficult to read between the lines of Uncle George's letters that he and the Company are worried pink, and that you're not his 'And Son' for nothing, eh? Though why didn't he come himself, one is entitled to ask? Why send you on this cloak-and-dagger effort to see what we're up to over here?"

Donna said a little desperately, "Look, I wanted to come. It *is* a holiday for me. But since, as you must know very well, Louvet hasn't been pulling its weight for ages, Father didn't see any harm in briefing me to see if I could find out why. For one thing, whether

Uncle Wilmot has cause for such a chip on his shoulder as he has, and for another, why *you* seem to have opted out."

Bran's hands, clasped behind his head, pushed his head forward in a leisurely nod. "Information straight from the grass roots of your wide experience of us and our land and our conditions, no doubt?" he mocked. "Well, maybe I can save you the trouble of a probe in depth. Dad's grouse is that his heart isn't in the banana industry and never was. And I'm getting out because there's no future in it on land that's in the state that Louvet is and has been for the last three years or so. Waste of energy to flog a dead horse. But you won't have seen Louvet yet, will you?"

"No," said Donna. "But I want to. Could you take me over it?"

"Sorry, no, not today. I've other fish to fry presently. You'll have to wait until Dad shows up. He may be over there now. It lies half a mile or so on, up the hill and on the far side of the road—" Bran jerked a thumb in that direction. "But he's taken the car, it's more likely he's ditched you to go off south into the rain forest on a botanising trip. Anyway, if you can walk, you could take yourself exploring alone."

"I might just do that." Donna added curiously, "What *is* it really about Louvet—apart from your and Uncle's lack of interest? *Why* has it gone to seed when, according to Elyot Vance, the actual land is no worse than that of Marquise, which he says it joins?"

Bran's eyebrows lifted. "There's loyalty for you? You resented having to be obliged to the man when he offered you a lift, but that didn't stop you from discussing Dad and the failure of Louvet on the way!"

"I did nothing of the sort!" Donna disclaimed hotly. "I've already told you I overheard him talking to his friend, which was when he said that about Louvet; not to me." Feeling the exchange was on the edge of acrimony, she changed the subject. "Tell me a bit about yourself," she invited. "How did you get here this morning from this hotel where you spent the night, wherever it is?"

"The Allamanda, Margot le Conte's place at Violon Point. I came up by mini-moke—there."

Donna shaded her eyes, following the direction of his finger pointing outside. "On that? In it?" she queried of the small square truck with foot-high wooden sides behind a driver's seat and a snub-nosed bonnet. "Calls itself a motorised vehicle, does it? You could have fooled me. I've seen hand-drawn dust-carts that could give it points for elegance. Does it go?"

"Like a bomb," Bran assured her. "Eats out of your hand and never turns a hair at the steepest of hairpins—pun, ha, ha. You'll see a lot of them around; they're handy for using on the plantation roads. Anyway, Margot le Conte is too keen a business woman to allow her hire-cars out on private journeys, so I have to have something for transport."

"I see." Donna suddenly laughed. "Guess how Juno announced that you weren't going to be home last night?" When she repeated the message as Juno had delivered it, Bran's own laugh was a shout.

"That—of the cubbyhole under the tiles which Margot almost begrudges me when I've been out on a night tour until the small hours?" he scoffed. "I must take Juno aside and mention that opportunity would be a fine thing—that the great Margot le Conte isn't for seducing by a mere minion like me."

"She's your boss? She owns this hotel, the Allamanda?"

"Uh-huh. She inherited it from her father when she was only eighteen; sacked its manager three years later, moved into his apartment 'over the shop,' and has run it on her own ever since. In five or six years she's made it one of *the* places of the island, and isn't content with that. I came into the picture when she decided that her tourist clients would prefer guides who weren't of the taximan type—chaps they could invite to lunch with them when they were out on day trips, without embarrassment on either side. So into the tours business goes Margot, all sails set. I qualified for the type she was looking for. I know every inch of the island from A to Z. I wanted out from Louvet; the job suits me, and so there you are."

Donna was doing mental sums. "Margot le Conte is still quite young, then? And is she French?"

"Only by extraction. She's from Antigua, born of European and Antiguan parents. English is her language, of course, just as it's ours."

"And is it this success of hers that makes her 'the great Margot?'"

"That, and her ambition, spelt with a capital A. In fact, two of a kind, you might say—she and Elyot Vance. Both of them convinced that there's room at the top for them, if for nobody else. And neither of them wholly averse to making the climb together, according to coconut radio."

Donna tilted her head. "Coconut radio?" she queried.

"Grapevine to you, my love. Dame Rumour."

"Oh—Yes, I remember. You mean they would combine business forces—or what?"

"Or what. Marital forces joined first, one imagines. Business ones to follow. Anyway, watch this space, all agog like the rest of us." Bran stretched and stood up. "Well, I'm off. A cruise ship came in yesterday, and I've got a date with a couple from Milwaukee. Care for a lift into town? I could drop you off half a mile this side of the Allamanda."

"No, thanks," said Donna. "I think I'll swim and then laze. Is it safe?"

"Perfectly." On his way down the steps Bran paused and turned. "Does Dad know that Vance brought you up yesterday?" he asked.

"Yes, of course. Their cars met at the foot of the lane, just as Mr. Vance was leaving."

"And did sparks fly?"

"No. How could they? Mr. Vance had done me a kindness."

"Which would irritate Dad rather than please him. I can hear him—'Under an obligation to the fellow.' Are you sure he didn't say as much later anyway?"

Donna smiled wryly. "In fact he did—word for word."

"How did I guess?" Bran chuckled, and went on his way.

DONNA HAD SWUM and floated and played in water which caressed like silk. It was still only mid-morning and now she lay prone on dry sand, letting it run through her fingers until she drowsed and presently slept.

She woke with a start and sat up. She hadn't meant to sunbathe for long on her first day and her back was beginning to tingle. She might swim again or—at a small sound behind her she turned to look back at the beach steps. Halfway down, on one of them, sat Elyot Vance, forearms resting on his thighs, some object between his hands.

"Oh," she said. "I didn't know—I fell asleep." Odd, she thought, this guilt at being caught and watched while sleeping. And equally odd, the vulnerable inferiority of the scantily clad in face of the fully dressed. Wishing she had brought a towel as a coverall, she stood up and was making a business of brushing sand from her body and legs as Elyot Vance joined her.

"Enter slave, bearing gift," he announced, proffering what he held in his hand.

It was an aerosol can. She took it from him. "What? Why?" she queried.

"For your private mosquitoes, which probably won't trouble you again, once having sampled your blood and found it tastes no better than ours, about which they're blasé by now. I found I had this unused can at home, so you're welcome to it. You spray it around you as a warning."

"Thank you, though in fact they haven't bitten me again, even last night, when I expected I'd be sleeping under a net. But my uncle's housekeeper scorned the idea, and I certainly didn't need one."

"You're making your own entertainment today?"

"Yes. My uncle and cousin are both out."

"Over on Louvet?"

"No. That is, Uncle Wilmot may be. But Brandon has gone to take an American couple on a tour." As Donna was wondering whether she ought to offer the hospitality of coffee or a drink in return for the insect-repellent, its donor said, "Yes, well, it's pay day on Marquise, and I'm taking my manager down to the bank for the cash. I must go. Do you mean to swim again, or are you coming up?"

She told him she must go to the house for some sunburn lotion and going ahead of him up the steps, aware of his critical view of her fiery back and shoulders, she wished again for the protection of a towel or a wrap. Almost any of the boys she knew would have made some such derogatory remark as "Who's a boiled lobster, then?" and have offered to apply the lotion for her. But this man's silent scrutiny merely made her self-conscious, she didn't know why.

He hadn't brought his car down the lane, and when he had left she went in search of Juno, who chided her for courting the sunburn, but was prepared to dab calomine to it with a willing and generous hand.

"You just like all strangers, but you learn in time, Miss Donna—old man sun, he is an enemy till he cook you brown like me," she said, and then, "Mister Vance, he is a good man. Mister Wilmot not think so, but he is good, very good. Pays his men well, build houses for them, send them to hospital when they sick, every time he see me he say 'Hey, Juno' and sometimes take me to Marquise, see my cousin Maria and her man. They are cook and man for Mister Vance, like me, cook for Mister Wilmot," she added in explanation.

This was a more generous assessment of their neighbour than Donna had been given to date. Average it out with her uncle's "outsider," Bran's "Midas" eaten up by ambition, and her own guarded reaction to his brusquerie, and what did you get? she wondered. Public Benefactor Number One, a monster of hard-bitten greed, the beau ideal of women (Bran again!), or the roughshod-cum-cavalier who could antagonise or disarm almost, as it were, in one breath?

But though she would have liked to demand that the real Elyot Vance should stand up, she was reluctant to discuss him with Juno, so with a non-committal murmur that he had certainly shown kindness to her, she switched the subject to Juno herself, to learn that she was a "widow woman," that she had no children, and that she had worked for Wilmot Torrence for "dunna many" years.

Dressed again in slacks and shirt and a coolie hat tied under her chin, Donna found a couple of vases in a cupboard, filled the low one with a spread of hibiscus blossoms, the taller one with sprays of magenta ixora and oleander, and placed them in the living room where she thought they brightened it considerably. Juno, however, serving a cold lunch of chicken and saffron rice soon after midday, disapproved.

"Those hibiscus only good for shoeshine boys, polish shoes. No use in house; dead by sunset every night," she averred in face of Donna's claim that meanwhile they were lovely, and that she wouldn't mind renewing the arrangement every day.

In the afternoon Juno disappeared into her own quarters and Donna decided to follow Bran's directions to the plantation. At the top of the hill, to the left of the road, a whole spacious valley was spread, lush with the dark green of row upon row of banana bullheads—Marquise and Louvet, side by side, the only boundary between them, Donna supposed, being the road which branched off the main one on which she stood, and became a track leading away down-valley as far as her eye could trace it. As she walked down the track, her guess that to her right lay Marquise and to her left lay Louvet was confirmed by a large roadside notice-board claiming the land on which it stood to be *The Marquise Estate. Property of Elyot R. Vance. Estate Manager, M. Couseau*, with a telephone number for the estate office. And as she walked on it became too painfully clear which was prosperous Marquise land, which was neglected Louvet.

Scattered about Marquise, men were working though none were near the road. Louvet, by contrast, seemed completely deserted. On Marquise, where wind and the weight of fruit had caused the main trunks of the plants to lean, they were carefully propped. On Louvet many had leaned, untended, beyond disaster point. Fallen bullheads everywhere added to the natural trash of decaying leaves and fibre which Donna's theory knew was left for the elements to turn to humus for the enrichment of the land. On Marquise every heavy swag of fruit approaching maturity was cosseted against wind and friction and toxic sprays, in enwrapping polythene bags. On Louvet the bullheads also carried fruit, but nakedly, the skins so brown-pitted that they must eventually become rejects, Donna thought.

The pity of it! The waste! Aloud she addressed an absent Elyot Vance. "I see what you mean," she murmured slowly, then bestrode the wide ditch between the track and the ranks of plants, treading trash and stumbling over hidden hazards as she walked down the length of one or two rows.

Conditions were no better further into the plantation. It was obvious that no one cared to keep Louvet in full production for the time that Elyot Vance had mentioned—at least two seasons. Another one in this climate of sun and rain and magically swift growth, and it could be a wilderness, she judged. Yet neither her uncle nor Bran cared enough for it to save it. Only Elyot Vance did, and he was denied it!

On her way back to the road she stopped to look more closely at a new season's plant where so far only the one "flower" it would bear had emerged—the fat, purple, pointed ovoid heavily a-swing at the end of its ropy stem, which wasn't in fact a flower at all, but a collection of bracts, protective sheaths for the embryo fruit.

She lifted a bract to marvel at the group of tiny downturned fingers beneath it; each finger blossom-tipped, each one a banana-to-be. Her imagination hurried the fingers into girth and length and their gradual upturn as they grew, until each group of fingers, emerging daily from its bract, indeed resembled a green open hand attached radially, hand above hand, to the stem which at maturity would be slashed from the parent plant.

Only her reading and her visits to Kew had taught Donna that this was how it was, and naturally she had never seen the cycle through. Nor was she likely to see even part of it here on Louvet, she realised, with no dedicated enthusiast to care that she should, from first ground shoot to harvest. Elyot Vance must know it all, but she couldn't see *him* troubling to act as her mentor, nor indeed herself accepting his patronage. For he would be patronising, she was sure. And caustic—as he had been already—to her ignorance. Besides, to Wilmot Torrence he was clearly the Enemy, and she supposed that that made him her enemy too.

A pity though that he was such a man-shaped man, so—alive. She would have liked to feel turned upon her that concentrated interest he had had for his friend at the airport; now serious, now genuinely amused, instead of the satirical approach he had used to her. She found herself wondering what was his relationship with his equal in success, the legendary Margot le Conte—what it meant to him and in what terms. Bran's assessment had made it sound rather cold-blooded, calculated. But Donna hazarded that Elyot Vance's blood ran coldly only for people who had little but passing interest and curiosity value for him—as she herself had, once he found out who she was. She had never given herself many marks for intuition, but she felt—wanted to feel—that the woman he meant to marry could rouse fire in him, desire, hot blood. Margot le Conte—it was a romantic-sounding name... Would the girl, little older than Donna herself, prove as romantic a figure to match?

As she walked on, past a Marquise acreage which was obviously a nursery for young banana plants, the Devil was massing his clouds again. The air grew heavy and the sudden rain began, at first only pitting the dusty track, but quickly turning it to squelch. The Devil's wife must have given him best, for the sky was totally overcast, and Donna was despairing of shelter when, ahead of her, through the curtain of rain, she discerned a building by the roadside on Louvet land.

She began to run. She would be wet through by the time she reached it, but she had to get out of this downpour. As she neared it she saw it was too solid an edifice to be, as her dim view of it had suggested, a packing and sorting station for fruit. It was a square, two-storeyed house, and suddenly for Donna a childhood memory stirred.

It was the sugar plantation house which Elyot Vance had said was still there, on the border between the two estates. He hadn't said that it was still occupied, and as she reached it she saw how forlorn and dilapidated it was, how cobwebbed its windows, how blistered and peeling its ancient paintwork.

It would be locked, of course, but the overhang of its upper floor balcony would afford some shelter. She ran in under it, shook herself like a spaniel, and tried the front door. It wasn't locked, and gave creakily to her push on it.

The inside door stood open to rooms which were thick with dust and rubbish, and they smelled musty. A back door gave on to a small walled courtyard. A staircase, some of its treads broken, led to the upper floor. Donna remembered none of it as it was now. She thought there had been a garden and a stone sundial, and that the balcony had been at the back, instead of at the front, facing out over what was now Marquise land. And then—it was built of wood throughout—it had been gaily painted in gypsy reds and greens. It had been as novel to her as if fashioned from gingerbread.

Although the rain had stopped and she meant to make her way back, hotfoot, to the bungalow, she went upstairs for a cursory look round. She crossed a room to the floor-to-ceiling window and found she hadn't to slip its catch to open it. She stepped out on to the balcony, took a step or two towards the outer balustrade, and didn't realise what was happening underfoot until it had.

With a tearing, splitting sound the flooring had given way beneath her weight. Too late to step back on to what may, or may not, have been sound boards, she went down into the V-gap of the broken ones. The V opened to the depth of her own height, and for a sickening moment she thought it would let her fall straight through. But at its point it held by what felt like mere splinters, leaving her in the ludicrous plight—if it had not been so frightening—of being upright with her back against one arm of the V, facing the jaggedness of the other, her feet down to the broken wood at its point.

She could get out. She *must* get out! But her cautious reach forward to the jagged arm only broke away more wood, and her attempt to turn back, in order to claw at the flooring behind her, caused the weakness at the point of the V to splinter further. If she did manage to turn, and it gave completely, she would be left hanging by her hands until she fell... She stayed where she was, not moving.

She felt sick with self-blame. She should have realised the state the woodwork would be in, unpainted and unpreserved against weather for years, it seemed. And how was she to be rescued? And when? Men were still working in the Marquise plantations, but they were too far off to hear her shout. Perhaps when they knocked off work some of them would see her if she signalled with—yes, her coolie hat would make a big flapping. Gingerly, hardly daring to risk the movement, she untied its strings, held it by one of them and waited.

Her shirt was sticking painfully to her sunburned back, and her slacks were clammy about her legs. Would those men out there work until sundown? If so, that was hours ahead! And supposing even then, none of them used the road?

But she hadn't to wait hours. At first, from the direction from which she had come, there was the sound of a motor vehicle, then the familiar sturdy shape of a jeep. Careful not to move otherwise, she waved the hat frantically, and the jeep stopped.

The driver was Elyot Vance. After he had jumped down he stood for a moment, staring. Then at a big stride he came over to the house. Donna heard him begin aloud, "What the—?" Then he went in under the balcony and she heard him run up the stairs and approach the open window.

Over her shoulder she called back, "Don't step out. The floor is rotten!" To which his reply was a terse "Obviously," as he knelt to crawl forward, feeling his way. The floor held, as it had done for her to that point, and when he reached her he ordered, "Turn round and face me."

"I—I can't. I've tried. If I move, I shall fall through."

"You must turn, and help yourself by holding on to the edge while I take the rest of your weight to haul you up. Now!"

She turned. The frail wood at the point of the V broke at the thrust of her scrabbling feet, and the jagged edge of the flooring crumbled again before she gained a firm hold on it. But the strong hands under her armpits upheld her as their owner, still kneeling, edged slowly backward, inch by inch, drawing her heavily with him until she too was able to kneel on firm wood, facing him.

While he had pulled she had looked at him and seen in his taut jaw and clenched teeth and glittering eyes something of the fire which his cool satirical outward bearing masked. But it was no smoulder of passion, nor even of physical effort. His tone left her in no doubt that it was a blaze of anger which drove him to his intensely breathed, "May the gods give me patience! That anyone could be such a fool—" He broke off, as if words failed him.

Still kneeling, Donna looked down at her clasped hands, trembling from shock and mortification. "Meaning me," she murmured, not making it a question.

"By the fool? Who else? If you'd gone right through and down, you might have been killed, or broken some limbs at least!" he retorted.

"I—I might have fallen on my feet, like a cat." It was a poor attempt at lightness which he scorned.

"Cats have unique fall mechanisms," he snapped. He stood and took both her hands to draw her to her feet. Without releasing her he went on, "A wooden house—*wooden*, in this climate!—standing derelict for years, and you choose to investigate, clamber about it—Why, the very state of the stairs could have told you what to expect of an open balcony, fully exposed to the weather! For pity's sake, come in off it while some of it's still underfoot. What were you doing down here anyway—alone?"

She followed him into the dusty room through the window and he slipped its catch shut. She explained, "I was exploring Louvet, and when it began to rain heavens hard, I saw this place and I ran for it. As soon as I got near, I knew what it was, even though it looked different—and smaller. But no one except you had mentioned it to me, and *you* hadn't said how long it had been derelict and rotting. So how was I to know it was dangerous?"

"'Nobody told me.' Famous last words," he mocked. "I'd have expected you to be canny to the sight of those stairs, not to mention the stink of dry rot in your nose. However—what's the damage? Are you hurt?"

"Only bruised, I think. And this—" She turned the outer side of one wrist to him to show a long angry graze.

"H'm. You'll need to watch that, keep it clean and covered. And you're still wet through." His hands had reached to feel her shoulders, and he allowed his touch to travel down her body to her hips. His glance ran down the line of her slacks to her knee, where a T-tear gaped, then lifted to her rat-tailed hair in an assessment of her woebegone condition which was as clinical and dispassionate as a doctor's. For a moment she wondered wildly whether she would have rated more sympathy from him if she had indulged in a fit of the vapours, whatever they were. But she decided not. The man was a cold fish who enjoyed putting people in the wrong and then blamed them as fools for being there. Well, anyway, as fools whom he was forced to rescue from their own folly. So where *was* his alleged attraction for women, eh, Bran?—an attraction which she had experienced initially herself, but wouldn't again while, bored, he looked at her and through her without really seeing her at all. And now, she supposed, he would dutifully round off his second bout of knight-errantry in two days by insisting on seeing her home!

He didn't trouble to insist. He took it for granted

that he would. When they went out to the jeep he lifted her bodily by the waist and dumped her on to the bench seat beside him, turned the vehicle and drove back up the track. Presently he remarked, "So your uncle sent you alone to look at Louvet? What do you think of it?"

"He didn't send me. He'd gone out before I was up this morning." Donna hesitated between loyalty and candour. And as she guessed loyalty would only make for argument, she chose candour. "It—it's pathetic, isn't it?" she said.

"It's more than that. It's near-criminal," he said grimly. But that was all. Donna was silent too, knowing he was right.

At the top of the lane to the bungalow she told him he could drop her there, and began to thank him. But he said, "No. If your uncle has returned, I'd like a word with him. If not, perhaps you'll tell him I shall look in again?"

"You aren't going to make trouble, I hope?" she ventured, as the car standing on the crab-grass was evidence that Wilmot was at home.

"Just as much trouble as the situation calls for." He braked, alighted, helped her down and made for the verandah. "Go and get out of those damp things," he added. But she stayed when she saw that Wilmot was sitting on the verandah, a glass of punch beside him on the table where he was extracting leaves and sprays of foliage from small plastic bags. He stood as they approached. "Ah, Vance," he said coldly, and sat again. "And Donna—where have you been?"

It was Elyot Vance who answered for her. "She's been exploring Louvet," he said.

Wilmot's brows went up. "With you?"

"No. She walked over on her own. Did you know she intended to?"

"Of course not. We haven't met since last night."

"Then I suppose I can't blame you for not warning

her about the state of the Dial House, but the fact remains that she went into it to shelter from the rain, and might well have been killed or badly injured when the balcony caved in as she walked out on it. Fortunately it held long enough until I happened by and was able to help her free. But that was her good luck and yours." Elyot suddenly exploded. "For Pete's sake, man, just how long do you mean to leave the place standing to rot away? Are you hoping that one day it will crumble to shavings before your very eyes, saving you the trouble of doing anything about it, or what?"

Wilmot blinked at this attack and looked at Donna. "You shouldn't have—You should have realized—"

"Of course she should. But she didn't." The words rapped out. "And no credit to you if she had. That menace—bang-on to our boundary road; no trespass board nor danger sign; doors and windows unbarred; open to the idle curiosity of any passer-by, and what about the risk to children? What about that?"

"There should be no children about there. They have no right on my land."

"No? Well, they have on mine—with their mothers, my women workers who can't leave them at home. Try telling an adventurous toddler not to wander, as we do constantly—still, sooner or later one of them or a bunch are going to make it over to the Dial—and then where might you find yourself in the matter of culpable negligence—tell me that?"

"The house is on my land. No one has the right to trespass into it," Wilmot maintained doggedly.

"When it doesn't boast so much as a fence or a gate to keep them out?" His opponent's gesture was contemptuous. "Try making that plea in a compensation court and see where it gets you!" He paused, then added in a less aggressive tone, "Look, man, *why* haven't you done anything to put the place together or raze it, until now?"

"Because I have neither the money nor—"

At that Donna was moved to put in, "Oh, Uncle, I'm sure the Company could bear the expense, if you would—"

Wilmot ignored her. "Nor," he repeated, "the available labour, as you, Vance, should well know, since you absorb it all at wages which I can't pay. What's more, may I ask whether you've jumped to conclusions on the condition of the Dial only from today's mishap to my niece?"

If Elyot saw the intended trap, he discounted it. "Oh no," he admitted. "I've inspected it thoroughly before now. I assure you, no jump."

Wilmot pounced. "Then you've trespassed yourself, but haven't seen fit to approach me about it until now?"

"That's right." The agreement was bland, almost good-tempered. "I've trespassed, but the place is your property, it's on your land, and protest was pointless until an accident happened. Now it has."

"And now—?" Wilmot invited.

"And so, protest, of course."

"Which you've made—"

"—And an offer to meet you. If, as your niece suggests, Torrence and Son will carry the cost, I'll personally see that you get the men and the tools. How's that?"

"To destroy the place?"

A shrug. "That's for you to decide. Though"—Elyot Vance glanced at Donna—"I imagine that for old times' sake, your niece would rather it were restored. She remembers it from her childhood, she says."

"And if I refuse to be 'met' in the way you suggest?" Wilmot demanded.

"Then I'm afraid it's ultimatum that you do something yourself, lest the Growers' Association should see fit—"

Wilmot stood again, drawing himself to his full lanky

height. "Are you *threatening* me with action by the Growers' Association, young man?" he questioned.

"Far from it." The other's smile was disarming. "I'm merely a humble member of the Association, and you're another, neither of us with a say in the high-ups' decisions on sanctions. But if you won't accept help from your own Company or from me, alternatively why not persuade your son that he could do worse by you than to take off his shirt and collect a few of his cronies to take on the job in their ample spare time?"

Wilmot was almost gibbering. "Thank you," he said. "When I find myself in need of advice from you, I'll ask for it. Until then—"

Elyot's nod appeared to accept the sweet reason of that. "Any time," he said, and to Donna, "Get in there and change, and have Juno bandage that wrist"—an order which she did not obey. As he turned from them both, he added to Wilmot, "Meanwhile, my offer remains open—indefinitely," and went down the verandah steps.

"You may consider it closed—definitely," Wilmot called after him, and sat down, drumming angry fingers on the table edge and muttering.

Donna ventured, "Uncle, I don't think you should have antagonised him so. That house *is* dangerous as it stands, and his offer to provide the men to work on it was generous, you can't deny."

Wilmot erupted. "Trespass! Nosing around! Telling me my own business! Hinting 'or else.' Trying the power game—with me!" He eyed Donna with suspicion. "That's twice in two days that the fellow has wormed his way in here; foisted himself on you first, and then on me. You haven't, I hope, encouraged him, by any chance?"

If Donna hadn't been so outraged by the accusation, she could have laughed. "It so happens," she reminded Wilmot, "that twice in two days he's been there when I needed someone—this afternoon, rather badly. He didn't have to be encouraged to do for me what any decent man would in the same circumstances, I hope. Both times he did it, and I'm grateful."

"Yes, well," her uncle yielded slightly, "I thought you might have been flattered. He has an easy way with women, one understands—"

"So Bran hinted of him as well," Donna cut in. "But I'm not as impressionable as all that, and I do rather object to being lumped together with 'Women' who may have fallen for his alleged charm."

"Yes, well," Wilmot conceded again. "I suppose I can trust you to take care of yourself and keep men like him at arm's length. I certainly hope so, for in Bran's set in and around the Allamanda and the beach clubs, you can hardly help meeting him. Just so long as you don't expect me to welcome him here!" he concluded sourly.

At that Donna felt she had had enough as the present pawn in this bitter long-drawn game between her uncle and his neighbour.

"After this afternoon, do you suppose he'd be overeager to come?" she asked and, getting no answer, went through to her room, feeling defeated and depressed and wondering whose side she was supposed to be on.

When she had discarded her soiled shirt and torn slacks, changed into a flowered shift dress and managed to bandage her wrist herself, she felt a little better.

But what a plunge from her blissful euphoria of last night! Where had the magic gone? The natural loveliness which had inspired her mood then hadn't changed. The sea and the sky, the warmth and the peace were still all there; only today's personal clashes were the despoilers. She hated quarrels, and she hated this old one because, through no fault of her own, it tore her two ways.

Odd, that yesterday she had been unmoved by, had

even welcomed the thought of having to see little or nothing more of Elyot Vance, and yet today she had resented Wilmot's edict against him. Whose side *was* she on, for goodness' sake? Two encounters with the man, both of them weighted against her, yet if he did keep his distance in future, she was actually going to miss a challenge which could be likened to the abrasive rub of sandpaper on the skin—painful, but stimulating at the same time.

So just how illogical, in the space of twenty-four hours, was it possible to get?

CHAPTER THREE

IT SEEMED that Wilmot saw nothing questionable in his having allowed Donna to make her own first foray to the plantation, and whereas in London and on the journey over she had visualised his being ready and willing to give the information which her father would want to hear, it was she who had to ask the questions and then to edit the lacklustre answers so as not to paint too dismal a picture of conditions on Louvet in her first letters home.

Of the Dial House incident she said nothing. Her father probably did not realise it still existed, and her own mishap would only worry him. She mentioned having met Elyot Vance, and for Laraye itself she was full of enthusiasm. There was time enough, she felt, to tell more when she knew more of the complicated issues at stake.

She swam and sunbathed every day; made one tentative suggestion that she might help in the office with paper work for the estate—an offer which Wilmot refused; went down to the town by jitney, the local bus, to shop for Juno in the markets, and at unpredictable intervals had fleeting encounters with Bran, who usually seemed to be on his way to or from somewhere else.

She walked often in the plantation where a few men worked, though not regularly and never, during Donna's first two or three weeks, on the weekly crop-consignment day, when they and their womenfolk defected freelance, to Marquise and other estates to earn more than Wilmot paid them, by helping to harvest and grade and pack and dispatch that week's crop for refrigerated shipment to England by the fleet of white cargo-ships which ran shuttlewise back and forth across the Atlantic.

During those weeks Louvet cropped nothing for consignment. That was how it was, Wilmot grumbled. If you harvested too soon the crop would be rejected as unready; if you left it too late you risked over-ripeness or theft. According to Wilmot the small grower just couldn't win; the titans like Marquise couldn't lose.

Marquise could corner the market in labour. Marquise could afford to spray by air against disease and pests. Marquise could build modern sheds for grading and packing. Marquise could coddle its growing crops in polythene. Marquise could keep five hundred acres in continual cultivation... so what could the small man do against competition like that? None of which seemed to Donna to add up to one good reason for Wilmot's retention of Louvet in face of Elyot Vance's willingness to relieve him of it. But that was an argument which at this stage of her ignorance she dared not put forward.

It was on the Saturday of her third week that Bran suggested taking her to dine at the Allamanda and to be "introduced around." Margot le Conte was giving a cocktail party to the hotel guests and had suggested that he should take Donna along.

"Do we have to go down in the mini-moke?" she asked, fearful for her hair-do and an evening dress in that primitive vehicle.

"No. Dad will let us have the car," Bran promised. "And doll up a bit, won't you? Those American women tourists do rather tend to lay on all they've got by way of window-dressing in the evening. You don't want to look country cousin by contrast."

Meaning *you* don't want me to look country cousin to your friends, thought Donna as she "dolled up" to the best of her ability in one of the lightweight evening dresses she had brought with her. It was of mist-grey chiffon over a satin underslip, the skirt falling from an Empire-style high bodice of silver lurex. She wore silver slippers, carried a silver tapestry bag and piled her hair high under a silver net snood.

Bran approved. Juno did not. "Grey colour—that for old women. Red, yellow, nice pink for young girl like you, Miss Donna. Gay shawl," she advised. Wilmot grudgingly allowed that he supposed she looked "all right." Donna herself had liked what her mirror had shown her, and went out to meet her evening in a light-hearted party mood.

Violon Point was one "horn" of the almost land-locked Violon Bay, one of the show-places of the island. The Allamanda Hotel, a long split-level building behind a many-arched colonnade of latticed stonework, faced the palm-fringed shore on a lengthy frontage. Every balcony on every floor was hung with trails of bougainvillea and morning glory, and the wide lawns behind the building were ablaze with the golden bells of allamanda blossom which gave the place its name. Though it was not long after dusk when Bran and Donna arrived, flood-lamps were already lighting and silhouetting the tops of the palms against the sky, and beyond the range of the lights, the deep jungle green of the surrounding heights had turned to impenetrable black.

"It's quite a place," murmured Donna in admiration.

"And quite a gal in possession," returned Bran. "Come and meet her. She's dying to meet you."

"Dying? She can't be!"

"She says so."

And that, Donna was to realise before the evening was out, was the very essence of the just-that-bit-larger-than-life character which was Margot le Conte.

Her greeting for Donna the stranger was a kiss on each cheek and a murmured, "Darling! Bran didn't say how pretty you are"—a compliment which might have pleased Donna more if she hadn't noticed that almost every other one of Margot's guests, including the men, was made welcome with a similar double kiss and word of flattery, implying a warmth which, Donna decided, Margot couldn't possibly feel for them all.

She spoke by gesture almost as readily as in the deep contralto of her voice. Everything she said or did was touched with extravagance, over-emphasis. With her, a beckoning finger became an imperious movement of her whole hand in her direction. She used it to call servants and guests alike, who, when she had done with them, were dismissed with an equally exaggerated backward wave. She smiled often, showing excellent teeth behind parted full lips. She carried her head on a long slender neck; her features were fine-drawn, her small nose a perfect aquiline; her skin—face, throat, bare arms and shoulders—had the velvet glow of a ripe peach; the heavier side of her black hair hung provocatively forward; her eyes were so dark as to be nearly black. In a bronze sheath of a dress which revealed every curve of her slim body she was as lissom as a yearling cat, as physically delicate as her manner was poised and assured. If she were indeed a tycoon she was a devastatingly glamorous one. In contrast with her, every other female in the room, including herself, had the makings of a country cousin, thought Donna, watching her.

She detached Donna from Bran almost at once, carrying her off in a babble of introductions to other people. It soon became apparent that it was as much a party for Margot le Conte's own friends as it was for her hotel clients, and after a time and some circulation the two sets tended to separate. Presently again some people drifted away to the dining room, others of the locals thanked their hostess and went home, leaving behind a few lingerers from the hotel set and a nucleus of Margot's own friends who had gathered to sit at a long oval table, seemingly prepared to make an evening of it for drinks and talk. Elyot Vance wasn't among them; he hadn't appeared at the party at all, surprising Donna who, after Wilmot's drear prophecy that she would have to meet him in the Allamanda set, had fully expected him to be there.

Meanwhile Donna's healthy young appetite was signalling its willingness to dine, and she looked about for Bran. But he was part of the hard core of the group at the table, and when she failed to catch his eye, she despaired of dinner in the immediate future. Instead she wandered off alone towards the soft murmur of the sea, lapping just below one of the arches of the ground-floor colonnade. She went to lean upon the waist-high stone balustrade where the flowers from the arch on the floor above trailed low enough to form a kind of scented pelmet for this one.

Behind her, people passed and repassed on their way to or from the car-park, but she was left alone to enjoy the night sounds and the sea sounds and the teasing of a tiny breeze until someone halted behind her and waited for her to turn about.

It was Elyot Vance. Without preliminaries he said, "I told myself, 'That's a back view I know,' and it was. How is the sunburn?"

Taken by surprise, she laughed awkwardly. "I've tanned now, and I don't burn," she said.

"And the mosquitoes?"

"They've left me alone since that first day."

"And the grazed wrist?"

"That's better too. You make me sound terribly disaster-prone," she added.

"Well, you weren't exactly among the blest of the gods when we last met, were you?" he countered easily. "But why are you alone? What about the party?"

"It isn't over. I was waiting for my cousin to take me in to dinner."

"Still involved, is he? And you're hungry?"

"Tending that way."

"So let's go and prise him free."

As soon as they appeared Margot hurried over from where she had been standing by the table, her hand on the shoulder of one of her men guests.

She held her arms wide to Elyot and offered her cheek for him to kiss. "Elyot, you're late," she said, and to Donna, "Clever of you to corral him, darling. Where?"

"I found her," Elyot answered for Donna. "Alone, communing with the night, but about ready to start chewing the carpet in need of her dinner."

Margot commiserated. "You poor lamb! I'll call 'Time, gentlemen,' to Bran this very next minute. But you, Elyot, you wretch, why are you so late? I declare, you've been *cinq à sept* with another woman!"

He laughed and pulled a strand of her swinging hair. "When I spend useful afternoon hours with a woman, that'll be the day," he said.

"Before now, you've spent an afternoon with me!"

"Talking business."

"But not *all* the time!" Margot sparkled archly. "Anyway, come and have a drink and I'll tell Bran he must take Donna to dinner—or else!"

But when Bran had detached himself from the group of drinkers Elyot declined a drink. "Maurice Couseau and I had one together at the Yacht Club, and I'm driving," he said.

"You'll dine, though?"

"I'd like to, yes."

Bran looked at Margot. "Then make a foursome of it, why don't we?" he suggested.

Margot hesitated. "Yes, well—" But Elyot took her masterfully by the elbow.

"I'm hungry too, so you'll eat now and like it," he ordered.

The whole length of one side of the dining room was

open to the warm night. Electric fans whirred from the ceiling, and a steel band beat out dance-rhythms at intervals for people to dance between courses. Margot had a word or two with her head waiter, approved the position of the table he offered, and before she sat down, made a tour of the other tables, chatting briefly with each of the guests.

When she rejoined the others Elyot quipped, "The conscientious keeper making sure all his valuable charges are fed and happy, eh?" At which she snapped a finger and thumb smartly against his hand.

"All part of the service, man," she said. "When I make you co-director of the Allamanda, you'll learn how a little bonhomie pays."

During the meal that was the keynote of their exchanges—a slightly brittle scoring-off each other, playfully by Elyot, less so by Margot, whose repartee was occasionally touched with malice. They evidently knew each other very well, thought Donna, envying them a little an association which seemed to shut other people out. Yet how close they really were it was difficult to tell.

The four were waiting for their coffee to be brought when Elyot asked Margot to dance. When they walked out on to the floor they were the only couple on it, and soon after they began to dance it was as if by common consent that they were left to a display which was not far short of exhibition quality.

The syncopated beat of the drums slowed and quickened, repeating phrases over and over, now sonorous, now wailing in the accompaniment to the repetitive words of calypso, all in a perfectly maintained monotonous tempo. And, encouraging and rejecting in turn Elyot's stylised advance and retreat, Margot forsook all decorum in her abandonment to the dance; in turn sensuous, provocative, tempting her partner and repulsing with mimed modesty the implicit invitation of his approach.

Her steps were nothing remarkable, an easy heel-and-toe movement only. All her expression was in her theatrical use of hands and arms, slim body, arched throat and wildly flung black hair. The whole performance became a man-to-woman question and answer, and Donna, fascinated, thought, *To this extent they know each other very well. They've done this together often before.*

The music stopped, their audience clapped them off the floor and several other couples moved on to it. Back at the table, poised and collected again, Margot ordered sharply, "Bran, do your duty by your pretty cousin—take her to dance," but Elyot cut in, "My privilege before a mere cousin," and held out his hand to Donna.

She went with him, dreading the inevitable contrast with Margot's expertise. But to her surprise and half relief, half chagrin that he didn't expect her to compete, he took her in his arms and steered her smoothly through the same old-fashioned slow foxtrot which the older couples were doing. Tactful of him, of course. But a shade belittling, all the same!

Presently Margot and Elyot danced with other people and Bran asked Donna if she wanted to. But she said no, and then urgently, "Bran, what does *cinq à sept* mean?"

He looked at her sharply. "Why, 'five till seven,' of course. You can count to ten in French, surely?"

"Of course I can. But what *does* it mean?"

"In what connection?"

"Well, when Elyot Vance arrived late, Margot accused him of having been '*cinq à sept*' with another woman, and he had to laugh it off."

"Yes, well—" Bran sounded embarrassed—"it's a French vulgarity for accusing a man of spending the late afternoon, say five o'clock till seven, with his girlfriend before going home to dinner with his wife."

"Oh," said Donna blankly.

"What do you mean—oh?" Bran retorted. "Why the surprise? I told you the kind of terms they're on. And you've seen them together."

"Yes, but—"

"And Margot's not the girl to be too delicate about claiming her monopolies, especially with another one there to be warned Keep Out."

"But I was the only one there to hear her," Donna objected.

"And you're feminine and you came in with Elyot, didn't you?"

"Yes, but she couldn't have thought—!"

"That you were any competition? No, probably not," Bran agreed with cousinly candour, adding sagely, "But I imagine women at the top like Margot don't care to suspect anyone of trying to climb their private ladder—anyone at all."

As that dance ended they saw a desk clerk approach Margot, and after speaking to him and excusing herself to her partner, she came back to the table, followed by Elyot. When he waited for her to sit she gestured, "No," adding to Bran, "It's your buddies from Milwaukee. They're flying home tomorrow and they've taken a fancy for a last night-view of the island from the mountains, so they want you to drive them."

Bran groaned, "Oh, *no*! It's my night off duty!"

"And he's been drinking," Elyot put in.

"Only punches, and he's had a meal since. He's all right," Margot ruled crisply. "No, Bran, I've sent back a message to say you'll go. Seems you've wormed your way into their affections and they won't have anyone else. Besides, The Customer Is Always Right."

Bran grumbled, "You said it, ma'am—I didn't." But he half rose, then stopped. "How long for?" he asked.

"As long as they want to be out, of course."

"I see. Maxim for maxim—he who pays the piper calls the tune, eh?"

"Exactly. It's the name of the game of success," returned Margot smoothly. "Go along now. They'll be waiting."

"But what about Donna? Do I take her home first?"

"No, she can stay here until you come back. You probably won't be more than an hour away at most." As he left, Margot added to Donna, "Sorry about this, darling, but it's all business, and you didn't want to go home yet, did you?"

This being one of those questions expecting no for an answer, Donna said it, and Margot went on, "Besides, I want to talk to you. Can you drive?"

Surprised, Donna said "Yes."

"And you've got one of those international licences?"

"Yes. Why?"

"Time on your hands too, I daresay? Not much going for you up there at Louvet, hm?"

"Well—" Donna hesitated, not sure where all this was leading. But as certainly, with Bran so often absent and Wilmot indifferent to her company, she was thrown much more on her own resources and Juno's than she had expected, she admitted she did have time to spare, and again asked, "Why?"

"Because I've been thinking I could use you. How would you like to work for me? Doing the same as Bran—playing guide to my tourists?"

Donna's first reaction was of astonishment and recoil. "Oh, I couldn't," she demurred. "I don't know the island as Bran does, and your roads are pretty hair-raising, aren't they?"

"If you enjoy driving and can, you'd soon get used to them. Besides, all my cars are automatic, and they eat out of your hand. And my idea was that, whenever Bran has only two passengers or one, you should go along with him for a while and learn the island. He tells me you spent some of your childhood here, so you probably will find you remember parts of it. And if, as he says too, you were hankering to come back, how else can you get to explore it in comfort and in company, tell me that?"

That was an adroit argument on Margot's part. Donna had wondered what prospects she had of travelling much farther afield than to Calvigne by jitney or the occasional trip in her uncle's car, and she was tempted. But her memories of Wilmot's disapproval of Bran's defection from Louvet held her back. "You are right," she told Margot. "I've wondered how I could see more of Laraye while I'm here, but I don't think my uncle would care for me to take a job."

"It wouldn't occupy you every day. You would only be on call when I needed you—say, to take out ladies who would rather be driven by a girl than a man. You might make some very good friends that way," Margot urged.

"Yes. Well, supposing I went out with Bran as you suggest, and tried handling a car, and spoke to my uncle, perhaps I could help out when you needed someone. I don't think I'd like to promise more than that," Donna said.

Margot shrugged. "Fair enough. Go out with Bran, make him let you take the driving sometimes and use your eyes and ears when he does his running commentary on the sights. Particularly, get hold of the names of the flowers and the trees and have the life-cycle of the crops—the bananas and the aubergines and pineapples and coconuts—at your fingertips. People pay to be informed, and informed they will be, or know the reason why."

"And you may be sure, with Margot in control, that they *pay*." Elyot put in, in a dry aside to Donna.

"Of course. I'm a businesswoman. But I give value for money by using people like Bran and Donna, instead of taxi-boys, a lot of whom only know the names of things in *patois* and consequently can't even spell them out, since *patois* isn't written," Margot snapped back.

"And when Donna has acquired all this gen do you propose putting her on a formal test?" he asked.

"I'd like to. And you'd like to show off, wouldn't you, darling? Rather fun, don't you think, if I played the dumbest of dumbwits who's never seen a banana or an aubergine except in a supermarket or on a fruit barrow, and thinks orchids are rare hothouse freaks that only rich brides' bouquets can afford?" Margot appealed to Donna, who smiled and agreed, realising she was meant to.

An hour passed; nearly two. There was more dancing—Donna partnered once with Elyot, again in a sober waltz, and with a couple of men to whom she had been introduced before dinner. When Elyot went to the bar with a friend, Margot took Donna to see what she called "my modest pad"—her private apartment on the top floor, the decor and furnishing of which were exotic in the extreme.

Margot took her leisure in a twenty-five-foot salon, glass-panelled all along the seaward side; sunbathed on a screened verandah, bathed in an emerald green marble sunken bath and slept in a king-size bed under a white satin canopy in an all-white bedroom. Though Donna found the whole effect rather overwhelming she murmured in suitable awe, "It's terribly *luxe*," to which Margot replied complacently, "I planned it that way. I'm a bit of a *luxe* person myself, and I do need the best of everything around me—you know?"

She had sat to comb her hair at the dressing-table mirror when Elyot came up to say that Bran had telephoned and that he had taken the call. "He's in trouble," Elyot announced.

"Trouble?" Frowning, Margot swung round on the stool. "What?"

"Not serious, and not his fault," Elyot assured her. "It seems he's had a difference with a jitneyful of revellers, the driver among them, on their merry way home from a Saturday night hoedown. The jitney had stopped—to put down some passengers, Bran supposed—just ahead of his car. But instead of going on when it did start up, it charged backward on to his bonnet and tried to climb it."

"Tch, the fools! Is our car damaged?" Margot demanded.

"Apparently not much, but when they'd prised them apart, the whole busload of passengers fell upon Bran, accusing him of running them down. They wouldn't listen to reason, so the upshot is that he and his own passengers have had to go to the police station in Marc d'Assau to give evidence. That's a one-horse place in the mountains," Elyot explained to Donna. "Everything is being taken down in longhand with a well-licked pencil, and Bran's bother is that he doesn't know when he can get free to take you home."

Margot said again, "Tch! That car was new last month. Are the other two, the Milwaukee couple, very annoyed?"

"Why should they be? They've suffered no damage, they wanted a night out and they're only delayed. They'll probably dine out on the story as a bit of Caribbean local colour for weeks to come. Meanwhile, what about Donna?" Elyot asked.

"Oh. Yes. We'll send her home by taxi, of course."

"No, I'll take her myself."

"Please don't bother, I can easily—"

"But, Elyot, you don't want to go yet?"

Donna and Margot had spoken together, and he answered Donna, "It's on my way," and Margot, "Yes, I'll go now, while my alcohol intake is minimal," ignoring her annoyed, "Tiresome of you!" which embarrassed Donna, but which he ignored.

In the foyer they said their goodnights to Margot, and as they got into Elyot's car, Donna remarked, "This is becoming a bit of a cliché, isn't it?"

"A cliché?"

"Stereotyped, repetitive—your having to volunteer transport for me so often, I mean."

"And should I reply gallantly that for me it's a pleasure which bears repeating, or risk offending you with a blunt reference to Hobson's choice? Perhaps I'd better play safe with a neutral 'You're welcome,' which can say as little or as much as you care to let it. Anyway, what are you feeling about Margot's proposal?" Elyot asked after a pause.

"I think I'd like to try it occasionally, but it depends on what Bran will say to toting me around while I learn the ropes, whether I can master the driving, and my uncle's reaction to the idea," Donna said.

"Well, you should find the driving nothing of a problem, once you've had a bit of practice; your cousin will like anything that Margot orders of him—she's that kind of woman, and with your uncle you must use all the diplomacy you know."

"Yes, though I shouldn't care to take it on if he doesn't want me to." She changed the subject. "Tell me, on these guided tours, *may* one take people quite freely on to the plantations? For instance, since there wouldn't be much profit in showing them Louvet, could I take them on to yours, Marquise?"

"Be my guest. It's all publicity for the trade."

"Thank you."

There was silence then until Elyot suggested, "I suppose tonight was your first experience of dancing to a genuine, dyed-in-the-wool steel band on its own home ground?"

"You mean out here, where playing on steel originated? Yes."

Originated of necessity, when the boys couldn't afford any instruments but cut-down dustbins. Do you like the rhythm?"

"It grows on you."

"It does more than that for some people. It gets deep

into their blood. Into Margot le Conte's for one. You may have realised that she hasn't many inhibitions to start with, but to a Caribbean beat of any quality, she abandons the lot and dances, stripped of every rag of reserve, as it were. As *you* couldn't, I take it, to anything like the same degree?"

Donna agreed, "No. It must be quite an experience, dancing with her?"

"It is. Unique."

"Which was probably why—" she couldn't help asking to make sure—"you chose to do only sedate foxtrots with me, knowing I couldn't compete?"

He appeared to ponder the question. Then—"You could say that. You're English. Margot is not. One couldn't look for the same kind of verve. On the other hand—"

Donna waited. At last she prompted, "On the other hand—what?"

"Well, I'd also admit that a man does like to vary his style—refreshing, you know, to get away from the jungle tactics that the drums demand, to the Blue Danube approach of having a girl in your arms, close enough to know she's really there, not one to five yards away and retreating."

"I see," said Donna gravely.

He laughed. "You don't. You'd have liked to show off what you could do. But let it ride for now, and perhaps I'll let you—next time."

When they reached the top of the lane, as she had done once before, she asked him to drop her there. But he refused.

"When I take a girl home after an evening out, I don't dump her on the area steps as if she were a Victorian housemaid," he claimed, and knowing that, if not from her, Wilmot would hear the story of her homecoming from Bran, she gave in.

At the foot of the verandah steps he took her hand. "I'm wondering what a reluctant Blue Danube girl expects of her escort when he takes her home these days?" he said.

"Expect of him? Why, nothing—"

"No? Well, just in case, I shouldn't care to disappoint," he said, and kissed her lightly but purposefully on her lips.

CHAPTER FOUR

THINKING OVER THE EVENING, Donna realised she had had as little relish for being called a Blue Danube girl as she had for having been kissed in her escort's line of duty, because he thought she expected it. Blue Danube indeed! It was a wonder he hadn't chosen the mazurka or the gavotte if he wanted to date her dancing in the past. And since they both knew his taking her home was a chore that had been forced upon him, why should he suppose she regarded him at all as someone who had invited her out and who, when he brought her home, might have kissed her goodnight when they parted?

Both epithet and duty kiss seemed to docket her as a type, and this she resented. In any future encounters with Mr. Elyot Vance, he would have to learn that she wasn't as predictable as all that; that occasionally she could pack some surprises of temperament and mood too! (Too? All right, by "too" her thought *had* meant "as well as" Margot le Conte, even though her honesty had to admit that the man was right—with a mercurial spirit of that calibre her own verve and versatility would have a pretty hard job to compete. But one could always try...)

When she went to breakfast the next morning she found that Bran had already told her uncle about Elyot's having brought her home. "The fellow's making a bit of a habit of it, isn't he?" Wilmot grumbled to Donna. "Let's hope he hadn't the gall to come into my house and stay?"

"No. He just dropped me at the door and left," Donna said.

"Good. He can evidently take a hint." Wilmot returned to his consumption of grilled flying fish, and Donna watched Bran trying to persuade the tiny bananaquit who flew in every morning at breakfast-time to take sugar from his outstretched palm. The little bird nodded and fluttered and quirked his tail, but wasn't to be tempted. He preferred to perch on the rim of the sugar bowl and help himself.

Presently Bran said, "Margot tells me she's enlisted you on the job as well, and that I'm to take you along with me until you've learned the ropes. Is that so?"

"Well, I hadn't given her a firm answer." As she spoke Donna glanced in her uncle's direction and Bran took the hint that she needed help.

"Okay. Leave it to me." He cleared his throat loudly to call Wilmot's abstracted attention. "Look, Dad, there's an idea afoot that as Donna ought to get around and see more of the island while she's here, she might as well come along and take a turn at driving when I go out on a tour."

"And whose idea is it that we're not doing our duty by Donna? Is that more of the Vance fellow's interference in our affairs?" Wilmot demanded.

"Not a bit of it," Bran assured him. "It was Margot le Conte's suggestion, in fact. Besides, it's not a question of either of us failing Donna. You need the car and I've my job, so she couldn't expect to see much except Louvet and the town unless—" Bran paused, then took the plunge. "Well, to be frank, the object of the exercise is that, when I've briefed her thoroughly, she might act as a stop-gap guide herself. Margot needs a woman to fall back on, you see, in case some of her timid ladies won't go out with a man. So how would you go along with that? I mean, Donna wouldn't consider it unless you agreed."

"Though you seem to have it cut and dried between you before I've been asked to agree," Wilmot commented, at which Donna was moved to protest, "Miss le Conte only put it to me last night, Uncle, and to Bran when he got back to the hotel. Of course I'll go no further with it, if you'd rather I didn't. Though—"

"Though what?"

Later Donna could not have told by what flash of inspiration she had hit upon the one note likely to appeal to him when she said, "Well, it had occurred to me that in one aspect of Miss le Conte's idea of my 'learning' Laraye, you could help me tremendously if you would. About the flowers and the trees, their names and their seasons—all that. I just wondered," she added lamely in face of his unrelenting stare.

"And to what end, this information that you want to glean from me?" he asked.

"Just so that, if Miss le Conte ever did call on me to help her out, I could pass it on to the tourists, who, she says, want to know it all."

"I see." For the first time there was a gleam of interest in his cold eye. "You get the geography from Bran and the natural science from me and feed it piecemeal to these guests of Miss le Conte's; though to whose lasting benefit, would you say?"

"Well, to mine, for one," she retorted with spirit. "*They* can forget anything I'd been able to tell them as soon as they like. But *I* shan't. *I* want to take it all home with me—to remember and enjoy and relive as far as I can. So that's mainly why I'd like you to agree to my going out with Bran, and to helping me yourself if you will."

"Helping you, in the time you will have, to a mere smattering of all that it's taken me a lifetime to learn, and still without having been able to put it to any rewarding purpose?" He stood up, crumpling his napkin. "Very well. You may do as you please, which I've little doubt you would, with or without my say-so—"

"I wouldn't, Uncle, really!" she disclaimed.

"And to anything you want to know what I can tell you, you're welcome."

She smiled. "Thank you. I'll be coming to you, notebook at the ready," she promised. But she spoke to his back as he left the verandah.

Bran said, "Well, I congratulate myself with having conducted that with a rare turn of diplomacy."

"You!" Donna scoffed. "I did more than half of it, by suggesting he could help."

"M'm—a stroke of genius, that. But who was it who had to go into action in answer to your silent, melting appeal, you tell me?"

"All right. It was you," she conceded, then worried aloud, "What did Uncle mean about his having achieved 'no rewarding purpose' from all he knows about the Caribbean flora and fauna and all that? If you won't resent my saying so, it was the first time I'd heard him sound sad, not just sour."

Bran nodded. "I know. It's his pipe-dream, you see, that he's never likely to realise. He has neither the money nor many people's sympathy for his scheme for clearing part of the rain forests for a kind of natural park, with everything that's indigenous to Laraye and the other islands growing there, wild but labelled as what each specimen is. He'd see the planting of it and the care of it as the fruit of all his know-how; his gift to posterity, as it were. But it just isn't on."

"A kind of Kew Gardens, do you mean?"

"A bit like, though wilder, and without any marked boundaries—just an acreage of the forest cleared and planted and blending with the rest. But to get it going would cost more money than we've got."

"Aren't there any rich Larayans who would sponsor it?"

Bran shrugged. "If there are, Dad is no salesman of anything—even of ideas."

"Well—" Donna thought she had the solution—"there's Louvet itself, isn't there? I know it's Company owned, but as Uncle isn't making much of a success with bananas on it, and you aren't interested, mightn't the Company let him have part of it for his scheme? I could put the idea to Father, you know."

"No dice on Louvet." Bran shook his head. "The conditions—soil, rainfall—aren't suitable. It's too exposed to wind and the spraying of neighbouring crops. No, it has to be further south where it's much more lush, with a lot more rain and where everything, but everything, will grow."

"There can't be *that* difference in conditions in an island not much over thirty miles long," Donna objected.

"Which is all you know," Bran retorted. "And which reminds me that you can see for yourself. I'm taking a couple down to Boiling Spring and the volcano tomorrow, and you may as well make it your first L-trip."

There followed for Donna many days of exploration of the tortuous roads of the island—deep into the interior, east through vast banana groves to the Atlantic coast, north to fashionably developing residential estates, south through the steamy jungle of the tangled forest land, up into the mountains for views of azure blue bays far below, following the coastline through nestling fishing villages, driving to the very rim of the acrid-smelling volcano, edging along the lower shelves of gargantuan outcrops of rock which rose sheer from the sea. She surprised herself both by how much she remembered and how much she had forgotten; a scent could recall her nursery days vividly; places, such as the town park where she must often have played, meant nothing to her at all.

There was not always room for her in the car, but as larger parties usually preferred to tour together in minibuses, there often was. Bran obviously had a distinct flair for his job; he made his guide patter interesting and amusing; he was patient with questions and never grudged his passengers time to stand and stare. Quite soon—after asking their permission—he allowed Donna to drive, at first on the easier roads, and then increasingly in the haphazard Calvigne traffic and corkscrew mountain tracks. At first she dreaded Bran's "Here—change places with me and take over," but as she grew in confidence she became quite greedy for the time he allowed her at the steering-wheel.

She wrote home enthusiastically about this, stressing her opinion that as this, and not reluctant banana culture, seemed to be Bran's forte, he should be allowed to develop it. Of her uncle she still wrote guardedly, saying she hadn't really got through to him yet, hoping her father would remember and appreciate what a difficult man to know his brother Wilmot was.

Meanwhile she was glad that Wilmot hadn't to be reminded of his offer to identify the island's flowers for her. He lent her books of coloured prints, told her where to walk to see particular herbs and trees and the shyer flowers which didn't flaunt themselves everywhere as did the typically tropic rosy hibiscus and frangipani and anthurium, and once or twice took her further afield in his car, driving slowly and naming for her the towering forest trees, the flamboyants, the pink pouis and the cassias, and the massive fan-spread of the tree-ferns.

He knew and could relate how most of the decorative and useful growth had begun—roots and cuttings cultivated by Spanish missionaries, seeds borne in upon the relentless trade winds, orange-trees imported by the Portuguese, native yuccas and maizes and cassavas turned for use as food by Christopher Columbus. Telling all he knew on the subject he had made his own, Wilmot came alive, and Donna, interested and listening, could only suppose that his lack of enthusiasm for the banana trade was because it offered him too narrow a field. To him it was too regimented, too commercial. His true love was for all growing things, but the more wildly rampant, the better. How tragic to have your life forced into one narrow groove, when it hankered to amble gently along a wider one, she thought. And in thinking it, she decided that this was enough to have killed the man in him, the drive, the warmth—souring and deadening him into the negative figure he was. But that in this conclusion she was only partly right she was not to learn until Madame Hué erupted upon the scene.

Donna was alone and sunbathing on the lawn one afternoon when, in an open vintage car with a strapped bonnet, Madame Hué drove down the lane at a speed conducive to hurtling herself and the car through the croton hedge and over the bluff; braked just in time, alighted and came across the lawn, both hands outstretched in greeting to Donna who had sprung to her feet in alarm, prepared for the imminent crash.

Madame Hué was small, round, dazzlingly white-haired, with a tanned face deeply creased by laughter-lines at mouth and eyes, the latter bright black buttons beneath brows which were still as black as the hair on her head was white. She announced, "I am Irma Hué. I live on Mousquetaire Hill. I am widowed. And you are—? No, no need to tell me, except your first name. The coconut radio has already told me—you're Wilmot's niece from England. Is that not so?" Her voice grated and her accent was French.

"Yes," said Donna, smiling. "I'm Donna—Donna Torrence. How do you do?"

"And you will have heard of me?"

Donna hadn't, and said so.

Madame Hué clucked with annoyance. "Bah, it is always the same with these Larayans—out of sight, out of mind, as you say. Me, I go up to Florida to visit friends—a month, two months or so—and I am forgotten until I return. Where is Wilmot? Is he at home?"

Donna said he wasn't, and offered drinks, coffee, lemon tea and a chair, all of which her visitor declined.

"No, sit down again, child, and I shall sit with you while you tell me about yourself," she ruled, plumping down upon the lawn, sitting cross-legged and encircling her fat knees with her clasped hands to stop her rotundity from keeling over to one side or the other.

"Now," she said. "Now I am wearing my listening hat. And so—when did you come? Are Wilmot and Brandon entertaining you as they should? How long are you staying? And which of us all have you met yet? Have you fallen in love? Or have you left a beau—perhaps more than one—behind you in England?"

Donna laughed. "That's quite a list of questions, Madame Hué!"

"No matter. Take your time. Let us start with the most interesting—are you in love?"

"Yes," said Donna, and paused. "With Laraye."

"Bah, you tease me! You know I meant with a man," Madame Hué accused. "This is a romantic island, but you cannot marry an island. So tell me the names of some men to whom you have been introduced, and I, who know everyone, will tell you which one of them might make you a suitable *parti*."

Donna's memory was able to produce the names of some of the men she had met at Margot le Conte's party, then she added, "There's another one to whom I wasn't introduced, but just—met."

"You—a girl of good family, and you picked him up?" Madame Hué's shocked tone was belied by the twinkle in her eye.

"Not exactly, though you could say he picked *me* up." Donna admitted. "At the airport, when Uncle Wilmot had mistaken the day I was arriving and hadn't met me. So he—Mr. Elyot Vance—made himself known, and drove me up here on his own way home."

"Ah," said Madame Hué. "Elyot Vance—what a pity."

"A pity?"

"That you should list him among the men who have interested you."

"You have only asked me about some I had met," Donna pointed out.

"Yet you remember to include Elyot Vance. And so I repeat—a pity. For though he is not married, is a charmer, of about the right superior age for you, and rich, one understands that he is already registered, labelled—what is the word I want?—ah yes, *booked* to Brandon's employer, Margot le Conte of the Allamanda. So if you have an eye for Elyot, I'm afraid an *affaire* would be all you could hope for. Marriage to you would not be in his mind."

"But I haven't! I don't—!" protested Donna, taken aback, though for some reason intrigued, rather than irritated by these mental gymnastics on the part of her companion, who ignored her outburst to continue, "Not that Wilmot would countenance either for you, considering how matters stand between him and Elyot. Has he—Wilmot—seen you with Elyot?"

"With him, actually only once."

"And?"

"Well—" Finding Madame Hué an avid listener and that she herself wasn't averse to discussing Elyot Vance with a third person, Donna told the whole story of their encounters and of her uncle's reactions from beginning to end. "It's always been sort of chance, you see," she concluded.

Madame Hué snorted. "Huh! Not always chance, if I know anything about Elyot's eye for a pretty girl."

"But I'm not pretty, and it *was* chance—at the airport, and at the Dial House and when Bran couldn't drive me home. Anyway. I only mentioned him because you asked me, and because Uncle made so much difficulty about it."

"Difficulties for which he sincerely believes he has reason."

"Oh, I know," Donna agreed. "Bran told me, and we already know something about it in London—about Uncle's resentment of the competition of Marquise with Louvet, and his consequent feud with Mr. Vance."

"Which doesn't stem only from Wilmot's jealousy of Marquise; it goes much further back than that. And if you want to know how far, and what it is all about, probably only someone of Wilmot's age or of my own could tell you. I doubt if Brandon knows or would show much sympathy if he did. You young people"—the black button eyes gleamed in reproof—"you resent our generation's ever having loved or been loved. But that is what Wilmot's enmity for Elyot is all about."

Donna was silent, suspecting she was about to hear the story, and she was right. Madame Hué continued, "Both Elyot's parents died in the town fire of over twenty years ago."

"Yes. He told me that," said Donna.

"But not, one supposes, since he may not know, that almost on the eve of their wedding, his mother had broken her engagement to Wilmot and eloped with Noel Vance. They had just the one child, Elyot, and were very happy, one heard. But Wilmot never forgave Noel for taking her from him, and although Noel lost his own life in the fire, Wilmot never ceased to blame him for exposing his wife to it. Wilmot's mania ran—If she had married him, they would have been living up here in the country, safe. She would still have been alive. And even I couldn't make him see that it was all chance, and that he was wrong and vindictive to blame Noel, who died too himself."

Donna asked, "Uncle confided in you at the time, Madame Hué?"

"*Only* in me, I think. I was for him what you would call 'the girl next door.' You understand this term?"

"Yes, I think so. But he married my aunt later, and they had Bran."

"And so did I marry too. I went away and only came back to Laraye after I was widowed. And what do I learn of my old friend Wilmot? That he is still eating out his bitter heart, not now against poor dead Noel Vance, but against his son for *being* Noel's son. But still in secret, I believe. To most people, as to your family too perhaps, it is just a business rivalry, with Wilmot always the loser. But I tell *you*, my child. Do you know why? It is because when you are in danger of being a little dazzled by Elyot's empty attentions to you, in your enchantment you may side with him against Wilmot, which would be unkind of you and less than the poor embittered man deserves of his own kin."

"But I never would! That is, I'm not *in* that kind of danger. I hardly *know* Elyot Vance," Donna protested. "Besides, as I told you, at our very first meeting, I defended Uncle Wilmot against him, and always would again, especially after what you have told me."

"Then that is good, and I am sure I can trust you." Madame Hué rocked perilously to her feet and brushed clinging crab grass from her ample trousered *derrière*. "And now that I am back on Laraye with plans for no more trips abroad for some time, I must take Wilmot in hand myself and arrange a cure for him. A cure being a wife, which all men need."

"He has had a wife," Donna pointed out.

"And cherished her as he should, one hears, for all his other discontents. And so we must marry him again. I myself shall put it in train."

"Must you go, Madame Hué? Won't you wait to see Uncle, though I can't say when he may be home?" Donna asked.

"No, I must go. Tell him I called, and you must come to see me, child."

"How far away is Mousquetaire? I haven't a car," said Donna.

"Then Wilmot must bring you, or Brandon, or I will fetch you myself. And call me Irma, my dear. Everyone does; I am a byword in Laraye."

Donna laughed. "I'm sure you're not. A byword—whatever for?"

"For minding everyone's business but my own!" With a wicked chuckle Madame Hué turned the vintage monster in its tracks and roared off up the lane, leaving Donna to pray that she would encounter no passing traffic at the top.

BRAN'S REACTION TO THE NEWS of Madame Hué's call was a laconic, "So she's back again, is she?" and Wilmot's dour "That woman! Did she say what she wanted of me?" sounded to Donna singularly unwelcoming to his one-time confidante.

"No. Just that she had hoped to see you," Donna told him.

"Though as if I couldn't guess. She fancies herself as a water-colourist and has some fool idea that if I wrote a tourists' guide to the island's flowers and trees, she could do the illustrations in colour. So no doubt she came to pester me again," Wilmot grumbled.

The idea seemed a good one to Donna, and she would have thought he would consider it. "But you aren't interested?" she queried.

"If I ever wrote a book which I could hope any tourist would put his hand in his pocket to buy, I'd have it illustrated by someone who knew better than Irma Hué which was the right end of a paintbrush," he ruled, dismissing the subject and causing Donna to wonder what he would say if he learned of the lady's plans, not only for a book but for a marriage of convenience for him which she intended to arrange.

How serious could she possibly have been about that? Donna wondered. Probably no more so than in her claim that Elyot Vance wasn't unwilling to allow chance to help him to add Donna's own scalp to his belt. She couldn't have meant either to be taken as fact. Donna couldn't see Wilmot ever arousing himself to marry again, and Elyot hadn't attempted to pretend he was interested... He had simply done what her chance emergencies had asked of him at the time. Even his peck of a goodnight kiss had been a duty chore, he had implied. And who wanted to be a mere duty to any man?

Irma Hué had not visited again by the time Bran said he had told Margot le Conte that he thought Donna was now practised enough to stand in as a spare guide whenever Margot needed her. Margot, he reported, had said, "That's fine, the darling. But remind her that I threatened I'd put her through her paces," and had named a day and time, which Bran had accepted for Donna.

Donna didn't relish the prospect too much. Why need Margot make it sound like the taking of one's original driving test? But on the afternoon in question a car was sent to take her down to the Allamanda, where she supposed she would be picking up Margot in one of the tourist guide cars.

On the way the Larayan driver was chatty. "Miss le Conte she go Barbados," he volunteered.

"Barbados? I suppose she'll be flying down? When?" Donna asked.

He shook his head. "No. She go today. She fly, yes. But she gone."

Donna stared. "Gone?"

"That's right. Hear tell she have tooth pain bad. Say no good tooth doctor, Laraye. Doctor on Barbados better. So she go, fly back tomorrow."

"But she had arranged to see me! She must have forgotten that."

"No, Miss remember. Me, I know so, for I drive her airport, and as she mount car she say to Mister Vance who there, tell you not to come, as she called away. But he say he see you instead. She say no need. But he say yes, and she say—" A shrug of the man's massive shoulders indicated Margot's reply—"and Mister Vance tell me come up for you, miss, after I take Miss le Conte airport. This I do," he concluded.

"Oh," said Donna blankly. Stepping into the breach again, was he? She had been right to call a cliché the circumstances which forced her company upon Elyot, for his coming to her aid—quite unnecessarily this time—was indeed becoming a habit. Why, she wondered a shade irritably, had he apparently overruled Margot about putting her off? He could so easily have telephoned, and saved both the driver and her a fruitless journey.

But that he didn't intend it to be a fruitless journey was made clear when, at the hotel, she found him waiting for her in the passenger seat of one of the guide cars. He got out, and before she could tell him she already knew of Margot's emergency, he said, "Margot has had to fly down to Barbados to see her dentist, so, rather than subject you to butterflies in the tum to no purpose, I've offered to play test-examiner myself."

"You mean *you* want to take me round on a trial trip, as I think she meant to?" Donna asked.

"On the contrary, you're going to take *me* round." He opened the car door for her and waited as, seeing protest was useless, she strapped herself in. As he got in beside her he produced a large-scale map of Laraye and remarked, "You were having butterflies, I hope, as all worthy examinees should?"

"A bit," she admitted. "I think Miss le Conte meant to make it a serious test of what I could do."

"Let her be 'Margot' between ourselves, may we?" he said casually. "Yes, well—" his forefinger traced a route on the map—"around the town first, I think; points of interest there; then up to the Lighthouse; round the Military Cemetery; over to Government House. All right, I'll brief you again when we've done all that. Off you go."

Donna moved "off" rather nervously, overconscious of both his scrutiny and his unreadable silences between the questions he put to her about anything of interest which they passed, not always spacing them considerately of the main task in hand—her driving of the car. He would bark, "Look, what's that?" quite suddenly, and when she jumped and said, "What's what? Oh, that's—" and told what "that" was, he showed no emotion at all, not even interest in her reply. But gradually she found she could interpret his every slight movement of foot or hand or clearing of his throat as some message he was putting over to her.

I'm getting on to his wavelength, she thought. *We're on the same beam*, and surprised herself at the quiet, almost warm sense of achievement which that gave her.

When he stopped her to suggest their further itinerary ("We haven't time to go full south, but drive as far as Carrière through the rain forests; on the way back, take in an avocado farm and we'll finish on Marquise") he advised, "You're going to have to expect questions, some of them pretty fatuous, I daresay. So if you want to ward them off, you should volunteer more patter than you've offered me. Stop in your own time and hold forth about the views or whatever, and point out things off your own bat as you go."

She did so, finding herself more at ease, even making a joke or two and repeating for her imaginary passengers' benefit some Larayan proverbs which she had learned from Juno and which amused her. She was enjoying herself; didn't want the tour to end.

At last they came down from the mountains where, on the highest roads, they had been level with the tops of the flamboyant trees and the coconut palms towering from the lower slopes. The red dust road dropped down to a valley which was the vast acreage of Marquise, one dark green mass of banana plants, with a group of Elyot's workers' cabins huddled in the middle of the mass.

He stopped Donna, told her to get out and helped her across the wide ditch which was the only barrier between the road and the growing crops. He pointed to a young plant with its pendant purple "head" which had not yet dropped any of its bracts to reveal the tiny green fingers underneath.

"Now give me a rundown on the whole banana cycle from A to Z," he ordered.

Donna smiled. "Doesn't that rather amount to teaching my grandmother to suck eggs?" she quipped.

"In this instance, I'm not your grandmother, thanks be. I'm a tourist straight from the heart of Chicago or Manchester who has hitherto only thought of bananas in terms of comic songs. So let's be hearing what you can tell me," he said.

When she had finished he nodded. "Very lucid. And the rest—harvesting, the washing, the grading, the shipment overseas?"

"I know about it, of course. But I haven't seen it; Louvet hasn't sent out a consignment since I've been here."

"You should rectify that. As long as you wouldn't expect me to spare you much attention, I could bring you out one banana-boat day to see the whole process through. The loading from the quays is a spectacle your passengers are sure to want to see. One thing you haven't mentioned—why, out here, the banana is known as 'fig'?"

She shook her head. "I know it is, but not why."

"The reason is a bit involved, but it's picturesque. The plant's botanical family is Musacoe, which derives from the Arabic Mouz, and the banana, probably in its wild state one of the oldest plants known to man, appears in the Koran as the Tree of Paradise. When it first came to Europe the name held and, by association I suppose, it became the fig-tree of our Christian Garden of Eden. The Caribs are still reluctant to hear it called anything else."

Donna murmured, "Tree of Paradise—I like that."

"Yes, it appeals to the romantic Eve in most women," he agreed, then indicated the lengthening shadows cast by the plants upon the road. "Time for sundowners, I think. Change places now, and I'll take you up to the house, where you'll meet my Maria and Choc, your Juno's relations who do for me, as Juno does for you."

"I must deliver the car back to the hotel," Donna reminded him.

"No hurry. When I've given you a drink, I'll take you home in it, deliver it myself and collect my own which I left down there. How's that?"

At the top of its winding driveway Marquise, unlike many houses in volcanic Laraye, was two-storied, with wide balconies to each floor, looking down over dipping lawns fringed with palms, and in the distance across to the sweep of the estate. Such of the interior of the house as Donna saw was beautifully furnished and beflowered; obviously the house of a bachelor who need deny himself nothing, but still a house which any woman would be proud to be asked to share.

Choc was a mountain of a man. Maria was tiny, with a voice so small that Donna could hardly hear her when she asked what "Miss" would like to drink. "Miss" chose a fruit punch, but was persuaded by Elyot to a daiquiri. He had one too and as he took the long chair beside hers on the lower balcony, asked, "Don't you want to know how I shall report on you to Margot?"

"Why, how will you?"

"Very favourably, I think."

"Thank you. I've had some good teachers—Bran for the geography and Uncle Wilmot for the flower names, not to mention Juno for the Caribbean proverbs."

"Don't I get any marks for the Tree of Paradise bit? Your passengers will fairly eat that. But it's evident that, as they say in the theatre, you're a quick study."

"When one wants to learn anything enough it comes easily," Donna said sincerely.

"How sententious of you! That sounds like a maxim from a copybook. But you mean Margot didn't press-gang you into it?"

"No, I'm grateful to her. I should never have got around as I wanted to, in any other way. I shall go back as full of impressions and memories as I hoped I might before I came."

"Only to be rather let down by the reality of Louvet?"

He had no right to be so shrewd! "A bit, perhaps," she admitted.

"But now you'll go back happier? And you'll *go* back?"

"Of course. I've a job in England, and I shall be going home."

"And so? Girls of your age have been known to leave home—quite a lot of them to marry in 'furrin parts.' Laraye, for one. I could point you to a dozen English and American girls who've married happily and successfully here."

"I daresay. But I don't happen to have marriage in mind, here or anywhere else."

"Oh, come! Don't tell me, when you knew you were coming to Laraye, that a tropical island and a rich planter who couldn't resist you weren't synonymous in your dreams?"

"They certainly weren't. And if they had been, they would have taken a knock. I don't know any rich planters—"

"You know me."

"You?" Donna sat upright in such blank surprise that she spilled her drink. Elyot laughed, reached for the jug and refilled her glass.

"Take it easy. No need for a double-take of that intensity," he teased. "I wasn't springing a proposal of marriage, even on a couple of daiquiris. I was only quoting myself as an example of several quite well-to-do planters on Laraye who aren't married. One or two of them would like to be, I know."

"Thank you. When I find I'm in need of a marriage bureau, I think I'll go to a real one, licensed by the London County Council. Meanwhile—"

"Meanwhile, you'll thank me not to tread on your dreams. *And* you are in a huff."

"I'm not," she denied, wishing he hadn't said that

about treading on her dreams. It assumed too much, it was emotive and for some reason it hurt. She went on, "This has become such a silly, hypothetical argument that it isn't worth getting huffed *about*, would you say?"

"*I'd* say not," he agreed. "But—" He didn't finish as Choc came out on to the balcony.

"Miss le Conte on telephone, sir. Want speak to you."

"Coming." Elyot excused himself to Donna and went back into the house.

She sat on, sipping her drink, watching the crimson-purple of the clouded sky clear slowly to the pale lemon it took on at full sundown. She knew she was a little too relaxed, not thinking very clearly. The time, the place, an early evening drink with a man had all the makings of a flirtation, she supposed hazily. So that was all their verbal sparring had amounted to—flirtation. Nothing to take seriously nor in offence. Nor even to mull over later, making more of his brittle interest in her than it deserved. They would have talked just so at a drinks party in all probability. But she still wondered why he had bothered to spare her the afternoon from his busy schedule. She would have liked to ask him, if she couldn't already foretell his bantering reply.

He came back and sat down again. "Margot, after a nasty session with her dentist and faced by a lonely evening, in need of sympathy and moral support," he said.

"Did you give it to her?"

"To the best of my ability from this distance. Poor Margot needs the direct touch; she suffers her own company only by dire necessity. She wanted to know whether I had done my duty by you; I reported on you as I told you I should, and said I was giving you a drink before taking you home."

"Thank you." Donna put down her empty glass, and then with a recklessness which only the unaccustomed drink could have encouraged, said lightly, "Well, at least no one could accuse you of being *cinq à sept* with *me.*"

She was totally unprepared for his sudden start and the dark frown he turned on her. "Of being *what* with you?" he demanded.

"*C-cinq à sept,*" she hesitated.

"And how on earth do you come by such a phrase?"

"I heard Miss—I mean Margot le Conte—tease you with it at her party at the hotel. I didn't know then what it meant, but I asked Bran, and he told me."

"Well, forget it." His tone was terse. "Even in joke, as Margot would have used it, it hasn't the most tasteful of implications, and with reference to our afternoon together, it makes no sense at all."

Feeling like a small child under reproof, Donna protested, "But that's precisely what I said just now—that it couldn't apply. It was only a joke anyway," she added, aggrieved.

"As was Margot's. All right, leave it." He let the silence lengthen into one minute, two. Then, just as Donna was about to suggest she would like to go home, he voiced aloud the question she had been asking herself. "Haven't you wondered why I volunteered to act as Margot's stand-in today?"

Her eyes met his frankly. "Yes," she said, "I had. It seemed so unnecessary that you should."

He shook his head. "I needed to talk to you, and since I'm *persona non grata* in your uncle's house, this was the first chance I'd had of getting you alone."

"To talk to me?" Donna's mouth went dry and there was a flutter of excitement in the region of her heart. "What about?"

"This," he said. "Listen—"

CHAPTER FIVE

For a long time afterwards Donna was to cringe inwardly at the thought of her hope that it was some personal confidence, some small intimacy, which Elyot had wanted to share with her alone. For what he had to say was so much an anti-climax that she wondered with shame whether her disappointment had shown in her face.

"It's about the Dial House," he said.

"The—Dial House?" She knew her surprise sounded blank.

"Yes. My ultimatum fell flat. Your uncle hasn't done anything about it, has he?"

"About repairing it? No. After the way you and he parted, did you expect him to?"

"Frankly no. That's where you come in, and why I needed to get you alone."

"*I* can't force him."

"I realise that, but I want you as a fellow-conspirator. I suggest that you make an urgency of it to your father, asking him that the Company should bypass your uncle and make a direct ruling as to the repair of the place."

"But in writing home I haven't mentioned it at all."

"Why not?"

"Because—well I suppose I was ashamed of my foolhardiness that first day, and I didn't want to worry them."

"Nor admit to the hornets' nest you stirred up, Louvet versus Marquise-wise?"

"That too, though they know something about that. But if I did appeal to Father, and the Company did act,

Uncle Wilmot would guess what I'd done, even that you'd put me up to it."

"Why should he?" Elyot parried. "He must realise that the Company knows what property it owns, and if you enlist your father on our side, your uncle could be led to suppose it had been decided at company level that it was time the Dial was put in repair, with or without his consent."

"Mm, perhaps," Donna mused. "But wouldn't that be riding a bit roughshod over him?"

"Roughshod? In the interest of my workers' toddlers, not to mention the risk of the whole crazy structure collapsing like a pack of cards, come the hurricane season? Thank you, but I'm not going to get any satisfaction from chanting 'I told you so' if or when it happens. So if you won't co-operate, I'll write to your Company myself."

"I will, of course," Donna promised reluctantly, though having known all the time that she must.

"Good girl! I knew I could trust you. And one other thing—since I'm an extremely interested party, I'd like you to mention that I'd supply the planning and the labour, as I said in the first place I would."

Donna shook her head. "Uncle would never wear that."

Elyot laughed. "Don't put goat mout' 'pon it—which, on the parallel that a goat can destroy anything with his nibbling, is vulgar Larayan for 'Don't crab the chances of success.' If the Company accept the reason for my offer, and the whole operation comes as a directive from them, what can the man do?"

Donna smiled thinly. "Be difficult," she said. "At the very least."

"And at the very most? He's already forbidden me his house, yet I survive."

She did not answer, not wanting to look at an immediate future which Wilmot could make quite untenable for her if he chose to forbid her to see even as little of

Elyot as she had done until now. To a guest, while she remained under his roof, Wilmot had the right to do that. Yet the prospect of no more contacts with Elyot appalled her. Which meant—?

It meant, she realised after they had parted that evening, that by some emotional about-face she had thought never to experience where he was concerned, his challenge to her, their frictions as well as their agreements, were becoming important, too important. And not only his challenge. The physical man himself—manner, voice, movement—all the dynamic virility she had sensed at her first stranger's awareness of him—had begun to matter too much. He was too often in her thoughts; in the expectation with which she woke each morning to the little secret question, dismissed at once, of "Am I likely to see him today?" An on-the-brink-of-love question, that. Her feminine instinct knew the signs, but hadn't warned her against caring whether the answer had to be yes or no.

How had it happened? That other time of their parting at night she had resented the spirit in which he had kissed her; this evening she would have made treasure of it, however little he meant by it. But he had not kissed her. On his own admission he had only wanted to see her today in order to enlist her help. So what had her hunger for his interest to feed upon? Just that he had said he trusted her enough to know he could look to her as an ally. But that was all. At best, she was only on the fringe of his life. And on the fringe of her own was where, if she were wise, she would learn to keep him. If she were wise...

SHE WROTE FULLY TO HER FATHER about the Dial House, admitting now her own escapade, relating Elyot's timely rescue of her, and telling of the subsequent violent clash between him and her uncle on the matter of its repair. She emphasised Elyot's understandable concern for it, and suggested that he be contacted directly, if the Company could see its way to falling in with his plan.

She was still awaiting a reply to this when Margot called her to her first guide tour.

Over the telephone Margot gushed, "Darling, Elyot gave you the full thumbs-up over your driving. *So* gallant of him to save me the bore of going out with you myself, and sweet of you to help me out. Now I have for you an advertising woman who is collecting copy about the Caribbean; if you get on together, may I assign you to her for later trips she may want to make? Okay?"

Though she went to her first appointment in some trepidation Donna enjoyed it herself and was thanked, congratulated and re-booked by her client, an Englishwoman intent on selling Laraye and its sister islands in rivalry to the more popular West Indian resorts.

There followed other pleasant assignments. Donna found herself in demand by the hotel's women tourists needing a guide, and she was expecting nothing unusual when she went down one day to keep an appointment with two American ladies, newly arrived overnight.

They were not waiting for her outside, nor in the foyer, which was empty but for a man who at first was chatting to the girl desk-clerk, then idly scanning the bookstand between glances at his watch. Donna returned to her car to wait for her passengers, but when they had not appeared after another ten minutes, she went back into the foyer to check with the clerk.

"Mrs. and Miss Bellew, Rosa—have you seen them waiting for me?" she asked.

Rosa shook her head. "Don't know lady that name."

"You might not. They are new guests. But anyway, two ladies whom I was to take on a tour?"

Light dawned for Rosa. "Oh—yes, two ladies. But they go with Louis just now."

"With Louis? But they were my passengers, and I wasn't late."

"I send them with Louis, all same. I think that right. This gentleman for you, maybe yes, Miss Torrence? Perhaps he wait for someone drive him," Rosa said hopefully.

Donna shook her head. Margot had never engaged her for a man passenger; that hadn't been in their arrangement. "Not for me, I think," she said. But the man was already at her side, smiling and saying, "But as there seems to have been some mix-up, you'd take me, I daresay? I'd be honoured if you would. Take pity on me, won't you, and say yes—*please*?" His accent was American with a drawling Southern inflection, he was darkly handsome in what she thought of as a film-star way, and his ready smile invited hers.

She hesitated, her native caution none too willing to drive him alone. In order to gain time for decision, she told Rosa, "I'd better look at the bookings ledger" and while she did so, checking that the Bellews were indeed rightly her passengers and that no man on his own was booked for that hour at all, she sensed Rosa's worry over the mistake, and made up her mind to help the girl out.

"Very well," she told the man. "Since I seem to be free, I'll drive you. Where would you like to go?"

He held out his hand. "Thanks a million. Anywhere, everywhere. I was hoping to fix up something, but I didn't expect—" His glance was openly admiring of her as he went on, "Names, first? I'm Mel, short for Melford. Who are you?"

"Donna *Torrence*." She laid deliberate emphasis on her surname, and he laughed. "Okay, hint taken. Mel *Drinan*—will that do? But does all the heavy stress mean that we're not to be Mel and Donna as we go on our way? *Mr.* Drinan and *Miss* Torrence—it *is* Miss, and not Mrs., I hope?"

"It's Miss." Donna relented. "I only meant that I

don't usually call people by their first names, until I'm asked."

"As I'm asking you and warning you I'm going to call you Donna. Pretty name, Donna, a gift. Does that mean your people saw you as rather a special gift when they named you?"

"I shouldn't think so," she said, remembering her father's prejudice in favour of a son, but doubting whether this readily amiable young man would appreciate the Dickens reference as Elyot had done. *Elyot!* By contrast with his blunt demanding approach, this one's was positively honey-tongued! "You are American, aren't you?" she asked him.

"Uh-huh. From Houston, Texas. But to save your asking, I'm not in oil. I'm in real estate, prospecting for possible developments on Laraye. And you are English, of course?"

"Yes." As he took the passenger seat beside her, she asked again, "Where would you like to go? If you are interested in housing, perhaps you would like to see the development that has been done already in the north of the island?"

"No hurry," he said easily. "Unless of course it's on the way to anywhere particularly romantic that you fancy yourself. Take me there and let me share it, won't you, please?"

"It would help me to plan a route, if you would say how long you would like to be out," she told him, and he waved an airy hand.

"Just as long as you can spare for me. Do you have another fare after this?"

"No."

"Well then, let's play it by ear. *I've* got all day. Meanwhile I'm counting my luck that you didn't have to pick up those two dames. Let's go."

By no means averse to showing off her driving skill, she chose the most tortuous road into the mountains which she knew, offering him sea-views and inland panoramas and a patter of folklore in her best professional vein. She realised, from his reference to her "fares" and his questions to her about the job and whether it paid, that he thought she did it for a living, and it amused her not to disillusion him.

She lived out in the country, she told him, on a not very prosperous banana estate, part-owned and managed by her uncle. Her cousin also acted as a guide-driver for the Allamanda. And yes, she enjoyed her work, and no, so far she hadn't had any "difficult" clients.

When, at around noon, they dropped down to the coast and she drove through a succession of fishing villages nestling in the lee of beetling cliffs, his interest in various restaurants they passed told her that he was thinking in terms of luncheon and perhaps debating whether to suggest her joining him.

At last he made up his mind. "Would it be in order for you to lunch with me?" he asked.

"Thank you. I think so," she said demurely.

"Then where?"

She took him to a quiet restaurant, palm-shaded, on the very edge of the shore, where she knew the seafood to be excellent and the service unobtrusive. But when he didn't approve it, saying it looked a bit tatty to him, she went to the other extreme and drove to one of the newer hotel-restaurants catering for tourists, where the guests were lodged in pseudo-Tahitian thatched cabins on the beach, from where the dining-room was reached by cable car up the mountainside. This her companion liked, though she thought it rather ostentatious. At the bar she chose a soft drink as she was driving, and took only half a glass of the bottle of wine he ordered with the meal, leaving the rest to him.

They talked. He told her he would be taking a few days' holiday before getting down to his firm's assignment to him to prospect for available building land and negotiate its price. As soon as he started work in earnest, he would be hiring a car himself, but in the meanwhile, perhaps she would take him out again? And when he had his own car he would hope for some dates with her. *Might* he hope?

She agreed guardedly, keeping up the fiction that she was not entirely a free agent while, though he talked about himself and his work, she learned nothing personal about him nor his background. Meanwhile, he was pleasant company and never lost an opportunity for a compliment, either oblique or direct. Everything about his appearance spoke of affluence—pale lilac silk shirt, impeccable grey slacks, casually knotted Charvet neckerchief, broad signet ring of plain gold—leading her to conclude that he was probably at executive level in what sounded like a very prosperous firm, though, in keeping with his reticence about his personal affairs, he hadn't told her its name.

On the drive back his manner became more intimate and his attention more concentrated on her as she talked than on what she was telling him about the scenery they were passing. Once he slid an arm across the back of her seat, but when she sat slightly forward, showing she knew it was there and that it irked her, he withdrew it at once. "Sorry," he smiled disarmingly. "Getting cramp in that elbow; just flexing the muscles, that was all," which was so adroit a retreat from what might or might not have been a tentative pass that she gave him the benefit of the doubt with her concerned, "Oh dear—is it better now?"

At the hotel he thanked her warmly and made an embarrassed gesture towards his wallet. At first she thought, horrified, that he was going to offer her a tip, but when he asked, "Whom and how does one pay?" she told him she would put in a chit and the cost would appear on his account.

"Fine," he said. "And now, could we have a swim in the pool and an early drink before you go home?"

Donna refused. She didn't keep a swimsuit at the Allamanda and besides—a white lie—she had an appointment to see Miss le Conte, the owner-manageress, before she left, she told him.

"Dinner, then? Tonight? Tomorrow?" he pressed. "Here, or wherever you like instead?"

She hesitated. A dinner date for which she could dress up would be nice, and though she had taken to him only moderately, the man was no wolf. But though she had no appointment with Margot, she had meant to find what were Margot's reactions to her having taken out a man passenger alone and, now that he had asked her, how Margot would view her acceptance of his invitation to dine. So she said she wasn't sure about the evening, but she would ring him—with which he seemed satisfied, and after he had named a time, they parted.

Rosa, questioned as to where Margot might be, said she was in her apartment. Donna said, "Well, ring her for me, will you please, and ask her if she can spare me a few minutes?"

Rosa's brown eyes widened. "You not make trouble with Miss le Conte about those two ladies?" she pleaded.

"Of course not," Donna assured her. "Are they back yet? How did they get on with Louis?"

"They say super. Fine." Rosa was beaming now. "Louis great chap, they say; good type, want him again. Ring Miss le Conte now; tell her you here."

After a minute or two she reported, "Miss say she occupied; she dressing, but if you won't keep her long, you go up."

Margot was in her opulent bedroom. Clad in a frilled silk negligée, she was doing her nails at the dressing-table; a valise, half packed, was open on the bed.

She spoke to Donna over her shoulder while fanning out her fingers to see the effect of a silver pearl polish. "You find me terribly pressed, darling—just half an hour before Elyot Vance calls for me. He has to go to Grenada on business by the evening plane; staying the night, and I'm going along for a ride; back tomorrow. Was it anything madly important you wanted?"

"Not so very," Donna said. "It's just that the Mrs. Bellew and her daughter who were booked to me this morning thought they were supposed to go with Louis Trapontine, and went. That left me without a passenger, so I took instead a Mr. Drinan, who hadn't booked, but wanted a tour. Was that all right?"

"You took him alone?"

"Yes—on a pretty comprehensive drive. He gave me luncheon. Was all that in order?"

"In order? But of course, darling. You should know me—I never turn down business, and if you were free and felt you could handle him, why not? Anyway, who did you say he was? There was such a crowd of new people in yesterday."

"His name is Drinan—Melford Drinan."

Margot turned then. "Melford *Drinan*?" she echoed. "Well, what d'you know? I knew he'd booked in, but I haven't seen him yet. So aren't you the canny girl to leap to his aid? For I suppose he told you who he is—one of *the* Drinan family of Houston, who trade as Hexagon Development Inc.—just about the major land prospectors in the States? Florida, Bermuda, Jamaica—you name it, and wherever there's real estate to be negotiated, Hexagon will be there. So if you made any kind of a hit with Melford Drinan, cultivate him, do. He could be well worth your while. Did he say he would like you to drive him again?"

"Until he hires a car of his own, he said, and he asked me to dine with him tonight or tomorrow. I said I would let him know."

"So go ahead. What are you waiting for? Make it here tomorrow night; it's a gala evening and more fun than just dining. And what did I tell you—that this way you would meet people? Men, of course I meant, because you English girls who used to get yourselves invited out in India to find husbands now holiday in the

West Indies with the same idea. And why not, bless you? It's a universal game, and all of it good for the tourist trade."

"Some of us come out for different reasons from that," Donna observed, her tone dry.

Margot shook her head. "You don't fool me. You wouldn't be human if you didn't keep one eye lifting in that direction—"

She broke off as the telephone rang. "Excuse me." She reached for the receiver. "Ah—Elyot." Her deep voice made a caress of the name. "Yes—coming. Almost at once. Just must *throw* on a clout and *fling* a few more things into my case. While you're waiting, have them send a bellboy up for it, will you? What's that? I know...I know, but I've been delayed a bit by—guess who? Your young protegée, Donna Torrence. And guess what, too? She's on the verge of hooking herself a prize fish—Melford Drinan of Hexagon Inc.—*you* know, and she came to ask if it was all right for her to encourage him. Isn't that sweet? Too utterly *ingénue* for words! Been out with him for hours today; dining with him tomorrow. Yes, all right, she's leaving this minute, and I'll be down. 'Bye, monster—" She turned with a smile to Donna. "You don't mind if I have to rush you, honey, do you? I just had to tell Elyot that you've found yourself a boy-friend—relieve him a bit of having to look after you as he has done to date. But now I must *dash*. Good luck with the date, and be sure to keep me posted, won't you? I adore watching love-affairs burgeon; at the beginning they're so naïve!"

"It isn't a—" But Donna wasn't allowed to finish. Margot's hands, gently but firmly at the back, propelled her from the room.

THERE COULD HAVE BEEN several reasons why she told Melford Drinan that she would have dinner with him that night, rather than the next. It might have been sheer contrariness; or that, in asking Wilmot for the loan of his car to drive herself down to the hotel, she couldn't wait to assure him, in answer to his growled, "You'll be bumping into that fellow Vance again, I suppose," that she knew Elyot to be away, and that her date was with someone else. But at heart she knew it was because she couldn't bear the thought of Margot's goldfish-bowl scrutiny of her evening in Melford Drinan's company. She could just hear Margot patronising her; even enlarging on the theme of Elyot's alleged responsibility for her. As if he had ever felt any in depth! Whatever he had done for her had been thrust upon him, and the only time he had sought her out voluntarily he had wanted something of her. No, she felt she would like to tell Margot, as far as obligations were concerned, honours between her and Elyot were easy.

Meanwhile, throughout that first evening with Melford, her thoughts were following Elyot and Margot to Grenada; intimately together in the little island plane, staying in the same hotel. They must both be too well known to risk scandal, but their rooms might not be far apart. They would dance during dinner and Margot would make a spectacle of it with the same abandon she always brought to dancing to the insistent beat and rhythm of a West Indian band. They would talk. If Margot enlarged on Donna's alleged "catch," would Elyot be interested? And if he were meeting the friend he had been seeing off to Grenada at the airport that first day, would he remember to relate how the "And Son" of Torrence And Son had turned out to be the mosquito-beset girl who had overheard every word of his disparagement of Wilmot and Bran? Or had he already forgotten the incidents of a day which to her had marked her first sight and awareness of him, yet which for him was just an ordinary one in his calendar, without special importance at all?

She went out with Melford Drinan several times after that. Whatever his business interests on Laraye, he seemed to be master of his own time, and when he hired a car for himself, he asked her often to lunch or dinner or for drinks and a swim. He was punctilious with chocolates or flowers, and when, on parting from her at night, he expected to kiss her, she let him. Unlike Elyot, he didn't claim it as a duty he owed her expectations of him, and while she was light-years away from its meaning anything to her, and he saw it as a pleasant way of bringing an evening to a close, why not?

Since their first date they hadn't always met at the Allamanda, giving Donna to hope that, by spreading their patronage to other hotels and swimming pools, Margot would be deprived of capital for gossip to Elyot or to anyone else.

But they were due for dinner at the Allamanda on the day that Wilmot received a letter from the Company, committing him, at the Company's expense, to the immediate repair of the Dial House, the condition of which had been adversely reported upon in strong terms by Mr. Elyot Vance of the Marquise estate, whose concern for the public danger was such as to cause him to offer both his own architect's services and the necessary labour for the restoration of the property—which offer the Company had been grateful to accept; and had so informed Mr. Vance by current airmail, understanding that as soon as he received the Company's agreement he would put the work in hand.

While Donna read the letter which Wilmot had handed to her, he was echoing aloud some of its formal phrases which he seemed to find particularly offensive, "'Strong terms.' 'Concern for the public danger.' The wheeling and dealing of the fellow! Knew the Growers' Association couldn't give him the go-ahead to interfere, so he creeps behind my back to get a ruling from the Company which he knows I can't ignore!"

Donna returned the letter, grateful for her father's tact in keeping her name out of the affair. "Mr. Vance did give you the opportunity to act with him yourself, without his going to the Company," she reminded Wilmot. "On the same terms too—that he would undertake the actual work."

"Under threat that he would go to the Company if I didn't agree. That's blackmail, no less! Does he realise, I'd like to know, that every man-jack he puts on the job will be a trespasser on my property?"

"I'd doubt that, if he has our Company's permission to put them there."

"Bah! And I suppose he'll expect me to be grateful to him for doing it?"

"And I should doubt that too," said Donna. "He didn't sound very much bothered about getting your approval, and since he has gone over your head, I can't think he will look to you for an about-face on something he'll be doing for his own satisfaction."

It was difficult, this sitting on a peace-fence between the two men. Previously, after Madame Hué's visit, Donna had asked Bran what, if anything, he knew of the deep causes for Wilmot's antagonism for Elyot. But Bran, sceptical and only vaguely interested, had proved Madame Hué's contention that the younger generation did not easily appreciate that its elders could love or suffer for love, and it was left to Donna, seeing both sides through the eyes of loyalty and dawning love, to wish she dared say to either man—"Enough is enough, and it's all been water under the bridge for a long, long time." But which of them was likely to listen to her if she did?

Sometimes on their dates Melford Drinan would call for her. Usually, when they were to meet at the Allamanda, she would drive down herself in Wilmot's car, and she did so that evening. They were to rendezvous in the salon adjoining the main bar. She couldn't see him when she arrived, so as there was a great crush there, she found a seat fairly near the door, in order to intercept him as soon as he came in.

She saw him before he saw her. As he came through the open swing doors abreast of several other people, Donna's glance went beyond him to notice Elyot not far behind him. She looked back at Melford and moved towards him, getting ready to smile a greeting. But he came on, seeing her, she knew from his direct look at her, but giving no sign of recognition; instead making some observation to the tall, ash-blonde girl beside him, who in turn passed it on to the exquisitely groomed, statuesque woman on her other side.

The three laughed, and Donna, seeing Melford's solicitous hand beneath the girl's elbow, halted so suddenly that she was jostled by someone behind her.

So they hadn't just happened to be level at the doorway. The two women were *with* Melford, and in consequence he had cut her dead! That he was not alone had to be the reason, for Donna was quite certain he had seen her. Moreover, when she allowed them to pass within a yard or two of her on their way into the salon, he had looked at her again, his eyes vacant as a stranger's.

She couldn't believe it. It was an experience she had never suffered before. She stood as if rooted, a lone island of a figure around whom people had to divide. She felt waves of mortification and anger flood hot colour into her face. Had anyone who knew her seen her humiliation, she wondered—and found the question answered when a hand clamped about her wrist, holding it low, out of sight of those around her, and she found herself staring into Elyot's blazing eyes.

Almost through clenched teeth he muttered. "We're getting out of here. Come—"

"What—?" She pulled against him, but his grip on her wrist was like a handcuff as he shouldered a way for himself and for her, out through the doors, across the bar and taking the opposite direction from the carpark, drew her the whole length of the adjoining colonnade to a point where it was deserted and shadowed.

There he released her, freeing her with so abrupt a turn of his own wrist that she was flung round to face him. "So," he accused her thickly, "it took *that*, did it, to show you how the drip regards you? As a pretty pass-the-time at best, and at worst, only just this side of a common call-girl—!"

At that she flared, and her open palm only failed to make violent contact when he caught her hand within an inch of his cheek, and jerked it back at her.

"That was vixenish and kitchenmaid. Don't do it again," he warned her.

"You called me something worse than a kitchen-maid!" she flashed.

"Well, was I wrong to conclude you've let yourself be treated so? Just now you *were* ready to greet the guy with a wreathed smile—right?"

"We—we had a date for dinner," she said faintly.

"And he meant you to get the message that he didn't want to know, being otherwise engaged—right again?"

"He cut me deliberately—yes."

"Spelling it out that, as I've said, you've been nothing better than a fill-gap for his leisure all these weeks. Or do you deny that he's only had to beckon, and you've gone running? Dinner, lunch, drinks—you name it. Well?"

"It hasn't been like that. He has asked me out quite often, but I haven't always gone."

"No? I'll believe you if you can name six occasions when you've turned him down."

"There haven't *been* many more than six times in all. And anyway, how would you know if there had?" she demanded with the false bravado of a child caught out in a lie.

"Oh, my dear—!" His tone was mock-pitying of her naïveté. "Haven't you learnt yet the extent to which, in a tight little community like Laraye, we *all* know *all* that goes on, and anything we happen to miss, someone is bound to tell us, whether we're interested or not?"

"In other words you, not interested, as you were, couldn't escape hearing about me and Melford Drinan?"

"If no one else told me, Margot would have done. As Nature abhors a vacuum, she abhors uneven numbers among the sexes, and getting them neatly matched up, two by two, is by no means the least of her many, many talents. A pity she seems to have been wrong about Drinan's pursuit of you being for real; her instinct for romance doesn't usually betray her like that, but she may have been misled by the stars in your eyes, perhaps."

"There haven't *been* stars in my eyes for him!"

"There were tonight when you looked at him. Who is your glamorous rival, do you know?"

Donna shook her head. "I've never seen her before."

"Nor the social dragon type with her? Her mother? An aunt? No matter. We'll find out. And now—what for you?"

"Now? I shall go straight home, of course."

"Run away and hide and lick your wounds? You'll do no such thing. You'll dine here—and like it."

"Alone? In full view, when you say everyone knows?"

"You'll dine—with me. And what's more, you'll be *seen* to like it."

"I—can't. You'll be dining with Margot."

"Margot has joined a party on board the banana boat for dinner. I dropped in for a drink and wasn't staying for dinner. I shall now, so come along and show some spirit. You aren't the first girl to be taken for a ride, and you won't be the last. So come."

At the entrance to the dining-room he took some time choosing a table, even consulting the head waiter's chart before accepting a centrally placed one where he seated Donna facing the whole room before he excused himself for leaving her while he telephoned

Choc to say that he wouldn't be dining at home. He was away for some time, and while he was gone a waiter showed Melford Drinan and his guests to a table apart from Donna's by only a few yards, leaving her in little doubt as to the reason for Elyot's choice and his insistence on seeing the table plan. He had meant to embarrass Melford with her proximity and he couldn't have chosen better; already Melford was avoiding looking in Donna's direction, and it was going to be difficult for him to glance about him in any natural way at all if he were not to catch her eye while she was so near.

Elyot came back. As he sat down he announced, "Latest arrivals—Mrs. Clara Berger and her daughter Ingrid; the latter, fiancée of Melford Drinan of Hexagon Inc.; the two ladies having descended on him unheralded, to surprise him for his birthday."

Donna drew a sharp breath. "How—how do you know?"

He shrugged. "Reception desks know everything and will tell it all for a small fee. And now—if it hurts like nobody's business and as if your life depended upon it—*smile*!"

Donna smiled, and wished she could tell him why it didn't hurt a bit.

CHAPTER SIX

SINCE SHE WAS more angry than hurt, and it was only her pride that was in shock, Donna found she could despise Melford Drinan's efforts to ignore her. What a snob and a coward the man was! Though—her scorn checked guiltily on the thought—wasn't she perhaps equally a coward to have let Elyot force his protection on her in order to save her face with Melford? Oughtn't she to have had the dignity to refuse his offer of shelter?

In fantasy she saw herself doing it—drawing upon hauteur to tell him something like, "If you think *that* of me, you can't want to be seen with me, except from pity, which I don't need." That would at least have been in keeping with her primitive impulse to slap his face for his insult.

But somehow fantasy couldn't stand up to the hard fact of his dominance; of his refusal to be thwarted in any purpose he saw as right. He thought she needed moral support against Melford; he meant to afford it, and from experience Donna had learned that a No to his will was not a word he would tolerate. Not that—for quite other reasons than he would understand—had she really wanted to say No...

During dinner he made a business of his attentions to her—ordering for her an orchid spray from the flower-girl, calling acquaintances over to be introduced or for chat between courses and inviting her to dance whenever Melford and his fiancée were also taking the floor. And since only Donna knew that the show was staged merely for Melford's discomfiture, she wondered how the story of Elyot's elaborate entertainment of her would reach Margot's ears.

Would the gossips make capital of it—(When the cat is away...) or would Elyot relate it and its reasons to Margot himself? And would Margot agree magnanimously that it had been the least he could do for darling Donna in face of so blatant a snub? Donna viewed the latter prospect with distaste. Elyot had acted tautly and promptly on his pity for her; Margot would make such a meal of hers!

At the end of the evening Elyot insisted on seeing her home.

"That's not necessary," she told him. "I drove myself down in Uncle Wilmot's car."

"Mean to say our two-timing friend hasn't been calling for you on dates and taking you home?"

"Not when I was able to borrow the car."

"As I might have guessed. Sultan summons his current favourite houri and she hastens to his command. And when you had wined and dined or whatever, he saluted you chastely in the car park and waved you away?" Evidently concluding—rightly—that she would scorn to answer this, he went on, "Where are you parked? I'll get one of the hotel drivers to ferry your car back, and I'll drive you in mine."

Having yielded to him on the major issue, Donna felt this was too minor a one for argument. She indicated her car, saw him approach a man, watched money pass, and then Elyot was handing her into his own car.

Donna never ceased to marvel at the magic of the island by night. It had been raining earlier, and as they skirted the town the pavements shone cleanly and the street lamps wore nimbuses of gold in the humid air. The lights on the quays cast broken paths across the water of the harbour; music and laughter came from the open doors of taverns, and the residential hills were dotted with domestic lights to a certain level, above which the heights were uniformly black. It was not until the last house had been left behind and they were into the dark of the forest trees and not now very far from Louvet, that Elyot remarked, "Well, I hope the exercise has done something for your self-respect. But what are you going to do when the fellow comes creeping to apologise?"

"If this evening was anything to go by, he isn't going to look my way long enough to apologise," Donna said.

"But if he does, are you going to let him get away with explaining he had grit in his eye, and chant, 'Not to worry. All is forgiven'?" Elyot persisted.

"Which would get me a long way, wouldn't it, in face of a life-sized fiancée with a prior claim?" she retorted.

He glanced at her quickly. "Was that the voice of cynicism, or of wounded resignation to your having been conned?"

"Neither. Just accepting the fact that a very pleasant interlude is over." Donna's tone was dry.

"There wasn't much 'acceptance' in your face when he cut you dead!"

"Because I didn't care for the way it was done. But there's no question of his deceiving me. We both enjoyed each other's company, but that was as far as it went."

"By his will or yours? All right, you don't have to answer that. To my reading of it, that look on your face said it all."

"Said *what* all?"

"That you were looking at a man you had begun to care about, and couldn't believe he could treat you so. With cause, I daresay, because between his allowing you to chauffeur yourself to your rendezvous and bidding you goodnight, no doubt he made love to you?"

"It depends on what you mean by making love."

"You know perfectly well what we mean by it these days, and it isn't your chap manoeuvring to hold your hand after he's picked up your dropped fan. Presumably he kissed you?"

"I don't have to answer that either!"

Elyot laughed. "My dear, you've answered it by refusing to. And if it was all so platonic, why was he guilty enough to hand you the frozen mitt?"

Sensing that he saw that as unanswerable, Donna said nothing. She realised too the futility of suggesting that he drop her at the top of the lane to the house, and when he reached it he drove down it in silence and stopped the car.

"Thank you." She stirred in her seat and bunched her long skirts preparatory to getting out. But when he made no move himself she added, "Thank you too for thinking you had to come to my rescue; I do admit I'd never been cut so deliberately before, and for the moment I *was* shattered."

He shrugged. "Feel free to appeal for a repeat performance any time," he said.

"There won't be another time."

"Meanwhile you enjoyed our evening?"

"Very much."

"Good. So there only remains some unfinished business—"

She turned her head quickly, looking a question to which her senses knew the answer. For his arms were round her, his head bent, his lips too close to hers for any intent other than the long searching kiss they extorted, urging a submission she was tempted to yield to the reality of his nearness, his touch, the warmth of his breath on her cheek, the pressure of his hold. This ought to be a dream come true... But "unfinished business"! Making a duty of kissing her, and expecting her compliance because she had admitted her gratitude for all the rest!

No. She didn't think she had uttered the word aloud, but whether or not, as she stiffened within his arms he held her off from him, his wry scrutiny measuring her reaction.

"That was totally unnecessary," she said.

"Unnecessary? What a dreary word! Anyway, who-ever kisses a girl of necessity?" he parried. "I can think of a dozen reasons for, and necessity's not one of them. Competition, for instance—"

Her heart quickened, but she mustn't let herself be-lieve it. "You're not in competition for me against any-one," she snapped.

"For this evening's you, I am. Against friend Dri-nan. When a guy has been allowed to cut in, you shouldn't underrate his urge to do better than the other fellow. Matter of male pride, you might say, and a really co-operative girl would indulge it."

"*Would* she? Would she indeed?" Donna raged. "Indulge him in something completely pseudo, just to boost his ego, or—maybe—to do a Tommy Tucker act in payment for her supper?"

His hands, still holding her lightly, dropped away. "If I may say so, that was well below the belt," he re-marked.

She knew it and regretted it, but couldn't bring her-self to apologise. Instead she murmured lamely, "You can hardly blame me for wondering—"

"On the contrary, I can and I do. I told you I kissed you just now for competition's sake, and however shady you consider that, it's not as low as expecting payment for services rendered. Anyway, forget it. You can quit wondering from now on. It won't happen again," he retorted, his dismissive tone a rebuke she couldn't take.

Making that his exit line, was he? Well, she had one to deliver too. "With me, perhaps not," she said. "But to-morrow night, with another girl, in competition with another man? And the night after that—" She checked, daunted by the ironic lift of his brows.

"*Three* different girls inside a week?" he mocked.

"Promiscuous opportunist I may be, but that's achievement indeed!"

Later Donna was to realise that if she had accepted that as lightly as he said it, she might have laughed with him and they would have parted friends. But at the moment she was too hurt, too disillusioned, too cheated of dreams. She had to hit back.

"Is it so very much more than your reputation says of you?" she queried, and then added the unforgivable thing. "It isn't as if, either, you were all that free to play around, competing. There's—Margot," she said.

His immediate answer to that was to open the door on his side, go round and open hers. He helped her out and with a hand beneath her elbow, marched her to the foot of the verandah steps, where he said, "You can leave Margot out of this, do you mind? Goodnight."

He didn't wait to see her into the house, and as she watched him return to the car without looking back her heart was crying, "Fool! Fool! He kissed you, wanted to, even if only just for tonight. And you could have tried to understand, even gone along with him in that spirit, enjoyed it, however little real promise it had for you. Instead—"

But the Instead was so shame-making that she couldn't bear to recall it. *Blot it out. Forget it. Think of something else.*

She only wished she could. It had lost her a friend.

SHE SUFFERED A RESTLESS NIGHT, but daylight brought more balance, more detachment, and she was able to persuade herself that the situation was not all of her making. She had been goaded into her spiteful mudslinging, and if only in return for Elyot's initial contemptuous name-calling—which showed what he really thought of her?—she could almost justify it.

Admittedly it wasn't the done thing, to taunt a man about his reputation with women, nor to accuse him of exacting payment in return for his hospitality. But Elyot had asked for it—hadn't he?—by kissing her in the intense way he had, tempting her to believe in its promise, and then claiming it as the unfinished business of proving himself the better man of two!

Donna's veering from her overnight mood of self-blame and regret was so complete that from there she went on to wonder whether Elyot too might be having second thoughts. Perhaps he would telephone. He might want her to know that he had had the green light from the Company to go ahead with the restoration of the Dial House. Or he might just ring to say Hello, How goes it?—which he would intend as face-saving for them both. Or he might be there, and normally friendly, the next time she went down to the Allamanda.

But he was not there. He did not ring on any pretext. He gave no sign of having anything more to say to her or to do with her at all.

Meanwhile events proved him wrong in his forecast of a situation where Melford Drinan would excuse his conduct to Donna and she might be weak enough to forgive it. For the situation did not arise. Three days later she heard from Rosa at the hotel's reception desk that Melford and the ladies Berger had checked out that morning on their return to America by non-stop jet.

"Throw big party last night. For 'm birthday, the Mister's, they say," Rosa reported with relish. "Chef make 'm big cake on towers—" her flattened hand demonstrated the tiers of a ceremonial cake—"ask plenty hotel guests. Miss le Conte, she there. Not Mister Vance. Not you, Miss Donna. But they ask you for sure—yes?"

Donna replied truthfully that she hadn't known about the party, and not so truthfully that she couldn't have accepted if invited. So that was that, she thought. Incident closed. And in this, she conceded, Elyot had been right. She had been no more than a fill-gap for Melford Drinan after all.

Naturally she couldn't escape Bran's comments on Melford's pursuit of her and his sudden defection.

"Why all the enthusiasm for you, only to stand you up?" Bran wanted to know. "Or did you stand *him* up before or after he imported a fiancée ready made? Down at the hotel they'd all decided it was a case, when surprise, surprise! he's off and you're not telling. So what did happen to break it up, for goodness' sake?"

"Nothing in particular." Donna was grateful that no one who mattered, except Elyot, had witnessed or questioned Melford's blatant snub. "It just wasn't a case in the way you mean—ever," she added.

"Meaning you weren't ever turned on about him?"

"Meaning just that. Nor was he about me."

"Well, obviously, since he had this other wench in tow all the while," Bran agreed. "Anyway, I'll believe you that you don't care. But you could have fooled *me*."

It was a day or two later that Donna had a letter from her father asking if she had now learned enough about conditions at Louvet to feel she could sound Wilmot as to its future.

"We can't afford much longer for it to be as unproductive as it is at present," he wrote. "So as you say you know Elyot Vance of Marquise is interested in it, perhaps you're in a position to find out what terms he has in mind, and then from your uncle whether he would do a deal? Of course the Company would not care to ride roughshod over him, but if neither he nor Brandon are prepared to keep it up, we might have to go over his head in disposing of it.

"So I'm trusting you, dear, to approach both sides with tact and see what emerges. Meanwhile, make the most of your time to enjoy Laraye, as I know you will."

Donna put aside the letter with a grimace. Easier said than done! One side—Elyot's—she couldn't now approach at all, with or without tact, and she doubted how far the same quality would go with Wilmot. Of course the Company would have to deal with both parties formally, but she understood her father's need to test the atmosphere first, so she supposed she must try. She decided to ask Bran to approach Elyot, and she tackled Wilmot herself.

As she had feared, her first exploratory questions brought his reaction that she had been put up to them by Elyot's coveting of the estate. This she was glad to be able to deny with truth, but she had to admit to her father's interest in the answers.

"Then you can tell him that he'd be better employed telling me how to conjure labour out of thin air and how to grow a commercially viable crop on soil as poor as Louvet's," snapped Wilmot.

"But it's so close to Marquise. Is it possible for its soil to be very different and poor? Besides, if it's as poor as all that, would Mr. Vance see any potential value in taking it into Marquise?"

That was a mistake, and Wilmot pounced on it.

"So now we have it!" he triumphed. "If, as you say, you aren't in league with the fellow, how do you know he's after it?"

Donna did her best to recoup ground. "I've neither seen him nor spoken to him about Louvet," she said. "But you know he would like to buy it, don't you, and I think it was Bran who told me so, soon after I came. And as Bran is quite frank that he isn't interested in Louvet, and you regard it as a burden in its present condition, I'd have thought—"

"Oh, you would, would you? Well, let me tell you this, young woman. While Elyot Vance is in the market for Louvet, and could outbid anyone else for it, no doubt, I'm no party to its being put up for sale, and so you can tell brother George when you write whatever report you may have promised him—"

It was at this point of deadlock that Madame Hué descended—literally, since her car hurtled down the lane at breakneck speed—upon the interview, and being Madame Hué, she had no compunction in listening in and taking sides.

"The Greeks had a word for the likes of you, Wilmot," she admonished him. "Needn't remind you what it is, need I? Don't want Louvet yourself; bare your teeth at anyone else who'd relieve you of it; won't do what you could do better than any man—write a book—with illustrations—that all the tourists would flock to buy. Bah, Wilmot Torrence, you haven't got the sense you were born with, man! But I, Irma Hué, your friend, know just what you are lacking. Shall I tell you what it is, hm?"

Wilmot's teeth could be heard to grind. "Not until I've told you, Irma Hué, to keep your nose out of my affairs," he growled.

Her fat shoulders shrugged. "Is that all that is new? Why, you tell me the same thing every time we meet, my friend. And so, for your lack of originality, I shall not now tell you what I know you need." She turned to Donna. "Run, child, and fetch the covered basket from my car. On the seat, yes. It is mangoes from Mousquetaire. You haven't a tree here, I know. We will take them together to Juno. Come."

On the way to the kitchen quarters she suddenly chuckled. "But you know what I threaten your bear of an uncle with, don't you, child?"

Donna thought back to their first meeting and smiled. "Perhaps I can guess. A—wife?" she ventured.

"But of course, a wife. He has been without one for too long."

"And have you anyone in mind?"

Madame Hué's eyes widened. "Naturally," she said. "Myself."

IN THE KITCHEN they found Juno in an unusually sombre mood. Her smile did not flash and her tongue did not prattle, and in answer to Madame Hué's brisk questions as to what was wrong, she admitted she was "troubled."

"Troubled!" echoed Madame Hué. "You are not ill; you have a good master and a secure place and no wild children to worry about. Nor, you should be thankful, a bad husband. So what ails you?"

Juno shook a head on which even the ribbon topknot was limp. "You say so, mistress, and all true. But it is not for myself that I worry. It is for my cousin Maria and her man Choc at Marquise."

"And what ails *them*, then?"

"They think they lose their places, Mister Vance's cook and man."

"Nonsense," scoffed Madame Hué. "Maria and Choc Baptiste belong to Marquise as a banana does inside its skin. Elyot Vance would be a fool to get rid of them, and Elyot Vance is no fool."

"A good man too," Juno confirmed.

"So why should this good man dismiss them? Has he told them they are to go?"

"Not yet he say to them go."

"Then why should they think he means to?"

But Juno either did not know or was not to be drawn as to the reason for their fears. She stated again, "They think so," and, further pressed by Madame Hué, added, "They hear so" and "People, they talk, tell them," but beyond that she would not go.

Madame Hué collected her basket from which Juno had emptied the mangoes, advised astringently, "Tell them they make volcano out of anthill, and not to heed people's talk," and then made a royal command of inviting Donna to luncheon at Mousquetaire.

As Donna feared it might be, the drive was a skin-prickling experience. At one point Madame Hué drove the nearside wheels of her car into a foot-deep rut at the road verge, whereupon she made a loud-hailer of her cupped hands, hollaed through them, summoning from an apparently empty landscape four or five youths who shouldered the car free, were rewarded with smiles and money, and melted again into their background as surprisingly as they had appeared out of it.

"When a woman finds herself in trouble, a man always comes along," commented Madame Hué comfortably as she was enabled to drive on towards the next hazard, whatever it might be.

Mousquetaire perched on its steep hillside as if it had been flung there and had stuck. Donna never ceased to marvel at the narrowness of mountain shelves which had been judged wide enough to accommodate Larayan houses, and Mousquetaire was no exception. It jutted out above its precipitous approach like a beetling cliff.

For luncheon there was flying fish and a chicken-and-rice dish. With it Donna drank cool coconut water—a novelty to her—poured from a green coconut, hacked in two with a cutlass by Madame Hué's garden man.

Afterwards, as they sat on her verandah, she asked suddenly, "You think me mad to suppose I could marry Wilmot, I expect?"

"Well—" Donna sought for a tactful answer, "somehow I'd never visualised his rousing himself enough to marry again. He's so—so negative about anything outside his own interests."

"Which is why a positive person like myself must take him in hand. I agree—he would not *marry*; therefore he must *be married*—find himself so, and I am working on it. You will see!"

Donna, remembering Wilmot's scathing criticism of her hostess, doubted whether any amount of the latter's "working" would bring him to the altar. But she was spared any comment as Madame Hué went on. "Not that even I would take him on while he is so pigheaded over Louvet. *No* woman in her senses would marry herself to a brokenbacked banana patch by choice, and as I have all my senses about me, I think, he must sell it to Elyot Vance before I even consider giving him my Yes."

Which, if it were true, gave Wilmot some breathing space, Donna thought with relief. For if Madame Hué were not going to lay concentrated siege to Wilmot's affections until he had sold Louvet to Elyot, she was likely to have to wait a very long time! And even her subsequent musing, "Though who knows?—one may find ways, perhaps, of working on that too," did not unduly disturb Donna for Wilmot's sake. On that score she could not see Irma Hué's power to budge him an inch.

At about four o'clock they set out on the return journey to Louvet. But nearing it by a few miles, Donna was puzzled at the road her companion was taking, and said so.

Madame Hué nodded. "That's right. I am not going straight to Louvet. We are making a detour first—to Marquise. If he is at home I am going to ask Elyot Vance the truth of these fears of the Baptistes, and if he is not, I shall find out from them."

"But ought you to expect that you'll be told?" Donna asked, aghast, not only at her companion's interference, but that she herself was being carried uninvited to Elyot's home.

"I mean to be told. For how can one help, if one doesn't know what the trouble is?" Irma sounded satisfied with the sweet reason of her reply. "And didn't I tell you that I am known for solving other people's problems—so long as they confide in me what they are—which, sooner or later, they usually do?"

To Donna's relief Elyot was not at home when they arrived. But when Choc answered the door to tell them so, Donna was shepherded ahead of Irma to the kitchen quarters, where Maria was dispiritedly chopping peppers for a salad.

"And now what's all this about your having to leave Mister Vance?" Irma demanded of her.

Maria's eyes widened. "How you hear, Miss Hué?"

"From your cousin Juno at Louvet. Who else? And so?"

Maria hung her head. "Not right to say," she said woodenly.

"Tcha!" Irma turned to Choc. "You then—you tell me. What is it all about?"

"Well, Miss"—he hesitated, then plunged without his wife's permission—"Like this, see. Miss le Conte, she come up Marquise; say Maria not do things right; tell me *I* not do things right; grumble, find fault. Say she tell Mister we no-goods, and she make big change; send us away, get fine valet-man for Mister, and proper chef."

Irma Hué nodded. "Margot le Conte, eh? And when does she say you are to go?"

Choc shrugged. "Don't know. Just say."

Irma turned to Donna. "She means when she marries Elyot, no doubt. Interesting, that. One hadn't heard he had decided on double harness just yet." Of Choc she asked, "Does Miss le Conte tell you this when Mr. Vance is there? Did he tell her to say you must leave?"

Again Choc said, "Don't know. But she not say it for sure, 'less he agrees?"

"We'll see about that," Irma ruled crisply. "When do you expect Mr. Vance to be in?"

But her question was not answered when there was a shout for Choc from the front of the house, and he leaped to obey it, followed through from the kitchen by Madame Hué and, reluctantly behind her, by Donna.

"Ah, Irma Hué. I saw your car." Elyot took her hand. Without being told, Choc picked up a drinks tray and carried it off, and Elyot's glance went beyond Irma to Donna. "Donna too. How are you?" he asked.

It was not a question to answer literally, and Donna hated herself for blushing at the memory of their last parting. Irma was saying, "Donna has been lunching with me and I am taking her home to Louvet. No, we aren't staying for drinks. I only looked in to learn the truth of a monstrous thing we heard of first from Wilmot Torrence's Juno about your Choc and your Maria—that, at Margot le Conte's say-so, you are sending them packing. *Is* that so? Are you?"

Watching Elyot's inscrutable expression, Donna wondered how Madame Hué could possibly have expected that his loyalty to Margot would allow him to give a straight answer to the impertinence of the question. Nor did he. He said smoothly, "You heard this from Juno, you say?" addressing Donna rather than Madame Hué, who cut in.

"*She* didn't. We did—just this morning, and only the smallest hint from Juno. But I've coaxed the details out of Choc, and now, Elyot Vance, I mean to hear from you whether or not it is true."

"Why?" he asked.

It was the first time Donna had seen Irma nonplussed. "Why?" she echoed. "Well—"

"Would you perhaps be thinking of taking them on yourself?" Elyot pressed.

"No, of course not. I have my Winston and my Sadie—"

"Or could you, I wonder, have persuaded yourself that it's any of your business?" Elyot went on, as if she hadn't spoken.

"But of course it's my business!" she snapped back. "As it would be the business of any of your friends who saw you making a fool and a knave of yourself at the behest of a woman! Don't forget, young Elyot, I first knew you when you were knee-high to a footstool, and over six feet tall though you may be now and cocksure with it, when I give you advice for your own good, you will kindly listen to it."

He nodded. "Willingly. *When* I've asked you for it in the first place."

The sound which issued from Irma's lips was a small explosion. "Come, Donna!" she ordered, stalking away. "Doing a kindness; saving a man from his own folly—and what thanks does one get for one's trouble? None—none at all!"

Elyot, making no attempt to stop her, followed her out abreast with Donna, to whom, to her surprise, he said, "Haven't we a provisional date for you to spend a shipment day on the estate? What about the next one—Thursay of next week?"

An olive branch? Or a sign of how trivially he remembered the acrimony in which their last meeting had ended; of how little a difference with her mattered to him? Donna heard herself saying, "Thank you. I'd like that—if you can spare the time for me," only to feel rebuffed by his careless, "Good. I'll tell Couseau that you want to see the whole thing through, and he'll look after you. Do you want him to send a car for you?"

"No, I can walk over. It's no distance."

"It means a very early start—soon after first light."

"That's all right. I wake early."

"And go prepared for any weather. If the heavens fall the shipment has to get away."

"I'll do that." His use of the word "go" emphasised for her that he was consigning her to the care of his estate manager; that he wouldn't be there himself.

Madame Hué's parting shot to him, delivered from her driving seat, was, "If you part from good faithful people like the Baptistes you will regret it, Elyot Vance!" To which he replied, "You think so?" and waved the car away.

Presently, after some minutes of wordless huffing and puffing, she said to Donna, "Of course what I really meant was that he's a fool if he allows Margot le Conte to wear the trousers for him already. Do you suppose he understood that?" And then, without waiting for Donna's reply, added, "And what was all that about a date with you?"

"It was just that, as I haven't seen a consignment harvested or shipped from Louvet, he once suggested I should spend a whole shipment day on Marquise, and so suggested next Thursday."

"You have been in touch with him then, since you met him by chance on your first day?"

"From time to time. He has been very kind."

"And what does Wilmot say to that?"

"Mr. Vance doesn't come to the house, but Uncle Wilmot knows I have seen him sometimes, and doesn't mind."

"Which is more than you can expect of Margot le Conte, if she suspects Elyot of being too kind to a pretty girl like you. But that is no bad thing either—some corrective jealousy for that young woman who has always been too sure of her men by half." Madame Hué nodded sagely. "Yes, I for one would not be desolated for Margot le Conte to learn the hard lesson that a man like Elyot is only as faithful as his lack of opportunities allows."

Donna said drily, "Well, she also has been kindness itself to me and must know she could have no possible cause for jealousy of me over Elyot."

"Then you would still claim, as you did at our first meeting, that you are not, as you would say, turned on by him, or as I would say, *bouleversée*, bowled over? Extraordinary!" marvelled Madame Hué.

"Why should it be?" Donna hedged.

"Because—" Madame Hué actually slowed the car for the plunge into the house lane—"because if he weren't the high-handed, self-satisfied tycoon that he is and just about as pigheaded as Wilmot Torrence, which makes two of them, I might fall for him myself," she concluded as she rocketed down the lane and brought the car to a standstill within a yard of the cliff-guarding crotons for the second time that day.

CHAPTER SEVEN

WHEN DONNA HAD TOLD Madame Hué that Margot had been kind to her, she had been entirely sincere. Though they had little in common and a very little of the other girl's extravagant company was more than enough for her, she supposed that Margot probably tolerated her to about the same degree. So that Bran's blunt question of the following day found her totally unprepared for it.

"And what have you been up to, to get so thoroughly on the wrong side of Margot?" Bran wanted to know.

"I? On her wrong side? So far as I'm aware, I've done nothing to upset her. What do you mean?" Donna frowned.

"Well, having just gathered that you're by no means one of her favourite people, I wondered why," said Bran.

"You gathered? How? What has she said to you about me, then?"

"About you, but not to me. I happened to be listening in uninvited."

"Oh, Bran—eavesdropping?"

"Why not, when I realised she was talking about your Melford Drinan fiasco?" Bran paused. "You do seem to have let her make a fool of you over him, don't you, my pet?"

"I don't know what you're talking about," Donna sighed. "For goodness' sake, begin at the beginning and explain."

"Well, it was at her last night's weekly cocktail party.

Margot was gossiping with her dearest rival, the manager's wife from L'Hotel Atlantique on Bayonet Bay. I was standing solo nearby. The two of them were swopping boasts about the Top People they'd landed this season; the Court Circular and New York's Four Hundred had nothing on the list of the names they dropped. And when Margot quoted Melford Drinan of Hexagon Inc. and Mrs. Tours came back at her with an oil-sheik plus bodyguard, Margot switched the interest back to Drinan by saying next, 'The joke was that while he was here alone, before his fiancée and her mother—they're Bergers, you know—came down to join him, he took a temporary fling with one of my little girl tourist guides, a young innocent without a *clue*, my dear. Flattered to her eyebrows, of course, but dropped flat when the Bergers arrived and the Berger girl retook possession.' Or words to that effect," Bran concluded.

Donna felt suddenly cold, but tried to brace herself. "And by the 'little girl,' Margot meant me, you knew?"

"Who else?"

"Of course. So what did Mrs. Tours say then?"

"She sounded sorry for you. She said, 'Poor child! But if she was as green as all that, shouldn't someone have warned her not to get involved?' And then, as if she'd been sharpening her knives in readiness for Margot, she went on very sweetly, 'You, dear, for instance? Do you mean to say *you* didn't know all about Melford Drinan's having a Berger daughter for a fiancée before any of them came down to Laraye?' Which—as no doubt the Tours woman intended—rather put Margot on the spot, didn't it?"

"How did it?" asked Donna dully.

"Well, either she had to admit that she wasn't all that well informed, or that she could have warned you and hadn't. Anyway, she threw you to the lions by snapping back. 'But of course I knew. What are gossip columns for?' Not being willing to have it supposed that she wasn't entirely *au fait* with all the details of her clients' social life, you see, she preferred to take any blame that was coming to her for not putting you wise when she could have done."

"And did she really know Melford was engaged, do you think?"

"Sure thing, I'd say. Trust Margot," said Bran with conviction.

"So did Mrs. Tours hand out any blame?"

"Mildly. She murmured something about, In her place, she'd have thought it only fair to put you on your guard, etc. etc.... But Margot only shrugged and said, 'Who would suppose nowadays that any girl out of her teens couldn't recognise and avoid a wolf—if she wanted to?' And then something about, So whose fault was it, if you took a tumble when he let you down? Which, when she switched the talk to something else, left me with the distinct impression that she might have been gunning for you for quite some time, and I asked myself why then, and now I'm asking you," Bran finished, slightly out of breath.

Angry and bewildered, Donna couldn't tell him. "Did you do anything? Say anything? Intervene?" she asked.

"How could I? It wasn't as if she had slandered you or lied about you. She'd only shown herself to be supremely mean."

"Though she did lie about me without knowing it. For as I told you at the time, I didn't take any tumble over Melford Drinan. We were never on the terms she concluded we were. But it does show I've been wrong in thinking she liked me—well, moderately at least, whereas now it seems she hasn't had any use for me ever since—"

As Donna paused, searching her memory, Bran prompted, "Ever since when?"

But she couldn't name a precise point in time. All she knew was that if Bran were right about Margot's pre-knowledge of Melford's engagement, she must somehow have earned Margot's enmity before that afternoon when Margot had congratulated her so expansively on her capture of his interest and had enthused in the same vein over the telephone to Elyot.

So early then in their relationship? Donna questioned. But since when or why, she had no idea, and told Bran so, convincing him, she thought.

When she was alone she wondered whether she could expect Bran to challenge Margot on her behalf, though she realised she couldn't. To do so would be to admit his eavesdropping, for which Margot was likely to give him short shrift. Besides, he enjoyed his work for her too much to risk her displeasure merely in defence of a cousin. But if Margot represented a rewarding meal-ticket for Bran, Donna had no such need to placate her, nor to oblige her any longer as a "little tourist guide," and Donna couldn't wait to opt out as soon as she had fulfilled her current appointments. She did so by asking Rosa to take no more bookings for her, and she notified Margot in a guarded letter, thanking her for asking her co-operation and affording her the chance to explore the island, but claiming that now, possibly within weeks of her return to England, she ought to give more time to Louvet and her uncle's interests, hoping that Margot would understand.

In the circumstances she didn't really expect Margot's complacence, and she wasn't going to get it, as Margot, having sent no reply in writing, made clear as Donna was leaving the hotel after her last assignment.

Margot waylaid her and asked her into her office, where with her usual overemphasis of the most ordinary remarks, she declaimed tragically, "Darling, this is so *sudden*! You can't mean to do it to me—you really can't!"

Donna cringed from the falsity of "Darling." How completely insincere was it possible to get? "I must, I'm afraid," she said shortly.

"But why, my pet, *why*? At the very height of my season and you such a total success with everyone you took out—why?"

(If you don't know why, you'd better start guessing.) Aloud Donna said, "I told you my reasons in my letter. I came to see my uncle and Bran and Louvet and to discuss some problems on my father's behalf, and we've made very little headway yet. I've got to give them more time than I have up to now."

"Pff! As if we didn't all know Louvet is past hope, darling. And, hand on heart, *would* you say Wilmot Torrence either notices or cares whether you're there or not?" Margot coaxed, but after Donna had doggedly said nothing, her tone changed, turned ugly.

"I *see*," she nodded. "It suited you to make a convenience of my offer to give you a free run of the island, a lot of free meals, social openings, but as soon as it suits you better not to honour your side of the bargain, you decide to skip—isn't that so?"

Donna allowed fairly, "It could look like that to you, but I did give you notice in writing and I told the desk not to book any more tours for me."

"For reasons which a blind man could see through!" Margot scoffed. "Oh no, my dear. I know perfectly well why you are piqued enough to let me down. You were so flattered by Melford Drinan's attentions and you set such store on snaring him that when his fiancée turned up and you realised he had just been playing around, you felt you had to blame someone, and you've picked on *me*! This was the only way you could think of getting back at me, and so—"

Donna said evenly, "All I've done is to end an arrangement which suited us both when we made it, and I think I've honoured it as far as I was obliged to." Looking Margot straight in the eye, she held her glance as she added, "And how could I, in all justice, blame you, when you couldn't have known any more than I did that Meford Drinan was only marking time with me? Because if you had known, you wouldn't have encouraged me to cultivate him, would you? Even as a casual friend, you would have warned me against taking him seriously? Surely—wouldn't you?"

Margot bit her lip and looked away. "Of course," she snapped. "What do you think?"

"That if you didn't, I couldn't possibly blame you, and don't," said Donna. "But equally I'm asking you to accept my reasons for not helping you any more, though at the same time thanking you for giving me the chance."

"Oh, cut the formalities! You sound like a model letter of resignation from Every Business Woman's Primer!" Margot declared. "And meanwhile, since I *don't* accept your reasons at their face value, you will forgive me, won't you, if I make a shrewd guess that, since the job only produced for you a woman-chaser as a lover, you feel that, given the time for the hunt, you could do better on your own? Now let's see—what men have we introduced you to? Whom could you have in your range. Even Elyot for one, I shouldn't wonder. For another—"

"If that's your guess, I've no choice but to forgive you for making it, have I?" Donna cut in.

"No—have you?"

"Even though it's wrong."

"Ah, but is it wrong?"

"Yes," said Donna flatly, and turned on her heel.

Now she had made an open enemy, and it did not occur to her until later that she had probably allowed Margot to believe she had been deeply hurt by Melford's defection. She thought she had convinced both Elyot and Bran otherwise, but for the want of a firm word to the contrary, she had given Margot the petty triumph of thinking she had been painfully jilted. Later too Bran accused her of making too much of Margot's inexplicable hostility. He himself hadn't many illusions about Margot, but since Donna had enjoyed her tourist guide work, wasn't she doing the proverbial cutting off her own nose by opting out of it? To which Donna said "Probably," but that her nose would be less injured than would her self-respect if she continued under any obligation to Margot.

Now her time was her own again, and contrastingly empty. She swam and sunbathed and walked alone, and when Bran was not using the mini-moke, she mastered it sufficiently to drive it into the town to do shopping for the house. It was while she was down there on the afternoon before she was due to spend the day on Marquise that she was hailed across Navarre Street by Irma Hué in her car, stopped so abruptly that it rocked on its ancient springs and evoked hoots and angry yells from the frustrated drivers behind it.

Unperturbed, Irma waved them through and repeated her call to Donna. "Hé, Donna child—something to show you! Come over, will you?"

Donna, who had parked the mini-moke and was walking, went across. "Get in," Irma ordered and, as casually as if she and her car had a deserted racetrack to themselves, went on, "What do you think? After being so rude, as good as ordering me out of his house, Elyot Vance—"

"Yes, well—" Donna cut in, in favour of the increasing stream of traffic the car was holding up, "oughtn't you to move on, find somewhere to park? You aren't very popular, stopping here, you know. People sound as if they're getting mad."

"M'm, so they do. Can't wait a moment nowadays, folks." Glowering at the first car she waved on, Irma went into gear and shot forward herself, grazing a kerb as she turned abruptly on to St. Vincent Square where she found a parking slot under the saman trees and halted the car again.

"Now," she turned to Donna, "about Elyot. Just as if we had last parted with kisses, he rang me up the other day—something he wanted me to do for him; something he thought that only I could do."

"And you said?" Donna prompted.

"Forgave him, of course, as one does with men like Elyot, and asked what it was, though he didn't tell me until he asked whether I remembered the appearance of the Dial House before your uncle let it go to ruin, and even further back than that, to the time when the whole area was under sugar and the estate planter had lived there. To which I said of course I did, but why did he want to know."

"So why did he?"

"Because he wanted me to do a painting of it—in watercolour or oils, as I pleased—to give his architect the idea of how he wanted it restored, exactly as it was, say, up to twenty years ago, before sugar failed entirely, and when Marquise and the rest of the area were not fully on bananas. About when it was singing its swan-song, he said, before it was left to stand empty for years."

"I remember it faintly myself from about twelve or fourteen years ago," said Donna. "It was painted bright red all over, picked out in green, and there really was a sundial in the courtyard."

"And so I've shown it—look!" Irma produced a portfolio from which she drew an unmounted painting in watercolours. "He can have it in oils instead if he wishes," she said. "But I'm taking this up to him to see if it meets his idea of what he wanted. Does it meet your memory of it, child—tell me?"

Donna was prepared to be pleased, and was. The walls of Mousquetaire were hung with tasteful paintings of flowers, still life studies and landscapes, all proving Wilmot's scorn of Irma's skill as an artist to be yet another of his sour prejudices. And the Dial House, as Donna's childhood memory pictured it, had come to life under her brush.

Irma's angle of view of it was just right. Its reds were gaudy, its greens were vivid; the tub flowers which bedecked its balcony a flamboyant mass of colour, its surrounding paved courtyard and its sundial a sombre grey by contrast. Donna breathed, "It's *just* like! Exactly as I think I remember it!"

Irma shared her appraisal of the painting. "You think Elyot will approve it for his architect?"

"I'm sure he should. But—" Misgivings had struck Donna.

"But what? You have doubts, child?"

"Well, it's my uncle's property. Is he likely to give Elyot the right to restore it as he wishes?"

"Huh! Who pays the piper—"

Donna took that as a literal question and answered it. "The Company will," she said.

"Tch! Such ignorance of your own proverbs! It's to be Elyot's time and Elyot's men, and Elyot's right to call the tune of how it's to be done, isn't it? Not your Company's, all the way from England, and certainly not Wilmot's, who could have rebuilt the place as Noah's Ark or the Taj Mahal, *if* he hadn't preferred to watch it fall apart about his ears," ruled Irma tartly. She put away the painting and made ready to move off. Donna got out and waved her away, not relishing at all Wilmot's reaction to Elyot's latest move to override him. But she was pleased. If Elyot had his way—and she backed him to, though wondering what whim had prompted his plan for an exact restoration—she was going to like the thought, when she went back to England, of the Dial House a ruin no longer and of its sundial telling the hours.

SHE WOKE THE NEXT MORNING to a tropical downpour, the Devil's heavy curtain of cloud showing no break anywhere.

"What happens when it's as wet as this?" she asked of the sleepy Juno who had called her at first light. "Do the men start cutting the crop, or do they wait until it clears a bit first?"

"Oh, they cut," yawned Juno. "Banana ship sail

midnight latest, wait for no man. Crop cut, carried, sorted for trash, washed, graded, packed, loaded, down on quay by eight evening—or else. But no need you go over Marquise yet, Miss Donna, do you drown on the way."

So Donna waited until the storm abated somewhat, when she set out clad in her own good raincoat, overshoes contributed by Juno and sheltered by the huge carriage umbrella which was the common property of the house.

She carried a picnic lunch in a deep pocket and with no wind to drive the rain either into her face or against her back, she rather enjoyed the walk over to Marquise, and by the time she reached the big main store and packing-station, the rain was already giving over. And as evidence that the cutting had indeed begun to time at dawn, the first loads of sorting were already coming in from the plantations in open trucks running on narrow-gauge rails, which were the legacy to the banana industry from the sugar harvests it had superseded.

Watching the waiting sorters' concerted rush upon the trucks, Donna reflected amusedly that the cliché for all this would be "All was bustle and confusion." But that it was an ordered confusion was proved by the speed with which the trucks were cleared, the huge stems stripped of their protective wrappings and the dexterity with which the women workers separated the bands of fruit and picked the spent florets from the tips of each single banana.

Next came the first washing under a conveyor-belt stream of running water, and the discard of bruised or spotted fruit. A second washing left a film of natural latex upon the surface of the water; a third cleared the skins of traces of pest-sprays, and then the expertise of long experience graded and packed the bananas into the cartons in which, softly nestled, they would travel under refrigeration to England.

The crop came in; went through its routine; the piles of cartons became of the area and height of average rooms before the transport lorries checked them out and away—the whole process one of swift precision in sharp contrast to the consequent welter of discarded polythene, trash of leaves, stems, damaged fruit, tyre-tracks and trodden mud which formed the store's inevitable underfoot approach.

Time passed; it was noon and the meal-break before Donna realised it. She was preparing to eat her sandwiches when Maurice Couseau, who had had little leisure to spare for her during the morning, insisted on taking her to lunch at his bungalow. This, as was Elyot's house, was perched high, with a full view of the rolling acreage of Marquise. Over the meal with his young wife the talk was of the day's crop, its unexpected heaviness and the battle for the time needed to get it all away to the deadline of eight o'clock at the docks.

"What happens if you can't make the deadline?" Donna asked.

"It *must* be kept—by us to eight p.m., by the loading dockers to an hour before sailing time," was the blunt reply. "We can ask for an extension, but we can't be sure of getting it, and as bananas begin to ripen at once, any that were left behind would make for dead loss."

"And have any ever to be left behind?"

Maurice Couseau met that with a short laugh. "On Marquise, never without very good reason, and to my respected employer nothing much short of a major Act of God which struck his whole work force at one fell blow would be likely to constitute a 'good reason,'" he said. At which Mrs. Couseau protested, "Oh, Maurice, that makes Elyot sound like a positive monster!"

"Monster? Not a bit of it. Just a man with a flair for gauging just what he can expect of people and usually getting it—that's all," he defended Elyot stoutly.

When they drove downhill again he dropped Donna

among the banana lines, for her to watch the hacking down of the bunches and their loading on the heads of the waiting girls who would carry them so to the trucks. Amid cries of encouragement and a lot of laughter Donna tried on one of the coltas—the hard fibre crowns which spread the weight of the load without the girls' having to put up a hand to balance it. Their carriage was superb, long custom making nothing of the weight, but when a stem was placed on Donna's colta, her knees buckled and after a few tottering steps she had to beg to be free of it.

Towards the end of the afternoon she rode back to the sorting shed on one of the trucks which, arrived there, had to take its place in a queue of at least a dozen others as yet unloaded. The activity inside the shed was frenzied and matters were not eased by its having begun to rain again. The great wooden doors had to be slid to and the humidity behind them was intense. Trucks which had been emptied turned and squelched away through the mud for fresh loads, the raw material of the skilled work which went inexorably on—against the clock.

Just inside the door where the truck put Donna down Maurice Couseau stood with Elyot, who nodded a greeting to Donna and said "Just a minute—", delaying her from moving away as he turned again to his manager. "How many more?" he asked him.

A figure was named, and both men looked at their watches.

"Going to be tight," said Elyot.

"Too tight for comfort. Any chance of an extension?"

"Doubtful. Anyway," Elyot glanced out at the pounding rain, "this should slow things up a bit on the lines, and if we can absorb this backlog of stuff, we could catch up and be ready for the rest that's to come in. Let's go."

As the manager moved off Elyot turned again to Donna. "This is Marquise with its shirt off—the tatty end of the business deal which finishes up on the ice-cream counters as a banana split. What do you think of it?" he asked.

"I'm glad to have seen it. It's exciting. Is it always as hectic as this?"

"Not always, though when it isn't, our pride needs to pretend that it is, it being a tradition in the local clubs that no planter worthy of the name ever admits to having suffered a light shipment day. It isn't done; honour must be served."

Donna looked about her. "Is there anything I could do to help?"

"Is there anything you think you could do?"

"I don't know. Perhaps—well, I might pick off the little flowers on the bananas."

He shook his head. "A bit of a puny contribution. Our girls have quicker fingers than yours. But something that would help—could you collect all these moppets who are hindering their mothers, and keep them quiet in a corner? Are you any good with children?"

Donna looked about her at the toddlers who were underfoot, variously pulling at their mothers' skirts, fighting among themselves and playing improvised games with discarded bananas. "I don't know," she said. "I'm very fond of them. But would they come to me?"

"If you do a Pied Piper act with the lure of some goodies that Couseau keeps in the office against emergencies like today's overtime working for the girls, who'd be taking their babes home about now on a less busy day. Then perhaps you could tell them a story or organise a game. Anyway, wait around, and I'll lay on the operation!"

The children came willingly enough, squatting round Donna, round-eyed and eager as she shared out the sugared biscuits and sweetmeats which Elyot brought to her before rolling up his sleeves and making one of the team of men clamping shut and stencilling "Marquise" on the cartons of fruit.

A game? Or a story? A round or two of Hunt the Banana proved popular; Oranges and Lemons, less so, since no one wanted to make an archway with Donna, thus missing out on the heady excitement of being caught under it. They played Tig until the younger ones tired, and then Donna, despairing of choosing a story acceptable to such mixed ages, hit on the idea of suggesting that they tell her a Larayan story instead.

She did not want for volunteers. Though the stories, charactered for the most part by over-proud cockerels, villain snakes and mild-mannered cows, were only a few sentences long, each was followed by a clamour of "I tell now!"—"I tell 'bout—!" and the narrators had to wait their turn.

During the recital the apparent babe of the party, a chubby ball with a curly black cap of hair, climbed on Donna's lap and went to sleep there, and she was still nursing him when she was aware of Elyot standing behind the group, watching and listening, not interrupting the stories. Her glance met his. He signalled a thumbs-up and smiled, then came across to her. "Nursery session over," he said. "Thanks a lot." He patted the sleeping boy's head, his touch gentle. "The girls have finished, and we shan't be long. Would you like to deliver this one to his mother, or shall I?" he asked.

"I will." The mother came to meet Donna, clucking her thanks and inviting Donna's admiration for her son's ability to sleep wherever he found himself. "This one—he good boy, sleep proper in bed. But papa say, put him in coop with chicken, peg him on line with washing, he sleep just the same," she claimed as she tossed him up to her shoulder and bore him away.

Emptied of the chattering women, the big store quietened. Both the manager and Elyot had disappeared; men were loading the last of the cartons, and Donna stood alone, irresolute as to whether she ought to see Elyot before she left. Then the telephone rang in the office near which she was standing. No one was in there, and no one came to answer it. Donna let it ring for a time, then decided it had better be answered, as a call here was sure to be a business message which ought to be passed on.

She picked up the receiver. "Marquise store office here. Yes?" she said.

There was silence. Then Margot le Conte's voice came, sharply questioning, "Who is that, then? Who is speaking?"

"Donna Torrence."

Another silence. Then a smothered exclamation, "What the—? What are you doing there? I'm calling Elyot. Choc said he was down there. So where is he?"

Donna said, "I don't know for the moment. He's been here—"

"And left you in charge of his telephone—how cosy!"

"I've been watching a shipment at his invitation. The last of it is just about to leave, as I am myself. I was alone in the store when the telephone rang, and as nobody seemed to be going to answer it, I did. And I daresay I can find Mr. Vance for you if you'll hang on," Donna offered coldly.

"No, I can't wait. You can give him a message instead," said Margot ungraciously. "Tell him, will you, that Ella and George Martin—have you got that, the Martins?—are going back to England by the banana ship tonight. I'm seeing them off, and I want him to join us in their cabin for drinks as soon as he can get here."

"And where is 'here'?" Donna asked.

"On board. We're waiting. He's coming down to see the shipment loaded, I daresay?"

Donna had wondered whether she might be asked to watch the loading, but if Margot was to be there, she felt nothing would persuade her to accept the invitation. She told Margot, "I suppose he will."

"Well, just give him my message, will you?" Margot replied without, Donna was thankful, the extravagant gloss of endearments which, from almost the beginning of their acquaintanceship, must have been false. The hostility which had been none of Donna's making was open on both sides now.

She was replacing the receiver as Elyot and his manager came back. "I took a call for you as you weren't here," she explained, and gave him the message as she had had it from Margot.

He nodded. "Right. Thank you. Then let's go," he said.

The three of them went out of the big main doors, which Maurice Couseau locked behind them. It had stopped raining, but between them and the men's two cars there lay a quagmire-cum-lake of richly churned mud and water. Elyot looked at Donna. "We can't ask you to ford that," he said.

"I could. I borrowed some overshoes from Juno."

"All the same—" An arm went across her shoulders, another behind her knees and before she could protest he was cradling her and squelching out across the morass, Couseau following. Setting her down beside his car, he tapped the glass of his watch and said to the other man, "We shall have made it, after all." Then he opened the passenger door for Donna, who shook her head and stood back.

"I'll walk home," she said. "It's a lovely evening after the rain. And thank you very much—" she shared a glance between both men—"it's been a fantastic day."

Elyot stared, his expression hardening. "You're seeing it through? You're coming to watch the loading?"

"No. I've seen that part before—from the dockside. I'll walk back now, if you don't mind."

He compressed his lips. "Very well." He took his

own seat, said, "Maurice, see Donna back to Louvet, will you? She isn't walking, after being on her feet since heaven knows what hour this morning. I'll go straight on down. See you there—" and drove away. Away to join Margot at Margot's imperious invitation, leaving Donna to guilt at having rejected him and with nothing for comfort but the memory of the smile he had sent her across the heads of the children and of the too-brief experience of his carrying her across the mud. The former had been no more than approval of her role as nursemaid; the latter merely a piece of male chivalry. But her imagination needed to see them both as his willing bridging of the rift between them. For they were all she had to set against her jealous mind-picture of him and Margot together, laughing, drinking, making love... All.

CHAPTER EIGHT

HOWEVER EXAGGERATED had been Margot's taunt that Wilmot scarcely noticed Donna's presence, he was certainly the last of anyone close to her to realise that she no longer had Melford Drinan's escort, nor kept any appointments at the Allamanda.

Even Juno had commented with a hearty, "You stay home more now, Miss Donna. That good. For one thing, feed better here with Juno's cooking, and maybe make the Mister eat proper, you feed with him."

And Irma Hué had been quick to see Donna as a new leisured special pleader of her own cause with Wilmot. "You spend more time together now. So—just a hint here and there that you are surprised he doesn't get rid of Louvet and feel free to do his own thing, as you young people would say. Or tell him perhaps how much you admire my work and how well you think he and I could collaborate on a book. Nothing too blatant, you understand, child? Just the odd word in his ear which should keep me in his mind," she urged, happily blind to the fact that Wilmot's sales resistance to the mere mention of her name was absolute.

But though Wilmot's reaction was tardy, when it came it was unexpectedly compassionate. A propos of nothing, he said one morning, "That fellow who used to call for you, take you out—you don't see him any more? Why not?"

Donna said, "Melford Drinan? He was only on a business trip, as I think I told you, Uncle. And he's gone back to America now."

"Gone back—just like that? Amused himself, then took off—was that it?"

She shook her head. "It wasn't like that. He already had a fiancée—"

"Was frank about having one? Told you so straight away?"

"No," she admitted. "In fact, I didn't know he was engaged, until his fiancée and her mother came down to Laraye, and they all went back together later."

"Jilted you, eh?" Wilmot took a long draught of coffee and wiped his lips. "Well, it happens," he said.

"Yes—" Expecting that to be the sum total of his sympathy, Donna was about to assure him of how little but her pride had been hurt, when he went on to repeat,

"Yes, it happens. But when you're young and it does, it seems to split your world apart, eh?"

When the man you love doesn't want you, it *stays* apart, was Donna's swift thought, though not of Melford Drinan. Aloud she agreed, "Yes, I suppose so."

"And yet—" Wilmot paused. "Well, if it's any help, there's a Larayan saying that you might do well to think of and remember. You wouldn't understand it in *patois*, but its gist is, 'One ship gone to the bottom won't prevent another's sailing.' You understand how its meaning could relate to a broken love-affair. It makes its point?"

"Yes indeed." Donna knew she ought to disillusion him as to how little she had been hurt at Melford Drinan's hands, but her thoughts were racing in another direction. She had never talked on any intimate level with Wilmot before, but it sounded as if he were trying to console her from his own experience, and if that meant he had realised at last the futility of enduring bitterness over the might-have-been, could she hope it had dispelled at least one cause for his hostility to Elyot?

In face of his own ineptitude, he might still resent Elyot's success, but if he had rid himself of the deeper canker of holding Elyot's mother's faithlessness against her son, wasn't that one step towards a tolerance which might make them, if never friends, something less than the open enemies they were now?

Donna said again, "Yes," and treading warily, added, "are you telling me, Uncle, that you yourself have found it to be true—that in time one gets over anything and is able to—to set sail again?"

He sighed. "In time, yes. Though it can sometimes take a lot too long. You shouldn't let it rankle too long for you."

"I won't," she was able to promise frankly. "In any case, my affair hadn't gone very far. But you're telling me that at some time there was someone for you whom you had to 'get over,' and that you did in the end?"

"When I was a young man, yes, and my affair had gone deep. But I married your aunt Winifred, didn't I? And it's she whom I've missed since she died. Not the—other one."

Donna said warmly, "I'm glad you were happy with Aunt Winifred, but thank you for telling me as much as you have." It occurred to her that here Irma Hué would expect her to dash in with a suggestion that, having known contentment in one marriage, he might be prepared to consider another. But for Donna by far the more important issue was the possibility of the end of Wilmot's cold war against Elyot; Louvet, cultivated and fruitful once more; Wilmot himself with cause no longer for his sour frustration; Elyot's ambition for Marquise and Louvet fulfilled.

When she went back to England she would go heart-empty. But at least that was a picture she would be glad to remember she had left behind. None of it would be her doing, of course—simply a change of purpose and direction on Wilmot's part. And if he were already on the way to that—?

But that he was not, at least in the matter of the sale of Louvet to Elyot, was evident from his reception of her tentative suggestion of how much she would like to see Louvet in as full production, comparatively speaking, as Marquise.

"As conditions are, that's impossible," he snapped.

"I know. For one thing, without Bran's help, you've had no choice but to neglect it," she soothed. "But isn't that an argument for getting rid of it while you can, before it deteriorates so far that nobody will buy it? And if you were prepared to sell it, you must know the Company would back your decision, surely?"

"Just so—expecting me to take the offer of the highest bidder!"

Though fearing what was coming next, Donna said, "Well, naturally. That's business."

"With which I'll have no part, while that fellow Vance is in a position to be able to outbid anyone else."

Deadlock. Donna tried another tack. "Bran says," she remarked, "that your real ambition is to set up a reserve in the rain forests for all the native Larayan flowers and shrubs. Will you ever be able to do that?"

"No money to buy the land."

"Who owns the land?"

"It's mostly Government owned, and it would require acres." Wilmot paused, then, as if making the offer were an effort, added, "If you're interested enough, I could drive you over the area I have in mind—down south, inland, where a lot of the soil would be virgin and ideal."

"I'd like that," Donna told him. And it was from that talk and his keeping of that promise that she was able to date a closer understanding with him, confirming her earlier guess that it was the commercialism of Louvet which irked him. He loved all nature for its own sake; trading in it was obnoxious—a principle which admittedly wouldn't have got humanity far on the way to civilisation, but which she supposed the few eccentrics like Wilmot must be allowed to indulge and live by, as far as they could.

At least Madame Hué claimed to take hope for her own plans from his airing of his ambition to Donna. Nodding thoughtfully as she worked it out, "So that if he could get the land for his old reserve, he might be willing to let Louvet go," she pondered.

"Not, I'm afraid, if it meant Elyot Vance could buy Louvet," Donna warned.

"Bah, the stubborn old mule!" Madame Hué exclaimed disgustedly. "Here you have one man with his hand in his pocket, ready to buy, and another who should have sense enough to sell something he doesn't value. But put them each side of a table to discuss a deal, and where are you? Why, exactly where you were before, my friend! And yet...and yet," thoughtfully again now, "there must be ways. Yes, indeed there should be ways. One must just continue to work on it, that's all."

Changing the subject, she reported that Elyot himself had had enough sense to listen to her plain words on the subject of Margot's threat of dismissal to Choc and Maria. When she had taken her painting of the Dial House up to Marquise, she had made it her business to question them, to hear—as Donna had already heard from Juno—that he had no plans at all for getting rid of them; that Miss le Conte had made a mistake in believing he had.

Unfortunately for Donna's peace of mind, Juno's version had been slightly different. For Juno, reporting that Elyot had used a word she didn't know, but which meant Miss le Conte had been "afore herself" or "aforehand" with her threats, offered Donna no comfort. If Elyot had said Margot had been "premature," which was likely, then "premature" was probably all Margot had been—jumping the gun of her future sway over Marquise when she was Elyot's wife, but already very sure of the rights she would demand of him and get, once she was.

Meanwhile, with no choice but to bow to the Company's ruling about the Dial House, Wilmot maintained his dignity by ignoring the fact that anything was going on there.

But something was. Donna too had indulged him by refraining from mentioning the place, but she did go down one day with Madame Hué, who, since Elyot's acceptance of her sketch, claimed a designer's right to see how her ideas were being carried out. And considering how little noted for speed Larayan artisans were, Donna was surprised by the progress the builders had made.

The walled courtyard had been repaved and a new sundial set up. Though it was still littered with builders' rubble, there were the makings of a garden; the rooms were clean and refloored; the broken stairs had been torn out and replaced, and the balcony of embarrassing memory for Donna was sturdy and brave in its new gaudy dress of red paint, in startling contrast to the bright emerald of the main structure.

Madame Hué approved it. Elyot, she told Donna, had had to fight his architect to have it restored just so. The man had advised razing the house to the ground, rebuilding it one-storeyed and flat-roofed, the finish to be white overall. But Elyot had insisted that it be executed exactly to the sketch. "'For sentiment's sake,' he told the architect," Irma reported. "Though what sentiment he could possibly feel for a house that he didn't own and wasn't on his land, I suppose he must have left the poor fellow to guess. But he got his way. As always."

"Considering how everything in Laraye gets the treatment of the brightest colours anyone could dye or mix, Elyot probably meant for tradition's sake, not sentiment's," Donna suggested. "And as I told you when you showed me your sketch, I remember this place exactly as you had it. Except—" She paused, shading her eyes as she looked up at the end gable beneath which they were standing. "Except that there was a clock up there in the wall, just under the eaves."

"A clock? *I* don't remember any clock," Irma claimed.

"But there was. I remember—" Donna broke off and turned as Elyot's car stopped on the road and he got out and came over.

"Donna says there used to be a clock in this gable. But there wasn't. If there had been, I'd have remembered it," Irma attacked him.

He looked at Donna. "Clock—or no clock?" he inquired.

"Clock," she affirmed with a nod.

"No clock," Irma insisted. "She was only a little girl when she left Laraye, and she must be mistaken. Besides," she added with simple logic, "if they had an outdoor clock, what did they want a sundial for?"

Elyot laughed. "Probably so that each could shame the other into telling the right time, Irma, *ma mie*, don't be so innocently literal, for Pete's sake. And Donna would hardly have imagined a clock, would she?"

"She might have seen a clock on some other house-gable, and thought it was here."

"Still, I think we'll let her have her clock," he adjudicated. "I'll arrange to have one installed."

Irma shrugged. "I thought you wanted the restoration to be exact. But you'd rather take Donna's version than mine?"

"Just in case Donna is right," he said quietly, causing Donna to wonder why he should choose to champion her in the petty argument, as if it mattered either way.

Fortunately Irma never remained ruffled for long, and when Elyot excused himself, saying he had to speak to his foreman, she stayed him.

"About our affair—are you expecting me at Marquise tonight?" she asked.

"So we arranged." He paused. "Does Donna know?"

"No."

"Nor Brandon?"

"Yes. After I saw you yesterday, I rang him at the Allamanda and he promised to bring Donna along."

Donna looked a query at both of them. "What is all this about?"

Elyot said, "Irma will tell you," and left. And Irma, slightly on the defensive, said, "Of course I was going to explain. It's a business matter I brought up with Elyot which indirectly involves you and your cousin, and Elyot suggested we all meet at Marquise to discuss it. Will you come?"

"If you think I should. But what kind of business?" Donna puzzled.

"I don't know that I ought to tell you before Brandon knows," Irma evaded.

"I thought you said he did?"

"No, I only meant that I had asked him to come to meet Elyot tonight, and he's coming. So let's leave it until then, may we?"

Reluctantly, her curiosity aroused, Donna left it, and Bran, questioned, knew no more than she did. He borrowed his father's car, and all the way over to Marquise they canvassed each other's opinions as to what "it" could be all about.

Irma was there before them. Elyot poured fruit punches and they settled on the verandah. "Shall I explain, or will you?" Irma asked him, and did so in answer to his, "It's your idea. Go ahead."

"Well, it's about Louvet," she began. "We all know how things stand. Wilmot doesn't want it and won't work it. Elyot wants to add it to Marquise and make a success of it." She looked at Donna. "If it were put on the market for sale, your Company would expect Wilmot to take the offer of the highest bidder, and Elyot would see to it that his was the best offer. *But* Wilmot wouldn't sell to Elyot, he says. And so, as it's to the interest of all of you that it should be sold, I've suggested to Elyot that there is a way round that. Always supposing that we agree to take it, of course."

There was a momentary silence. Then Bran said, "I'd say I'm game for anything that would rid us of Louvet. But why should you bother?"

Irma flushed slightly. "Because Wilmot is my friend, and he has been saddled with that white elephant for too long—"

"Which conjures up a most bizarre image—Dad buckling at the knees, while this milk-white elephant rides high. Wish I could draw," murmured Bran. "But go on—what's the scheme?"

"This," said Irma. "That somebody makes a private offer—of a size that it would be madness to refuse for Louvet in its present state—either through the Company or to Wilmot direct, and as it would come from quite a different quarter than from Elyot and would even appear to cut him out, mightn't Wilmot be fairly likely to take it?"

Again silence as Donna and Bran digested this. Then Donna repeated. "'Somebody'? Who?"

Irma shrugged. "Just someone. It wouldn't matter who."

Donna felt a chill of foreboding. "A—a *fictitious* person, you mean? A cover for someone else who was really putting up the money? It would all be done under wraps—through solicitors or something, until it was signed and settled? But all the time there wouldn't *be* this mythical purchaser." She looked straight at Elyot, through him. "The offer would really be—yours?"

He inclined his head. "That was the idea."

"And Irma's, you say? But you go along with it? You're willing to play? Just as Bran says he's game for anything to be rid of Louvet, so you're game for anything to get your hands on it? You'd even stoop to this—this charade of a scheme to deceive Uncle Wilmot, and I don't know how you dare!"

She broke off, her features working, as Bran put in,

"Easy, girl, easy! What's so wrong with it as a scheme, anyway? It would sell Louvet, which everyone agrees would be a good thing, and in doing it, it would save Dad's face, don't you see?"

"Save his face!" Donna echoed, almost beside herself. "Save his face—for how long? For just so long and no longer, I suppose, than it suited you all to pretend that it wasn't Elyot who clinched the deal? So that when the time arrived for the cover to be dropped and for Elyot to start working Louvet, which would have to happen sooner or later, what about Uncle Wilmot's 'saved' face then, you tell me? *What?*"

Her glance had travelled from one to the other of them, her outraged questions addressed to them all, and each of them answered her in turn.

Irma said uncomfortably, "But once Wilmot learned the truth, it would be too late, and he would have to come round in the end."

Bran said, "It sounds to me like the classic case of 'ends and means.' If the end result is satisfactory, what's wrong with the only means that are likely to bring it about?"

Elyot said, "It doesn't seem to have occurred to you that we could have laid the thing on and carried it out without any obligation to consult you. Bran, yes, since he, as his father's son, has a financial interest in the future of Louvet. But you, no. It was simply that I, for one, wanted your reaction, and I'm sure Irma thought it fair to get it too."

"And you've got it, haven't you?" she retorted furiously. "Or must I spell it out that I think the whole thing is despicable and unworthy of any of you?"

"No, you've made yourself quite clear as to that already," Elyot said evenly.

"Good," she snapped, and looked at Irma. "I *meant* I thought it was unworthy of you," she said. "I know you've interests of your own with regard to Uncle Wilmot and you want to see him rid of—how did you put it?—his broken-backed banana patch, but that you would hatch a plot like this and think I'd be a party to its going through—no? You say you're his friend, but who needs enemies with friends who can scheme like this?"

She dealt with Bran next. "And you see nothing wrong with it? Just because it's a way of getting rid of Louvet, you'd stand by and see Uncle Wilmot tricked into the only way that could be achieved. Well, *I* won't. You'll all have to think again. And as for you—" she turned on Elyot, her voice shaking—"I suppose you are so used to getting your own way that it didn't occur to you you might fail this time if you backed Irma's scheme? Well, Bran warned me about you very early on—said that everything you touched was a success and there was nothing that power or money couldn't get for you. And it's money here, isn't it? *Secret* money. You've only to wave a big enough cheque, signed by any other name than yours, and you are home and dry—you hope."

She broke off, needing to still her quivering lips. Still loving the shape, the presence, the potency of the man she'd thought he was, she hated the complacent duplicity which had fallen in with Irma's scheme; assuming that if money and deception would make it succeed, he'd go along with the deception, and the money—his—would be there to be used.

"You *hope*," she repeated meaningly, and stood up, wiping off her damp palms, one against the other, as if ridding them of a taint. More controlled now, she added, "Meanwhile, if any private offer for Louvet comes to Uncle, either through the Company or from anywhere else, I shall advise him to put it straight into the nearest rubbish bin, which is where it should belong. Is that clear?"

When no one answered her, she thrust aside the drink which she had scarcely touched, and moved far enough away to cause Elyot to rise and demand sharply, "Where are you going?"

She turned. "Home to Louvet," she said.

"How?"

"If Bran isn't ready to come, I'll walk."

"After dark? That distance? You'll do nothing of the kind. Brandon—!"

Bran didn't move. "She's had her say, calling us all twisters. She can darn well wait until I'm ready," he said sulkily.

Elyot's eyes flashed anger. "She's going now, and she's not walking back alone. You will take her, and if she refuses to get into your car, I'll put her in bodily myself." His imperiously jerked head brought Bran to his feet. Finishing his drink, he nodded "See you—" to Irma and Elyot and followed Donna out, muttering as he opened the car door for her, "Nice matey trip back *this* is going to be!"

BRAN'S SARCASM had been right about the drive back to Louvet, and was equally so with regard to the relations between himself and Donna during the time which followed.

When they had to do so, they spoke with studied politeness. Otherwise they avoided each other as far as was possible, and though Juno worried that young Mister now spent too much time at "that hotel," neglecting Donna, Wilmot's detachment from the everyday scene appeared to notice nothing amiss.

Irma Hué rang up once when Donna was out and left a message with Juno, suggesting that as she had something of interest to tell Donna, Donna should ring back. But Donna did not ring; nor did Irma telephone again, and she did not come over. Elyot made no sign at all.

Thus isolated, Donna spent more time alone and increasingly more with her uncle. To her father she wrote that she saw no prospect ahead of his willingly quitting Louvet; that if the Company decided it must cut its losses, it must, in her opinion, act independently of Wilmot, and that, her trouble-shooting mission having failed, perhaps she ought now to return to England. If the estate were disposed of, she thought Bran could be trusted to be able to make his way in fields of his own choice, but she supposed and hoped that the Company would adequately pension Wilmot and perhaps allow him to retain the Louvet bungalow. She had not yet had a reply to this letter when Wilmot received a small bulky package by post from Elyot—the keys to the completed Dial House.

Wilmot showed them to Donna with a grudging, "Something, I suppose, for the fellow to acknowledge that it's my property he's been tinkering with. Want to go down and see what he's done with it?"

The suggestion surprised Donna, for on his own reluctant forays on to the neglected land, he must have seen the work in progress. But she went with him as willingly as she did now on any expedition he offered her.

The workmen had all gone, their rubble cleared; tubs of flowering plants were in place on the balcony, the floors were scrubbed, the windows were clean and there was a clock in the end gable. Wilmot tramped all over the building and the courtyard and said finally, "It's as close to the original as I could have done it myself. But why should *he* bother, when his only concern was for his brats of trespassers? And how did he know what it looked like in the sugar days?"

Donna said, "He must have remembered something about it; *I* could, and I think he asked Madame Hué to paint a picture of it as she remembered it, and his architect worked from that."

"And how do *you* know all this?" Wilmot asked suspiciously.

"She showed me her painting before she took it to him," Donna was able to answer with truth.

"Huh! Paint—Irma Hué? Wonder the architect was able to tell which way up to look at it," Wilmot snorted.

"Well, I thought it was very good," Donna felt obliged to admit.

"And what sort of judge of art are you?" he retorted tartly—a question to which he obviously expected no answer.

So the halcyon days of the dry season passed—cool blue mornings turning white with heat by noon, watered less often now by rain flurries which never lasted long, calm golden evenings when a clear sky paled to lemon, or a cloud-wracked one to purple and flame as the sun went down.

Anxious to learn the pattern of the climate and conditions in the months ahead when she would not be there—what about the torrid heat, the tropical rains, the risk of typhoons which the tourists shunned?—Donna heard from Juno the Larayan rhyme which said it all about the hurricane season—

"June—too soon;
"July—stand by;
"August—if it must;
"September—remember;
"October—all over,"

and though Juno assured her, "Long time passing since hurricane catch Laraye. Cyclone no blow now'day," Donna regretted that she would not know the heady, dangerous excitement of looking for a hurricane which might or might not come. Long before September or October she would have gone back to England.

Immediately ahead there loomed a day of Carnival for Calvigne. It would mark no particular event, no saint's day, no special reason for making public whoopee. But periodically the town needed both to let off its high spirits and to put on a show for the tourists, and for this purpose one day was as good as any other.

Donna heard of Carnival's promised delights from Juno and saw the preparations for it when she went down into the town. Bunting was looped between the lamp-standards; all the windows on the route of the carnival parade sported flags of every possible significance. Donna spotted among others the Red Ensign and the yellow cholera flag—Calvigne wasn't a cosmopolitan port for nothing! The shops and the market would be closed; the bars would be open. The schools, the town council, the Banana Growers' Association, the Yacht Club would be represented; five steel bands would accompany the parade; everyone's house-helps and gardeners would expect the day off, or if not granted it, would take it. All the hotels were laying on parties and dances for the evening; the night-clubs expected to be serving breakfast the following day.

On the day itself Juno, peacock-garbed and flower-hatted, went down by bus to meet Maria and Choc. Bran offered Donna no invitation to go with him; he merely announced that he would be sleeping at the Allamanda that night. Wilmot said that one Larayan carnival was just like another and that in his lifetime he had already seen too many. Donna would probably like to see the parade, but she couldn't have the car as he would be needing it. So Donna, lacking both escort and transport, decided to go by the next bus to watch the morning's procession and displays, planning to get back before Wilmot did, probably in the afternoon. On leaving to catch the bus she asked when she could expect him and where he was going, and he told her, naming an area she knew in the rain forest. He would be back in time for dinner, well before dark, he said.

In the town the streets were a kaleidoscope of moving colour as a surging tide of Larayans, clad in their best and gaudiest, flowed over pavements and roadways, looking for the best vantage points from which to watch the parade. There was singing, there was laughter, there was picnicking on punches and hamburgers; the few cars which had ventured on to the streets were jeered and catcalled as they came virtually to a standstill against the stream.

The very mass of humanity might have been frightening if it hadn't been so lighthearted and good-natured in expectation of a day which it meant to make its own.

Donna found a spot, shaded by a shop awning, from which to see the parade, which had begun at ten o'clock and was taking upward of two hours to snake and curvet and gambol its way round the town. The bands were spaced along its length, vying with each other to maintain a beat to which people could march; the banners of countless fellowships ballooned above the company; the decorated floats were the signal for screams of excited appreciation from the audience along the route. There were hideously masked devils and dragon men, children in space-gear, clowns, angels, cowboys. Every now and then things were held up while the clowns gave a tumbling act or the cowboys mimed a shoot-out against Indians. The ultimate goal of the parade was the town cricket-ground where a grandstand had been erected from which the floats would be judged.

Donna ordered a light lunch in one of the marquees on the ground, knowing she must exercise more than usual of the necessary patience in waiting to be served. She hadn't seen anyone she knew, but she didn't lack the companionship of people ready to chat and to invite her comments on the fairness or wicked prejudice shown by the judges. She stayed until the awards had been made, the parade disbanded and it was time to catch the return bus. She was glad to have seen Laraye at its gayest, most innocently jubilant. For all she had had to spend it alone, she was going to remember this day...

Back at the bungalow in the late afternoon, she had a swim, made herself a pot of lemon tea, collected the makings of a prawn vol-au-vent and fruit salad for dinner, then lay on the sun-lounger on the verandah, reading, until the sun went down.

Until then she hadn't expected Wilmot, and though he had promised "well before dark," she didn't question his lateness until it was really dark. She busied herself laying the table, preparing the salad, mixing his pre-dinner punch and getting ready to put the vol-au-vent in the oven as soon as he came in.

But he did not come. Anxious now, more than an hour after sunset, she fidgeted from verandah to kitchen, making jobs to do, telling herself she mustn't worry. He had the car; it could have broken down where he could neither get help nor telephone. The road through from Soubion, his objective, was a lonely place after dark... too lonely, no more than a mountain track for part of the way. Donna shivered at the thought of Wilmot marooned somewhere up there, and though her reason argued that he must have been benighted by accident many times before, nothing of the sort had happened while she had been in Laraye, and she didn't know what to do.

At any other time Juno would have been there. So, about now, would Bran have been. But Juno, who would wait for the dancing and the bonfires, wouldn't be back for hours, and Bran had said he wouldn't be home that night at all. But something had to be done, someone must be told, someone who could help her, who had a car, as she hadn't one at her disposal.

She stood, hesitant, looking at the telephone. If she hadn't rejected Madame Hué's call to her, she might have rung Mousquetaire for advice. But Irma, anyway, was probably at the Carnival herself. It had to be Bran then. By now he was probably at the Allamanda for its evening party. Though supposing he weren't—?

She picked up the receiver, got the number, gave her message to the porter who answered. "Mister Brandon? Don't know if he here, miss, But wait. I go find."

He was a long time away. Donna fiddled with the

telephone cord, picked at a stray thread on her dress, listened too for the sound of the car coming down the lane, and jumped in foolish dismay when a crackle in the receiver indicated that the porter had come back and was at the other end of the line. Or was it Bran?

"Yes? Yes?" she croaked impatiently. "Is that you, Bran? Listen—"

But the voice which cut in upon her was neither Bran's nor the porter's. Of any voice she least expected to hear, it was Elyot's.

CHAPTER NINE

ELYOT SAID, "Donna? You wanted Brandon? Well, he's been paged, but he doesn't seem to be here. Would you like to leave a message? He shall get it as soon as he turns up."

She didn't know what to say. She had banked on being able to summon Bran and the mini-moke. "Yes... no. That is—" she hesitated. "Leaving a message won't do. Do you know perhaps where I could reach him?"

"Not a clue. He could be living it up anywhere in the town or at any other of the hotels. No message then to say what you want him for? Where are you ringing from, anyway?"

"From the bungalow, from Louvet. I'm alone here, and I need Bran to get back here—now."

"Alone?" Elyot's echo was sharp. "Where is Juno, then? And your uncle?"

"Juno is at the Carnival, and Uncle Wilmot drove down to Soubion, saying he would be back before dark. But he hasn't come, and I'm worried. Something must have happened to him, and that was why I was calling Bran. But if he isn't there—"

Considering the bitter tirade she had hurled at Elyot the last time they had met, she hadn't meant appeal to sound in her tone. But she couldn't keep it out, and when he responded to it she was ashamed.

"*Soubion?* That's all of thirty miles!" he exclaimed. "Why there?"

"He's on one of his nature forays. I know the area he'd be making for—I've been there with him. There's a point where he leaves the car on the road—it's a terrible one—and walks up into the forest. And supposing he had had an accident, fallen perhaps, and couldn't get back to the car, or—" Now her defences were down and though she had thrown away the right to expect Elyot's willing help, she was openly begging that he wouldn't grudge it to her.

He didn't. He said, "Right. Stay where you are. He may turn up yet, and you could be panicking without cause. But I'll leave straight away and drive up." He rang off and she replaced her own receiver, looking at her watch then, wondering how she could fill the many slow minutes until he arrived. By now she didn't expect Uncle Wilmot to confound her fears for him. Her only lifeline to hope had to be Elyot.

He came in his estate car, which seemed to be loaded with an assortment of gear at the back—two powerful torches, an axe, a banana-worker's cutlass, a thermos flask, a bottle of cognac, a first-aid kit, a blanket, pillows and a stretcher—all the latter, he explained, borrowed from the Red Cross post in the town which planned to be open for carnival casualties all night.

"A useful tool, a stretcher, when you can command four hands and you don't know what you're going to find," he remarked, which afforded Donna the wry satisfaction that he took her fears seriously.

"You'll have to come with me to show where he's likely to be if he isn't held up on the road," he told her.

"Of course."

"Then get a warm coat and stout shoes; we may have to stay out and to climb."

She joined him in the car after fetching the topcoat and lace-up shoes which had been comfortable autumn wear on her journey from England as far as Antigua, though not beyond. As he drove he put one or two questions as to times and Wilmot's habits of movement on his forays, and Donna broke the ensuing silence by apologising. "It was good of you to come, when I couldn't contact Bran. I don't know what I should have done—called the police, I suppose."

He shrugged. "You would have preferred Brandon, naturally. But you should be glad it was only the shank of the evening as far as my carousing went; I hadn't got down to any serious debauchery. The police, yes, perhaps. Or did you think to try the hospital? No? Well, I was intent on getting up here, so neither did I. But we go through Anse Lima; I'll ring from a kiosk there."

But the casualty ward had only the occasional punched nose and small fracture to report; nothing from farther afield than the town. When he returned to the car, presently Elyot asked, "How is it you weren't doing the party round yourself with Brandon?"

"He didn't ask me. We aren't—exactly—speaking."

"No? Sounds childish, that. Since when? Or needn't one ask?"

Donna said uncomfortably, "I'm sure you know. Bran didn't like the home truths I came out with that night. But they had to be said."

"On the evidence you thought you had against all of us?"

"On the evidence you'd all admitted to," she retorted with spirit.

"On which you set up as prosecuting counsel, judge, jury, the lot. Though you could have allowed your cousin the point he made for the defence—that the end sometimes justifies the means."

"That's just a cynic's excuse! The thing people always say when in their hearts they know they're in the wrong, or are being shabby at least. And in my opinion *nothing* justified those means, nothing at all."

"As you made abundantly clear at the time," Elyot agreed, paused, then added, "I was glad."

"Glad?" Utterly surprised by the admission, warmed by it, given hope, she turned to him. "But I'd trounced you all, and meant to. How *could* you have been glad? Why?"

He threw her a brief glance. "Because, I suppose, it showed you were prepared to stand by your principles, and one has to admire that."

Hope died. "Glad" was a friendly, olive-branch word. "Admire" was cold, impersonal. She said, "Oh. You admired my standing up to you, but you didn't agree I was right."

"The scheme wasn't pursued any further," he pointed out.

"Only because I'd warned you what would happen to it if it had been!"

"More likely because we weren't in unanimous voice about it."

"But you were! Mine was the only odd voice out—" Donna broke off and sat forward, peering. "That—that shape ahead at the roadside—it's Uncle Wilmot's car!"

Elyot nodded and slowed down. "It's certainly a car."

"It's his. But it isn't where I expected. Not as far." She looked about her in bewilderment. "I don't know this part."

Elyot stopped, reached for his torch and went forward. The other car had no lights, showing it had been where it was since before dark. "The key is in the ignition and it's not locked," he reported.

"No. Uncle always says someone would have to need a car very badly to steal his."

Elyot got in, switched on, and the engine purred sweetly. He examined the petrol gauge and got out again to turn his torch on the tyres. "No reason for abandoning it," he mused, then pointed the beam on a path leading up into the woods. "That's a well-trodden path, and he may have used it. Come on, let's go!"

He gave her the other torch and led the way up the path, holding back branches and entangled lianas for her. At what seemed a long way into the jungle of giant ferns, wild banana and trees whose tops were invisible in the darkness, the track branched. "How is your hailing voice?" Elyot halted to ask. "Or shall I try?"

But only silence answered his prolonged Hallos, and with a "This one first," he started off on one branch of the track. "Needle in a haystack, but one can but try," he was saying over his shoulder to Donna when he suddenly stopped, directed his torch downward and stooping, picked up something from the path.

"Recognise this?"

Donna reached for the square of linen he held from one corner. "It's a handkerchief!"

"And ten to one it's his. Look—reasonably clean, dry—which means it hasn't been here long enough to be trodden in by any creatures or birds. Come on. We could be right."

They were. A turn or two in the path further on they were in a small clearing and at the foot of a giant tree, face downward head resting on his arms, lay Wilmot.

"Uncle!" He gave no sign, and Donna's heart beat achingly as they both knelt beside him. "Is he—is he—?" She choked on the dread word, but Elyot, feeling for a pulse, shook his head.

"No. There's not much more than a flutter, but it's there. Has he any history of heart trouble, do you know?"

"Not that he or Bran have ever mentioned."

"Lying fairly naturally too—doesn't seem to have broken anything, but just collapsed." Without attempting to move him Elyot examined the inert form, gently touching here, lifting there, and raising each eyelid, turning the beam of his torch on each pupil.

"What is it?" Donna breathed.

He sat back on his heels, pulling at his underlip. "Don't know for sure—"

"But what do you *think*?"

"Could be—" He paused. "Can you take this? I've seen a case before, and it could be—snake-bite."

"Snake-bite? Oh no!"

"M'm. Ever heard of a *fer-de-lance*?"

She nodded, aghast. "But it's extinct on Laraye. The mongooses you imported accounted for them all!"

Elyot sighed. "The brochures again! No mosquitoes, no *fer-de-lance*—which means we aren't plagued by them, but the odd few survive."

"But the bite is quite fatal—there's no hope!"

"Used not to be, but with modern serums used in time, only the very young and the very old are at the greatest risk, and your uncle seems to have been pretty wiry." He stood up. "But we're wasting time, and speed is of the essence. We've got to move him, get him down to the car. Will you stay here while I bring up the gear, or do you want to come with me?"

"I'll stay, of course. I couldn't leave him now."

"Not too scared?"

She suppressed a shudder. "No. I'll stand, and keep my torch alight and moving all the while. I couldn't bear Uncle to come round and find himself alone—"

"Good girl!" Elyot's hand pressed her shoulder and then he was gone, the nimbus of his torch receding, leaving blackness behind.

Donna tried not to think of how long she might have to wait until he came back, hauling the stretcher and blankets up that hazardous track. The air was very still, but the essential silence of the night was punctuated by the chirr-chirr of the cicadas and the occasional startled shriek of a bird disturbed at roost.

It was impossible not to remember and compare the blissful promise of her first night on the island with this one. What a lurch her personal world had taken since then! And yet—and yet, had she been able to look ahead, would she have chosen a way very different from that which had brought her from there to here? Knowing Elyot, loving him, caring about his approval; drawing closer to Wilmot as she believed she had done; even the challenge of Margot le Conte's hostility—all of it had been experience, and experience was something the wise ones said you must have, or become a cabbage, neither enjoying nor suffering—just being.

So her thoughts churned as she kept on the move patrolling the small area. Her legs ached and she would have liked to sit by Uncle Wilmot and hold his hand. But the slightly sinister stirrings underfoot kept her going, and at last she heard the louder sounds of Elyot coming back.

His breathing was heavy with effort. "I've hacked the way clearer as I came up, to make it easier to get the stretcher down. You'll have to manage one end of it, taking your time," he said.

After that it was all action, though not so difficult nor prolonged an action under his careful guidance. As Wilmot was still unconscious, neither the brandy nor the thermos was used. But when room had been made for the stretcher on the floor of the car Donna asked, "What about the other car—Uncle's? I could drive it back behind yours."

But Elyot would not let her, saying he had to drive fast and he couldn't afford to be concerned about her keeping up. He would send a couple of his men up for the other car in the morning.

At the hospital Donna waited in an ante-room while he went with a doctor and nurse into a cubicle with Wilmot. When he came back he brought with him the contents of Wilmot's pockets and his shoulder-haversack containing some wilting plants which Donna found infinitely pathetic. "What—?" she asked, her chin trembling.

Elyot said, "It's as I thought—collapse from snakebite. They've found the puncture marks on his thigh. They're keeping him in, of course, but they're pretty sure they can pull him through. We were in time, you and I."

"*You* were in time. I mightn't have contacted Bran for hours, and I could have done nothing without you." Donna wondered what he would say if she confessed the bitter uncharitable thought she had had while she sat there waiting. *If Uncle Wilmot dies, that will be the problem of Louvet's future solved for him,* and the guilt of having thought it for an instant brought tears of shame to her eyes.

She tried to blink them back, but one or two rolled down her cheeks and she was aware of Elyot's scrutiny as she brushed them away. And then, somehow, he was holding her close, stroking her hair, and as she gained control, patting her shoulder and finally holding both her hands—none of it in the love she craved of him, of course, but in more spontaneous kindness and compassion for the weakness of her tears than she had had from him yet.

As she stood back from him, murmuring, "I'm sorry—" he released her hands and said, "You're overwrought, and no wonder. We must get you home."

"Yes." But the thought of the house, empty of Bran and Juno and full of her worry for Wilmot, dismayed her, and as if Elyot read her thought, he said, "But you aren't going up there alone. I'll take you along to the Allamanda until I can rustle up Brandon from wherever he may be."

"Oh—not the Allamanda, please," she begged.

"Why not? If I can't track Brandon, it's where he will eventually show up."

"Yes, but—"

"But!" he echoed, his tone impatient now. "The Allamanda is a public place; you don't have to regard it as forbidden ground, just because you chose to walk out on Margot for the flimsiest of trumped-up reasons—"

Donna gasped. "I gave her notice by letter, *and* adequate reasons," she claimed, though realising too late that Elyot would have heard Margot's distorted version of why she had left. She hadn't convinced Margot that Melford Drinan had meant nothing serious to her life, and Margot had made pretty capital out of that omission by telling Elyot that under cover of "trumped-up" reasons, she had resigned from the job out of pique at her failure with Melford. And now Elyot confirmed her guess by saying, "Well, Margot felt you had behaved rather shabbily for reasons which she was pretty sure weren't genuine. But that's water under the bridge and your private quarrel is no excuse for your not making use of the Allamanda tonight. So come along, don't make difficulties. You're not going back to Louvet until Brandon goes with you."

They were back where they started—he with no tolerance of empty qualms; she with no more than nuisance value to him. Their shared ordeal had bridged the rift between them, but even his compassion for her tears had been no more than kindness, the comforting "There, there!" he might have offered to a frightened child. Donna's depression was complete.

IN FACT Bran had been at the hotel when they arrived, and he and Donna had gone back to the hospital before returning to Louvet in his mini-moke. Juno was already there, having shared a taxi with her cousins, who had gone on to Marquise before Juno had found the house inexplicably empty and had suffered a crisis of nerves in consequence.

"Me, I say to me—Miss Donna still at Carnival with her beaux. But where Mister, this hour of night? Tell you, young Mister and Miss Donna—till you come, feel good f'nothing; like no more than a cent's worth ice melting in the sun," she had declared, and had listened in dramatic, exclamatory horror to Donna's story and Elyot's part in it before she had pronounced the unarguable truth that, "Fact, don't know who your friends are, till you got trouble. The Mister, he say he got no friends, least all Mister Vance. But who run, like Good Samaritan in Bible, when he in need o'help? Maybe now Mister listen when I tell him Mister Vance good, kind—But maybe not," she had concluded resignedly. "Maybe take more than old man snake t'make Mister Wilmot change his spots."

But though Donna agreed as to the improbability of Wilmot's change of heart towards Elyot, certainly his misfortune proved that he had more friends and people concerned for him than he would have claimed. During the days he was in hospital he professed indifference to inquiries made about him, but after he came home he was reasonably gracious with callers who dropped in. Donna suspected, though she was sure he would have denied it, that he was touched by the attention his accident had caused.

Their common worry for him forced Donna and Bran to bury the hatchet of their quarrel, and Madame Hué made opportunity from Wilmot's convalescence to assume tacitly that whatever had been amiss between her and Donna was now happily resolved. She arrived, unannounced and bearing gifts, as she had done before their rift, and Donna had no choice but to welcome her, and to speed her parting tactfully when Wilmot, her captive victim, showed irritable signs of speeding her brusquely himself.

In fact, it was she who surprised Donna by telling her that Elyot was one of the few people whom Wilmot had received in his room while he was in hospital. Donna realised that Elyot would have telephoned or called to ask about him, but that they had met at Wilmot's invitation was news to her.

"Uncle hasn't told me or Bran about it. How do you know?" she asked.

"From Elyot."

"Elyot called at the hospital, and Uncle asked him to his room—just like that?"

"Well, considering Elyot had saved his life, should Wilmot have done less? But it wasn't quite like that," Irma admitted. "Elyot asked to see him, and Wilmot agreed."

"Well—!" Donna breathed. "What did they say to each other? Did they manage to part amiably for once? Or did the sparks fly?"

"Elyot wasn't telling, except that he had put a business proposition to Wilmot, which Wilmot—"

"Tch!" Donna's exclamation was in utter distaste. "Surely not *another* one, and Uncle still in hospital? What was it this time? An outright cash offer for Louvet? Or another devious scheme of Elyot's own; one that didn't need partners to help it on its way?"

Irma had the grace to look abashed. "I thought you had forgiven and forgotten all that," she said plaintively. "And you did not allow me to finish—whatever was Elyot's suggestion to Wilmot, he did not turn it down, and they parted, Elyot said, with it left on the table between them. Wilmot allowed that he might be willing to discuss it again."

"Then it couldn't have been anything to do with Louvet," Donna decided. "Uncle has always been quite adamant that he would never parley with Elyot over that."

"But that would be before he had to owe Elyot his life, and might one not think that should make for a little charity between the worst of enemies?" Irma queried with reason, though Donna doubted whether either charity or gratitude stood much chance against Wilmot's deep-rooted jealousy of Elyot and his stubborn pride.

All the same her curiosity drove her to leading up to the subject of Elyot's proposal by asking Wilmot what, when she returned to England, she could tell her father about the future of Louvet.

"You must tell him that I see no more success for it in the immediate future than it has had for a long time," Wilmot replied unhelpfully.

"But you wouldn't consider its being put up for sale?"

"On the open market—definitely no. In any case, it would have little value there in its present condition."

"Though Bran says Mr. Vance would be willing to buy it from you at any time as it stands," Donna ventured.

"Vance, yes." As Wilmot showed no sign of enlarging on that Donna tried again.

"Has he said anything directly to you about it?" she asked.

She got no answer to that. Wilmot said, "Is Bran about? If so, call him, will you? I haven't spoken to him yet about this matter, but you should both hear it now."

Bran came. "Breakthrough at last? Dad has decided to sell to Elyot privately? Well, what d'you know? And what price now all your virtuous dudgeon over our scheme to get him to do just that, young Donna?" he had said to Donna's hasty summons. But the shape which Elyot's proposition had taken was a surprise to them both.

Wilmot said stiltedly, "You'll have realised of course that as soon as I recovered, I asked my doctor to carry my thanks to Elyot Vance for his help on the night of my accident. And when he asked to see me we found ourselves on—er—tolerable terms. He congratulated me on my escape; I thanked him again for giving Donna and myself such prompt and expert help. He made light of it—said he was only standing in for you, Bran, and that you would have done as much."

"I doubt if I'd have rumbled snake-bite as surely as he did," put in Bran modestly.

"Yes, well, that's as may be," Wilmot allowed. "But from there he and I chatted a little, and in the course of talking it came out that he has the ear of the Government on certain of its plans, and that he had volunteered to sound me about them."

"Plans, Uncle? Plans for what?" asked Donna.

Wilmot's rare smile lifted one corner of his mouth as he turned to her. "Oddly," he said, "for a long-cherished ambition of my own—the laying out of a natural part of Caribbean flora and silviculture on a suitable area of the rain-forest. The Legislative Council, Vance said, would appreciate my advice as to the best site for such a scheme and would be prepared to ask me to draw up plans for it and, once it was in being, to act as its curator."

"Oh, Uncle, how marvellous for you! And you could? You would?" urged Donna.

"Plan it? Of course. I've had my own ideas and plans for such a reserve for a very long time, as I think I've told you. Soubion would be the ideal area, and Vance agreed."

"And the Council would allow you to plan it to be as wild and rambling as you like?"

"I have no intention," said Wilmot loftily, "of co-operating on anything which would approximate to a municipal park. They can accept my plans, or they must employ someone else."

Bran nodded. "No bandstand, no clock golf, no miniature lake, no Teas. Sounds just what the doctor ordered for you, Dad. I suppose the Council would put up all the cash, the labour and so on?"

"I understand so. As a tourist attraction they would see the cost as well spent."

"And the curator bit? Would you take on that?"

There was a moment's silence. Then Wilmot said, "Provided I weren't also saddled with the trouble and worry of Louvet, yes."

Both Bran and Donna suppressed gasps. "You would consider selling it, then?" asked Bran.

"If I took the job as curator of the reserve, I should make Louvet the responsibility of the Company, to deal with as they think best. If they wish to sell, that must be their decision. Or if they decide to buy me out of my share in it, that's their affair too." Wilmot fixed his son with a steely glance. "You realise, I daresay, that there may be no place for you in the Council's nature reserve scheme?"

"Is that a threat or a promise? Either way, it's okay with me," returned Bran gaily. "You go cosset your trees and your flowers, Dad, and leave me free, without a bad conscience, to do my own thing. In fact, I'm thinking of asking the bank for a loan to set up my own car-hire and guide firm any day now."

"Leaving the Allamanda and going into competition with Margot le Conte?" asked Donna, surprised. "She won't like that, will she?"

"And am I harrowed by Margot's troubles? Anyway, she's too big a fish, with too many irons in the fire, to worry about the competition of small fry like me—*if* I may mix my metaphors," Bran retorted, and turned to his father as Wilmot was about to leave. "Thanks for putting us in the picture, Dad. And keep us posted from here out, won't you?" he said.

Wilmot nodded. "Anything I learn or decide myself, you shall both hear all in good time," he promised, and paused. "It occurs to me, niece," he added, addressing Donna, "that it might make for goodwill and show good manners if we invited Elyot Vance to dine with us sometime. Perhaps you would see to it, would you?"

When he had gone, Bran and Donna looked at each other, shook their heads in bewilderment and laughed aloud.

Bran exploded, "*He* won't sell to Elyot, but the Company can, if it likes! Of all the arrant side-stepping get-outs I ever saw—!"

And Donna said, "Bless him for saving his face as gracefully as he managed to. He's a polished diplomat, that's what. And do you think he really meant what he said about welcoming Elyot to dinner?"

"Perhaps you'd better invite Elyot and see," advised Bran.

CHAPTER TEN

IT SEEMED TO DONNA that Wilmot's hatchet-burying overture should properly come as a man-to-man invitation from him to Elyot—a casual, "Drop by for drinks and take a bit with us one evening" approach. But when Wilmot declined to be a party to anything so informal she realised such hail-fellow terms were beneath his dignity. Elyot's summons to dine at Louvet had all the makings of a royal command and as such, must be issued by its hostess, if not by gild-edge card marked R.S.V.P., at least for a definite date and time at due notice to all concerned.

But when Donna, co-operative but diffident, telephoned Marquise to suggest an evening, it was to hear that Elyot was in Barbados on business, and before the day when Choc expected his return, Irma Hué, that human gossip column, came over from Mousquetaire with some astonishing news, of which even Bran knew nothing. Margot le Conte had sold the Allamanda to an American syndicate and was in process of buying an even more de-luxe hotel in Barbados!

Barbados? Donna suffered a jealous pang. "I suppose that's why Elyot Vance is down there now?" she hazarded.

"Is he?" queried Irma, interested. "Well, so is Margot too, one hears. So it could be more than coincidence—their both being there, I mean. Though I did understand—and from an *entirely* reliable source—that the new venture was solely Margot's own baby. She'll be moving to Barbados to run it, of course; which would make any kind of partnership with Elyot rather difficult, as obviously he won't be leaving Marquise. No, I think you can take it there's nothing like that between them. Elyot isn't the man to take on any deal in which he didn't own fifty-one per cent of the shares, and Margot's not the woman to be content with forty-nine," Irma decided to her own evident satisfaction, though without convincing Donna, who demurred,

"But they do have some kind of a business relationship now. I've heard them refer to it. And doesn't everyone suppose they are going to marry some time? And if that isn't going into partnership together, what is?"

Irma smiled indulgently and patted Donna's hand. "You have ideals, child, and rightly so. But with two sophisticates like Margot le Conte and Elyot Vance, it is a different story. When they marry—if, after all this time of keeping us guessing, they ever come to terms agreeable to them both—it could well be no more than a business affair, with the shares arranged as I have said."

Needing to turn the knife in her own wound, Donna said, "So Bran told me about them a long time ago—when I'd only met Elyot once, and Margot not at all. 'Two of a kind,' he called them, and it seems he was right."

"And the truth makes you sad for them? For Margot most? Or for Elyot?"

Donna felt her colour rise. "For—for the kind of marriage it sounds as if it would be," she evaded. "Cold-blooded. Mercenary."

"H'm," said Irma non-committally, and changed the subject to ask if it were true that Wilmot was to free himself of Louvet without loss of face.

It was both refreshing and revealing to tell Irma something she didn't already know and to follow her train of thought at the news.

She basked visibly. "Once free of that millstone, you will see the difference in him," she claimed happily.

"He will lose ten years of his age, gain a new outlook. Saddled with Louvet, naturally as a man of honour he has not felt himself free to consider marriage again. He has been too modest for too long. But now one can hope he will realise that, without loss of loyalty to a first wife, it is good and intended for a man to share his life with a second—a helpmate for what need be no more than his middle years. Yes indeed, he should begin to see the worth of a wife to him," she nodded in conclusion, and departed, leaving Donna to speculate on how far Wilmot's change of circumstances might persuade him towards marriage, or whether Irma, faint but pursuing, might have to propose to him herself.

Donna did not see her nor hear from her again until she rang up with an invitation to join her for dinner that evening. It would be a cold meal, as she had given her couple the night off. So Irma would be alone and would appreciate Donna's company for a chat. So much was happening to people within their circle lately that it was both amusing and important to keep abreast of what was going on, was it not? Say seven o'clock, then? That would suit Donna, yes? Donna said it would, provided Wilmot would lend his car, and Irma said, "Good. I shall expect you, dear," and rang off.

Donna was punctual. She parked the car, expecting to find Irma awaiting her on the back verandah of the house, but though drinks were ready there and the table in the dining-room was set with places for two, Irma was nowhere in the house, nor in the garden, which Donna searched, singing out news of her arrival.

Puzzled, she wandered back to the house. Irma *had* meant this evening, hadn't she? And the welcoming drinks and set table bore this out. So where was she? The vintage tourer was not in the car-port which served it as garage, so Irma must have taken it somewhere, though Donna would have expected her to leave a message, telling her guest where.

Then Donna saw the note. White envelope against

white-painted verandah table, it had escaped her notice until now. It seemed to have been penned in a hurry and was only vaguely explanatory.

"So sorry, *chérie*. Called away. A sick friend—you know how one is obliged to answer such appeals. If I am not back to greet you, promise me to wait just half an hour for me, will you? There are drinks ready, and if you feel inclined to wait longer and need your dinner, the meal I planned is in the refrigerator. If nothing happens and I don't get back, still allow me that half-hour of grace, won't you?"

Not much enlightened as to whether Irma hoped to get back reasonably soon or not, Donna re-read the message after dropping ice into a tumbler and pouring herself a lime squash.

"If nothing happens?" Why, what should? Irma must surely have meant to write "If something happens"—to prevent her return before Donna left. Then that repeated plea for half an hour's grace—why so definite a period? And did Irma really expect her guest to plunder the larder and munch through a meal alone, just because her hostess had been called away?

Giving it up, Donna glanced at her watch and stretched out on a sun-lounger to enjoy her drink and watch the scarlet ball of the sun go down.

At the sound of a car climbing the long drive to the house, she sat up abruptly and scrambled to her feet, ready to greet Irma when she arrived, well within the promised half-hour. But Irma would have brought her car straight into the car-port; this car had stopped on the front drive as a visitor's might, and after a minute or two, round the side of the house came its driver—Elyot.

Donna stared at him. "Oh—I thought you were in Barbados," she said. "Did you want to see Madame Hué? I'm afraid she's out. Was she expecting you?"

He nodded. "In a manner of speaking, yes. Seven-fifteen precisely, she said, and not after seven-thirty at my peril. But I knew she wasn't to be here." He eyed the array of glasses, ice-tub and bottles. "Do you suppose she would have offered me a drink? I see you have one. What do you recommend?"

Donna ignored this appeal as she worked on the enigma of the rest. "I don't understand," she said. "Why should Irma have invited you at an exact time for dinner, if she knew she wouldn't be at home? Besides, she couldn't have known. She had to leave a note for me—"

Intent on mixing a punch, Elyot said, "I wasn't invited for dinner, specifically."

"Then for what, if, as you say, you didn't expect to find Irma here?" Donna demanded.

He used a swizzle-stick and laid it aside. "Ah, but Irma had promised that though she wouldn't be here herself, someone would be," he said.

Donna's heart thudded. "Someone? Who?"

"You," he said. And then gently, indulgently, "As if you couldn't guess—!"

Her protests came staccato, a little shrill. "I couldn't! I didn't! Irma said in her note—! Anyhow, *why*?"

He left his own drink on the table, came over to her, took her glass from her nerveless fingers and urged her into a chair, drawing up one beside her.

"Because—want to know?—we've been saying no to each other for too long, and it's taken a Meddlesome Mattie of an Irma Hué to put us in the way of saying yes and *yes* and again yes," he told her.

"What do you mean—yes?"

His hand, which somehow was holding one of hers, shook it gently. "Come," he said. "According to Irma, though she could be wrong, you've been saying it to me for quite some time. And I, without needing her to tell me so, for a lot longer than that."

"You've been saying Yes to what?"

"To the inevitable. To a truth I couldn't believe at first—that I'd fallen for you, my lovely, prickles and thin-skinned dudgeon and all. That I wanted you, want you, shall always want you. That I needed to tell you so; *must* tell you some time, or better still, show you—Almost got around to it more than once. But always, always you dodged away, kept me at arm's length, flaunted your affair with Melford Drinan at me, and finally laid about me with a barbed tongue, the night of that foursome at Marquise with Irma and Brandon. Though oddly," he paused to play with the fingers of the hand he held, "it took Irma to give me a ray of hope that same night, after you'd swept out, that you might be saying yes to me too. *Were* you? Had you already? Was Irma right?"

Donna answered that indirectly. "You say Irma—knew? How?"

"Women's topsy-turvy reasoning, I guess. She said that only a girl who was deeply in love, only to believe she had discovered her idol's feet of clay, could possibly scourge a man with words as you did me. It was your disillusion talking, Irma said; your betrayed faith, your caring—" He stopped short, his grip on Donna's hand tightening. "You said—just now—I mean, you asked me how Irma knew! Then it *is* true? No, don't look away. Face me. There *was* something for Irma to know, and the something was—?"

She faced him. "The same as for you, I think," she said.

"That you do love me? Since when?"

"I—don't know. It just sort of dawned."

"For me too."

"But I had to deny it—because of Margot."

"Margot! After you had happened along?" He shook his head. "No way. Though if you hadn't happened, I might have considered Margot. And a huge mistake that would have been, if I'd taken any alliance with her to the point of marriage."

"But why me?" Donna marvelled. "I'm plain—"

"You're beautiful."

"And ordinary."

"Unique."

"And touchy and thin-skinned—you said so yourself."

"And honest. And plain-speaking. And loyal to a fault. And essentially *good.* And sweet and loving with children—"

"How do you know?"

"One has only to see you with them, as I did once with my girls' children at the store. I looked at you that afternoon and thought, What I'd give to see some of her own and of *my* own at her knee! Wishful thinking then; reaching for the moon. But now—" He turned to her and took her in his arms. His voice coming thickly, he murmured, "There are other ways than words, my love, to tell you how I worship you. This way, for one—And Answer me, if you can. Show me—"

They clung together, allowing touch and smile to express their wonder and gratitude and promise. At first Elyot's kisses were shyly exploratory—the merest brushing of his lips on Donna's cheek and brow and throat, and she was tense within his arms, not quite trusting the miracle...

If rumour about him were true, this must have happened for him many times before—propinquity with a girl, solitude for them, a romantic tropical dusk, flirtation. And yet...and yet—in these modest kisses there *was* supplication, there *was* worship. He was asking, not demanding her response as his right. Content to wait for it, he was showing her that she was special to him; not any girl, but his girl, his one-and-only—and then, when at last his lips sought hers in passion her response came alive and leaped to answer him in an excitement and desire which matched his.

Now she too was demanding, seeking, sharing delight with him on a mounting tide which engulfed their senses until it broke with Elyot's sudden release of her and his muttered, "That was too dangerous—the ache of it, the wanting. I had to let you go, or—But you understand?"

"Yes." She knew what he meant, and treasured the knowing for what it told of the depth of his feeling for her. With any other girl—! She allowed him to draw her down beside him on a wicker seat for two where he said ruefully, "I'll have to content myself with looking at you, marvelling, wondering why the heck I took so long about it; why I never chanced my arm before."

"You never showed any signs of wanting to!"

"On the contrary, there were at least two occasions when I made what might be called scouting forays to test the climate."

Donna blushed, remembering. "You've always been so brusque with me, impatient of me," she went on.

"Only with your resistance to me. I'd never been used to that and I didn't take to it willingly. But you can't say I haven't tried to serve you in kind—what about the Dial House, for instance?"

"The—Dial House?"

"Done up faithfully to period—*your* period as you would have known it before you left Laraye—even to disputed clock in end-gable, because *you* claimed it had been there."

Donna drew a long breath. "You did *that* to please me? Oh, darling—!"

"Otherwise I could have patched up its walls, slapped a flat roof on it and pleased my architect instead. Do you realise, my girl, that I had to track down that sundial in a mason's yard in Grenada; have it shipped and set it up with my own bare hands? And since we're on the subject of my silent service and forebearance, what about my allowing you to assume I went all the way with Irma's scheme to hoodwink your uncle into selling Louvet, when I could have floored you with a word of denial?"

"Then why didn't you?"

"Because you were enjoying your indignation too much, and it seemed a pity to spoil your fun."

Donna thought back. "You did tell me later you admired me for standing up to you."

"And so I did. It made me like you as well as love you, and liking's just as important in its own way as love. That's the huge difference," he mused. "Margot and I have never liked each other—"

"You must have done once!"

Elyot shook his head. "No, never. There was always this thread of near-rivalry between us; this hostility, her need to score off me and my urge to score off her. I'd give her full marks for business flair, and I've considered more than one financial partnership with her. But we couldn't have built a good marriage on the kind of armed neutrality which was all our personal relationship was."

"She has always implied it was more than that," Donna pointed out.

"Again, probably, because she can't bear to have it thought she isn't on top of every situation—in my case, that she could marry me at any time she wanted. And she has always been so sure of herself that I'd have said jealousy was beneath her, until she showed she was jealous of you."

"Of me? How did she show it?"

"In various ways. Losing no chance to make a snide remark about you. Referring to you as my 'little protegée.' And once, in a moment of rare candour, admitting that she knew Melford Drinan was engaged all along, and had rather enjoyed your discomfiture when you found out."

Donna nodded slowly. "Yes, Bran had heard her boasting of it to Mrs. Tours one night, and though I faced her with it, I did my best to help her deny it. She did, and though I knew Bran couldn't have made it up, I couldn't imagine then why she should resent me, even hate me, as I realised she must."

"With good reason, sweetheart, once she saw you as a rival. And don't pretend," Elyot chided, "that you're 'way above jealousy yourself. *I* can't. I was jealous as hell over Drinan. And you too—over Margot?"

Donna smiled. "'I cannot tell a lie,'" she quoted. "And so—ever since, I think, the night when I watched you dancing with her in *her* way, and later you taunted me with being a Blue Danube type. But I didn't know why I cared at the time."

"But now you do?"

"Yes."

"Then say it. Tell me—"

"I suppose—because even then I'd begun to fall in love with you," she admitted.

"Then if that was when it began for you, I beat you to it by aeons and leagues," he triumphed. "Flowers, theatre tickets, a promise to show you my etchings—tell me, have I ever paid court to you with any of them?"

"Not that I remember."

"Exactly. Pretty old hat, the lot. But to woo a girl with an aerosol of mosquito-spray, can a man come any more original than that?"

Donna bubbled with laughter. "You weren't courting me as early as that, so don't pretend you were!"

"And if I weren't, why didn't I leave our allegedly nonexistent mosquitoes to do their worst?" Elyot handed her drink back to her and took up his own. "Anyway, let's finish these, and I'll escort you into dinner on my arm."

Donna protested, "But we can't! We must wait for Irma to come back!"

"But she isn't coming back for hours."

"How do you know?"

"She said so when she gave me my instructions. Told me she was taking herself on the town for a cinema show and supper after it, giving me a clear run with you until midnight, and that dinner would be laid ready for us on the table."

"Which it is," Donna confirmed. "Places laid for two."

"Well, there you are. Irma didn't mean to play gooseberry as well as matchmaker. She did her bit, and then relied on our self-help."

"How did she know we should want to eat together? She assumed a lot. And to think I believed her story of a sick friend!"

"Only a very pale grey lie; just an extension of 'All's fair—,'" Elyot countered. "Besides, she's probably hoping we shall do as much for her when she steps up her campaign to get Wilmot."

"I didn't know you knew about that," Donna said.

"Who could help it—the unfortunate man!"

Donna laughed. "Does that mean you think she'll win in the end?"

Elyot shrugged. "I shouldn't like to say. Up to date it's been a case of irresistible force against the immovable object, but once Louvet is off both their backs, they may come to terms."

Donna tucked her arm into his as he moved towards the house. "And you'll be taking on Louvet?" she asked.

"Just as soon as your Company will make a deal with me. I can hardly wait," he said.

They found cups of Vichyssoise soup, a cold fowl, salad, and a chocolate mousse in the refrigerator and pretended, at Elyot's suggestion, that they were eating their first meal at Marquise. "This is how it will be every night, once we're married," he said. "You there; I here. But no, not so far away. Near enough to be kissed between courses if I feel so disposed. As I do now, even before we begin."

Afterwards they debated how they could thank Irma, and decided to leave her a posy, though it had to be of her own flowers. They wandered round the garden in the darkness, gathering some golden allamandas here, long chenille tails there; sprays of pink crape myrtle, short-lived hibiscus, with a cluster of passion flowers for the heart of the posy. Donna arranged it deftly and they left it at the base of the table-lamp where Irma could not fail to see it.

Then they turned out all the lights but that one lamp, and Elyot insisted on driving Donna home in his car. He would return for Wilmot's later.

They talked intermittently on the way—"Do you remember?" and "This reminds me of—" and "Supposing—?" and "I never thought—;" happy, cosy chat, sure of eager response. When they reached Louvet they took a long time to say goodnight, and when at last Elyot agreed that they must part, he asked idly, "How did you know I'd gone to Barbados?"

Donna told him.

"So does the breach-bridging invitation to dinner with Uncle-in-law-to-be still stand?" he asked.

"Of course."

"And what do you suppose he's going to say about Us?"

"Perhaps," said Donna, "you'd better come to dinner and see."

THE AUTHOR

Jane Arbor once owned a bookshop and lending library, experience that gave her an insight into the kind of books that people love to read. With their lively characters and fascinating situations, her books, such as *Tree of Paradise*, have become favorites with her readers everywhere.

Sherringdon Hall

Sheila Douglas

As the only woman doctor in her new job serving a tiny closed-minded community, Kate expected to be tested by her new patients. But she resented having to prove herself to her professional colleagues, too—especially the stern and skeptical Robert Montgomery.

Kate remembered all too well how Robert's effortless superiority had exposed her own schoolgirl gaucherie when they'd met once long ago.

And now, when she was so much more mature, more sophisticated, more polished, it seemed unfair that he could still rattle her with such ease.

CHAPTER ONE

GLASGOW WAS over four hundred miles from the village of Sherringdon. Kate Ferguson, who wasn't used to driving so far on her own, had taken two days over the journey.

"You'll probably get lost a dozen times," her brother Angus had teased as he had said good-bye yesterday morning. "You're the world's worst map-reader, Kate!"

Determined to prove him wrong, Kate had planned her route carefully. She had made no mistakes until now, but since leaving the main road she had become entangled in a network of narrow lanes, half of which weren't even sign-posted. By her reckoning she should have reached Sherringdon some time ago.

Kate sighed and wound down the window. It had been chilly when she had left Glasgow yesterday, but here in Sussex it might have been midsummer instead of early October. She came to another crossroads and slowed down to read the signpost. Sherringdon wasn't on it, and there was no house in sight where she could ask the way.

"What I need is a drink," she thought, and swung the car on to the grass verge. She tossed her sweater on to the back seat, opened a can of lemonade and drank with relish. Feeling better, she was even prepared to admire the view. It lacked the grandeur of the Scottish Highlands, but in a gentler, more pastoral way Sussex was beautiful too.

She was just trying to decide which of the four roads to take, when round the corner came an old man walking slowly with a stick. He looked hot and tired and rather cross. When she called to him he stumped over to the car.

"Lost, missy? Where are you heading for?"

"Sherringdon," Kate said, and his glum face brightened.

"I live there. I'll show you the way."

Seated beside her he became patronizing. "Females have no sense of direction. Turn and go back the way you came." He studied her quite openly while she drove. "Visiting in Sherringdon?"

A nosy old man, Kate thought, but there was no harm in telling him. "I'm going to Dr. Nicholson's. I shall be working for him until his father is better."

The old man gave a disbelieving grunt. "You're a doctor, miss? It's hard to credit!"

"Certainly I'm a doctor," Kate said with dignity, then she caught a glimpse of herself in the driving mirror and had to smile.

Windblown red hair, shiny nose and flushed cheeks! She looked more like a schoolgirl than a general practitioner. It had always been a problem for Kate that she looked younger than her age, which was twenty-four.

"You're just a slip of a girl," the old man grunted. "Folks in these parts aren't used to being looked over by young females."

"Females have been in medicine for nearly a hundred years," Kate said firmly. "Haven't you met a woman doctor before, Mr.—er—?"

"Beaney. No, I haven't. We're old-fashioned round here. Turn left and we're in Sherringdon. Pretty, isn't it?"

A number of old cottages and a few larger houses were grouped around the village green, their gardens bright with dahlias and michaelmas daisies.

"Not much of it, is there?" said Kate, filled with an unworthy desire to deflate Mr. Beaney. "I can only see one shop."

"One's enough if it sells everything," Mr. Beaney

retorted. "That's Dr. Nicholson's house, miss, the big white one at the corner."

Kate cast another glance at herself in the driving mirror. She didn't want to meet Ben Nicholson looking so untidy. "I'll drop you here, then, Mr. Beaney."

He made a great business of getting out, entangling himself in his stick and muttering about his arthritis. Kate switched off the engine and waited impatiently for him to go, but he lowered himself on to a convenient bench and watched her steadily. Somehow she couldn't bring herself to do her face in front of him, so she started up again and drove the car round the green to the house Mr. Beaney had pointed out.

She sat in the car for a minute or two, trying to conquer a sudden attack of nerves. This would be her first experience of general practice, a far remove from hospital work, where a young doctor always had someone more senior to turn to for advice and reassurance. It wasn't like coming to work for a stranger, though. Ben Nicholson and her brother were old friends, who had met at Cambridge and gone on to the same medical school. Later her brother had worked as a trainee assistant for Ben's father in this very practice, and had formed a deep affection and respect for the older man. Although Angus hadn't seen the Nicholsons for several years they had always kept in touch.

That was why Ben had written to her brother when his father had a coronary thrombosis. "Do you know a reliable chap who could do a six-month locum?" he had asked. "I have a temporary one who leaves in two weeks, thank God, as he's absolutely useless."

Angus had shown Kate his reply. "I can't think of a reliable chap offhand, but I know a very reliable girl. My sister! She's just finished her hospital posts, six months each in medicine, surgery and obstetrics. No G.P. experience, but she's a quick learner. She has to fill in time until our senior partner retires, when she's taking his place."

Ben's answer had been unflatteringly lacking in enthusiasm. "After one locum fresh out of medical school I'd have preferred someone more experienced, but if you say she's O.K. I'll believe you. Robert disapproves because she's a woman. He sends his regards, by the way."

"And who," Kate had asked, "is Robert?"

"Robert Montgomery—you know, Bill's brother. You met him once, didn't you, while you were engaged to Bill?"

Kate had had an instant and shaming memory of her one and only meeting with Robert Montgomery, when shyness and lack of social poise had made her talk too much. It had been in London during the brief and disastrous period of her engagement. Bill had told her a great deal about his older brother, who worked in Canada, but was coming back to England for a short visit.

"Is Robert in England again, then?" she'd asked, and Angus said yes, he was back for good, because his father had died and he had inherited the family estates.

"What's it got to do with whom Ben employs?"

"Nothing really, but they're the most important local family, so naturally Robert takes an interest in village affairs."

"It sounds absolutely medieval!" Kate's disapproval made her vehement. "I didn't like the man when we met, and he's probably worse now."

"I thought he was a decent chap. Of course it's years since we've seen each other. Not since he went to Canada."

It was this connection between Angus and Robert that had led to Kate's meeting with Bill. Bill had been a registrar at Queen's College Hospital when Kate was a student there. He had introduced himself when he learnt who she was, and their initial friendship had quickly blossomed into a love affair, that had been as intense as it was transient.

"Anyway," said Kate, "I've no intention of taking

the job. It would be awkward living in the same village as the Montgomerys."

"Because of your broken engagement? But that's old history now. Bill's married and living in Australia. You never went to Sherringdon, did you, so none of the local people will know you. I doubt they even heard Bill was engaged, it was all over so quickly."

Kate sighed. She didn't like being reminded of that not very creditable episode in her past. The decision to end the engagement had been hers, and Bill had taken it badly.

"Robert knows about me. It would be awkward," she repeated. "Probably part of his objection is personal, and not just against women doctors in general."

Angus had referred again to Ben's letter. "No, he states specifically that Robert doesn't approve of a woman in the practice. A pity Ben mentioned it, but tact was never his strong point."

After that Angus had had a hard time persuading Kate to change her mind. He had stressed his own debt to old Dr. Nicholson, who had been kindly and tolerant when he was a raw and inexperienced trainee G.P. "This would be a chance to repay him. Do it for my sake, Kate, if not for theirs, at least until they can find an adequate replacement."

So against her better judgement Kate had been talked into coming, and now she wished she hadn't been.

She was just about to run a comb through her hair when someone called, and Ben Nicholson walked down the path to meet her. "Hallo, Kate." His smile was warm as they shook hands. "When we met last time in Glasgow you were still a schoolgirl. Angus didn't tell me how pretty you've grown. I expect you could do with some tea after that long journey?"

He was just as she remembered him, a sturdily built young man, solid and reassuring, and Kate began to cheer up again.

"I'd love some tea," she agreed, and dropped her comb back into her handbag.

"In there." Ben waved her into a room where French windows opened on to a pretty garden. "Robert, come and say hallo to Kate."

The man standing on the terrace was taller than Ben, and when he turned Kate remembered him at once. Robert Montgomery had the sort of striking good looks not easily forgotten, black hair and dark blue eyes in a deeply tanned face. She remembered the good looks and the cool self-assurance, but surely there was an added quality of hardness that hadn't been there before?

He came into the room and stood for a moment, looking down at her unsmilingly, then he extended a hand. "We've met before, Miss Ferguson, of course." There was no warmth in his voice, which was hardly surprising, for he was probably regretting this unexpectedly early meeting as much as she was.

"There's been a lot of water under the bridge since then," said Kate with equal coolness. She made this remark deliberately, to stress the fact that she was a very different girl from the gauche young student of four years ago.

He still had the power to make her feel uncomfortable, however, or perhaps it was her guilty conscience about his brother. As his eyes travelled slowly over her Kate was reminded of her dishevelled appearance. "I could do with a wash," she told Ben, hoping that Robert was only a casual caller and would have left by the time she returned. She was a little put out to find him still there, looking very much as if he intended to stay for some time.

"You pour, Kate," said Ben. "You know I'm not married?"

"Yes, Angus did mention it." The silver teapot was heavy and Kate handled it awkwardly, aware of Robert's eyes on her. There was delicious home-baked bread, scones and a large fruit cake. Kate, who had only had a sandwich at midday, ate as heartily as Ben did. As she accepted a second slice she saw the faint smile on Robert's face and felt compelled to excuse herself.

"I don't usually eat so much, but I didn't have a proper lunch."

"Don't apologize," Ben said cheerfully. "You always were a good eater, Kate. Could clear a plate in minutes," he added for Robert's benefit.

"That was when I was a schoolgirl," Kate said crossly. Embarrassed, she took a large gulp of tea, choked and suffered the additional humiliation of having her back slapped heartily by Ben. "For heaven's sake!" She wiped her eyes and cast a furious look at Robert, who was staring fixedly out of the window, probably to hide his amusement.

"Where am I going to live?" she asked as a diversion. "Here, I hope, Ben?"

"No, not here. With Robert's cousin Maggie."

"Oh," Kate said rather blankly. "But why can't I stay with you?"

"It wouldn't do. If I was married or had a resident housekeeper it'd be all right, but we only have a daily woman now. People would talk. You know how it is in villages."

"Let them talk!" Kate exclaimed scornfully. "It wouldn't bother me."

"Perhaps it would bother Ben, though," Robert interposed quietly.

She swung round to look at him and they stared at each other in silence, Kate with mounting resentment because she sensed that this man had a good deal of influence over Ben.

The telephone rang in the hall and Ben went to answer it.

"You must see that it's an impossible suggestion," Kate said crossly, "my staying with your cousin."

"Why Miss Ferguson?" Robert asked evenly, and she scowled at him.

"Because of—oh, you know. My being engaged to your brother. It would be embarrassing."

"Unfortunately there's no alternative," he said. "Accommodation is limited around here. We're off the tourist track and there's no hotel within ten miles. If Maggie hadn't come up with this offer I don't know what Ben would have done."

"Been forced to offend the susceptibilities of the locals," Kate suggested. "But there must be somewhere else."

He gave her an exasperated look. "I assure you there isn't. Please don't be tiresome. Ben has enough on his hands already."

Kate took a deep breath and pressed her lips tightly together. She decided it would be more dignified not to answer, so she picked up a medical journal and leafed through it. She tried to concentrate on what she was reading, but she was acutely conscious of Robert Montgomery, stretched at ease in an armchair, swinging a well shod foot back and forth.

An important local family, Angus had said, and there was undeniably a look of breeding about the man. It showed in his well shaped dark head and the good bones of his face. Kate, who noticed hands, saw that his were long and slim and very tanned. He made no attempt to break the silence, which Kate was beginning to find oppressive, when Ben came back into the room.

"That was the call I've been waiting for. A difficult delivery. I must dash." He grabbed his black bag from a table and paused a moment in the doorway. "Robert will take you round to Maggie's place."

"But we haven't discussed work yet!" she protested.

He waved an impatient hand. "I'll see you later at Maggie's."

Robert stood up. "Shall we go, Miss Ferguson?"

Kate realized that he wasn't, as she had thought at

first, a casual visitor. Ben had expected to be called out, and had asked Robert to look after her. Tactless in the circumstances, but Angus had said Ben wasn't strong on tact. She would have to sort things out with him later, but meanwhile she supposed she would have to put up with Robert's cousin for a night or two.

They walked out to the drive and Robert opened the door of a blue estate car. "I'll lead the way. It's about two miles from the village."

They set off down a narrow winding lane. Losing sight of the other car on a bend, Kate accelerated and then had to tread hard on the brake. The blue car had halted just round the bend, where a herd of cows completely blocked the road. Kate missed the other car by inches, tyres squealing as if she was the worst kind of road hog. She gripped the steering wheel tightly, shaken by the narrowly averted accident.

Robert stuck his dark head out of the car window. "These lanes are too narrow for speeding. If you don't watch out you'll need a doctor yourself."

"If I'd hit you it would have been entirely your own fault," Kate shouted back. "No one should stop on a blind corner."

He got out of his car and strode towards her, giving one of the cows a hard slap on the rump to get it out of his way. Resting one hand on her open window, he bent towards her till his face was only inches from her own. "Are you suggesting I should have mown down a cow or two?" he asked sarcastically. "And perhaps the lad who's driving them as well?"

Kate stared up at him, flustered by his closeness, and annoyed with herself for feeling flustered. She edged away from him and slipped the gear into first. "Is it really necessary for you to come any farther?" she snapped. "Surely you can tell me the way?"

"I doubt if your driving ability is equal to getting past me," he pointed out unkindly. "Besides, Maggie probably won't be back yet from work."

He strolled back to his car and as soon as the cows were past drove on, while Kate followed, fuming. Such a silly little incident really, and so much more sensible if she had simply laughed it off, but there was something about the man that made an apology difficult.

They passed a large farm, on the far side of which the road ended in a private drive. She saw tall chimneys through the trees, caught a glimpse of water, and then Robert turned off the drive into a walled courtyard. Kate drew up beside him and got out.

"Maggie's car isn't here, so she can't be home yet." He walked over to her and gave her a long thoughtful look, which made Kate shift uncomfortably. "I realize that you don't like the idea of sharing with my cousin, but I hope you'll have the decency not to show it."

It was hot in the courtyard and very quiet. Robert just stood there looking down at Kate, waiting for her to reply.

Kate, whose training had given her a fair degree of composure, felt curiously ill at ease with him. She tried to tell herself that it was because he was so tall and she was quite a small girl. It put her at a disadvantage to have him towering over her. But in her heart she knew that it was more than his size that made Robert Montgomery a formidable man. There was a compelling air of authority about him, that reminded Kate of the most brilliant and also the most alarming of the teachers at her medical school.

"Of course I shall be polite to your cousin," she managed at last. "Though I shall make a great effort to find something else as soon as possible. And if I can't I shall look for another job."

Ill-advised words which she instantly regretted when she saw his scornful expression. "You'd let Ben down because of a little personal inconvenience? Haven't you any sense of loyalty at all?"

"Naturally I wouldn't leave him in the lurch." Indignation made Kate's voice rise. It sounded shrill and unattractive to her ears and with an effort she controlled herself. "I'd wait until he found another locum. And while we're on the subject of locums, I don't care for your attitude to women doctors."

His dark brows drew together in a frown. "I'm not with you, Miss Ferguson."

"You told Ben you didn't want a woman doctor here. I find that quite fantastic—the sort of thing you'd expect from an ignorant farmhand, not an educated man. And anyway," she ended hotly, "what's it got to do with you?"

She didn't get the reaction she had expected. After a moment's silence he started to laugh. "Actually it might have something to do with me, because the Nicholsons are our family doctors. I wonder which of us would hate it more if I had to consult you in a professional capacity?" and he laughed again, not very pleasantly.

"You look disgustingly healthy, so that's not very likely."

"Disgustingly, doctor? Do you prefer people to be ill?"

Kate took a deep breath and fought hard for control. "I picked up an old man on the way here, who had a similar outlook to yours. It was excusable in him."

"But not in me?" He leant against her car, his smile sardonic. "Since you have such a chip on your shoulder perhaps I'd better spell one or two things out. I was only expressing an opinion when I advised Ben not to employ you, and that opinion was based not on personal prejudice, but on a lifetime's knowledge of the people round here. They'd be slow to accept any new doctor, Miss Fergusion, let alone—" his gaze travelled slowly and critically over her—"a pretty little redhead who looks no more than a schoolgirl."

Kate wished that she'd worn something more formal than a shirt and trousers. She was still trying to think of a reply when he went on, "And just for the record, my objections have nothing to do with past history. You made my brother very unhappy for a time, but you did him a good turn in the end. He's happily married now to an extremely nice girl."

The implications of his remark made Kate flush, but before she could answer a car came down the drive and turned into the courtyard. A girl of about Kate's own age got out and came towards them.

"Sorry I'm late. I got held up at school."

Robert made the introductions. Maggie looked nice, a rather plain girl with a charming smile. Not at all like her cousin, which was a point in her favour! "Might as well take your luggage up now," she said, "then Robert can cope with the heavy things."

She led the way upstairs to a large bedroom with white walls and dark exposed beams. Through the windows Kate could see other buildings. She was looking down at the forecourt of an old country house.

"What is that place?" she asked Maggie, an unpleasant suspicion dawning in her mind.

"That's Sherringdon Hall, Robert's house. Didn't he tell you? I live in what used to be the servants' wing. Robert had it converted for me last year. It's old, but I hope you'll find it comfortable."

Kate was too taken aback to make even a conventional polite reply. It was bad enough living with Robert's cousin, however pleasant she might be, without having the odious man practically on her doorstep. He came into the room now and dumped her cases on the bedroom floor. He must have heard Maggie's words, and he had certainly noticed Kate's reaction.

"Don't look so horrified, Miss Ferguson," he said. "Maggie's house is quite self-contained, and she's completely independent of us."

Maggie was obviously puzzled by the tension between the other two. "Is something wrong?" she asked. "Doesn't Kate want to stay here?"

Robert put his arm round his cousin and gave her an affectionate hug. "Kate is most grateful for your hospitality, Maggie dear." He threw Kate a look over Maggie's head which plainly dared her to contradict that. "I'll leave you two girls to get acquainted."

When he had gone Kate felt obliged to add something to his words. After all, Maggie was doing her a favour by putting her up. It was really most generous of her to take in a complete stranger, and Kate said so with genuine appreciation. "We'll have to work things out on a businesslike basis," she ended, but Maggie looked faintly offended.

"I don't expect any rent. We can go shares on the food, though I get a lot from the farm and Robert refuses to accept a penny for it."

Kate didn't care for the idea of being beholden to Robert Montgomery in any way, but politeness forbade her to say so to his cousin. She would just have to put up with the situation for the time being and do her best to keep a sense of proportion. After all, she was here to do an important job and where she lived was a very minor consideration—or should be. Besides, when she knew her way round she was sure she would be able to find somewhere else to stay. Cheered by this thought, she settled down to her unpacking.

Ben came round later than they had expected. He looked tired but cheerful. "Evening surgery isn't usually so long," he told Kate, "but I've been on my own for two days, so the work has piled up. Feel ready to start in the morning?"

"Of course," Kate smiled, but perhaps she wasn't entirely successful at hiding her nervousness, because Ben gave her a sympathetic grin.

"Butterfiies in the tummy? Don't worry, Kate. If you have any problems ask my advice."

He was kind and understanding. Kate said impulsively, "It's not so much that I'm worried about doing the wrong thing medically. It's taking over from your father. The patients will probably hate a new face."

"They always do, I'm afraid. I had the same problem

when I took over from Dad's partner. But if you do your work properly you'll soon build up a good reputation."

"Sounds very pompous," remarked Maggie, coming into the room at that moment with mugs of hot chocolate for them all. "Don't let him patronize you, Kate." She was joking, of course, because she and Ben seemed very good friends.

Ben threw a cushion at Maggie's head. "Maggie's the bossy one. Comes of being a schoolmistress, you know."

They discussed the routine of the practice, while Maggie lay on the sofa and rustled a newspaper. When Ben left his parting words were, would she please be on time for morning surgery.

"Nine o'clock sharp, because the first ones always come early and if you start late they pile up so quickly."

"I won't let her oversleep," Maggie promised. "I always set my alarm for seven-thirty."

Mindful of Ben's words, Kate arrived at his house while he was still shovelling down an enormous plate of bacon and eggs.

"Have to keep my strength up," he said with a grin.

In spite of the fact that he was five years older than she was his manner was that of an overgrown schoolboy. Kate couldn't help wondering how the patients liked having him as the senior partner while his father was away.

They walked through the garden to the surgery, which Ben told her had been built less than ten years ago. "Before that they used part of the house. Mother, being a good doctor's wife, and an ex-nurse to boot, put up with it, but it meant precious little private life for any of us. Unfortunately she died before the new set-up, so she never had any of the advantages."

They walked through the waiting-room to a chorus of "Good morning, doctor" and some interested stares at Kate. She heard one woman whisper to her neighbour, "Much too young for a doctor, isn't she?" and wondered how they knew who she was.

She asked Ben and he looked amused. "News travels fast in the country. Come and meet Miss Andrews, who keeps us in order."

Miss Andrews was officially the dispenser, but Ben introduced her as the most important member of the practice.

"She knows the family tree of every patient, which can be very useful if you're not sure how much of their illness is emotional and how much is physical. And she knows every stick and stone for a ten-mile radius, so she can give you directions when you go visiting."

"You've been here a long time?" Kate asked as they shook hands.

"Thirty years," Miss Andrews said abruptly, her handshake as firm as a man's. She was rather mannish in appearance too, with short rough grey hair and bony features, her immaculate white uniform buttoned over a flat chest. One of those formidable middle-aged women whose whole life was dedicated to her work, Kate thought uneasily. Probably no sense of humour either, and as unwilling to accept a newcomer as many of the patients would be.

"Andy didn't take to our last locum," Ben observed with cheerful lack of tact.

Miss Andrews gave a thin smile. "A very brash young man," she observed, and thrust a pile of patients' record cards into Ben's hands. "I've given Doctor Ferguson a light list today until she gets used to the routine."

Ben cast a rueful look at the thick pile of envelopes he was holding and disappeared into his office.

"You'll be using Dr. Nicholson's office," Miss Andrews informed Kate, ushering her into a pleasantly sunny room.

After she had gone Kate sank into the swivel chair and swung backwards and forwards a couple of times to relieve her tension. "If the patients knew how racked by nerves most young doctors are," she thought wryly, "they'd be a lot nicer to us!" Then she flicked her microphone switch to "on" and called in the first patient.

After half an hour she was so absorbed in her work that she forgot to be nervous. The years of training and the preregistration hospital posts were all directed to this end—to give her enough self-assurance to cope on her own. Most of the patients were pleasant, a few, mainly the older ones, were a little guarded in their manner and only one was downright disagreeable.

He was a large red-faced man in a loud check suit, and was hardly through the door before he was laying down the law to her. "I've come for my certificate, doctor."

Kate glanced down at his notes and saw that he had been off work for a fortnight with an attack of bronchitis. "Let's see how you're doing," she suggested. "Please take off your jacket and shirt, Mr. Nelson."

"That's not necessary, miss. The other doctor examined me last time and I'm not any better."

"That's for me to decide," Kate said firmly, "I'm not signing an insurance certificate without examining you," so looking very martyred, Mr. Nelson removed his clothes.

Kate listened to his breath sounds carefully and then said cheerfully, "That's fine, I can sign you off now."

"Thought you would, miss," he said with a satisfied smile.

"No, I mean I can write your final certificate. You can go back to work."

After a disagreeable few minutes he stormed out, refusing to take the certificate and demanding to see Dr. Ben. Miss Andrews came out of the dispensary to find out what was wrong. Like most bullies Mr. Nelson could be easily deflated, and it would have taken a braver man than he was to stand up to the dispenser's forbidding manner.

After he had gone, muttering under his breath, but with the disputed certificate clutched in his hand, Miss Andrews gave Kate an approving nod. "An old acquaintance, Mr. Nelson. I'm glad you didn't give way to him."

Later over a cup of coffee in the dispensary, Ben asked what all the noise had been about, and was much amused when she explained.

"Well done, Kate! That man has always been a trouble-maker. Do you feel up to dealing with a round of visits?"

Buoyed up by their approval and her own relief at getting through the morning more easily than she had anticipated, Kate felt ready for anything. "I'd love to do some visiting. I'll need a map, won't I?"

"I have one for you," said the efficient Miss Andrews. "And I've written the list out in the most convenient order. Also a few directions that should help you find the way."

"You think of everything," Kate said gaily. "You wouldn't like to visit them too?"

It was intended as a joke, but unfortunately Miss Andrews didn't take it that way. "I was trying to be helpful, doctor," she said stiffly. "I didn't intent to presume."

She snatched up their empty cups and busied herself rinsing them at the dispensary sink. Dismayed, Kate tried to explain. "Oh, goodness, Miss Andrews, don't be offended! I was only joking."

Still on her dignity and without turning round, Miss Andrews acknowledged this remark with a regal nod of her head. Kate pulled a face at Ben, who hustled her out of the room into his office. "It doesn't pay to be facetious with Andy, especially when you don't know her very well. She hasn't much sense of humour."

Kate felt sadly deflated. "I thought she liked me. She's been so helpful all morning."

"She's old-fashioned, doesn't expect people to be familiar with her until they know her really well. Now here's your list." He handed it to her. "And the patients' cards and the map. Think you can cope?" He gave her a rather dubious look.

"Certainly I can," Kate assured him, but more soberly now. It seemed that it was not only the patients who might take time to accept her. She had to prove her worth to her colleagues as well.

CHAPTER TWO

IT WAS A QUARTER TO TWO before Kate finished her round, and she felt ravenously hungry. Ben had told her not to bother to come back to the surgery, so she drove straight to Maggie's house, although Maggie, she knew, wouldn't be at home. She rummaged in the refrigerator, cut herself a cheese sandwich and poured herself a glass of milk.

The weather was still perfect, so she took her lunch out into the courtyard, and sat on an old stone seat in the sun. Bees droned in a clump of fading lavender. Geraniums spilt rather untidily from a decrepit old tub. They needed dead-heading, and so did a lot of other plants.

Maggie was obviously no gardener. The courtyard was delightful, but it needed tidying up, and Kate decided that if she tackled the garden it would be one way of repaying Maggie for her hospitality. There was absolutely no doubt that she was welcome. Maggie had assured her of that last night.

"It'll be nice having company," she said. "I've been thinking for ages of trying to find someone to share."

"It's good of you, Maggie, but I think I should make an effort to find something else. Your cousin isn't as welcoming as you. He made that pretty plain."

Maggie had stared, then shrugged. "You mean because of that old business of your engagement? Don't you think you're being over-sensitive? Do stay!"

Her face was so earnest and appealing that Kate hadn't the heart to say no. Perhaps she was being unnecessarily touchy and it was worth giving it a try. "It'll only be for a few months, though. When Ben's father is better I won't be needed here."

"Maybe you will. Perhaps they'll take on a third partner so that Dr. Nicholson has less work."

"I'm a city girl, really, I wouldn't fit in here. Besides, I'm joining my brother's practice in April."

"Don't you like the country?" Maggie had asked.

"For holidays and short visits, but not to live."

"It's the best place to grow up in, and you must admit this is a beautiful spot."

Kate sat on after she had finished her lunch, idling in the sun. Maggie was right, it was a beautiful place. The courtyard was mellow with age, the flagstones worn by many feet. She decided to explore, so she went out of the courtyard and round the side of Maggie's wing, into a much larger courtyard with buildings on three sides. The main house stood at right angles to their part, an old Georgian manor, imposing by virtue of its lovely proportions rather than by its size.

In spite of its charm, though, there was a shabby look about the place. The drive needed weeding and the central lawn was full of plantains. Robert Montgomery, it seemed, hadn't any money to spend on gardeners. Kate walked across the lawn to the building that stood directly opposite Maggie's house. She was admiring the old oak door when it opened and a boy and a girl came out, a good-looking pair in their late teens, who bore a marked resemblance to Robert.

The girl smiled. "You must be Dr. Ferguson. I'm Linda Montgomery and this is my brother Tim."

Maggie had told Kate that Robert's young brother and sister lived with him. She smiled back at them.

"I was just looking around. It's an interesting old place, isn't it?"

"Not bad," Tim said carelessly.

"Too big for us really," Linda added. She dug her hands into the pockets of disgraceful old jeans. "Do you like riding, Dr. Ferguson?"

"I've never tried. And please, you make me feel middle-aged! The name's Kate."

"Kate, then. Never even sat on a horse?" Linda asked incredulously.

Kate had to laugh. "No opportunity in the centre of Glasgow."

"But you like horses? Come and see ours."

The girl already had the stable door open again when Tim spoke. "Do shut up, Linda. Everyone isn't as besotted with the animals as you are." He gave his sister an affectionate but exasperated look. "Her last school report said definitely not sixth form material, but would make an excellent stable girl!"

"Shut up yourself!" retorted Linda. "So you can talk, pipping your A-levels."

The boy coloured. "I only failed one. I suppose you're frightfully brainy, Kate, to get through all those years of book bashing!"

"Not really," Kate smiled. "I failed chemistry in my first year."

"Did you really? That was what I came down in. Robert thinks I didn't work hard enough, but it's a tough subject, isn't it?"

"Very tough," Kate agreed. "You'll take it again, I suppose?"

Tim ran his hands through long untidy dark hair. "I haven't decided," he said glumly. "I feel like chucking the whole thing."

"High time you stopped brooding," Linda told him. "Would you like to look round, Kate? The gardens are nice."

They were a friendly pair, so Kate accepted. "Nice" was an understatement. Even in their present uncared-for condition the gardens were very beautiful. A flagged terrace ran the whole length of the back of the house, and beyond the terrace wide lawns sloped down to a large lake. There was a boathouse with an old dinghy in it.

"Use it any time," said Linda. "There's a tennis court too, but it could be in better shape. Robert thinks we should look after it, though he has all those men working for him."

"He can't spare the men from the farm," Tim pointed out. "And he certainly hasn't time himself. Robert works very hard, harder than any of his employees."

Kate thought of the elegantly clad man she had met yesterday and was surprised. She had thought of him as a gentleman farmer, living well while other people did the dirty work. When she said this they both laughed.

"He was wearing his best suit yesterday to impress his bank manager!"

"It's not the way you think, Kate. He doesn't have an estate manager. He does it all himself."

"We had a manager when Dad was alive," Linda explained, "but Robert was in Canada then. It was one of the things Robert and Dad quarrelled about, employing unnecessary people—"

"Shut up, Linda. Kate isn't interested in our family problems." Tim gave his sister a disgusted look, and Kate forestalled an impending argument by saying that she must go and finish unpacking.

"Come through the house," Linda invited. "It's quicker."

Kate hesitated, wary of meeting Robert. However, she was bound to bump into him now and then, and the sooner she learnt how to deal with him the better. Cool politeness would be more adult than verbal sparring. In the main hall she stopped, to admire the oak panelling and to shudder at the stuffed animal heads on the walls.

"Someone must have been pretty busy," she observed. "I hate to see them like that."

"Do I take it that you don't approve of blood sports, Miss Ferguson?"

Kate turned quickly. Robert had just come in

through a side door and was looking at her quizzically. In a dark shirt and corduroy trousers his appearance was very different from that of yesterday, although there was still an air of distinction about the man.

Kate found his manner irritating and reacted accordingly. "You're quite right Mr. Montgomery, I don't."

"Then you'd better keep out of our woods," he advised her, "or your sensitive soul might be affronted by the dead animals and birds my gamekeeper hangs on the trees."

"Why would he do that?" Kate asked, ignorant of country ways.

"To frighten off the others. Don't look so disgusted, my dear girl. Farmers can't afford to be sentimental. We leave that to townspeople."

"It isn't sentimental to try to preserve wildlife," Kate said indignantly, and was further exasperated by his contemptuous amusement.

"I'm on the side of the conservationists where rare species are concerned, golden eagles and such like. But rabbits and squirrels breed so fast and do so much damage that we have to keep them down."

Linda, who had been dancing around them impatiently, broke in now. "Oh, Robert, don't go on! I'm going to teach Kate to ride when she has time."

This was the first Kate had heard about it, and she said so. Linda gave her a cheeky grin. "Of course you must learn. Everyone rides in the country."

"I saw a bike in Maggie's garage. I'd feel safer on that," said Kate.

Even Robert laughed at that and Linda caught hold of her elder brother's arm. "It's hard to believe Kate's a doctor, isn't it?"

Robert looked at Kate and took his time about replying. "You're right, Linda, it is hard to believe."

Unexceptional words, but whereas Linda's had presumably been intended as a sort of compliment, his seemed to imply criticism.

"For that matter," Kate retorted, "You're not exactly my idea of a farmer!"

The words came out rather sharply and Robert raised his eyebrows. "Just what is your idea of a farmer, Miss Ferguson? I'm intrigued to know."

Mindful of her recent resolve, she made a great effort not to show her irritation. "Probably as off the mark as your idea of a doctor," she said lightly. "I must go. I've an evening surgery soon."

She walked back to Maggie's house thinking that at least the younger Montgomerys were nice. When she said this to Maggie at supper the other girl nodded.

"Yes, they're pleasant kids, but rather a trial to poor Robert."

Kate was inclined to think that it might be the other way round, but didn't say so. "A trial in what way, Maggie?" she asked.

"Tim's such a dreamer—lazy too. Robert made great sacrifices to keep him at school last year and he didn't work nearly hard enough."

"Yes, he told me he'd failed an A-level, but that can happen to anyone. And what's wrong with a state school? I went to one."

"Generations of Montgomerys have been to the same school. Robert wanted Tim to keep up the tradition."

So the man was a snob as well. One more black mark to him! "And Linda? In what way is she a burden to poor Robert?"

Maggie gave her an old-fashioned look and Kate hurried on. "She seemed an attractive girl to me—full of life, very friendly."

Maggie nodded. "She's that all right. Too friendly if anything. And not very discriminating. She goes around with a rather wild crowd that she meets at night school. It worries Robert because she's still so immature."

"Is their mother dead?" Kate asked.

"Yes, she died before their father. That was when Robert left home. He only stuck it for his mother's sake—" Maggie broke off abruptly. "I won't bore you with old history. How did your first day go?"

"It had its ups and downs," said Kate wryly, and indeed that was to be a fitting description of the whole of her first week. The surgeries went quite well, backed by Miss Andrews' commanding presence. The dispenser reminded Kate of the Outpatient Sister at her last hospital, a woman who had been triumphantly in control of the trickiest situation.

It wasn't the medical side of general practice which bothered Kate, it was knowing which form to fill in and even sometimes whether a form was necessary at all.

The routine home visits she enjoyed. Driving around the lush Sussex countryside was a pleasant relaxation after hours in the surgery, but her first few night emergencies were decidedly worrying. There was the added difficulty of finding the address in the dark, and the very real problem of having to decide, perhaps in the middle of the night, whether it was justified to call out an ambulance and to send a patient miles to the nearest hospital.

The first time she did this was a chastening experience. The house surgeon she spoke to sounded weary and bad-tempered, as well he might be at four in the morning.

"Yes, yes," he said impatiently, when he had heard Kate's story, "but what's the diagnosis?"

"I've been trying to tell you," Kate retorted in exasperation. "I'm not sure of the diagnosis, but he certainly needs admission."

"We're short of beds," the H.S. grunted, perennial complaint of all acute wards, "so if there's any doubt about it—"

"Look," Kate cut in, "I don't know the diagnosis, but I know an acute abdomen when I see one. Put me on to your registrar, please. I haven't time to argue."

At that the H.S. had climbed down and Kate telephoned for an ambulance. She stayed with the old man and his frail, frightened old wife until the ambulance arrived nearly an hour later. She drank so many cups of tea, sitting close to the comforting warmth of the old-fashioned kitchen range, that she was too wide awake to go back to bed.

At coffee time after morning surgery she could scarcely keep her eyes open. She told Ben about her night visit, and there was indignation in her voice when she described her argument with the house surgeon.

Ben's eyes twinkled. "Calm down, Kate. I expect you've done the same to some hard-pressed G.P. in your time. The trouble is that when one's a newly qualified doctor it tends to go to one's head. After years of being a medical student, which is just about the lowest form of hospital life, authority is very sweet."

Kate laughed a little ruefully because she knew that he was right. "They say all medicals should be patients at some time, and I suppose every hospital doctor should do a stint in general practice. I hope I was right about the old man needing urgent admission, or that wretched H.S. will take great pleasure in informing me I was wrong."

"I'll ring and find out," said Ben. "He's one of our favourite patients. Never calls us out unnecessarily."

That couldn't be said of all the patients in their practice. Kate found it hard to be pleasant when she was called out of her bed by a woman who had had a pain for a fortnight, but omitted to mention the last fact over the telephone. Then there were the patients who asked for a visit and were out when you arrived, and the over-anxious mothers who got in a panic if their children's temperatures rose above ninety-nine degrees.

"But I've some sympathy with them," Ben said one day, "because children can be very worrying, even to us."

Tolerance and kindliness were two of the qualities that Kate admired most in Ben. He might not be as clever as her brother, but he was one of the most conscientious doctors that she had ever met. It all added up to a very likeable person, so Kate wondered why he was still unmarried. She remarked on this one evening when Ben invited her to supper, but he refused to be drawn.

"I suppose the right girl never came along. And since we're being so personal, isn't there some lad up in Glasgow who's longing for your return?"

Kate had had lots of men friends during her years at medical school, but apart from the period of her engagement they had been gay, uncomplicated relationships without any serious involvement. So she smiled and shook her head, and Ben, studying her lively face over his dinner table, expressed disbelief.

"They must be a slow lot in Glasgow, then. You're a lovely girl, Kate."

It was so unlike Ben that it made her feel ridiculously shy, so she changed the conversation quickly to discuss the coming week-end, which was to be her first on call. After only twelve days in the practice Ben still had some doubts as to whether she could manage a whole week-end on her own, but Kate had talked him into it because he looked badly in need of a break. For over a month he had borne the brunt of the practice and he was still very worried about his father, who was not progressing as well as had been expected.

"I shan't be going away," Ben said, "so if there are any problems don't hesitate to ask my advice."

"All right, Ben," but Kate was determined that she would not under any circumstances disturb his well earned freedom. She told this to Miss Andrews after the Friday evening surgery, which the doctor on duty for the week-end took alone.

Miss Andrews' dour countenance registered approval. "You're right, Dr. Ferguson. He's been working much too hard. Thank goodness you were free to come or I don't know how we'd have managed."

That was probably as near as Miss Andrews would ever get to a compliment. Kate flushed slightly, pleased and touched. On an impulse she confided to the older woman that she felt a little nervous at the thought of a whole weekend on her own.

"So far I've only been on for a night. Oh well, I expect I can cope."

"I'm sure you can, doctor," Miss Andrews said in her positive way. "Though it's nice to meet a young person these days with some sense of modesty."

Kate was hard put to it not to laugh. That "young person" sounded like someone out of a Victorian novel, and she prided herself on being bang up to date.

"Thanks, Miss Andrews," she smiled. "See you tomorrow."

When she arrived back at the house there was an appetising stew waiting for her. Maggie was a splendid cook and insisted that she enjoyed doing it more, now that she had company. She was going away for the week-end, and over supper worried a little about leaving Kate on her own.

"Sure you won't mind? I've stocked up the fridge and you know where most things are by now."

"Of course I won't mind. Don't fuss, Maggie dear. I'm quite capable of looking after myself."

"But if you should have any problems Robert's right next door."

"I'd have to be desperate before I'd call on him!" Kate thought, looked out of the window and saw Robert enter the courtyard. "Talk of the devil," she murmured, "here comes the lord of the manor in person."

Maggie put her coffee cup down with a little bang. "Why don't you like Robert?" she asked quietly.

Kate coloured, wishing she hadn't uttered that flippant remark. "I—I don't know him well enough to like or dislike him," which wasn't quite honest and certainly didn't fool Maggie.

The other girl studied her silently and Kate's colour deepened before that direct gaze. "Heavens, Maggie! Is that how you look at your schoolchildren? You make me feel quite nervous."

There was a rat-tat on the door and Robert's deep voice in the hall. "May I come in, Maggie? Good evening, Miss Ferguson."

Kate was uncomfortably conscious of her flushed cheeks, and relieved that he devoted most of his attention to his cousin. He sat down with them and had a cup of Maggie's excellent coffee. "I've decided to go to London with you, Maggie," he announced. "The farm's fairly quiet this weekend and I could do with a break."

Maggie was delighted. "Splendid, then you can drive me, and come with me to Aunt Margaret. I hate going there on my own, she's such a bully."

He gave her an affectionate look. "That's because you let her see you're frightened of her. Stand up to her, my girl, like I do."

"It's easy for you," Maggie grumbled. "She'll take anything from you because you're her favourite."

He shrugged. "Only because I'm a man. Aunt Margaret is a firm believer in the superiority of the male sex." His eyes rested for a moment on Kate, and he added with a faint smile, "You'd think her hopelessly out of date, Miss Ferguson. In her opinion a woman's place is in the home."

"And educating girls is a complete waste of time," Maggie added with a giggle. "So you see, Kate, she doesn't really approve of me and makes no effort to hide it. I don't know why I go to see her."

"Because you wouldn't dare to neglect her," said Robert, "Aunt Margaret expects her full share of attention."

"And gets it," Maggie added. "You'll see the old

lady before long, Kate. She always comes down for the hunting season."

Kate disliked the idea of hunting, but mindful of a previous argument with Robert was determined not to show it. She made a noncommittal reply and sipped her coffee.

"I'm the odd one out in the family," Maggie went on. "I never hunt."

"Because you don't enjoy it?"

"Because I don't approve of it."

Robert rose and looked down at them both, his smile a little mocking. "I must go before I get involved in an argument. You'll be glad to know Miss Ferguson's on your side, Maggie. She's agin all blood sports."

Maggie rose too and walked to the door with Robert. "I wish I could convert you, but I'll keep on trying."

He laughed and raised a hand to Kate. She heard their voices in the hall for a few moments and then the slam of the door. Maggie came back, the smile still on her face. "Robert's such a dear, but he has this one blind spot. Of course he was brought up to shoot and hunt and fish, and though I don't approve of hunting I must admit that he looks magnificent on a horse!"

MAGGIE AND ROBERT left for London after an early breakfast, and Kate went off to her Saturday morning surgery. She had a few visits afterwards, but no real problems. In fact the week-end seemed to drag by, and she was very conscious of being stuck in the house with nothing much to do. By five o'clock on Sunday evening she was feeling really sorry for herself. Hating inactivity and by nature gregarious, she wandered out into Maggie's garden, wishing she had a companion.

She was weeding a rosebed when Linda Montgomery strolled along the drive, a couple of golden labradors at her heels. "Hallo, Kate. Feel like a walk?"

"I wish I could," said Kate, "but I'm on call. Such a

bore! It's all right if one's working, but I hate hanging around."

"And Maggie's away, so you're all on your own. Come and have supper with us." The girl went pink and twisted a dark curl round her forefinger. "That is—if you'd like to—" She wasn't nearly as sure of herself as she'd seemed on first acquaintance.

"Well, thanks a lot, Linda—but I wouldn't hear the telephone from your place."

"Ring Andy and get her to transfer the calls through to our house," and as Kate still hesitated she added with a grin, "Robert won't be back till late."

It was Kate's turn to colour now. "You do find him rather a pain, don't you?" Linda asked. "Well, so do we. Tim and I are jolly glad when he goes away. Wish he did more often."

"That's a fine sisterly remark!" Kate felt compelled to say.

"Come off it! We know you two don't get on, so why pretend?"

"Why indeed?" Kate gave a little laugh. "Thanks, Linda, I'd love to come."

"I'll pick you up on my way back, then. It'll only be a cold snack because our cook's off."

The cold snack turned out to be delicious home-cured ham and salad fresh from Robert's garden. Kate learned a good deal about the young Montgomerys, including their aspirations for the future. Linda longed to go to an art school in London, but Robert was dead against it, at least until she was older. The most he would agree to at present was that she should attend evening classes in their nearest large town. "And pretty crumby they are," Linda sighed. "Half the class can't even draw properly."

"She's easily their most talented pupil," Tim stated proudly, for once on his sister's side.

Tim himself, it appeared, had got down to the hard slog of revision. "Not just chemistry," he said glumly.

"Robert wants me to take all my A-levels again, because even in the ones I passed I didn't get very good grades."

Robert had made up his mind that Tim was to go to agricultural college. A top one too! None but the best for the Montgomerys!

"But what do *you* want to do?" Kate asked, and the boy shrugged.

"I don't know really. And it's easier to go along with Robert," a point of view of which Kate disapproved very much.

"Don't let yourself be pushed into a career you're not keen on," she urged, but Linda said that he had to do something.

"And if he does agriculture he'll be better equipped to help Robert on the farm," she pointed out.

"I don't want to spend the rest of my life helping Robert on the farm," Tim said with a touch of sulkiness, and Kate felt a good deal of sympathy with this view.

"*I* shall be working with *my* brother," she mused, "but I should say he's a lot easier to get on with than yours."

Tim had opened a bottle of vin rosé and they lingered on over the meal, talking and laughing. They were still at the table when they heard a car draw up in the courtyard. Tim went to the window to see who it was.

"It's Robert and Maggie!" the boy exclaimed. "And there's another car coming. Oh, lord, it's the Mitchells, of all people!"

The two youngsters gave each other dismayed looks, and Linda jumped up. "Let's clear off before it's too late," but Robert was already at the dining-room door.

"Hallo, you lot." He looked surprised to see Kate, who felt a little uncomfortable. She would certainly not have come if she had expected Robert back this early. It appeared that Maggie and he had had enough of London and changed their plans. On their way home they had stopped at the village pub, where they had met the people they had brought back with them.

Robert introduced them as Colonel and Mrs. Mitchell and their two daughters. The elder girl, Diana, was about Kate's age and wore smart expensive clothes. Diana's rather supercilious appraisal made Kate very conscious of the shirt and denim skirt that she hadn't bothered to change after gardening.

Handsome rather than pretty, with a high clear voice, but Kate thought the other girl very affected. A horsey type, apparently, as she launched into a hunting story that went on and on.

When it finally ended Robert offered Kate a drink. "None for you two," he remarked rather grimly to his young brother and sister. "You've been making pretty free with the wine, haven't you?" at which Tim coloured and Kate felt more awkward than ever.

Should she have tried to stop them? Or at least persuaded them not to have more than one glass? Did Robert think her a bad influence on them? She sipped her sherry and wished she hadn't come.

Tim, with a rather obvious attempt to change the conversation, told Robert that Kate had offered to help him with his chemistry revision. Robert received this information with marked lack of enthusiasm.

"I don't see the point. You'll be covering the ground again in your course at the college. Besides, Miss Ferguson's far too busy."

"It was her idea," Tim said sulkily. "She understands my difficulties because she found chemistry tough herself."

Robert raised his eyebrows, but before he could voice further objections Kate stepped in. "I shan't try to teach him anything, just ask questions. Less boring for him than slogging away on his own."

"I can see you've made up your mind," Robert said coolly, "but don't let him make a nuisance of himself."

Tim flushed and retreated into a corner. Kate felt sorry for the boy and angry with Robert for treating him so ineptly. "Must you be so blighting?" she asked under her breath, "especially in front of other people? He's not very happy at the College of Further Education because it's so different from his school."

"Then he should have worked harder, shouldn't he, and there would have been no need to go there."

"Haven't you ever failed an exam?" Kate exclaimed. "Couldn't you be a bit more sympathetic?"

"Sympathy is the last thing that lad needs. He's inclined to trade on his charm as it is. Look how he's worked on you."

"You don't know much about teenage psychology, do you, Mr. Montgomery?"

"Not a thing," he agreed with grim amusement, "but I do know my own brother. Please don't interfere, Miss Ferguson," and he turned away as Diana claimed his attention again.

From hunting the talk drifted to farming and the soaring cost of fertilizers. Kate gathered from the conversation that Colonel Mitchell farmed the land adjoining Robert's. Also that the two families were close friends and shared many mutual interests. The Mitchells were clearly in no hurry to go and Kate, sitting between the Colonel and his wife, waited for a break in the conversation so that she could make a move to depart.

Mrs. Mitchell, an older version of Diana, was a big woman with a booming voice, who competed with her elder daughter to monopolize the conversation. Having discovered that Kate was a town girl, who couldn't ride and knew absolutely nothing about horses, she showed no further interest in her. Diana too was inclined to be patronizing, but Kate was amused rather than offended by their attitude.

She allowed herself a small smile at Diana's enthusiastic discussion of Robert's pedigree bulls, caught Robert's eye on herself, and stared fixedly at a rather bad eighteenth-century portrait of a Montgomery ancestor.

"Miss Ferguson thinks farmers have limited minds," Robert remarked, "concerned with nothing but their animals and their crops."

She murmured a hasty denial, but at his sceptical look went on quickly, "Medicals talk shop too. A medical party must be terribly boring to outsiders."

"And you find our talk boring?" Diana asked sweetly.

Kate couldn't decide if she was being malicious or merely tactless. She was the sort of girl who made no effort to get on with her own sex, but played up to the men. She sparkled whenever Robert addressed her, and watched him when he talked to someone else.

"She's after him," Kate thought, "but she makes it too obvious." It was an unusually catty observation for her, but she hadn't taken to Diana.

The Colonel on the other hand was rather a dear. A ruddy-cheeked man with a large moustache, he didn't patronize her because she wasn't well up in country matters. He was soon chatting happily about his wartime experiences in North Africa, and from that they progressed to holidays abroad.

"Crete this year," the Colonel told Kate. "We leave next week."

"Your daughters too?"

"My youngest girl." The Colonel chuckled and tapped Kate's hand. "Diana prefers to stay here." He looked across the room at the girl, who was engaged in an animated conversation with Robert. "Crete can't compete as an attraction," he murmured with a fond smile for his daughter's foolishness, "and of course she doesn't want to miss her training sessions. She competes in point-to-points, and she's just starting show jumping. An absolutely splendid little rider, though not as good as Robert, mind."

"Very county," Kate thought sourly. "Way out of my class. The sooner I get out of this house the better," but at that moment the younger Montgomerys came up and detached her from the Colonel.

"How about a game of table tennis?" Linda suggested, and Tim added in a low voice, "I've had enough of Diana's hunting stories for one evening. Heard them all before, anyway.

Kate laughed, saw Angela Mitchell hovering in the background and hoped she hadn't caught this remark. Compared to her older sister Angela seemed sweet and gentle and rather colourless. Invited to join them, she blossomed away from the rest of the family, and an enjoyably noisy doubles game was in progress when Robert looked in an hour later.

"Sorry to break it up, but Miss Ferguson's wanted on the phone."

It was a distraught wife whose husband had a severe pain in the chest. "He's in agony, doctor, and he looks a dreadful colour."

It sounded very much like a coronary thrombosis and was therefore an acute medical emergency. Kate wrote down the address and the rather inadequate directions the frightened woman managed to give. Then she went back to the drawing-room to excuse herself.

"It seems to be quite a way from here. Do you think I shall find it fairly easily?"

"Glebe Farm? It's nearly ten miles away, and up a narrow track that you could easily miss." Robert looked at his young brother. "Tim had better go with you."

"I shouldn't be much help," said Tim. "It's ages since I've been that way."

"Linda, then?" but the girl shook her head. "Sorry, Robert, I've only the vaguest idea—"

"I really must get started," said Kate. "I expect I shall find it."

"That I doubt," Robert said crisply. "Give me two minutes and I'll come with you. The Martins are not the people to call you out unnecessarily."

"Please don't bother," Kate murmured, and Diana added in her high affected voice, "Surely you don't need to go? Draw the girl a map."

"I think I do need to go," Robert said quietly. "I might draw the map incorrectly. Shall we take your car, Miss Ferguson, to save shifting your medical gear?"

She could see he was determined to come, and arguing would only waste more time, so she nodded, smiled a general good-bye and turned towards the door. As she went out she caught the flash of irritation on Diana's face, and heard Mrs. Mitchell's fulsome comment.

"How terribly, terribly kind of you, Robert! Such a bore for you. I hope that young woman appreciates it."

Kate collected a jacket and her car keys and went down to the courtyard. Robert was already there, clad in a heavy sweater and swinging a torch in one hand.

"Might come in useful," he said, "if I remember the track to Glebe Farm."

"Do you want to drive?" Kate asked.

"No, thanks."

"Most men hate being driven by a woman," she remarked. "They seem to feel it's a slur on their masculinity."

"Perhaps I'm past the age when I need to assert myself in that way."

Or too sure of himself to need to impress any woman? Particularly one he disliked? Kate drove out of the courtyard and rather cautiously along the uneven drive. Even so the car lurched as she struck a pothole and she muttered something under her breath.

"Sorry about the drive," he apologized. "Some day I plan to have it resurfaced."

"I bet it would cost a lot."

"More than a thousand, which is why it will have to wait."

They turned out of the drive and Kate trod hard on the accelerator. On these narrow twisting lanes she preferred night driving, because the headlights of another car gave warning of its approach.

After a few minutes' silence she said a little awkwardly, "It's very kind of you to come. Really kind."

"Shall we say it's in the nature of an olive branch?"

"An olive branch?" she repeated rather doubtfully.

"Don't you think it's time we called a truce?" he asked.

"I wasn't aware we were at war!"

"Weren't you?" he asked dryly. "I find that a little hard to believe, especially after what Maggie said to me on the way up to London. She suggested I should try and be more friendly. So here I am—" he sounded faintly amused now—"trying to be friendly."

She felt this unexpected speech called for some sort of response, though he hadn't been exactly friendly when they were discussing Tim's affairs. "As we're—such close neighbours it would be—more agreeable—if we could be on better terms," she agreed cautiously, and was put out when he began to laugh.

"Not sure how far you want to go, my dear Kate? I may call you Kate in view of our improved relations?"

Kate didn't like being laughed at, and suspected that his feelings towards her hadn't really changed. If he was trying to be pleasant it was only to please Maggie.

"Call me what you like," she said ungraciously, and concentrated on driving and on following his directions. Although she would have preferred not to have him with her, she had to admit that she would never have found the way on her own.

"Slow down," he said at last. "I think it's just round the bend."

In the glare of the headlights she saw a sign with "Glebe Farm" painted on it. "Thank goodness," she muttered as they bumped up the rutted track. "We've been a long time getting here and his wife sounded so frightened. Let's hope it turns out to be indigestion. Not every pain in the chest is due to a coronary."

This one was, however. Five minutes later, standing by Mr. Martin's bed, she was in no doubt of the diagnosis. Sweating, apprehensive, his lips colourless, he could only clutch his chest when she asked him about the pain. His pulse was thready and irregular, his blood pressure alarmingly low. She gave him an injection of morphia and told him that he would have to go into hospital.

"Stay with him while I ring for an ambulance," she told Mrs. Martin, who was standing in the background, rigid with apprehension. For urgent calls the ambulance men showed a praiseworthy promptness. Mr. Martin, strapped on to the stretcher to get him safely down the steep stairs, was on his way to the hospital less than half an hour later.

Robert had been invited into the house by Mrs. Martin, who was quite plainly very much in awe of him. Her manner irritated Kate, though she had to admit that Robert did his best to put the woman at her ease. As she climbed into the ambulance after her husband, Robert called after her, "I hope all goes well, Mrs. Martin." Turning to Kate as they walked back to the car, he added gravely, "Is he as bad as he looks?"

"I'm afraid so. He's had a massive coronary and I doubt if he'll pull through. Yet when his wife asked me I hedged. We tell such lies to people," she ended on a sigh.

"I doubt if she could take the truth right now. It wouldn't help her husband if she went to pieces in front of him. Relax, Kate. Unwind." He looked down at her, his face clear in the bright moonlight, and more kindly than usual. "You look very tired. I'll drive you home."

"I feel tired," Kate admitted, and slid gratefully into the passenger seat. The tiredness was as much due to tension as to the lateness of the hour. As such a new G.P. she still found it a strain handling grave emergencies, not because of the medical problems involved but because of the human ones. If you were young and not very sure of yourself, it wasn't always easy exuding the calm self-confidence that the patient and his relatives required for their own peace of mind.

"You said you found it difficult to believe I was a doctor," she murmured. "I wonder how many other people feel the same way."

"I don't remember saying that, but if I did I take it back. I have nothing but admiration for your professional poise and expertise."

He sounded sincere, but Kate peered at him suspiciously in the dim light. "You have to be joking. I was nearly as worked up as Mrs. Martin."

"But you didn't show it, and that's what counts. I do remember that remark now. I only meant that you looked too young to be a doctor, not that you look inefficient. Ben says you're doing surprisingly well."

"Big of him," Kate said flippantly to hide her pleasure at this unexpected praise, and then as she took in his words more completely, "Why surprising? Why are men always surprised when a woman's moderately competent at her job? I tell you it's downright insulting—" she broke off, aware of his amusement. "That's right, laugh! It's a man's world all right."

"Yes, I'm afraid it is," Robert agreed blandly, "but there are compensations in being feminine. If you'd been a man I should probably have left you to find your own way. But women are such hopeless map-readers!"

"And that's a stuffy, pompous thing to say!" Kate retorted hotly.

"I was joking," he said mildly. "You rise very easily, don't you?" He shot her a quick glance. "You want to watch that sharp tongue of yours, my girl. Your brother has a much sweeter nature than you."

"We've always been considered rather similar. If I'm sharp with you it's because—because—" She tried again, mindful of the fact that he had done her a favour—"Maybe it's my fault, but you're so—so—"

"Irritating?" he supplied pleasantly.

"Overbearing," she snapped, good resolves flying out of the window. "I suppose you're so used to talking down to the peasants you do it without thinking."

"Could it be that you're a bit of an inverted snob, Kate?" he asked softly, and she made an exasperated gesture.

"I expect you're right. I can't get used to the village squire scene. It's an anachronism in the seventies."

"It's that all right," he agreed grimly. "Sherringdon Hall is decrepit and hard to run, and eats up any profit I make on the land, but it's been in my family for over two hundred years. Before it was built there was a house on the same site that dated back to the fourteenth century. My forebears owned that too."

He stopped abruptly and sighed. For such a self-assured man he seemed for a few seconds as vulnerable as the next person. It made him more human and more likeable.

"It must be a great responsibility," Kate said seriously, and fell silent, trying to imagine what it would be like to have roots that went so deep into the past. Perhaps she had judged Robert too hastily. Autocratic he might be, but he took his responsibilities very seriously, and looked after the welfare of his workers most admirably.

"A fine man," one old lady had told her at the surgery. "My husband worked on the estate all his life, but when he died I expected to be turned out of my cottage. Only Mr. Montgomery said I was to stay."

"I should hope so too!" Kate had exclaimed, and the old lady had smiled at such ignorance.

"That's not the usual way, doctor, with a tied cottage. His father would have turned me out. It was a good day for Sherringdon when Mr. Robert came back from Canada."

The car turned on to the drive and when Robert drew up in the courtyard she climbed out wearily. Robert, looking irritatingly fresh, walked round to hand her the car keys.

"Maggie must have gone to bed," he commented, glancing at the darkened house. "I hope you don't have any more calls tonight."

"So do I," Kate said fervently. "Thank you for coming with me. It was a great help." On a sudden impulse, she held out her hand. "Mr. Montgomery, I think we began on the wrong foot somehow. After tonight perhaps we could make a fresh start?"

He took her hand and held it for a few seconds, his fingers cool and firm. "That would be a good idea. Could you bring yourself to drop the formality? Robert would be more friendly."

She was very conscious of the contact between them, of his closeness and the attraction of his smile. "All right, then." She hesitated for a moment. "If you disapprove of my helping Tim—"

He shrugged. "Why should I disapprove? It's decent of you to bother with the boy." A faint smile came and went. "Perhaps I should make more effort to understand him," which Kate took to be a half apology for his sharp words earlier that night.

"I wish you would," she said earnestly. "Good night, Robert," and she turned away quickly, overcome by a sudden and inexplicable shyness.

As she prepared for bed she thought over the events of the evening, wishing rather absurdly that she was older and more mature—poised and polished, unruffled by a man like Robert, with his cool self-assurance and effortless superiority.

CHAPTER THREE

THE FINE WEATHER continued throughout October. Kate had her half day on Thursdays, and on her next afternoon off she decided to explore the grounds of Sherringdon Hall. She took the path round the lake and on the far side was tempted into the woods, which stretched for miles until they ended by a long stone wall on the main road.

She walked slowly, scuffling through the fallen leaves, came to a chestnut tree and stopped to fill her pockets. Maggie and she could roast them on the sitting-room fire. She was bent double, searching for the best ones, when she heard voices close by. She straightened up as a boy and girl came round a bend in the path, closely entwined and intent only on each other. The boy stopped and turned the girl towards him, his hands sliding over her possessively, his kiss passionate.

Kate felt embarrassed. While she was trying to decide whether to let them know she was there, she saw the girl's face properly for the first time. It was Linda Montgomery, flushed and happy, and looking quite beautiful, in spite of the disreputable jeans and skinny sweater that were her permanent attire.

The boy was lanky and long-haired, a tough-looking lad with a cocky walk. He tugged Linda by the hand and they turned down a side path and disappeared into an old stone building that Kate had noticed earlier, a little pavilion that gave a view over the lake. She didn't think they would be wasting much time on the view, though.

She pushed her way through the low undergrowth

and set off again, down the main path, hoping that they hadn't noticed her. It was disagreeable playing a peeping Tom, even unintentionally. The incident worried her a little, because this was no casual boy-and-girl friendship, and Linda was very young. She wondered if Robert knew of the lad's existence. Presumably he did if Linda brought him home, though it was unlikely that the elegant Robert would approve of such a scruffy young man. She hadn't particularly liked the look of him herself.

She went back to the house and was doing some ironing when the telephone rang. "Linda here. Could I talk to you about something, Kate?"

"Talk away," Kate invited.

"Not on the phone," the girl said quickly. "Can I come over? Maggie's not back yet, is she?"

"No, she'll be another half hour or so. All right, come over," but Kate sighed as she looked at the pile of unironed clothes still to do. Women doctors didn't have much time for domestic chores, and had to fit them in whenever possible.

When Linda arrived she looked ill at ease and fidgeted around for a minute or two, making disjointed remarks about nothing in particular.

"Get to the point," Kate suggested. "You didn't come here to discuss the weather!"

Linda coloured. "No. I wanted to talk about this afternoon."

Kate had already guessed what was coming. "I didn't think you'd seen me. It seemed best to just fade away." She gave a half smile. "You were pretty wrapped up in each other and I felt an intruder."

Linda went redder still. "The point is—you won't say anything to Robert, will you? About seeing me with Dave?"

"What an odd idea, Linda. Why should I discuss your affairs with Robert?" said Kate.

"Not discuss—but you might make some casual

comment. Robert disapproves of Dave, you see. I'm not supposed to meet him."

"So you meet secretly in the woods? A bit risky! Suppose it had been Robert walking along that path?"

"Robert doesn't have time for casual walks. Hardly anybody goes there. You're the first person we've met in weeks."

So the affair had been going on for some time. Kate wasn't happy about it, and yet she didn't want to get the girl into trouble.

"Do sit down, Linda, and stop fidgeting. I'm trying to think what I should do. Why doesn't Robert like that boy?"

"Because he's such a snob!" Linda exclaimed passionately. "Dave's father used to work on the estate, but he got tired of being pushed around by Robert and went into the garage business. He's built it up from a grotty little place into something really good, and Dave works with him."

"As a mechanic?"

"That's right. So what?" the girl asked belligerently.

"So nothing," Kate said soothingly. "Good luck to them if they've made a success of their venture. But are you sure, Linda? Is it really Dave's background Robert objects to?"

"Of course I'm sure. Robert's a hopeless square—can't adjust to modern life, doesn't even try."

The girl sounded so positive that Kate was almost persuaded. Perhaps that was half of it, and yet—and yet—she hadn't liked the look of the young man. What if Robert had more personal reasons for disapproving of him?

"Linda, you're very young," she persisted. "How old is Dave?"

"Twenty."

Older than Kate had realized and not likely to be content with a few kisses. Worried, she stared out of the window and saw Maggie's car turn into the courtyard.

"We'll have to break it up now, Linda," she said hurriedly. "I'm not entirely happy about it, but of course I won't give you away. I think we ought to talk about it again—"

"You're a doll!" Linda cried. "I knew you'd under-understand. She planted a smacking kiss on Kate's cheek and rushed out of the room before Kate could say any more, yelled a remark at Maggie in passing, and disappeared.

Kate was still sitting in the window, half amused and half annoyed, when Maggie came in. "What was all that about?"

"Oh, girlish confidences," said Kate, wondering if it might not be a good thing to discuss the matter with Maggie. She dismissed the idea, however, because Maggie and Robert were very thick, and Maggie would almost certainly insist on bringing him into it.

She liked Robert better than she had done in the beginning, but she still thought him very high-handed in the way he treated his young brother and sister. He would have no sympathy at all with Linda's behaviour.

Kate hadn't forgotten her teenage years, the problems, the enthusiasms, the frequent crushes. With any luck the affair wasn't all that serious and Linda would have another boyfriend by next month, in which case all Kate would have done by betraying her confidence would be to lose the girl's trust for ever.

And she needs help, Kate thought, but not from an older brother or a cousin. From someone disinterested, whom she likes and trusts.

And so Kate rationalized her actions in not giving Linda away, and stifled the faint unease she felt about the whole affair. She did, however, make several attempts to talk to Linda again, but either by accident or design they only seemed to meet when there were other people about.

One morning she was further afield than usual on her round of home visits. Glancing at the petrol gauge she saw that the needle was nearly at empty, and pulled into the next garage she came to. Waiting behind another car for her turn at the pumps, she thought that the attendant looked vaguely familiar. A patient, perhaps? She had never been good at remembering faces, and doctors saw so many in the course of their work.

She rolled down the window to make her order and the young man gave her a broad grin. "Remember me, doc?"

"Should I?" Kate asked, but even as she spoke she did remember. Linda's boy-friend, Dave! There was a swagger to his walk that could have been due to nervousness, though she didn't think it was. He smiled again as he saw recognition dawn.

"Linda says you're on our side," he grinned.

A little stiffly Kate said, "I'm not on anyone's side. Because I've kept quiet so far you needn't think that I approve."

He stopped smiling. "Look here, you've got the wrong idea. It's Linda who insists on meeting secretly. She's afraid of that toffee-nosed brother of hers, not me."

He sounded sincere and he looked cocky enough to be afraid of no one. Robert, after all, had control only over his sister. Kate dug in her handbag and watched him lope off to the office for change. When he came back the smile was once more in place.

"Do me a favour, doc. Give this to Linda." He passed a small packet through the window and Kate stared at it suspiciously. "It's just some tubes of paint she asked me to pick up in town," Dave said impatiently. "What did you think it was? Dope?"

The thought had crossed Kate's mind, and was not as bizarre as all that, because even in this remote country practice she had met a few young people on drugs.

"All right, I'll give it to her. I've been trying to talk to her for days, so this will give me a good excuse."

"About us?"

"That's right. You met at evening classes, didn't you? And you still see each other there? So why not leave it at that and avoid the risk of getting Linda into serious trouble?"

"The College canteen's a bit limiting," he smiled, but it wasn't a nice smile. It was intended to mock her.

A car tooted behind and Dave raised a hand in careless salute. "You're holding up the traffic, doc."

"A brash young man," Kate thought, as she drove out of the garage. What she couldn't decide, though, was whether there was any real harm in him. It was not the first time she wished she hadn't become involved. She decided to make a real effort to have things out with Linda.

That evening Maggie went out to practise carols with the local madrigal society. Kate was on duty, but by nine o'clock had had no calls. She telephoned Robert's house and asked Linda to come over.

"I've something for you from Dave," she told her.

That at least might be expected to bring Linda over, but the girl stalled with obvious embarrassment. "It's not very convenient. I'm just going out."

"Then I shall bring it over," Kate said firmly. "Is Robert in?"

The implied threat did the trick. "I'll come right away," Linda said hastily, and less than a minute later was banging on the door. "What is this?" she asked breathlessly. "Where did you meet Dave?"

"Not by design," Kate said coolly. "I happened to stop at his garage. I was surprised he recognized me after such a brief glimpse."

"There's a small window in the summerhouse. We watched you through that," said Linda, and giggled self-consciously. "We wanted to make sure you'd gone before we—well, you know."

"I do know. And I think, Linda, that the time has come for some plain speaking. Why have you been avoiding me?"

Linda protested, not very convincingly, that she hadn't been. "I've had a lot to do in the house," she said virtuously. "Aunt Margaret arrives tomorrow and it's the one time in the year when the place is really tidy."

Kate had a vague memory of Robert and Maggie talking about a formidable old aunt who paid them a yearly visit. "The one who comes for the hunting!" she exclaimed, and Linda giggled.

"That's her. She's really a great-aunt and absolutely prehistoric. We all dread her visits—well, not Robert, nobody frightens him—but Tim and me, and Maggie too, I think."

"You're off the point," Kate said gently. "We were discussing your affairs."

She gave a little push and the girl subsided into an easy chair. From there she looked up at Kate with a mixture of apprehension and wariness, Dave's parcel clutched tightly in her hand. Kate told her quite plainly that she wasn't prepared any longer to keep quiet about the secret meetings. That Linda must promise not to meet Dave any more, except openly and with Robert's approval.

"And if you won't," she ended gravely, "I shall tell Robert all about it."

Flushed and sulky, Linda twisted a strand of hair round her forefinger. "I thought we were friends," she mumbled. "I didn't think you'd do a sneaky thing like that."

"I'd much rather not. You only have to say the word, Linda. But it's because we are friends—because I do like you—that I'll do it if I have to."

"What's that supposed to mean?" Linda muttered.

"You're awfully young to be so involved with a man. Meeting in the woods—it's very unwise—" Kate hesitated, afraid of offending the girl, but she needn't have worried. Linda was a product of her time.

She laughed with genuine amusement. "Oh, Kate, I wasn't born yesterday. I can look after myself."

"That's a remark a good many girls have made," Kate said dryly, "and a lot of them have ended up pregnant. I meet them in the surgery all the time, some of them no older than you."

"Dave says I ought to be on the pill!" Linda exclaimed, and then put her hand to her mouth in a childish gesture of dismay. "But I don't expect you'd approve?"

"No!" Kate snapped. "Well, Linda? Which is it to be? A promise from you? Or a talk with your brother?"

"I don't have much choice, do I? But we'll still meet at night school," she added defiantly. "You can't object to that."

"Of course I don't. What does Dave do there?"

"He's taking an engineering course. He's bright," said Linda proudly. "School bored him, but he sees a point to this, because it's for the business."

Remembering Dave's jaunty manner and the sharp knowing eyes, Kate was prepared to believe that. "I admire ambition," she said. "I like a person who'll work hard for what they want. But play it cool, Linda. Meet him with other people around. And please—please—don't see yourself as some sort of a martyr."

She smiled at the girl, but Linda looked back resentfully. "You're just like all the others, and I thought you were different."

How young she was, Kate thought, and tried again to bridge the gap between them. "I can see I'm not your favourite person right now. How do I rate beside that aunt of yours? Better or worse?"

That did bring a flicker of a smile. "No one could be worse. She's quite awful,' 'and then the telephone rang and Kate went off to answer it. While she was writing down the name and address of a patient who needed visiting, she heard the front door slam. Linda, doubtless with relief, was making her escape.

"HAVE YOU MET Lady Howard yet?" Ben asked a few days later, when Kate and he were sharing a cup of coffee after morning surgery.

Kate stared. "Lady who?"

"Robert's Aunt Margaret. She's staying with them now."

"Not to speak to, though I've seen her in the distance. On a horse! So she's Lady Howard! Maggie didn't tell me."

"She's the widow of a colonial governor in the days when we still had colonies," Ben said with a grin. "Actually I'm quite fond of the old warhorse." He looked thoughtfully at Kate. "I wonder what she'll make of you."

"We're not likely to meet much," Kate said carelessly. "I don't think governors' wives are quite my thing. Much more in the line of that snooty Mitchell girl."

She had noticed Diana's red Mini parked outside Robert's house quite a few times this week. She had seen Robert and Diana in the distance riding together round the estate. Once, chafing with impatience, she had had to sit in her car for nearly ten minutes, while the hunt blocked a narrow lane. Arrogant so-and-sos, she had fumed, and had not been placated when Robert, riding up on a magnificent black horse, had told them to clear a way for her.

She had rolled the car window down, red with annoyance, and told him exactly what she thought of a bunch of people who could waste time on such an idiotic pursuit. He had smiled down at her, more attractive than ever in his hunting gear, and doubtless aware of it, Kate thought sourly.

"I've already said I'm sorry for holding you up. I didn't realize it was your car."

"And that makes it all right?" Kate queried sarcastically. "You thought it was O.K. to keep one of the local yokels waiting? Doubtless they know their place better than I do?"

His good humour evaporated a little. "You've got the wrong idea about some things, my girl. The average countryman isn't in such a hurry as you townees. And we don't deliberately cause an obstruction." He gestured with his whip at the excited pack and the cavorting horses. "Some of those people don't ride as well as they think they do."

"Then they shouldn't be out at all!" Kate snapped, and he nodded rueful agreement.

"Try telling them that, though." He bent down towards her. "Cheer up, young Kate. Perhaps someone will fall off. Think what fun you'd have then, being horrid to the poor devil in your surgery!"

Over coffee she regaled Ben with this incident. "Don't you think it's fantastically arrogant, the way they spread themselves all over the road?"

Ben shook his head. "They don't mean to be arrogant. Hunting's in their blood. Robert was probably right, that most of the local folk don't really mind. And you must admit that they're a splendid sight."

Kate had a vivid memory of Robert on horseback, looking like one of the portraits at Sherringdon Hall. "Overdressed dummies!" she snorted, because she hated to admit, even to herself, how impressed she had been. "What do you think of the Mitchell girl?" she asked as an afterthought.

"Diana?" Ben shrugged. "Not my type. I like a girl with a bit of warmth in her." He flicked a glance at the half open door of his office and pushed it shut with his foot. "It's a pity we're never off duty together, Kate. It would have been great showing you around." A large hand covered hers. "Perhaps when Dad's better?"

"When your father's better I won't be here," Kate said firmly, because she was a little ruffled by Ben's behaviour lately. He had asked her to eat with him on a number of occasions and dropped in at Maggie's more and more frequently. He made no secret of the fact that he found Kate attractive. In his rather heavyhanded way he complimented her on her clothes or her hairdo.

"Beats me how you manage to look so gorgeous when you work so hard," he said admiringly on more than one occasion, for Ben was inclined to repeat himself. Kate knew the danger signals when she saw them, and took care to be cool and aloof. She liked Ben, but that was all. She hadn't come within a million miles of falling in love with him, and it would be awkward if he fancied himself in love with her.

Their easygoing relationship would be strained—was a little strained already, perhaps. Once Ben had leant his solid frame against Miss Andrews' workbench and drunk his coffee in the dispensary. Now he would find reasons to invite Kate into his office. "That patient you saw yesterday? What did you think of her?" or "Let's go through next month's duty roster." Things like that. It didn't fool Kate and it most certainly didn't fool Miss Andrews, whose back had a habit of stiffening alarmingly when she was displeased about something. Kate wanted to tell her that that made two of them who didn't approve of Ben's behaviour, but of course she couldn't. It would be both embarrassing and petty.

So she did her best to avoid being alone with him, and wished she hadn't denied so vehemently the existence of that young man in Glasgow, whom Ben had inquired about on an earlier occasion.

CHAPTER FOUR

NEXT WEEK-END Kate was on duty again. When she got home after her Saturday morning surgery and her round of visits, Maggie produced a bottle of sherry. Kate sipped and leant her elbows on the wide window-sill. They were in the big sitting-room which over-looked the drive. The sun was hot through the glass even in November.

Kate looked out on the rose garden, agreeably tidy after her recent efforts, and felt deeply contented. She had just made the surprising discovery that she enjoyed country life, the clean air, the space, the blessed quiet.

"I've never before lived in a house where I could see cows from my bedroom window," she remarked. "It sort of gets you after a time."

Horses' hooves sounded on the drive. Robert and his aunt rode by, the reins loose on their horses' necks. The old lady rode as easily as her nephew, straight-backed and proud. For some reason Kate moved to the next window so that she could watch them disappear into the stables.

"I forgot to mention it. We're invited to dinner this evening." Maggie gestured towards Robert's house.

Kate frowned. "I don't think I should go. I'm on duty."

"Of course you must. They'll think it rude if you don't. Besides"—she gave her engaging smile—"Aunt Margaret wants to look you over, she's heard such a lot about you."

"Oh? From whom?"

Maggie waved her hands vaguely. "Different people.

I heard Robert telling her the other day that if she didn't behave herself and take her pills, he would call you in. Said the old lady wouldn't be able to browbeat you the way she does Ben."

"You mean she's our patient?" asked Kate.

"While she's down here."

"There can't be much wrong with her if she can ride like that."

"I think it's only will power that keeps her going," said Maggie. "She's old and ill but refuses to admit it."

That evening, meeting Lady Howard at close quarters, Kate knew that Maggie's assessment was correct. The careful make-up couldn't conceal her condition from a trained eye. Her face had the haggard look of someone who suffered a good deal of pain. The twisted hands on the ivory cane gave a clue of the possible cause. Arthritis, Kate thought, and marvelled that the old lady could ride at all. The fine eyes, so very like Robert's, examined her from top to toe.

"So you're Kate Ferguson. Not a scrap like your brother, are you?"

Kate murmured a conventional reply, her democratic spirit already rebelling at the old lady's autocratic manner. Lady Howard patted the sofa beside her.

"Sit down, child. I'd like a talk with you," so Kate sat down a little unwillingly, with a quick glance round to see if there was any chance of rescue.

Lady Howard laughed a shade maliciously. "You're just as my nephew described you. He said you were no good at hiding your feelings."

A little stiffly Kate answered, "Which nephew, Lady Howard?"

"Robert, of course."

"I'm at a loss to understand why you should have been discussing me at all." The stilted phrase didn't sound like Kate, but the old lady's manner had put her back up.

The reddened mouth with its network of surrounding wrinkles tightened ominously. "He also said you were the most argumentative girl he'd ever met. What he failed to mention was that you're a pretty little thing. Is that red hair out of a bottle?"

Kate had never approved of those elderly people who used their age as an excuse for rudeness. "Certainly it isn't," she said coolly. "And just for the record, I've heard a good deal about you too." And you can make what you like of that, she thought, meeting the old lady's suddenly sharpened glance with a touch of defiance.

A voice spoke behind the sofa—Robert's. "Sherry's your drink, isn't it, Kate? Well, Aunt Margaret, what do you think of her?"

He rested both hands lightly on the sofa back and smiled down at them. Lady Howard took so long in replying that Kate buried her nose in her sherry glass to hide a sudden and unexpected feeling of awkwardness. They were impossible, the pair of them, discussing her in this highhanded way, but she should have been more tactful and not made that indiscreet, indeed almost rude remark.

"I like her," Lady Howard said at last. "At least she's got spunk. I'm getting rather tired, my dear boy, of everyone agreeing with me," and she favoured the surprised Kate with a broad smile.

A little uncertainly Kate smiled back, but it was Robert who spoke. "Then you shouldn't be such an old autocrat. The others are too terrified of your abrasive tongue to argue with you."

"And so they should be. I don't approve of young people answering back their elders," said Lady Howard with scant regard for consistency.

Kate choked on a mouthful of sherry, recovered and felt it was time that she put a word in. "Have you quite finished discussing me?" she asked in a long-suffering voice. "It is a little embarrassing, you know."

Robert looked amused by this act. "Come off it,

young Kate. You can give as good as you get and well you know it. But our discussion had a point, because Aunt Margaret is thinking of consulting you." His expression had sobered now as he waited for her reaction.

"Medically?" Kate didn't relish the idea at all. "Oh, but that wouldn't do," she added quickly and with all too evident relief. "You're Ben's patient, Lady Howard. It would be quite unethical."

"Rubbish, my dear. Ben won't mind," Lady Howard said briskly.

Won't have to, more likely, Kate thought with mounting irritation, wondering if she was expected to conduct a medical session in Robert's drawing-room. A surprising number of people, who should have known better, insisted on telling doctors their ailments in the most unlikely places.

Lady Howard, it appeared, was not one of them. "I'll see you in the surgery on Monday morning," she announced, and Kate shot back, "*If* there's an appointment free, and *if* Ben doesn't mind."

"You can ask him right now." Robert straightened and went forward to greet the new arrivals. Diana Mitchell had just come in, followed by Ben. It appeared from the conversation that Diana's car was out of action, so Ben had given her a lift.

"But you'll run me back, Robert, won't you?" Diana gushed, sliding a possessive hand through his arm.

"She tries too hard," Lady Howard observed. "Robert's the sort of man who prefers to do his own chasing."

While Kate was trying to decide whether this uncharitable remark called for an answer, the old lady crooked an imperious finger at Ben, who approached rather warily. "I am not going to bite you, young man," she said tartly. "I have a request to make, that's all." It came out like an order, however, and Ben gave his consent most willingly. Too willingly, Kate thought resentfully. Lady Howard was most likely a terrible patient and he was glad to get rid of her.

"No need for you to come to the surgery," he said amiably. "Kate can call in at the end of her round when she comes back for lunch."

Manoeuvred into a position from which it would be difficult to extract herself without giving offence, Kate agreed to this arrangement reluctantly. "Beast!" she hissed in Ben's ear, when Lady Howard had indicated that she wanted to talk to Maggie for a change.

They had wandered off together to an unoccupied corner of the large room. Ben wasn't quick to pick up her meaning. To his puzzled face she added sharply, "Fobbing that old dragon off on me. Honestly, you've got a nerve!"

He gave her a guilty smile. "I've had her for years. I didn't think you'd mind."

"Well, I do mind, though I suppose I shall have to put up with it."

She scowled at him and he laid a placating hand on her arm. "Don't be cross, Kate, though you look very pretty when you're roused." His eyes crinkled and he squeezed her arm. "You're the prettiest girl here, by far."

That had to be the moment that Robert appeared, a glass in his hand for Ben. The look on Robert's face told Kate that he had overheard Ben's remark—a look compounded of surprise and something else. Annoyance? Disapproval? But why on earth should Robert disapprove, if Ben chose to make advances to his young assistant?

Kate reacted predictably to Robert's manner. She drew closer to Ben, stood on tiptoe and whispered some nonsense in his ear. Ben laughed loudly and she echoed his laughter, watching Robert out of the corner of her eye. She was a little discomfited when he just stood there, waiting for them to stop.

Self-consciously she drew away from Ben and Robert remarked in a neutral sort of voice, "I was going to offer you another drink, but I can see you've had enough."

Kate bristled. "Well, of all the—I've only had one sherry, as well you know. And anyway, I don't drink much on duty."

"Good for you. And just as well, since you seem to get lit up so easily."

Ben gave them both a puzzled look. "What goes on? And why are you looking so cross, Kate?"

Kate took a firm grip on her temper, remembering just in time that she was a guest in Robert's house. "Robert enjoys ribbing me," she murmured. "I'm not really cross," but the fierce look she flung at their host belied her words.

Robert gave a smile that Kate labelled superior, and nodded in the direction of his aunt and cousin. "Go and rescue Maggie, Ben. She's wilting under Aunt Margaret's attack."

Alone with Kate, he planted himself squarely in front of her and added softly, "Do you think it's wise to encourage Ben? Work and romance are a tricky combination."

This was Kate's opinion too, but coming from Robert she thought it outrageous interference, and said so. Aware that one or two other people were looking their way, she managed to keep her voice down, but she couldn't control her mounting colour. Kate had a fair skin that flushed easily, and was a great source of irritation to her. She turned her back on the rest of the room and waited for Robert's reply.

"I agree, Kate, that what you do is none of my business, but Ben's my friend and I hate to see him making a fool of himself. He never could resist a pretty face and usually it's of no consequence, but with you"—he made a comprehensive gesture—"the reputation of the practice is in Ben's hands while his father's away."

"You can't seriously be suggesting that Ben and I fool around at work!" Kate cried. "You don't know much about doctors if you believe that. Some of the young ones can be pretty wild, but they don't misbehave on duty."

"No, Kate, of course I don't think that. I know you're both good and dedicated doctors. I only meant that Ben's got enough problems already without you adding to them."

Before Kate could answer the cook came in to say that dinner was ready, and in the general move that followed she found herself separated from Robert. A good thing, she thought, because she had felt a powerful urge to hit him with one of his own, probably expensive china ornaments, which were in her opinion too lavishly scattered around the drawing-room.

From Kate's point of view it was not a successful dinner party. They ate pheasant, perfectly cooked, and a superb damson pie accompanied by a huge jug of cream.

"Bad for the coronaries," Kate murmured to Tim, who was sitting next to her.

He grinned and poured a liberal amount on to his portion of pie. "I'm young enough to get away with it, doctor."

"Don't you believe it," Kate retorted. "Research has proved that the damage is done in early childhood."

The rector of Sherringdon, who was on her other side, had turned to listen. An earnest man, who weighed the lightest remark carefully, he embarked on a solemn discussion of the perils of overeating. Bored Kate glanced up the table and met Robert's ironic gaze

"Serves you right for showing off your medical knowledge," that look seemed to say, but surely he couldn't have heard her, though he did have an unusually acute ear. The rector droned on and Kate pretended to listen, and was careful not to look Robert's way again. At least she was sitting well away from the head of the table, where Lady Howard, on Robert's right, was effortlessly dominating the conversation. Diana was looking rather sulky—bored, probably, because Robert wasn't paying her enough attention.

Kate was brought back to the rector's conversation with a jolt by the realization that he had asked her a question. "Er—I didn't quite catch that," she stammered, embarrassed that her lack of attention had been exposed, and it had to be that moment when other people were momentarily quiet.

Robert, looking amused, came to her rescue. "Poor Kate! It's a shame the way we laymen give doctors no respite."

"I only asked—" the rector began, to be ruthlessly cut off by Lady Howard.

"My dear man, I think it's positively indecent discussing medical matters at mealtimes." She bent the full force of her powerful personality on him, and he subsided into silence.

Tim touched Kate's arm and grinned at her. "What a family! What chance have Linda and I of growing up into normal well-adjusted adults?" which Kate took to be an oblique criticism of his aunt.

"I rather like the old lady," she muttered, and he pulled a face in return.

"You wouldn't if you had to live with her."

"But surely she won't be here for long?"

"Till the New Year," he said glumly. "She always spends Christmas with us and returns to her London flat on New Year's Day. It's become a family ritual, worse luck."

When dinner was over Kate went to the table tennis room with Tim and Linda. Rather to her surprise and the ill-concealed disapproval of the young Montgomerys, Diana came after them.

"You don't mind me joining you?" The girl's usual self-confidence seemed to have been dented by Lady Howard, or perhaps by Robert's failure to signal her out for special attention. Kate, who was kindhearted, felt sorry for her, even though she didn't like her. She suspected that Diana had hoped for great things while her parents were away, frequent visits to Robert's house culminating perhaps in an engagement. The other two, with lamentable lack of manners, had simply ignored Diana and embarked on a game of singles.

Kate sank down on a disreputable old sofa at one end of the room. "I'll play you when they've finished," she suggested, "and the winner of each game can play each other. O.K.?"

"O.K.," Diana agreed, and sat down beside Kate, her face brightening a little. "I can't stand that old bitch," she grumbled. "Robert's a saint to put up with her, don't you agree?"

"Not really. He seems genuinely fond of her, in which case where's the virtue in it?"

"Robert's... funny," Diana mused. "Everyone else hates her coming. Mother says she's the rudest woman she's ever met." (Which was the pot calling the kettle black with a vengeance, Kate thought, remembering the contemptuous way Mrs. Mitchell had dismissed her, as being of no importance.) "What did she say to you? You had quite a long chat with her before dinner."

"Oh, this and that," Kate said vaguely.

But Diana was not easily put off. "And what was Robert saying to make you look so cross? You'll think me very nosey," the girl, a little pink, patted her hair, "but I couldn't help noticing. I find personal relationships so fascinating. You know—what makes other people tick, and all that."

Kate had a shrewd idea that all this was merely a blind. She had labelled Diana self-centred and entirely absorbed in her pursuit of Robert. The girl was only interested in Kate's argument with Robert, because everything he did was of interest to her.

Kate looked a little pityingly at this girl, who had such an obsessive and apparently unrequited passion.

She seemed lacking in dignity and self-respect, but then people in love so often did.

"As a matter of fact," she said carefully, "Robert and I were having a pretty sharp disagreement. Not the first one, I may say. However hard I try we seem to rub each other up the wrong way."

"You mean you don't like him?" Diana exclaimed, astonishment mingling with relief in a most comical way. Kate had suspected that the other girl considered her a potential rival, and had chosen her words deliberately to dispel such a ludicrous idea. She had obviously been successful, because Diana became positively friendly, and embarrassingly eager to pour out confidences.

Kate learnt that Diana had known Robert since she was a young girl, and he a boy in his late teens. He had always been her hero, and when he quarrelled with his father and went to work on a ranch in British Columbia, she had cried for ages. "For simply ages," Diana sighed, sounding still the schoolgirl she had then been. "I know it's wrong to be glad when someone dies, but when I heard that Robert's father had had a heart attack—" she cast a guilty look towards Tim and Linda, but they were totally immersed in their game—"I thought at once, Robert will be coming home from Canada."

"Why did he quarrel with his father?" asked Kate.

Diana thought for a moment. "The old man was hopeless at running the estate. Took more out of it than he put in. He had a succession of bad managers. Robert was only a boy, but he had a mind of his own."

"I'll bet he did!"

"Well, after all, it was his inheritance that was being wasted. They had awful rows, but he hung on for his mother's sake. Then when she died he couldn't stand it any more. He never came back here while his father was alive, though the old man begged him to at the end."

"Somehow I wouldn't have expected him to," Kate said thoughtfully. "He's a hard man, isn't he, and doesn't have much sympathy with other people's weaknesses."

"Those years in British Columbia made him tough and self-reliant," Diana nodded. "He's a—a proper man, isn't he?"

"Oh, indeed he is," Kate agreed dryly. "Though myself I don't regard gentleness and sensitivity as being amiss in either sex."

"Don't you?" Diana seemed a little puzzled by this remark, then she smiled broadly. "It's just as well we don't all like the same things—or people, isn't it?"

Their conversation was brought to an absurd end by Tim, who drew up his bat in a sign of victory, whereupon Diana took on Kate and beat her easily.

"I never had a good eye for a ball," Kate smiled, losing with a good grace. She wandered off to do her face in the downstairs cloakroom. Emerging, she lingered for a minute or two in the hall, examining some silver-framed photos on a table in a corner. She picked up one of a beautiful dark girl in an oval frame. Robert's mother? There was a family resemblance, but that frilled and tucked dress surely hadn't been worn when she would have been a young woman.

"You know who that is?" Robert asked emerging from the drawing-room and coming over to her side. She shook her head. He took the portrait from her hands and gave a sigh as he stared down at it. "Aunt Margaret," he said, and though he must have looked at it many times there was still sadness in his voice. "Old age can be very cruel, can't it? And harder to take if you were a great beauty once. Bear with Aunt Margaret, Kate. She won't be the easiest of patients, but those who fight against the advancing years seldom are."

Kate stared at him, her feelings very mixed. Her initial reaction at meeting him in the hall had been one of irritation, that he had apparently quite forgotten their disagreement before dinner. This had been replaced by the sharp realization that he wasn't as insensitive as she had labelled him—not to those he loved, anyhow. Had he hated his father, that he had shown so little compassion when the old man begged him to come home?

"What goes on in that funny mind of yours?" Robert asked, replacing the photograph on the pretty inlaid table.

"You're very fond of her, aren't you?" she murmured, avoiding his question, and he nodded.

"I'm not blind to her faults, though. The trouble is most people don't see beyond the 'great lady' manner, which frightens them if they're timid, or annoys them if they're like you."

"Like me?"

He gave her a quizzical smile. "Independent and modern-minded." Whether he intended to or not he conveyed the impression that he disapproved of these qualities, at least in a woman. The thought made her bristle so that she came out with a gauche remark.

"I can just imagine the sort of woman you'll pick as a wife, Mr. Montgomery."

"I thought we'd progressed to christian name terms," he reminded her. "But do tell me, my dear Kate. I'm most intrigued."

She blushed like a schoolgirl, furious with herself for that naïve remark, but determined not to back down. "Old-fashioned in her attitude to men. Accepting without question their belief in their own superiority. Oh, she'd be attractive, of course."

"Why of course?" he asked mildly, and she gave an exasperated snort.

"Because men like you"—her words tailed off and her colour deepened—"you know what I mean," she ended lamely. Handsome men who had been around didn't pick plain wives.

His expression was curiously rueful. "Well, now I

CHAPTER FIVE

"VERY SENSIBLE OF YOU to stay in bed. I should have recommended you to do just that."

Kate rose from her perch on the edge of Lady Howard's bed, folding the cuff of her blood pressure machine, while she pondered on how much it was wise to tell the old lady.

"I only stayed in bed because I thought it would be more convenient for you. I'm usually up by eight."

Kate walked over to the window and stared out at the lawns and the distant lake. "I'd suggest, Lady Howard, that from now on you alter that routine. Make it normal to get up at midday, at least for some weeks."

"What are you trying to tell me, young woman? Come on, out with it!"

Kate reflected for a moment on Lady Howard's medical records, which she had read carefully in the surgery before her visit. "You know you have high blood pressure, which has in the past been satisfactorily controlled. Well, it isn't now. We'll have to alter your treatment a bit, add another pill or two. But in addition you simply must take more rest."

"I refuse to become a vegetable!" the old lady exclaimed fiercely.

Kate smiled. "I can't imagine you ever being that! Besides, a little gentle exercise is better for your arthritis, or you'll stiffen up too much."

Lady Howard, enthroned among a mountain of pillows, and clad in an extremely ornate quilted and beaded bed-jacket, picked up a heavy silver mirror from her bed table. She began to comb her still thick white hair, and said with dignity, "I shall take the medicines you prescribe, Doctor Ferguson, but how much I do is my own affair."

Her manner was dismissive. So might she have spoken to an offending servant when she was still the governor's lady. Kate, stifling a desire to giggle, moved back to the bed and picked her words carefully.

"I'm sorry, Lady Howard, but you're wrong. Medicines alone won't bring down your blood pressure. The way you live is important too. You must be guided by me in this. I am your doctor, for the present at any rate."

"Must! Must indeed!" The colour deepened in the old lady's heavily powdered cheeks.

"Hasn't your doctor in London urged you to ease up?" Kate probed, refusing to be intimidated.

"I don't pay any attention to *him*. Man's a complete fool. I thought a woman would be more understanding."

"For understanding read complaisant," Kate murmured, and tried the effect of a smile. It was met, however, with a frosty look.

"If you'll go now, Dr. Ferguson, I shall get up. It takes me longer to dress than it used to do."

It was usually the doctor who terminated the interview, not the patient, but Lady Howard was a law unto herself. Kate nodded and moved towards the door. "I'll bring your new pills round from the surgery this evening, and I'll call in to see you at the end of the week."

"That will be quite unnecessary."

"You must allow me to decide that." Kate paused, the door half open. "I want to see if you're taking my advice."

"I've already told you that I shall do as I want."

"Then I'm sorry, but I can't go on treating you. It's up to you. Think it over." She shut the door quickly before the inevitable explosion. Judging by her outraged expression, very few people had spoken to Lady Howard so bluntly.

"I'M AFRAID I didn't do her blood pressure any good," Kate confessed to Ben, when she met him later in the surgery to discuss her new problem patient. "Wouldn't it be better if you went on looking after her? I don't think she'll see me again."

"No," Ben said positively. "Robert has already been on the phone to me. He says that after twenty minutes of fulminating against your impertinence, the old dragon climbed down and admitted that she's been overdoing things lately. You frightened her quite a bit, Kate. She'll see reason."

Robert said much the same thing that evening, when he called in to talk things over with Kate. Maggie was out visiting friends, and Kate was snugly ensconced by the old-fashioned kitchen range, which they used when they couldn't be bothered to light the sitting-room fire.

"Give her time to get used to the idea," he urged. "She's stubborn, but not stupid. An occasional short ride won't hurt her, will it?"

"I suppose not, though it beats me how she rides at all with those hands and the degree of arthritis in her hips."

"She has to be lifted on to her horse," Robert admitted, "but riding's her chief pleasure. It would be too much of a wrench to give it up entirely."

He was silent for a minute or two, frowning. Kate watched him, admiring the strong planes of his face, that were thrown into prominence when he looked down, and the lean shapely brown hand which cupped his chin. She had never met a more physically attractive man, but she was still far from sure that she liked him.

He looked up suddenly and caught her by surprise. "I've been very worried about Linda lately," he told her.

"Linda?" Kate stammered, confused both by her own thoughts and his abrupt change of subject.

He leant forward in his chair, the frown still there. "I hardly see her these days, and when I do she's like a stranger. Do you see much of her?"

"Now and then," Kate said guardedly, uneasy because of a guilty conscience.

He misinterpreted her still manner. "I shouldn't burden you with my problems. It was just that Linda seems to like you—"

"Not any more," Kate said quickly, and could have bitten out her tongue, because he asked at once, "You've fallen out? About what?"

Uneasily she murmured that it wasn't important. "You know how touchy adolescents can be."

He looked at her in silence for a few seconds until, ill at ease, she glanced away. "Did it have anything to do with the Hickman boy?" he asked grimly.

"The Hickman boy?" she queried.

"Dave Hickman. Has Linda discussed him with you?"

"Er—the young man you don't approve of? Yes, she did mention him," Kate said carelessly. This inquisition was beginning to rile her, and in spite of her better judgment her sympathies were with Linda. After all, the girl had promised to be sensible, and Kate knew that Robert would be very angry indeed if he learnt what had been going on.

"Why don't you like him?" she asked, curious to hear his side of it.

"Young Hickman has been in trouble since he was out of short trousers. He was a real tearaway at school, against all authority. We've suspected him of poaching for a long time, though we've never caught him at it. And there's a local girl who's had a baby recently. Her parents swear this lad's the father."

"But none of it proven," Kate pointed out. "Perhaps rumour exaggerates. That cocky manner is definitely off-putting."

"You've met him?"

"Just for a minute or two while he filled my car up."

Robert leant forward in his chair, looking very serious. "But even first impressions count. Honestly, Kate, do you think he's a suitable friend for a young girl like Linda?"

"No, of course I don't. But I—I don't think she sees much of him, only at evening classes."

"I wish I could be sure," Robert frowned. "If the right moment comes up see what you can find out."

"I'll do my best," Kate murmured, and anxious to end an awkward conversation, asked him if he would like a drink.

"Coffee would be fine," he said, and they were in the middle of drinking it when Maggie returned. She looked less cheerful than usual and refused a cup of coffee rather brusquely. "Keeps me awake. I'll have Horlicks."

They heard her banging about in the scullery, and when she reappeared she threw herself into an armchair.

"What's up, Maggie?" asked Robert in an amused voice, and Maggie gave him an irritated look. "Oh, it's been one of those days. School was dreary and so was this evening, and on top of everything—" she stopped abruptly and shrugged. "Sorry, I'm tired, I expect."

Robert took this as a hint and departed soon after. Kate, who had grown very fond of Maggie, gave her an anxious glance.

"Is there something wrong? It's not like you to be so edgy. I've had the feeling for some time that you're annoyed with me."

"Whatever gave you that idea?" asked Maggie.

"You've seemed a bit—cool lately." Kate spread her hands appealingly. "If you've changed your mind about having me live here, for heaven's sake say so. I can look for something else."

Maggie went red and stared at her feet. "It's nothing

like that," she said gruffly, and added in a voice so low that Kate could hardly hear her, "You can eat your heart out for someone for years, and even though you know it's no good you keep on hoping. Until you see him getting interested in another girl." She took a deep breath and jumped up, her eyes bright with tears. "I'm not blaming you, Kate. You weren't to know," and she rushed out of the room, banging the door behind her.

Kate was dumbfounded. She had always known that Maggie was fond of Robert, but hadn't suspected that she was in love with him. The truly astonishing thing, though, was Maggie's assumption that Robert was interested in Kate. It would have been laughable if the other girl hadn't been so upset. At any rate Kate was determined to put her right as soon as possible.

She overslept and came down late to breakfast, to find Maggie just finishing her coffee. "Your bacon's in the pan," Maggie muttered, eyes on her plate, and added awkwardly, "I'm sorry I blew my top last night. I've been bottling things up for too long, I suppose."

"Oh, Maggie!" Kate turned the bacon over and spoke with her back to the other girl. "You've got it all wrong. He's not a scrap interested in me, and I'm certainly not interested in him."

Maggie pushed back her chair. "Well then, perhaps I still have a chance." Her voice was brittle, over-bright. It was plain that she didn't believe Kate. "See you," she added, and left Kate to a solitary and not too happy breakfast.

Was everyone in love with the wretched man? Diana and Maggie, and heaven knows how many other misguided females? Were they so taken in by the surface good looks that they couldn't see beneath them to Robert's less attractive qualities? "I don't like tough, arrogant men," Kate announced to the empty kitchen, and then laughed at herself a little uneasily, because she had felt the need to make the statement at all.

On Friday she paid her second visit to Lady Howard, and this time the old lady was much more amenable. "I've done as you suggested and stayed in bed till midday." She looked over the top of her spectacles at Kate, the *Daily Telegraph* open on her knee.

Kate smiled. "I'm glad of that. Let's see how your blood pressure's doing."

After a brief examination she stood up again, and was going to leave when Lady Howard said irritably, "You modern doctors are all the same—no time for your patients."

"I had the impression that the less you saw of doctors the better," Kate said mildly, and Lady Howard gave her a suspicious look.

"Are you being impertinent, miss? That's another thing I don't like about the modern young. No respect for their elders."

"And I'll tell you something I don't like about the old," Kate retorted, her smile robbing the words of most of their sting. "Their assumption that they can be as rude as the devil and get away with it."

There was no answering smile for her. The old lady drummed her twisted fingers on the silk bedspread, her mouth thin. "So you believe in the generation gap, Miss Ferguson?"

"No, I don't. It's one of those myths that have been overblown by the mass media. What really matters is being on the same wavelength as another person, not what their age is."

Lady Howard smiled at last. "My own view exactly. And if you'll come off your high horse, young woman, I'd like to point out that we agree on a good many things."

Astonished, Kate stared at her. "Such as?" she asked weakly, and the old lady chuckled.

"Such as coming out with the truth, even if it might be more tactful to stay silent. You remind me of myself at twenty, Kate. I may call you Kate, I hope?"

Kate nodded, preoccupied with the notion, surely incorrect, that there was any resemblance between herself and this formidable old woman.

"Of course," Lady Howard added, a twinkle in her eyes, "you're not a beauty and I was. But you're a very attractive young woman, and I often think men feel more at ease with a pretty girl than a beautiful one. Are you a feminist, Kate? Is that why you haven't married?"

"Do I believe in Women's Lib, you mean? Some of it, the sensible bits. I think the women who want an equal chance with men should have it, but on the other hand the ones who are quite content to stay at home shouldn't be made to feel inferior."

"Very reasonable," Lady Howard conceded. "But you haven't answered all my questions. What do you want for yourself, Kate?"

"Well, really! Do we have to be so personal?"

"You'll have to forgive my curiosity, child. Now that I can no longer lead such an active life, I take a great interest in the activities of others." Lady Howard laid her small clawlike hand on the girl's smooth young one.

"Well, I suppose I want the best of both worlds," Kate admitted. "To be a doctor *and* to get married. When I meet the right person. Most women want children, don't they?"

"I never did, which was as well, as I never had any. And fortunately it didn't seem to matter too much to my husband. He was a younger son and there was no property to pass on. But Robert now—it's high time he got married"—she relapsed into silence in the manner of the old, brooding over her thoughts, which appeared to be unpleasant ones. "What do you think of the Mitchell girl?" she asked, coming out of her reverie just as Kate was about to make a move towards leaving.

Her train of thought was obvious. "You mean as a

wife for your nephew? I don't know enough about her. She's obviously very keen on him."

"A stupid girl!" Lady Howard said with surprising viciousness. "Wouldn't have a chance if it wasn't for her money."

"Is she rich?" asked Kate. "I didn't know."

"She will be when she's twenty-five. Her father's comfortably off, but it's the mother's side who have the money. Something in trade—" Lady Howard waved a disparaging hand. "Her grandfather hadn't an aitch to his name, but you'd never guess it to listen to Diana. Just shows what a good school can do, eh?"

"And that's a fine charitable observation," said democratic Kate, "also quite impossibly snobbish."

"I am a snob," the old lady asserted unrepentantly. "At least, I object to people pretending to be what they're not."

Kate laughed, being more or less in agreement with this last statement. "It's all so silly anyhow. In this day and age it really is more important who you are than who your parents were."

"Not to me," the governor's lady said haughtily. "Quite apart from the fact that Robert is not in love with Diana, I don't care for the idea of him marrying into the *nouveau riche*."

An outmoded expression from an outmoded old woman! "I don't think we should be discussing your nephew like this," Kate demurred, but couldn't resist adding, "If he's not in love with her surely he won't marry her?"

"Money can be a powerful attraction," the old lady said cynically. "And Robert needs money badly. He was just beginning to get the estate on its feet again when the present economic crisis arose. Life's hard these days for farmers."

"It's hard for everybody. Robert strikes me as the last person to accept the position of a poor man married to a rich wife."

"He's scarcely poor when he owns all this." Lady Howard's expressive hands waved towards the window, and the lush acres of Robert's estate. "But he's short of ready cash and in six months Diana will control her own money. Robert's a realist, not a romantic boy, and the young woman is not unattractive if you can stand that awful voice."

She seemed to have made up her mind reluctantly to accept the inevitable. Poor Maggie, Kate thought, you'd think she'd know who her real rival was. She made her escape before Lady Howard could indulge in any more indiscretions, and as she stepped out into the courtyard met Linda coming in.

It was some time since she had seen the girl, and mindful of Robert's request she laid a hand on Linda's arm. "How are things going? We never seem to meet these days."

"I'm pretty busy. We're doing a Christmas show at College."

"Dave in it?" Kate asked with studied casualness, but Linda gave her a suspicious look.

"What is this? What do you want to know, Kate?"

"Whether you're keeping your promise," Kate said quietly. "Robert's worried about you. He told me so the other day."

A flicker of apprehension crossed the girl's face. "You didn't let on? About Dave and me?"

"I said we'd talked about him, that's all."

Linda squeezed Kate's hand, the antagonism gone at once. "You're a sport. I knew I could trust you!"

"I only hope I can trust you," Kate murmured to her departing back, but the girl moved so quickly that she probably missed the words.

CHAPTER SIX

ONE MORNING in the surgery Kate was writing an insurance certificate for her last patient. She signed it, added the date, November the twenty-ninth, and realized with surprise that she had been nearly two months in Sherringdon. Working hard and enjoying it, the time had gone incredibly fast. The early doubts and uncertainties common to nearly all young doctors had already been replaced by a quiet confidence that she could handle most things, and if she couldn't there was no disgrace in calling on specialist opinion.

Ben's father was home from hospital now, but making a very slow recovery, so that she would be needed for at least six months.

"Longer maybe," Ben had told her recently, but she had explained that the senior partner in her brother's practice was definitely due to retire in April. Ben had suggested that since this was a two-man practice and the one in Glasgow consisted of four doctors, his need was greater than theirs. Also that it was easier to get a locum in a big city, and even if this proved impossible there was always the deputizing service, which a hard-pressed G.P. could use at night.

This amenity didn't exist in the country, of course. Kate promised that she wouldn't let him down, would certainly not leave him single-handed, and suggested that he should discuss the problem with her brother.

When he joined her for coffee that morning Ben waved a letter at her. "From Angus. He says of course you can stay until Dad gets back. Working in a city where there's a medical school, they can always find someone to act as a stopgap. He says if you stay much longer you'll maybe opt for country practice permanently! You do like it here, don't you, Kate?"

"I love it!" Kate exclaimed, and he looked pleased by the warmth of her response.

"My own feeling is that Dad should never come back full time. He's nearly sixty and I want him to have some retirement to enjoy. This practice has grown lately with the new building in the area. We could do with two and a half doctors. Would you be interested in joining us permanently?"

The intentness with which he waited for her reply made Kate cautious. "That would depend on a lot of things. And anyhow, have you discussed it with your father?"

He shook his head. "Dad's obstinate. He'll be very unwilling to accept the idea of doing part-time. I don't want to upset him at this stage of his recovery."

"Well then, let's leave it for the moment." She sensed his disappointment at her rather lukewarm reply, but was determined to play it cool as far as their relationship went. Even though she did her best to discourage him, Ben's manner towards her was increasingly that of a man who was seriously interested.

"My housekeeper's away this week," he observed. "How about taking pity on me and letting me eat at your place? I'm not much good at cooking."

"Nor am I, I'm afraid, though Maggie's teaching me. She's a super cook. Of course, Ben. You'll be welcome any time."

Ben interpreted this to mean every evening, so Kate was relieved to discover that Maggie wouldn't be going out at all that week. Tête-à-têtes were best avoided. If Ben was disappointed at not having her to himself, his innate good manners prevented him showing it.

On Friday evening Robert called in with one of the surgery's medicine bottles in his hand. "Aunt Margaret dropped her pills and hasn't been able to find them all. Would you ask Andy for some more, Kate?"

Kate said that she would, and Robert, pressed to stay, lay back in an easy chair and accepted a cup of coffee. He looked tired and a little jaded, and when Kate commented on this he agreed.

"I've had a packet lately. Wet weather when we wanted dry, and no rain when we needed it. Prices of everything rocketing, and the younger men nothing like as good as their fathers were."

It was so unlike the proud and self-sufficient Robert to grumble that Kate could only stare. Maggie murmured sympathetically and his mouth twisted wryly. "I'll get by. I'm nothing like as hard hit as the poor devils of small farmers. Some of them face ruin if things don't improve soon. I'm having a break tomorrow and going to Chartmouth—I could do with some sea air."

"So could I!" Kate exclaimed. "I've been meaning to go to the seaside ever since I got here."

There was a little silence. Robert looked from Kate, to Maggie and Ben, then back to Kate again. "What's stopping you?" he asked. "This is your week-end off, isn't it? Care to come?" and he smiled at her with unexpected warmth.

"You mean with you?" His offer made Kate absurdly flustered. "Oh, heavens—you'll think I was fishing—I feel awful—"

She relapsed into silence before his impatient gesture. "My dear Kate, why all the fuss? I wouldn't have suggested it unless I'd wanted you to come. I have to see my solicitor first, but after that I shall be at your disposal."

Kate hesitated and glanced at Maggie, expecting her to look less than pleased. Rather surprisingly the other girl was in favour of the idea and said so with such enthusiasm that Kate was a little put out, wondering why Maggie wanted her out of the way.

The blossoming friendship of their early days seemed to have been nipped in the bud by Maggie's moment of self-revelation. She was never openly unfriendly, but the easy camaraderie which had been developing between them no longer existed.

Ben, who had sat silent throughout this exchange, observed dampingly, "Chartmouth's not much of a place. Why don't you go to Brighton?"

He was the one who looked put out and Kate guessed that he was disappointed. It would have suited him better if Maggie had been going with Robert, which in itself was a good reason for the trip. He must be made to understand, as painlessly as possible, that there was no future in his feelings for Kate. So she accepted Robert's offer and promised to be ready in good time, and at ten o'clock the following morning stood waiting by the dining-room window.

"You look very nice," Maggie told her with a smile. "That dark brown does things for your red hair."

"There's nothing to beat Scots tweed," Kate agreed, looking down at herself with pleasure. She knew that the well cut trouser suit fitted her perfectly. Over her arm she carried her sheepskin jacket, for the November day was damp and chilly.

The weather forecast was good, however, and her spirits were high. However much she loved her work the prospect of a day off by the seaside was exhilarating, and Maggie, oddly, seemed to feel no qualms about her going with Robert.

Robert's blue estate car turned into the courtyard. Kate picked up her handbag and Maggie accompanied her to the door. "Have fun!" she said brightly, and to Kate's astonishment landed a smacking kiss on her cheek.

Robert, who had old-fashioned manners, got out to open the car door for Kate. "Good girl! Some women can never be on time."

"The same goes for some men. I had a boy-friend

who thought nothing of keeping me waiting for half an hour."

"If you waited that long you must have been keen on him. Is he still around?"

"Sort of. He's a registrar at my last hospital. He always had a good excuse for being late—doctors usually do."

He laughed. "When you're in the same line I suppose it works both ways. Knowing what an ardent Women's Libber you are, I'm sure you made him kick his heels sometimes."

Kate was in too good a mood to take up his challenge and contented herself with saying, "I never tried keeping him waiting. I was too flattered by his attentions. I was very small fry compared with him."

"Does the past tense mean anything?" he asked casually, and she nodded vigorously.

"It certainly does! The competition was too fierce, and anyway, I found out that he was very conceited."

"So you gave him the push too," he observed dryly. "Quite a girl, aren't you, Kate?"

It took her a few moments to realize what he meant. Hot colour flooded her cheeks. "That's a beastly thing to say!" she cried. "Bill and I—that was quite different. I wasn't engaged to Michael—he was just a—"

"Passing fancy?" he suggested ironically, and she gave an exasperated sigh.

"If you like. It wasn't serious. I don't spend my time falling in and out of love, if that's what you're trying to imply. I've only ever been in love once—at least—" Incurably honest, she hesitated—"at least I thought I was at the time," she ended lamely.

"Unfortunately you made Bill think so too," he said with extreme coldness.

"I know, and I'm sorry," she began, but he cut her short.

"Why the hell are we dragging up old history like this? It's over and done with. Leave it alone."

She sighed and was silent, wishing she hadn't come. Whatever momentary impulse had made Robert suggest bringing her, it was obvious that he still didn't approve of her. When they reached the seaside she decided that it would be better if she went off on her own.

She looked out of the car window, pleased to see that the early morning mist was clearing, and it promised to be a good day. Half an hour later they were running through the outskirts of Chartmouth. It was a typical south coast resort, the sea-front lined with the usual hotels and cafés. Half-way along Robert turned into a side road and drove into a hotel car-park.

"I'll leave the car here and walk to my solicitors." He glanced at his watch. "Just time for a cup of coffee first." He took her arm and led her through the back entrance into the hotel lobby. "Aunt Margaret comes here occasionally when she fancies a few days by the sea. It's old-fashioned but comfortable and it serves the best sea food in town. Do you like lobster, Kate?"

"Yes, I do, but please don't order lunch for me. I plan to go off on my own. What time will you be leaving?"

They had halted only feet away from the reception desk. Out of the corner of her eye Kate saw the receptionist change from boredom to vivacity. "Hallo, Mr. Montgomery! Nice to see you again. What can I do for you?"

Robert might not have heard Kate's remark for all the attention he paid to it. "Good morning, Millie. You can order coffee for us, and lunch at one o'clock."

"Yes, Mr. Montgomery. How is your aunt these days?"

"Not too well. We'll have our coffee in the sun lounge. Come on, Kate." He stood aside to allow Kate to precede him into the big room, where a few scattered people were reading the morning papers.

Kate chose a sofa in the far corner and stared fixedly out at the sea sparkling in the autumn sunshine, until she felt well in control of her feelings. Then she said quietly, "I told you—I don't want lunch here. Please go and change your order to a single one."

"What the devil is wrong with you, Kate?" he demanded. "Since we came together we might as well eat together."

"Charmingly put!" Kate snapped. "But it's quite obvious that your friendly gesture doesn't mean a thing. That night when you came with me to the Martins' I hoped—I thought—we could be on better terms. Now, after your nasty remarks today, I realize we never can."

A waitress arrived with the coffee tray. While she busied herself with pouring Robert studied her in silence. "So that's it," he said at last. "Look, Kate, I'm sorry I upset you. Sorry I said what I did." He moved closer and picked up his coffee cup. "I've some dreary business to get through with my solicitor and I could do with cheering up afterwards. Please have lunch with me."

He smiled at her and Kate smiled back a little reluctantly. "Well, all right, but I'm only too conscious that I sort of asked myself."

He put his cup down with a little bang. "Don't start that again! It'll be a pleasure to have your company—" He looked her over slowly, and something in his eyes made Kate feel unaccustomed shyness. "A day by the sea, a pretty girl and even the weather's good. So let's make a bargain, Kate. No arguments for the rest of the day! I want to enjoy myself for a change."

He could charm when he wanted to all right, Kate thought a little warily, but she for one was well armed against him, because he wasn't at all her type. However, they were here and they might as well make the best of their day together. So she looked up, and this time she smiled without any reservations. "Then let's enjoy ourselves," she agreed. "It *is* a lovely day."

They parted, after arranging to meet again at a quarter to one, and Kate wandered along the broad promenade, where the old men and women sat in shelters enjoying the autumn sunshine. She reached the shopping centre, and remembered that she hadn't yet had time to buy any of her Christmas presents.

The time passed quickly and pleasantly. After years as a poor student on an inadequate grant, she got a real kick out of being extravagant. She bought toys for her brother's three youngest children, books for the eldest and for Angus himself, and a cashmere sweater for her sister-in-law, who was a dear and spent all too little on herself.

She would still be at Sherringdon for Christmas, so she added scent for Maggie and a tie for Ben. The Montgomerys? No, that would be overdoing it. Tempted by a smart little boutique, she bought a couple of dresses for herself, glanced at her watch while the salesgirl was wrapping up her purchases, and saw with dismay that it was already nearly one. Robert, she was sure, was not the sort of man who expected to be kept waiting.

She walked quickly back to the hotel, but it was farther away than she had realized. When she finally reached it she pushed through the glass doors, hidden behind a mountain of parcels that were rapidly getting out of control. The top one slid off and then the next. Kate halted, wondering how she was going to pick them up without dropping the lot, when Robert strolled over and bent to retrieve them.

"Do you always shop on this scale?" he asked with amusement, and nodded towards a porter. "Put these somewhere safe, please."

"No need," Kate murmured, rather hot and bothered both because of her lateness and because of her clumsy entry.

He removed the rest of the parcels from her arms and handed them over to the hovering porter. "I expect you want to tidy up," he observed, looking her over with a faint smile, so that Kate was reminded of her windblown hair and flushed cheeks. "I'll order drinks and wait for you in the dining-room."

She did her face quickly, wishing as she did so that she had the social poise to deal with a man like Robert. When she joined him he was already discussing the menu with the head waiter, who appeared to be an old friend. Robert was right about the food. It was excellent, and Kate, hungry after her walk, did it full justice. She drank several glasses of wine but declined a liqueur, because Robert had already told her that he was going to take her up on the cliffs overlooking the town.

"There's an old Norman castle, ruined but still impressive. And you can walk for miles and meet scarcely a soul, especially at this time of year."

They drove up a steep road to an almost empty car-park, wandered around the castle and then set off along the cliffs. Kate, who loved history, listened enthralled to Robert's stories of the past in this one little corner of England, and thought how well he told them. She had some trouble keeping up with his long stride. When they reached a stile she was out of breath and leant for a few seconds against the top bar.

"Tired?" Robert sounded surprised.

"Puffed. Your legs are a lot longer than mine."

"Sorry. You should have asked me to slow down." His black hair, blown by the sharp wind, fell into his eyes. He brushed it away impatiently, smiling down at her. She had never before seen him in such a light-hearted mood. He was—she admitted it reluctantly—quite devastatingly attractive, and also extremely good company.

When they left the cliff tops Robert took her into the old part of town, where fishing boats were drawn up on the beach and old men mended nets in the sun. They had tea in a delightful café with Regency windows, and beams so low that Robert had to stoop.

Kate, ravenous after her long walk, said apologetically, "You wouldn't think I could eat so much after that enormous lunch, would you?"

He laughed. "I'm hungry too. Besides, it's a pleasure to take out a girl with a healthy appetite."

Tea over they walked back along the promenade in the half dark. As they entered the hotel lobby a woman came out of the lift, stared and gave a joyful exclamation.

"Robert, of all people! What are you doing here?"

Robert turned quickly, looked startled for a moment, then gave a slow smile. "Elizabeth! It must be all of two years!"

"More," Elizabeth said. At close quarters she was older than Kate had thought at first, possibly a year or two older than Robert, not pretty but undeniably elegant. She had smooth dark hair, worn in a classical style, and a thin intelligent face.

Robert introduced the two women and Elizabeth said, "I was just going to have tea. Join me?"

"We've eaten," said Robert, "but we'll come and sit with you."

In the hotel lounge he and Elizabeth shared a sofa, while Kate lay back in a deep armchair feeling a little out of things. Not that Elizabeth wasn't charming, drawing Kate into the conversation as much as possible, but the other two were so obviously old and intimate friends, and wanted to catch up on each other's affairs. Kate gathered that they had known each other since childhood and progressed to Cambridge together.

"Elizabeth is terribly brainy," said Robert. "Beat all the men in her year."

Elizabeth dismissed this half teasing remark gracefully. "I worked very hard, Kate. Women do mostly, don't they, if they've been lucky enough to get a university place?" She gestured as she spoke and Kate noticed the wedding-ring on her hand for the first time. She wondered how much longer Robert intended staying, turned from contemplation of the lighted promenade, and found that Elizabeth was studying her with an intent and speculative look, that was wiped away so quickly Kate wondered if she had imagined it.

Robert was asking Elizabeth about West Africa, from which she had recently returned, but Kate had a feeling that the other woman was restive. Perhaps she wanted to be alone with Robert. Old friends, after all, might have things to say to each other that weren't for a third person's ears. Kate glanced at her watch and dropped a remark into a temporary silence.

"It's just gone five. I think I'll go back to the shops. There was something I forgot this morning."

"You won't have much time," Robert observed, but Elizabeth said quickly (and with relief?), "If you hurry you'll just make it."

So Kate walked to the town centre, bought some tights and dawdled back along the sea-front. She was gone the best part of an hour and when she returned Robert and Elizabeth were still sitting in the lounge, heads close together, talking intently. They had drinks in front of them now.

Robert rose when he saw Kate and asked her what she would like. Elizabeth greeted her with smiling charm and Kate knew that she had been right. The older woman was pleased because she had made that tactful withdrawal. They sat over their drinks for some time, and when they finally left Robert's last words to Elizabeth were, "Next Tuesday, then. I'll be looking forward to it."

When they left Kate's last glimpse of Elizabeth was of a smiling composed woman moving gracefully towards the stairs. As they settled themselves in the car Robert said, "It was good of you to leave Elizabeth and me on our own. We had a lot to catch up on."

"I thought you might have," Kate murmured, and added, "I liked her very much."

"It was mutual," he assured her.

"Is she a widow?"

There was silence for a few seconds. "Separated," Robert said at last, in the tone of voice that doesn't invite further questions. After they had been on the road for about half an hour he glanced at his watch. "Just on eight. There's a nice old pub in the next village. Shall we stop there for a snack?"

"I've done nothing but eat all day," Kate protested. "You're not in a hurry to get back?"

"Not in any hurry at all," he assured her. "And we'll need something, so we might as well eat there."

The headlights of the car showed a village green and a pub sign swinging in the wind. Robert turned into the car-park, and Kate shivered when she got out, but inside the bar it was pleasantly warm. Robert waved her to a small corner table close to a blazing fire. He ordered ham sandwiches, cider for Kate and beer for himself.

"This is one of the nicest old inns in all Sussex," he observed when he rejoined her, and he told her a little of its history, which dated back to Tudor times. Kate felt relaxed and happy in his company and thoroughly enjoyed listening to him. She had discovered today that Robert could talk well on a surprisingly wide variety of subjects. But why surprisingly? He had, after all, spent three years reading history at Cambridge. He was very far from being the sporting farmer she had at first rather scornfully labelled him.

"Care for another?" He picked up their glasses and turned towards the bar. Kate noticed with some amusement the interested glances he attracted, especially from the women, and her heart warmed towards him because he was so obviously indifferent to their interest. Here at least was one very attractive man who wasn't conceited.

Her thoughts went back to the registrar at her old hospital whom she had mentioned to Robert that morning, and to the rather disquieting end to that conversation. When he sat down again she frowned at him, trying to make up her mind what to say. He raised his glass. "Cheers. But why the ferocious look, my dear Kate?"

She hesitated, decided to speak, but found it difficult to begin. "We've had fun today," she said at last, "and—and I think we've got on quite well, but I know you still have—well, reservations about me."

He sat up straight and gave her a thoughtful look, but he said nothing to help her out, so she was forced to struggle on.

"I mean, " she floundered, "you're still critical of my behaviour to Bill." He said nothing, so she asked sharply, "Well, aren't you?"

"Since you've brought the matter up," he said slowly, "yes, I suppose I am. But must we drag up old history? Bill's happily married now. Let's leave it at that."

"But I don't want to," she persisted. "I'd like to try and explain. Then perhaps you'd have a better opinion of me..." Her words trailed off under his ironic gaze.

"I find it hard to believe that you care a rap for my opinion. Skip it, Kate. I don't particularly want to hear the story of your past."

She flushed at the snub and wished too late that she had kept quiet. He was wrong, however. She did value his good opinion and would have liked him to have listened. She sighed, and he leant towards her to put his hand over hers.

"Come on, snap out of it. I'm sorry if I've upset you, but it does no good to rake up the past. What happened between you and Bill is over, finished. Perhaps I've judged you too harshly, I don't know." He shrugged, then smiled. "You're certainly a different girl from the giddy young thing Bill introduced me to—what was it—over four years ago?"

Staring into the fire, Kate said unhappily, "I knew you didn't take to me then, but I was shy—and—and you seemed so superior—"

"Indeed?" he drawled.

"Well, I thought so at the time. I was young for my age and not very sure of myself—" She broke off because hadn't he made it very plain that he didn't want her to go on. "Anyway," she ended with a flash of her usual spirit, "you've changed too. You're more human, or have been today, thank goodness."

He laughed so much at this that several people glanced their way, and Kate tried to stop him. "Do be quiet! They'll think you've had too much to drink."

He dismissed her remark with a wave of his hand. "You're good for me, Kate. It's nice to go out with a girl who has a mind of her own. I've enjoyed today."

"I have too," she said a little shyly, glad that her attempt to resurrect the past hadn't entirely spoilt the evening. Robert seemed in no hurry to go and it was nearly eleven before they arrived back at Sherringdon Hall.

Lights showed through the windows as they drove into Maggie's courtyard. Ben and Maggie were sitting one each side of the stove, with newspapers on their knees, looking for all the world like an old married couple. Robert smiled as he looked at them and an expression that was almost smug crossed his face. Kate wondered why he should look like that, and then forgot about it in the general exchange of greetings.

Later, when the men had gone, and the girls were climbing the stairs to bed, Maggie said to Kate, "Glad we talked you into going? I knew Robert would give you a good time."

Kate halted outside her door. "I had a super time. But I don't understand, Maggie. I thought you wouldn't like Robert taking me out."

Maggie stared. "Why should I mind?"

"But you said—you were upset when you thought Robert was interested in me—not that he is, of course—" Kate began to get tangled in her own words and stumbled to a halt.

Maggie's astonishment was extreme. "Robert? You thought it was Robert I wanted? Kate, he's my cousin, almost a brother!"

She began to laugh, and Kate said with dawning comprehension, "Then who? Not Ben?" She was astonished that any woman could look at Ben when Robert was around.

Maggie's laughter came to an abrupt halt and her face grew strained. "Of course it's Ben. He's the only man I've ever cared about. I took the teaching job near here for his sake, and I'd begun to think I'd have a chance until—" she hesitated, then went on quietly, "until you came along."

"Oh, Maggie!" Kate put her hand on the other girl's arm. "He and I are thrown together so much over work, but when I leave here he'll forget me in a week."

"I hope so." Maggie made a brave attempt at a smile. "But Robert? What an odd idea!" She started off down the corridor to her own room, then swung round to stare at Kate. "How could you have thought I minded Robert taking you out? You must have known he was only being kind."

The words stung Kate because they confirmed her own opinion. Robert, exerting himself to entertain, could be very charming, but it meant nothing. He might in the future be a little more friendly towards her, but friendliness after tonight was not what she wanted. She was attracted to him, and she thought ruefully that she would have liked the attraction to be mutual. She undressed slowly, wondering if he would ever take her out again, and was a little cheered when she remembered his words, "I've enjoyed today."

Perhaps, when he knew her better, he would be pre-

CHAPTER SEVEN

KATE WOKE LATE on Sunday morning, to find Maggie still in bed. She felt like a cup of tea, so she went down to the kitchen. As she perched on a stool, waiting for the kettle to boil, something that had puzzled her last night became suddenly clear.

That satisfied, yes, almost smug expression on Robert's face was because he had been pleased to find Maggie and Ben so obviously enjoying each other's company. Which must mean that he knew Maggie was in love with Ben, and that was why he had asked Kate to go to Chartmouth with him. He wanted her out of the way.

It was silly to feel so let down. Even before she had realized the truth by no stretch of the imagination could she have believed that Robert was interested in her as a woman.

The kitchen was filling with steam. Kate jumped up and switched the kettle off. She stood, teapot in hand, and thought wistfully of the fun she had had yesterday. A sharp little picture of Robert on the cliff tops, hair blowing in the wind, looking younger and gayer than she had ever seen him, came into her mind.

She bit her lip and tried to dismiss all thoughts of him, but a fresh idea pricked at her composure. He hadn't lingered on in that nice old pub because he was enjoying her company. He had stayed because he wanted to leave Maggie alone with Ben as long as possible. She put the teapot down with a bang, then picked it up to make sure she hadn't cracked it, but the tears in her eyes made it difficult to see. She wiped them away crossly, and told herself that it was her pride that was dented and not her heart. Robert was without doubt the most attractive man she had ever met, but she had nothing in common with him. Nothing. Their outlook on life was totally different, and it was only a week or two ago that she had been asking herself if she even liked him. It would be as well if she didn't forget that again, otherwise she was in danger of making a complete fool of herself.

She hoped that she wouldn't see him for a few days, but she had arranged to visit Lady Howard on Monday afternoon, and as she was leaving Robert came into the hall.

"Hallo, Kate. Is the old lady doing all right?"

"She's doing fine," Kate said quietly, her calm manner concealing the turbulence of her emotions. She looked at his handsome, smiling face with a disturbing mixture of anger and resentment. He was in tough working clothes, corduroys, a thick dark sweater and boots, and to her eyes he was even more attractive than he had been dressed for their day in Chartmouth.

"I'm in a hurry. I have an evening surgery," she said, making for the door.

Robert followed her out, lengthening his stride to keep up with her. "Slow down. I wanted to ask you something." He caught her by the arm and she stopped unwillingly.

"I really am late." His touch and his closeness made her heart pound disagreeably.

He looked down at her curiously. "Something wrong, Kate?"

"Of course not! I told you—I'm in a hurry." She wrenched her arm away and walked off quickly, leaving him staring after her.

So much for her determination to be cool and aloof! The little incident niggled away in the back of her mind all evening, making her less agreeable than she usually was to the patients. It was bad luck for Mr. Beaney that he came in last at seven-thirty, when she was wilting after a hectic surgery.

Kate recognized him at once, the cantankerous old man who had shown her the way to Sherringdon on the day she had arrived. He walked in slowly, leaning heavily on his stick and looking decidedly grumpy.

"I thought it'd be Dr. Ben," he said crossly. Thus did the older patients refer to Ben. Dr. Nicholson was reserved for his father, even in the older man's absence.

"If you want to see a particular doctor you should inquire who's on," Kate replied evenly, determined not to lose her temper.

He took some time to settle himself in his chair, grumbling away under his breath. Kate flipped through his cards. Eighty-five—a good age. Probably senile, she thought, and he couldn't help being irritating!

"What's the problem, Mr. Beaney?" she asked.

"No problem," he retorted, folding twisted hands on his stick and peering at her with faded, watery blue eyes. "Come for me pills."

She checked the record card to see what he was on. Indocid for his arthritis. She wrote a prescription. "They don't give you indigestion—the tablets?"

"Course not, would I take them if they did?"

"All right, Mr. Beaney." Kate repressed an urge to snap. "Give this to Miss Andrews," and she handed him the prescription.

"Aren't you going to take me pressure?" he croaked. "Dr. Ben always does."

She glanced at his card. "Not if you feel well, Mr. Beaney. Not giddy? No swelling of the ankles? Good. I feel sure you won't want a female examining you unnecessarily."

She added this last sentence because she recalled his previous strictures on women doctors, but as the old man hobbled painfully out of the room, she felt very ashamed. It wasn't fair to take it out on Mr. Beaney, however provoking he was, because she was angry at Robert.

When she got back home Maggie had already gone out somewhere. There was a note on the kitchen table telling her that the casserole should be ready. She decided to eat it in the kitchen, and was doing Maggie's delicious beef stew less than justice when there was a rap on the window, and Robert looked in at her. Reluctantly she opened the back door.

"Sorry to interrupt. I thought you'd have finished supper." He sat down opposite her. Kate had a drink of water to give herself something to do. "You took off in such a hurry I didn't have time to ask you—would you like to come to market with me this week? Thursday is your half day, isn't it?"

"Yes."

"Doing anything that afternoon?"

"No." She took another sip of water.

"Care to come? It might amuse you if you've never been to that sort of thing."

Kate put her glass down. "Thank you, Robert, but I don't think it is my sort of thing."

The words were harmless enough, but there was a brittle quality to her voice that made Robert look at her very hard. "Pity," he said evenly, "it would have been nice taking you." He rose, but didn't move towards the door.

Kate, very conscious of his gaze, kept her eyes on her plate and took a mouthful of stew. Eating on your own and being watched is always rather an ordeal. She chewed for a few seconds, swallowed awkwardly and took another gulp of water. "I wish you'd go away," she said crossly, and feeling that this was unnecessarily rude, added quickly, "or at least go next door. Though Maggie's out for the evening, so there's not much point.'

"Don't like talking and eating? Then I'll be quiet," Robert said pleasantly, and to her intense annoyance sat down again, thereby spoiling what little appetite she had left.

Kate pushed the remains of her dinner aside. "Not hungry?" he asked sympathetically. "Or did you get out of bed the wrong side this morning?"

She jumped up and made for the room next door. "Look, I've had a wearing day and I don't feel like company. I'm sorry to have to put it so plainly."

He followed her through the door. "Oh, I got the message all right, Kate. I would like to know why."

"Why what?"

He made an exasperated sound, put his hands on her shoulders and spun her round, none too gently. "Why you're being so unfriendly. It's not tiredness that's making you bad-tempered. Last Saturday we enjoyed each other's company, at least I thought we did. So what have I done? I confess that I'm baffled." His hands slid down from her shoulders to her elbows and he gave her a shake. "Well, Kate?"

She was confused and alarmed by her conflicting emotions—anger that he wouldn't leave well alone, and distress because his touch affected her so powerfully.

She tried to pull away, but his grip tightened. "Well, Kate?" he asked again, and this time there was an edge to his voice. He was plainly not going to release her until she said something, but once started it was difficult to control herself.

"I enjoyed Saturday too until I realized why you asked me out. Why you wanted me to go." It was impossible to keep the bitterness out of her voice. His expression changed and he tried to interrupt, but she rushed on. "No one likes being made to feel a fool. Oh, I didn't kid myself that you were longing for my company, but I did think it was a friendly gesture, not a—not a—not a deliberate act to get me out of the way, so that Maggie could make the running with Ben."

He removed his hands at last and gave her a wry

smile. "That old cliché about redheads having a temper seems to be true! Come on, Kate, don't hold it against me. So all right, I did think it would give Maggie a lift to have Ben to herself—" he hesitated a moment—"but it was a spur-of-the-moment idea—not a deliberate act at all. And whatever my original motive for taking you out, I enjoyed your company very much, and would like to do it again."

It was a very handsome apology indeed, but she was too upset to be mollified by his words or his smile. She backed away from him angrily. "I suppose you thought you were very clever? Doubtless you and your friend Elizabeth had a good laugh at my expense, when I went off."

His smile vanished at that. "You're being very childish," he said coldly. "Don't you think you're making an unnecessary fuss about all this?"

His remark did nothing to soothe Kate's feelings. "I think you'd better go," she got out in a choked voice, "before I say something really rude!"

He shrugged and moved towards the door. "It's time you grew up, my dear Kate. You're almost as self-centred as Linda."

People in love were self-centred, Kate thought miserably, throwing herself into a chair after he had gone. Perhaps it was better to admit the truth. Perhaps the cure would come quicker once she had diagnosed the complaint! It was no good fooling herself any longer. The argument that she couldn't love Robert when she had known him such a short time was nonsense. No good either to dwell on her previous conviction that they hadn't a thing in common. She loved him in spite of that, and she had certainly come to respect him. To respect his concern for his employees, his kindness in helping the small farmers among his neighbours, who were less fortunate than he was.

Even his autocratic manner she had come to accept as an inevitable result of his birth and background. It no longer jarred on her as it had done in the beginning. The truth was that when you fell in love you accepted the whole person, and scarcely noticed the superficial characteristics that were so important on first acquaintance.

She gave a shaky laugh, remembering the mixture of contempt and pity she had felt—oh, so recently—for Diana Mitchell. But no one, she vowed, would ever know how she felt, and then wondered uneasily if she hadn't already given herself away to Robert, by showing such bitter resentment.

The thought made her cheeks burn. She would have to tread very warily indeed. It might be a good thing to apologize the next time they met, play it cool and sophisticated—point out that her reaction had been a perfectly normal one. Any girl would have been mortified by his behaviour.

She spent the next few days half hoping for and half dreading an encounter with Robert, but though she caught fleeting glimpses of him about the farm or garden, they never met face to face. On her next afternoon off she was in her bedroom, changing into a sweater and slacks, when Diana's red Mini turned into the main courtyard and drew up at Robert's front door. The girl jumped out just as Robert emerged and they stood for a moment, talking, then made off in the direction of the stables.

Kate stood at the window and watched them go, stabbed by a jealousy so intense that it frightened her. If only—oh, if only—she hadn't turned down Robert's offer the other day, she would have been with him and not Diana. For it was obvious from the farm produce piled into the land rover that they were on their way to market. Robert was not too proud to do his own bartering, if he had no man to spare from more important jobs on the land.

Pique had made her refuse to go with him, and now he would probably not ask her again. She slumped down on the bed, wondering how she was going to get through her half-day. She had no friends in Sussex apart from Ben, and while this hadn't worried her in the past, it mattered now. It would have done her good to let off steam to a sympathetic girl-friend, to tell someone what a fool she had been. But there was no one. She would have to get through the bad patch on her own.

THE NEXT TIME Kate visited Lady Howard, the old woman swept aside her professional questions impatiently. "I'm all right, but why are you looking so peaky? Ben working you too hard?"

Kate had been doing more than usual because Dr. Nicholson had decided to convalesce at his sister's home in Cornwall, and Ben had taken two days off to drive his father down. She tried to explain, but perhaps she didn't sound very convincing, because Lady Howard's expression was dubious.

"Perhaps you're sickening for something. Doctors never look after themselves properly. Or perhaps you're in love? Missing some young man?"

Kate's sharp denial made the old lady very thoughtful. "Well, I suppose it's none of my business." She patted the silk bedspread. "Sit down for a minute or two, child. I'm bored to extinction."

Their talk turned to the rapid approach of Christmas, which fell in the middle of the week this year. Lady Howard wanted to know if Kate was spending it in Glasgow, and Kate said regretfully that it wasn't possible. She was free on Christmas Day but on duty on Boxing Day, so Glasgow was too far away for even a flying visit.

Maggie had already mentioned that she always spent Christmas with her cousins, and had implied that Kate would be expected to go as well, and now here was Lady Howard saying the same thing. "Then of course you'll come to us on Christmas Day."

Kate had quite looked forward to the idea when it was first suggested. "I don't think so, Lady Howard," she said. "I mean—it would be awkward, wouldn't it? I'm not one of the family like Maggie, and Christmas is a family affair, after all."

This lame excuse was brushed aside. "Absolute nonsense! Of course you must come."

There was a tap on the door and Robert came in, dressed as for town, and smiling affectionately at his aunt. "I take it the professional part of the visit's over? I saw Kate arrive and got tired of waiting for her." He glanced towards Kate, his smile gone now.

She stood up, one hand clenched tightly at her side, saw Lady Howard's eyes on her and quickly uncurled her fingers.

"We were discussing Christmas," Lady Howard remarked. "Kate seems doubtful about coming, but she can't spend the day on her own."

"Certainly she can't," Robert agreed. "Maggie always comes for Christmas and Boxing Day, Ben and his father too. This year it'll be only Ben, of course. I think you'll enjoy it, Kate. We have lots of people in, plenty going on."

Impossible to refuse without being rude, though she was surprised that Robert seemed to want her. She agreed with careful politeness that it would be something to look forward to, saw the ironic gleam in Robert's eyes and moved quickly towards the door.

"I've stayed too long, and I've a clinic at two."

The child welfare clinic was at a neighbouring village and usually she enjoyed it. Today she felt that she would have to drive herself hard to cope with the problems of her young mothers. Meeting Robert had been even more of an ordeal than she had expected. The effort needed to maintain her outward composure had taken a lot out of her.

Robert followed her out. "You look as if you could

do with a drink. Come and have one while I talk to you about something."

Kate said "I don't think—" but Robert took her firmly by the arm, and held on to it all the way downstairs. "I never knew such a girl for arguing!" He piloted her towards the library, a beautifully proportioned room that Kate thought they should use more often.

"Does anyone ever open these?" she asked, gesturing towards the hundreds of books on the shelves.

It was something to say, and she wasn't really interested. Perhaps Robert guessed this, because he shrugged and said indifferently, "I do, when I've time."

A decanter and two glasses stood on a small table. He poured sherry for them both, sipped and gazed at her reflectively. "I've been trying to see you all week."

"See me?" Kate asked, and added, puzzled, "Well, you knew where to find me."

"I didn't want to talk in front of Maggie, and I didn't want to make an issue of it by asking for a private chat." He smiled faintly, looking for Robert a little less self-assured than usual. "I owe you an apology, Kate."

"You do?" Kate asked blankly, and took a large swig of sherry to hide her confusion. She coughed, put her glass down and looked at Robert suspiciously.

His smile was wider now. "Of course I do! Any girl of spirit would have acted as you did the other day. And I didn't help by being sarcastic."

She stared at him and tried to think of an appropriate answer, but she was overwhelmingly conscious of his powerful attraction and her own response to it. He misunderstood her silence, for his smile went and he frowned.

"So you're not prepared to forget it. Do you enjoy rows, Kate?"

"Of course not. You—rather took me by surprise."

"Because I apologized? You haven't much of an

opinion of me, have you?" He gestured to a chair and she sat down a little wearily.

"You're looking tired," he commented. "Any particular reason?"

"Work's been fairly heavy this week." She rested her head against the back of the armchair and shut her eyes, because she found it difficult to look at him.

"Are you unhappy about Ben?" he asked quietly, and her eyes opened at that. "You've no need to be," he went on, half irritated and half amused. "I was wasting my time the other day. He's quite besotted with you." He crossed the room to pick up the decanter again, and she stared at the back of his head, longing to touch his thick dark hair and angry with herself for wanting to.

It occurred to her that he had drunk his sherry very quickly, which probably meant that he was finding the conversation as difficult as she was. Or maybe, she thought wryly, he was simply a man who hated apologizing!

"You're talking absolute nonsense," she protested. "Ben likes me, that's all."

"That wasn't my impression last night. We had a drink together at the Red Lion and he went on and on about your splendid qualities, both as a woman and as a doctor."

"With which you doubtless disagreed! I'm sorry if he bored you."

He turned and walked over to her, put his glass down on a little table, and bent over her chair. With one hand on each of the arms he leant towards her, until his face was only inches from hers. She jerked her head back and her breathing quickened. She looked at his smooth tanned skin and his well shaped mouth, which was curling up in a mocking smile.

"I didn't exactly disagree," he said softly. "I said you were quite a girl, but only a fool would fall in love with you." She sat very still. "You're a career woman, aren't you, Kate, though you're feminine enough to enjoy attracting the men. Poor Ben!"

"I can't help it if Ben thinks he's in love with me," she protested.

"Can't you? If you really don't want him, try being a little less provocative."

"Oh, leave me alone!" She tried to rise, but he gave her a push and then straightened and picked up his glass.

"What is it about you?" he said ruefully. "I meant to make my peace and now here we are, near to quarrelling again." He laughed suddenly, but without real humour. "I suppose it's unfair to blame you, but last summer I'd begun to think Ben was getting interested in Maggie."

Kate jumped up, wanting only to get away. "I thought it was women who were supposed to be the matchmakers! Maggie would feel terribly humiliated if she knew we'd been talking like this."

He nodded. "Of course, but she won't know. I'm very fond of the girl and I'd hate to see her lose her chance of marriage. Unfortunately she's a one-man woman, and it's Ben or nobody for her."

"I shan't be here much longer," Kate said slowly. "Six months is soon over," and she was shaken profoundly by the pain this thought gave her. Never to see Robert again, to hear of him perhaps, occasionally through Angus. She wondered how she would be able to bear it.

She was wrenched away from these unhappy thoughts by his next remark. "It's gone one. Please excuse me, Kate. I'm meeting Elizabeth at two."

She drained her glass quickly, contrived a little smile and said politely, "Well, anyway, thanks for the apology. I suppose it's my fault that our conversations get so out of hand."

Afterwards, eating a cheese sandwich with total lack of appetite, she brooded on their encounter. It was no good, she thought forlornly, Robert's opinion of her would never alter. He saw her as hard and self-centred, indifferent to other people's feelings. A career woman, he had said, but she wasn't, she wasn't!

When she had met his brother she had been young and impressionable, swept off her feet by the Montgomery charm, and flattered that the most sought-after surgical registrar in the hospital should even notice her existence. He had rushed her into an engagement and almost into marriage, but just in time Kate had come to her senses and realized that she wasn't in love. What she had felt for Bill was a strong physical attraction, no more, and she didn't think that was a sound enough basis for a lifetime together.

There were already signs of strain in their relationship, centring chiefly around Bill's conviction that her career wasn't really important. His rather patronizing attitude to her enthusiasm for medicine was the cause of their final row. She had stalled when he wanted an early wedding, saying she would prefer to wait until she was qualified. He had tried a mixture of bullying and lovemaking to break her resolve, and when she resisted both had lost his temper and given her an ultimatum. She married him now or it was all off.

It was at times of crisis like this that Kate regretted more than usual the death of both her parents in an air crash. Angus had done his best to cheer her up, but his best wasn't the same as her mother's affectionate understanding. She could have done with their support now, Kate thought wistfully. Even after eight years she still missed them badly.

She wondered what version of the break-up Bill had given his family. Doubtless it hadn't been at all flattering to her. No wonder Robert disapproved of her, and thought of her as a single-minded career woman. Perhaps it would be a good thing if she made herself into one, at least for as long as she worked at Sherringdon. Hard work was an antidote to heartache, and at least she was one of the lucky women who had a really worthwhile and satisfying job.

"ANYTHING WRONG?" Ben asked her a few days later. "You're not looking as bonny as usual."

They were standing in the drive after morning surgery and were both just about to leave on their round of visits. "I've had one or two late nights," said Kate, and opened the door of her car.

Ben put a hand on her arm. "But we've had an unusually quiet week." His nice ordinary face was puckered into a frown. "You've changed since you came here, Kate. And you've lost that lovely colour you used to have." He touched her cheek lightly with a forefinger. "You're not worrying about the work, are you, because you've no need to. You're managing splendidly."

"No, Ben, it's not the work." The wind had a bite in it today and Kate gave an exaggerated shiver. "Not the weather for standing around! Besides, I've a lot of visits on my list."

After a couple of calls in the village her next was to see a child whose father worked for Robert. She was standing at the garden gate, repeating her instructions to the little boy's nice but foolish mother, when Robert's car came round the bend.

He drew up a short way from the cottage and came towards them, looking concerned. "Nicky no better, Mrs. Williams? I'm glad you changed your mind and called the doctor."

The young mother had hung on longer than she should have done and the little boy was quite ill. "I've been trying to talk Mrs. Williams into letting Nicky go into hospital," said Kate, and Robert raised his eyebrows.

"She's afraid he'd be unhappy. So we've compromised and I'll give him twenty-four hours on antibiotics, but if he's no better tomorrow she'll let him go in."

Mrs. Williams, who had already been in floods of tears in the house, showed signs of a fresh outburst, and Kate patted her on the arm sympathetically. "It won't do if you let Nicky see that you're upset. I'll look in again last thing tonight, but if you're worried about him don't be afraid to ring before then."

The young woman gulped and blew her nose. "You're awfully kind, doctor. You seem to understand better than the men."

"One up to women doctors," Robert said softly as they walked away from the cottage, and Kate smiled but didn't bother to answer. She was too preoccupied with presenting just the right casual façade to Robert, so that he shouldn't guess the wild surge of happiness she had felt when he had stopped to speak to her.

At least he had really stopped to speak to Mrs. Williams. He was a kind and concerned employer, and took a genuine interest in the welfare of the families who lived on his land. The feudal approach had some good points, Kate thought.

When she said so to Robert he looked down at her in some amusement. "Changing your mind about us, Kate? Village life beginning to appeal?"

"Yes, I think it is," she said slowly. "There are fewer social problems in a country practice. People are more neighbourly, more willing to help. My brother sometimes has to admit patients to hospital who aren't very ill, but simply have no one to look after them, especially the old."

She glanced past Robert and saw that he had a passenger in his car. The woman turned her head and smiled. It was Elizabeth Hannay, whom she had met in Chartmouth. Robert nodded, glanced at his watch and said that he must be going, because he and Elizabeth were lunching with friends.

Kate continued on her way, thinking about Robert's relationship with Elizabeth. He was quite obviously seeing a great deal of her at present. Were they in love, or just old and intimate friends? Robert had said that Elizabeth was separated from her husband. Would he marry her if she got a divorce? Kate sighed, thinking that the poised and experienced Elizabeth would make an excellent lady of the manor.

Maggie had told her often about the old days, when the Montgomery parties were famous throughout the district. Those days were gone for ever, but Maggie thought it a pity that Robert didn't entertain more often, even on a modest scale.

"He works so hard he could do with a bit more fun," she had said.

To Kate's suggestion that he was maybe anti-social she had shaken her head. "Robert's a splendid host. It's just that he's got in a rut, all work and no play. Mind, it was necessary until he got the farm on its feet again, but now that things are running more smoothly I wish he would ease up. He needs a wife," Maggie had said thoughtfully, not knowing how her words had turned the knife in Kate's heart.

The other girl had added something to the effect that he would have to make up his mind soon. Even Diana, besotted as she was, must have some pride.

Kate's reply had been tart to hide her despair. "How can any man even think of marrying a woman for her money? It's quite sickening, in my opinion."

At that Maggie had jumped to the defence of her cousin and pointed out that no one knew if Robert was thinking of it seriously.

"He's much too self-contained to give away his feelings. He's fond of Diana, I think, and if he can't have the woman he really wants, he might as well settle for a marriage of convenience."

After this remark she seemed to feel she had gone too far, and had steered the conversation to something impersonal, leaving Kate to speculate unhappily as to the identity of the woman whom Robert really loved. Now she thought she knew the answer. Elizabeth? Or yet another woman about whom she hadn't heard? There was no doubt, she thought bitterly, that Robert was one of those men over whom women made fools of themselves.

That night she mentioned to Maggie that she had met Robert and Elizabeth. "Is she the woman you meant?" she asked. "The one he really wants?" She coloured under Maggie's stare. "You said something about it the other day, and I couldn't help wondering."

"You're not the only one," Maggie said dryly. "We all are, but none of us dare ask, not even Aunt Margaret." She brooded for a few moments. "Robert was in love with Elizabeth years ago, when they were at Cambridge together. He asked her to marry him, but she turned him down for another man. What made it worse was that David Hannay was a great friend of Robert's. He took it pretty badly and not long after that his mother died, so he went off to Canada."

"And now she's separated from her husband, and they're seeing a lot of each other. I expect they'll marry if she gets a divorce." Kate kept her voice level with a great effort.

"I hope not!" Maggie exclaimed fiercely. "I never liked Elizabeth. She came down here years ago and walked around as if she was assessing how much the place was worth. She assessed correctly, of course, because it was in a bad way under Robert's father, which was why she chose David Hannay."

"Oh, Maggie, that's very unkind. You make her sound horribly mercenary."

"That's exactly what she is—a calculating, cold-blooded bitch. She messed Robert's life up once. I can't believe he'll let her do it a second time."

CHAPTER EIGHT

THE WEEKS FLEW BY until Christmas. Kate, in the throes of an influenza epidemic, had left her present-packing until the last moment.

"Thank goodness we don't have any decorating or cooking to do!" she exclaimed, on her knees in a welter of wrapping paper and ribbon.

Maggie, engaged on the same task, reached over for the sellotape. "Angus and his family all well?"

"They sounded fine," said Kate. Angus had just telephoned a few minutes ago to wish his sister a happy Christmas, and had been pleased to learn that she was spending the day with the Montgomerys. "You'll have a super time, Kate. A real country Christmas, and in that lovely house."

Kate had murmured agreement and hoped that it would indeed be so. Over the last few weeks she had come to terms with her feelings for Robert, and recognized the fact that she would have to get over them. Robert was not for her and never would be. The faint hope that he might ask her out again had finally died. He was seeing a lot of Elizabeth Hannay, who had arrived that evening and was staying with the Montgomerys over the holiday.

Having to watch Robert and Elizabeth together might be painful, but it would help her to accept the inevitable, and Christmas could still be fun if she allowed it to be.

It was past midnight before the girls had packed the last of their parcels. Maggie crossed to the window and drew the curtains back. "What a wonderful night! Just look at those stars. If the weather stays as cold as this we might well have snow before long."

Christmas Day was so cold that it took the breath away, but by eleven o'clock the sun was out. Maggie and Kate walked up the path to the church, exchanging greetings with friends and acquaintances. It was fun living in a small community. It gave one a warm sense of belonging. Kate, brought up in the impersonal atmosphere of a big city, knew that she would miss this side of her present life very much.

As they settled themselves in their pew the party from the Hall arrived, Tim and Linda looking tidier than usual, then Lady Howard, walking slowly with a stick and flanked by Robert and Elizabeth. Robert's hand was under his aunt's elbow. He settled her carefully in her seat, before slipping into his own place next to Elizabeth. Kate stared at the back of his dark head, and wished with a fierce intensity that it could be herself in Elizabeth's place, told herself not to be a fool and leant sideways to catch Maggie's remark.

"Ben's just arrived. He said he might come if he didn't get any calls."

Kate followed the direction of Maggie's gaze and waved at Ben. It's going to be quite a Christmas, she thought with wry amusement. Let's just hope that Maggie at least has some luck! Then the vicar arrived and the congregation rose, and Kate forgot her personal problems in the familiar but always heartwarming Christmas service.

When they came out the girls waited for the party from the Hall. Kate stood a little in the background, while Maggie, who was in high spirits, kissed Robert on the cheek and, after only a moment's hesitation, did the same to her formidable aunt.

The old lady looked amused, caught Kate's eye as Maggie turned away, and beckoned her forward. "You're looking very pretty, child, but then you always do. Pity Maggie hasn't got your dress sense. Can't you smarten her up a bit?"

"Lady Howard, please!" Kate looked anxiously round, but Maggie was already out of earshot, talking animatedly to another family group. The flagstoned path was slippery with frost and Kate put a hand on Lady Howard's arm, afraid that she might fall. Robert appeared on the other side and smiled across his aunt.

"Happy Christmas, Kate. I didn't get the chance to say it earlier."

"And the same to you." Kate vowed that she *was* going to be happy in spite of everything. There would be a bittersweet pleasure in being Robert's guest, and watching him dispense hospitality in his own rather lordly manner.

QUITE A NUMBER of visitors turned up for drinks before dinner, the vicar, the Mitchells, several local farmers and their families. Kate, exchanging pleasantries with a farmer's wife who had been a patient of hers and who greeted her like a long-lost friend, noticed that Diana Mitchell was hovering disconsolately on the edge of the group around Robert.

The girl had every reason to look glum. Elizabeth was by Robert's side, smiling her quiet Mona Lisa smile, cool, poised, perfectly dressed. The estranged husband must make her a generous allowance, or else she had money of her own. She laid a hand on Robert's arm and leant towards him, speaking into his ear. Robert laughed and threw out some remark, and the group around him laughed too.

Only Diana remained unamused, and as though giving up moved across to Kate's side. When the farmer's wife wandered away she said in a low angry voice, "How long is she staying?"

There was no doubt to whom she was referring. "Over Christmas. A few days, I suppose."

"She's an absolute bitch!" Diana said savagely, and Kate made a shushing noise.

"Someone will hear."

"I don't care if they do," snapped Diana.

"Then you should." Kate caught the other girl by the arm and led her into a corner. "I know how you feel, but try not to show it. If Robert's in love with Elizabeth that's it. You'll have to accept it." She had nearly said "we," which would have been a dead give-away. She gave a choked sort of laugh and thought how ironical it was that she should be consoling Diana, when she felt so wretched herself.

"Cheer up," she murmured, gave the other girl's arm a squeeze and looked round to find that Robert was watching them, Elizabeth too.

It was nearly three o'clock before they finally sat down to dinner. They were using the big dining-room today, and the magnificent old oak table was loaded with exquisite glass and silver. "Lovely to look at, but awful to clean," as Linda muttered when Kate commented on its beauty.

Kate sat between Ben and Tim, and well fortified by sherry, was as gay as anyone there. Alcohol was a splendid anaesthetic, she thought, smiled at the idea and looked up the table to where Robert sat, with his aunt on his right and Elizabeth on his left. Ben, who was on call but had so far not been needed, had limited himself to one pre-lunch drink and one glass of champagne.

"I shall make up for it tomorrow," he announced. "Then it'll be Kate's turn to be abstemious. Roll on Boxing Day!"

After dinner they sat round a huge log fire in the drawing-room. Maggie and Kate and Ben had added their presents to the pile under the Christmas tree, and now it was time to open them. Kate had a moment's anxiety, wondering if she shouldn't after all have brought individual presents for the Montgomerys. She had asked Maggie's advice, but Maggie had said no, a box of chocolates for the whole family would be quite enough.

Linda and Tim were picking up the parcels and reading out the messages on them. In the general gaiety Kate forgot her little worry and collected her presents as eagerly as anyone.

"To Kate from a very grateful patient. Why, it's your writing, Aunt Margaret. I thought you hated all doctors!"

Everyone laughed, and Kate added the small gold parcel to her pile. "And here's another for you," said Linda. "Kate from Robert."

Kate's heart gave a lurch and she looked across at Robert, but he and Elizabeth were already opening their parcels, sitting side by side on the sofa near to the fire. Lady Howard, who was opposite to them, called to Kate to come and join her, and Kate opened the gold packet first. It was a bottle of perfume with a famous name on the label, and Kate's delight was quite genuine.

"I've always wanted some of this. I shall feel quite different when I'm using it."

"And so you should," Lady Howard agreed. "You young things don't dress up nearly often enough." She herself was regally attired in an extremely pretty dress of blue silk, set off by a magnificent pair of diamond earrings and a matching brooch.

They opened the rest of their presents and Kate kept Robert's to the end, for no reason that she could explain. It was flattish and rectangular in shape. A book? She fingered it speculatively and wished that she had bought a special present for him.

"Well, hurry up and open it," said Lady Howard, giving the girl by her side a sharp look.

Kate pulled the tinsel ribbon off and then the deep blue wrapping paper, and read the book's title: *Sussex in the days of the Norman Conquest*. She turned the pages over slowly, smiling to herself because Robert had remembered their outing on the cliffs at Chartmouth. At no other time had they talked about the Norman invasion.

She glanced across at the other sofa just as Elizabeth kissed Robert on the cheek, looking very pleased with herself. No, more than pleased. Positively smug! In her hand she held something that winked and glittered, some sort of jewellery, a brooch apparently, for Robert was leaning towards her now and pinning it on her dress.

Kate turned away quickly, trying hard not to hate Elizabeth. She made a little pile of her presents, then searched around for Robert's card. He hadn't written in her book, so she would keep the gift tag as a memento.

"Lost something?" asked Lady Howard.

Kate shook her head, saw the gift tag on the floor and picked it up quickly, slipping it between the pages of the book. It would be something to treasure in the bleak days ahead, she thought, and sighed without realizing that she had done so.

Lady Howard watched her expressive face, then said with unusual kindness, "You're a good child. If he had any sense he'd realize it."

Kate didn't pretend to misunderstand. "He'll never really forgive me for letting his brother down. So we can't even be friends."

That "even" was a complete giveaway. She realized it as soon as she'd spoken, but she suspected that the old lady had already guessed her secret. At any rate she patted Kate's hand and said softly, "Now that I've met you I think you showed good sense. You and Bill could never have been happy together. What astonishes me is that you ever thought you could be."

"The trouble was we didn't think," Kate said with an attempt at lightness. "I was young and foolish then, and I mistook a temporary attraction for the real thing."

If only what she felt for Robert could be dismissed as

lightly, but she knew that the heartache she went through when she watched him with Elizabeth was the most painful experience of her life. She had an opportunity a little later to thank him for his gift. "It was kind of you. I'm sure I shall enjoy it."

He nodded and told her that he had already read it. "Elizabeth helped me choose it. History's her subject too."

Silly to feel so let down! They had probably shopped together on one of the days he met Elizabeth in Chartmouth. "It was a good choice," Kate said politely, and hurried away just as Elizabeth came up, to slip a hand through Robert's arm and ask him if he was ready for that walk.

"A walk?" Maggie exclaimed. "Great! We could all do with some exercise." But somehow Elizabeth managed to scotch that suggestion, smiling gently and hinting that she and Robert wanted a little peace and quiet after all the excitement. So they went off together, and the others gathered round the fire to play a noisy game of Scrabble. Kate's head was beginning to ache, and her eyes stung with the tears that she could so easily have shed. She would rather have sat somewhere on her own and given way to her misery, but that would have been to draw attention to her feelings. There was safety in numbers, and if she was quieter than the rest nobody seemed to notice it.

Robert and Elizabeth came back when the others were having tea, with the news that it was snowing hard. "Inches deep already," Elizabeth announced.

"Hope I don't get any night calls," Ben muttered, while Kate wondered if Elizabeth's faint frown had any significance. She looked less pleased than she had done when she went out. Robert's face gave nothing away. He accepted a cup of tea from Maggie, who was doing the honours with the heavy silver teapot, glanced round for a seat, and lowered himself on to a stool by Kate's chair.

"Enjoying yourself?" he asked casually, and Kate made the conventional polite reply, while her heart thundered in her chest because of his closeness. She longed to touch his brown hand, lying so casually on the arm of her chair, and thought despairingly that she was behaving like a lovesick schoolgirl.

Robert leant towards her. "You don't look as if you're enjoying yourself. Ben neglecting you?"

"That's a silly question!" Kate snapped, and he gave a short laugh.

"Do you know, Kate, I can't make up my mind about you. I'm half inclined to believe you when you say you're not interested in Ben, and yet—" he turned to look at Ben who was holding forth on something to an attentive Maggie—"why are you so glum? It's Christmas Day, after all."

"I am not looking glum!" Exasperation made her voice rise. She got a grip on herself and added under her breath, "I'm quite as glad as you are if Ben's paying more attention to Maggie. I've done my best to make him realize—" She broke off because Robert was looking at her with a disturbing little half smile.

"I believe you, Kate," he said. "So now it's up to Maggie."

IT WAS MIDNIGHT before Maggie and Kate returned to their part of the house, and by now they had to plough through knee-high snow in borrowed gumboots, carrying their thin slippers in their hands. From her bedroom window Kate looked down on their own small courtyard and the old outhouse where they parked their cars. She would have to be up in good time to clear a passage from the garage to the drive.

The snow looked even deeper at the back of the house, for it was drifting in the wind. If she got an urgent call tomorrow morning she couldn't afford to waste time struggling to get her car out. So she set her alarm for seven-thirty, had a quick breakfast, and was hard at work with a shovel and brush when Robert strode by, accompanied by his dogs.

"What on earth are you doing?" he demanded.

"What do I look as if I'm doing?" she countered pertly, to hide her pleasure at this unexpected encounter.

He ploughed through the snow to her side, the dogs slithering behind him. "I meant why are you tackling it on your own? I'll send over a couple of my men, or you'll be at it all morning." He smiled down at her, and flicked some snow off her hair. "You're on duty, aren't you? I don't think you should go out on your own in these conditions. We can't have you getting lost in a snowdrift."

She was touched by his concern, but perversely wouldn't show it. "I'm not that helpless. We do have snow in Scotland!"

"Even so you're not used to driving on country lanes in really bad weather." He glanced up at the grey sky. "More snow on the way. Let me know if you have any calls," and he went on up the drive.

Ten minutes later two of the farmhands arrived and made light work of clearing the rest of the snow. Robert had sent a message that she would be well advised to take the car up the drive, and park in the farmyard before any more snow fell. The men had to push for several yards before the car tyres began to grip, and even when she was moving she nearly didn't make it to the top of the hill.

She stopped by the gates that led into the farm's main yard, uncertain where to park. Robert emerged from one of the cowsheds and beckoned to her. "Run it under that overhang. You shouldn't be snowed up there, but if we get a lot more you'll have to swallow that stubborn pride and use my Land-Rover."

"Oh." She cast an apprehensive glance at the vehicle. "I've never driven one."

"Good God, I'm not suggesting *you* drive it!" She

snorted at his masculine superiority, and he laughed and marched her off down the lane. "How about giving me some coffee? I didn't fancy breakfast when I got up."

"Me neither. But I could do with something now."

Maggie was still in bed, so Kate took her up toast and coffee before settling herself opposite Robert at the kitchen table. She would look on this interlude as a bonus, she thought contentedly, and hoped that she had understood him correctly, and that he intended driving her himself if she had any calls. Elizabeth mightn't like it, though!

"Is Elizabeth up?" she asked without thinking, and he shrugged and said, "No. She finds our country habits of early to bed and early to rise very uncivilized."

"Then she wouldn't be much good as a farmer's wife." She bit the last word off in a panic, and coloured under his sarcastic smile.

"What a girl you are for jumping to conclusions! Have you forgotten that she already has a husband?"

"You said they were separated," Kate mumbled, and he frowned.

"Separated. Not divorced." He added slowly, "David's a great friend of mine."

So he did have a conscience about making love to a married woman, and his friend's wife at that. Kate was glad to hear it, because she wanted to think well of him. Besides, if he gave up Elizabeth—she broke off these foolish speculations to offer him another cup of coffee.

THE GIRLS WERE TO SPEND Boxing Day with the Montgomerys as well as Christmas Day. Kate was lucky and had no emergency calls all morning, nor were there any routine visits to make. When they arrived at the Hall soon after midday they found that a good many people had dropped in again for drinks. Robert appeared to keep open house over the holiday and certainly didn't act the role of a man who was hard up. Perhaps there was more of his father in him than he cared to admit.

"A penny for them?" he asked, appearing suddenly at Kate's side.

She was perched on a wide windowsill, alone for a moment. He sat beside her, handsome and casually elegant, and her heart began to pound in the familiar disturbing way. "I was thinking what a packet all this must cost," she murmured, nodding towards the noisy crowd. "I mean," she stammered, afraid that she had once again put her foot in it, "my family don't entertain on this scale. I—I'm not used to it."

His quick frown was replaced by a smile. "Hasn't anyone advised you to think before you speak, young Kate?"

Kate blushed, hating to be thought gauche. "You did ask," she muttered. "I don't know what it is about you—" The line seemed to be unwise as well, so she took a sip of sherry under his amused gaze and tried again. "You bring out the worst in me," she said crossly, abandoning all attempts at discretion, and he laughed and patted her on the shoulder as if she was a little girl.

"Come and meet the Langleys. You don't know them, do you? And if it'll relieve that frugal Scots mind, we only entertain like this once a year. It's always been a tradition which I'm reluctant to break, however hard pressed."

Kate was still talking to the Langleys when her attention was attracted by a noisy argument in the hall. The drawing-room door was open, and she saw Linda and Tim with another girl of around their own age, a girl who looked vaguely familiar. A blonde girl who had been to the surgery once with some trifling complaint. The blonde looked furious and wasn't bothering to keep her voice down.

"I warned you, Linda Montgomery! I told you to stay away from Dave—" At that moment Tim saw Kate watching them and pulled the door shut.

Rather perturbed, Kate turned away to find Robert

right behind her. "What the devil is going on out there?" he asked. "Linda and Tim are short on manners, but I don't expect them to quarrel with my guests."

"Just some teenage argument," Kate said quickly, and slipped a hand through his arm. "I could do with another drink."

"You still have some."

"So I have." She gave a nervous little laugh and downed the remainder, anxious to distract his attention. "Please," she said brightly.

He took the glass from her. "You're on duty," he reminded her, "and a short time ago you said you would just have one. What the devil are you playing at, Kate? Are Tim and Linda up to some mischief? The Watson girl's certainly capable of anything."

"Don't you like her?" she asked. "Then why invite her?"

"She came with her parents," he said shortly. "Decent hardworking farmers with a no-good daughter." He gave her a hard look. "Now come on, Kate—" but at that moment the president of the Women's Institute bore down on them, and Robert was engulfed in a chattering bunch of middle-aged women. Kate let out a sigh of relief. She had been afraid that Robert would walk into the hall and hear something awkward. She could imagine his anger if he found his sister and another girl quarrelling over Dave Hickman. Perhaps it would be better if she warned them.

She slipped out of the drawing-room, but the hall was empty. Voices came from the library, arguing, pleading. She pushed the door open and as she walked in the three young people swung round.

"Sorry to barge in," Kate said quickly, "but I couldn't help hearing, and I thought I'd just warn you, your brother is wondering what goes on. He saw you in the hall, though I don't think he heard as much as I did."

Linda bit her lip nervously. "He'll be furious if he finds out. And Susan means to tell him."

"Tell him what?"

The young girl flushed, avoiding Kate's eyes. "She found Dave and me together, in a car."

"Oh, Linda!" Kate's exclamation was reproachful. "You promised you wouldn't meet him except at the college."

"Then she's a liar!" Susan Watson snarled, her pretty face distorted by emotion. "And it'll just serve her right when I tell that snooty brother of hers!"

Her words died away and her mouth opened wide as Robert spoke from the doorway. "Yes, Miss Watson? What are you going to tell me?"

He stood there, tall and forbidding, his handsome face sterner than Kate had ever seen it. Linda went very white and retreated behind Tim, but Susan stood her ground with a sullen look of defiance.

"Dave's my boy," she muttered. "I told Linda to leave him alone, but she's been meeting him on the sly, and now she can take what's coming to her."

"Oh, shut up, Susan!" Tim cried angrily.

"I won't shut up! If she didn't want Mr. Montgomery to know she shouldn't have done it. Serves her right if she gets into trouble."

Robert's voice was coldly contemptuous. "You've made your point, Miss Watson. Now perhaps you'll leave. I want to talk to my sister—alone."

The blonde flushed and made for the door. "No need to be so unfriendly! I thought you'd like to know what your little sister's been up to—" He made a curt gesture of dismissal, and she left with a speed that would have had Kate laughing at any other time.

Right now, though, her only thought was to protect Linda from the coming storm. "Robert, it's the season of goodwill. Couldn't it keep for a day or two? Linda's sorry, I'm sure."

"Is she?" he asked bleakly. "Sorry to be found out would be more accurate. Please go away, Kate. You too, Tim."

Linda clutched her younger brother's arm, as panicky as a naughty child. "Why can't Tim stay? And Kate knows all about it anyway."

Robert turned abruptly and shut the door. When he faced them his anger was under control, but no less alarming for being suppressed. "I see," he grated, and flicked Kate with a look of scorching contempt. "You're a pretty pair, aren't you? Both dishonest as the devil. I always knew you were a liar, Linda, but I didn't think Kate was."

"Robert, please let me—"

"I don't want to hear your excuses, Kate. You knew Linda was carrying on this"—he made a gesture of extreme distaste—"this affair with young Hickman, yet when I told you I was worried you covered up for her, told me you knew nothing."

Linda, relieved perhaps that her brother's anger was momentarily diverted to Kate, edged towards the door. He swung round and grasped her by the wrist.

"No, you don't! I have a lot more to say to you." Over the top of the girl's head he looked at Kate with open dislike. "Will you please go away? Tim too," and accepting defeat they went.

Tim brushed his long hair back nervously. "Phew! Linda's in for an uncomfortable ten minutes. I don't feel like going back to the party, do you?"

"I think we'd better, though." Kate felt almost as shaken as he was. "Try and look as if nothing's happened, Tim."

As they returned to the drawing-room people were already beginning to leave. Susan Watson passed them with a middle-aged couple who were presumably her parents. "Bye-bye," she said airily, and gave a silly giggle.

Tim's haughty look made him for a moment remarkably like Robert. "I can't stand that little bitch," he whispered, and Kate nodded her agreement.

"I think we'll both keep out of your brother's way until he's simmered down."

They joined Ben and Maggie and several other young people, but although she stood with her back to the door and concentrated on the joke someone was telling, she was tinglingly aware of the exact moment that Robert returned, and knew that he was moving across the room in their direction.

She gave him a quick look, which he met with a blank face. If he was going to be disagreeable he was saving it for later. Thoughts of the inevitable showdown spoilt the rest of the day for Kate, so that she pecked at the excellent lunch, and allowed her mind to wander during the game of Monopoly that Tim insisted on her joining.

Lady Howard had retired to her room for a rest. Robert and Elizabeth were reading, and the others sat around on the hearth-rug with the board between them.

"Oh, come on, Kate!" Maggie cried. "It's your turn," and Kate jerked her thoughts back to the game.

Linda, who was quieter than usual, gave her a sympathetic look. "Don't worry, Kate. He was beastly to me, but you're a visitor, after all. I don't suppose he'll say much to you."

She whispered this in Kate's ear, but Kate shook her head doubtfully. "I think he's just waiting for the right moment. I shall do my best not to provide one."

Linda grinned and Kate, looking round, saw that Robert was watching them, grim-faced. She turned away quickly, biting her lips. It was a welcome relief when the telephone rang and it turned out to be an emergency call. Fortunately the patient lived in Sherringdon, as the road from the Hall to the village was still relatively clear.

"Sure you can manage on your own?" Ben asked, and Kate said that of course she could. She would have to get used to driving in bad weather. Robert, after handing her the telephone, kept his eyes on his book and didn't look up when she went out with Ben, who insisted on accompanying her up the drive.

"You may need a push to get started," he observed, and added curiously, "Any idea why Robert's looking so browned off?"

"Robert? Is he?" Kate stalled, head down against the biting wind.

"Of course he is. You're looking guilty, Kate. What have you been up to?"

It relieved Kate's feelings to unburden herself to Ben. He listened silently and when she had finished shook his head disapprovingly. "You've been very silly, my dear girl. Robert must be absolutely furious."

"Well, thanks for nothing," Kate said crossly. "When I've seen this patient I shall go straight back to Maggie's place."

It was nearly seven before she returned. The patient had a perforated duodenal ulcer, not uncommon following the overindulgence of Christmas time. She had to admit him, but the ambulance took a long time to plough through the snowy lanes. So Kate stayed with him until it arrived, and had a hard job making the short journey back. It was snowing heavily again and the snow was drifting. She left the car at the farm and struggled down the hill, her face stung by wind and snow. She remembered Robert's offer to drive her if she needed to go out, but presumably he had either forgotten or was too angry to care what happened to her.

She let herself into Maggie's house and sat by the kitchen range, trying to warm her frozen fingers. She was still there, reluctant to leave the comforting warmth, when the doorbell rang. When she opened the door a flurry of snow blew in and Robert stepped quickly through, brushing snowflakes from his dark hair.

Dismayed, Kate could only stare up at him, so he pushed her out of the way unceremoniously and slammed the door shut. "I want to talk to you, Kate." He gripped her by the arm and marched her into the living-room.

"There's no need to be so rough," Kate objected, trying to raise her courage for the coming battle. She sat down in her favourite chair, body tense and hands tightly clenched.

Robert stood in front of her and there was a brief unnerving silence. "Why did you do it, Kate?" he asked at last, but Kate could think of no answer that wouldn't increase his anger. "Well, come on," he said grimly. "You must have had some reason for your extraordinary behaviour. Misplaced sympathy? The pleasure of making a fool out of me? What?"

"I—" She gave him a despairing look. "You'd never understand, because you've forgotten what it's like to be sixteen, but I haven't, and I felt sorry for Linda. They didn't mean any harm."

"Didn't they? So you approve of a young girl like Linda making love in the back of a car? Do you think that boy was satisfied with a few kisses? Do you? Do you?"

He bent over her, caught her by the shoulders and shook her savagely until she was breathless and gasping. "I've never felt like hitting a woman before, but I do now. You knew all about it and you knew I was worried, because we discussed it, and yet you kept silent. You have a strange code of values, Kate."

Shaken by his violence, Kate managed a stumbling defence. "I did talk to Linda. I thought that was enough. Telling you would only have got her into trouble."

"Less trouble than she's in now," he bit out, and she tried again.

"I didn't want to antagonize her. I thought—if I

didn't give her away I'd have more influence with her. I had no idea she was still seeing Dave."

"Then you're a bad judge of human nature. Linda has always told lies if it suited her. Wouldn't it have been the wise—the decent thing—to discuss it with me? I am, after all, responsible for her until she comes of age."

Kate's feelings were an uncomfortable mixture of shame and resentment—shame because she knew his anger was justified, and resentment because honesty made her admit it. If it had been anyone but Robert she would have apologized. As it was she made a half-hearted attempt to justify her actions. He heard her out with compressed lips.

"I see, Kate. In your opinion I'm overbearing and unsympathetic towards the girl, and that excuses your irresponsible behaviour. Well, it's my opinion that you're as immature as Linda, and with less excuse, since you're a good deal older."

"I haven't explained very well," Kate said unhappily. "I don't think of you like that now. I—I meant that when I first knew you that was how you seemed—" She gave up that line as too dangerous and started again. "All right, I made a mistake. I trusted Linda when I shouldn't have done. But has it occurred to you that this whole affair is her way of rebelling against an out-of-date social code? She wants to be like the other girls she meets at college or wherever, not Miss Montgomery of Sherringdon Hall."

There was a little silence after her words. Robert still looked furious, but he seemed to be thinking about what she had said. In the end he admitted that there might be some truth in it, but had she analysed Dave Hickman's motives?

She stared at him and he went on slowly, "You've seen the sort of girl Hickman goes around with—Susan Watson. Now why would he show an interest in a little girl like Linda?"

"She's very pretty," Kate pointed out.

"And young for her age. Hadn't it occurred to you that the lad's chief motive might be malicious? To get his own back on me?"

"What a fantastic idea!"

"Not really. I sacked his father a few years ago for dishonesty, and I've had words with young Dave on more than one occasion. I don't doubt that the whole family hate my guts." He turned as if to go, but after a moment's hesitation sat down instead. "Indulging in a slanging match isn't going to help Linda, so let's try and be civilized about it. Maybe there's some truth in your comments, though God knows I've tried to be understanding." For a few surprising moments he sat with bowed head, looking tired and discouraged. Then he was himself again, straight-backed and controlled. "If I'm right you do realize Linda may be hurt?"

Kate fidgeted in her chair, only too aware that she had been gravely at fault. "I'm sorry," she said, low-voiced. "I do see that—that it was wrong not to tell you," and she waited hopefully for his response.

Perhaps her apology came too late, for he shrugged and his voice was cold. "Do you, Kate? But the damage has been done, hasn't it? I'm well aware of the principal reason for your behaviour, of course. You enjoyed helping to deceive me, didn't you? It gave you quite a kick."

"No!" she insisted, but he ignored her interruption. "You've never bothered to hide your dislike, though I had begun to think—Well, it's of no consequence except in so far as it affects Linda."

"But it does matter," said poor Kate. "I told you, it was only in the beginning I felt like that."

"Was it?" he asked with open disbelief. "Anyway, don't forget my offer if you have any night calls for the outlying farms. The forecast's bad. There's more snow on the way."

Hurt by his chilly response, she answered childishly, "If I need any help I'll ask Ben."

"Ben's car would be no better than yours. The Land-Rover is the only one that could make it. I'm offering for the patients' sake, not yours."

Unkind words, which hurt more than he would ever know. "All right," she agreed reluctantly, "but couldn't one of your men drive me?"

"My men work very hard, and it *is* Boxing Day. I shouldn't dream of asking them to turn out. So you'll just have to put up with me if the need arises."

"All right," Kate muttered, "but I hope it won't."

His smile was disagreeable. "No more than I do, my dear," and he went, leaving Kate to the turmoil of her unhappy thoughts, and the faint longing that she could put the clock back on the events of the last few months.

CHAPTER NINE

To KATE'S RELIEF she had no emergency calls that night, but she lay awake for hours brooding over the scene between herself and Robert. He had never really approved of her, but lately he had seemed more friendly. Now he must dislike and despise her very thoroughly for not being more honest with him.

Morning found Kate with smarting eyes and an aching head. She dragged herself wearily out of bed, envying Maggie's long school holidays, shivered at the freezing temperature, and went quickly downstairs to open up the kitchen stove.

It was Friday and the surgeries were back to normal, were indeed busier than normal because of the two days' holiday. Kate got through the work somehow, thankful that it was Ben's week-end on duty. The afternoon visits dragged on till five o'clock because of the bad condition of the lanes. The snow ploughs had been out on the main roads, but many of the minor ones were almost impassable. Miss Andrews had given Kate a spade and a length of rope when she left the surgery.

"Better be prepared for trouble," she explained. "If you don't need it someone else might."

In fact Kate had used neither, but she had twice had to leave her car and walk through snow to reach some isolated farm.

"My gumboots are soaking," she grumbled, back at the surgery to return patients' case notes.

"Have a cup of tea, doctor," Miss Andrews consoled her. "I've just taken one in to Doctor Ben before he starts evening surgery."

Ben gave her his usual cheery reception when she joined him, but commented with concern on her pale face. "This cold is enough to make anyone feel out of sorts. Have a good rest this week-end, and let's hope the worst of the weather will be over by Monday."

His hopes weren't fulfilled, however. It snowed intermittently all Saturday, with Sussex and Kent getting a special mention on the news for particularly severe blizzards.

"We haven't had such deep snow for years," Maggie observed, curled up comfortably on the sofa with the Sunday papers. "Why so restless, Kate? Haven't you anything to do?"

"Plenty," Kate sighed, and applied herself doggedly to a pile of mending. She had spent a wretched two days alternately longing to meet Robert and praying that she wouldn't. She had glimpsed him once, striding up the drive with his labradors, dressed in working clothes and looking very preoccupied. She guessed that such severe weather brought problems to farmers, but he had personal worries to contend with as well, and she felt very remorseful for the part she had played in them.

She was reluctant to unburden herself to Maggie, because the girl worshipped her cousin, and would never understand the complicated motives behind Kate's actions. "For that matter I find them difficult to explain to myself," Kate said ruefully over Monday lunch with Ben.

He had suggested that it would be less trouble for her to eat at his house than drive through the snow-packed lanes to Maggie's place. The housekeeper deposited an apple tart in front of Ben, and he concentrated on cutting it while he formulated his ideas.

"You're a real mixed-up girl," he said at last. "It's never easy to be objective about oneself, but for what it's worth I think I understand why you did it." He gave her his slow kindly smile and Kate waited for him to enlarge. "You were determined to dislike Robert right from the beginning—Maggie and I both noticed it. I wish you could see your way to making it up with him."

Kate dug her spoon into her apple tart, then put it down untasted. "He doesn't want to make it up, Ben. I did try to say I was sorry—" Her voice quavered in spite of all her efforts to control it. She fumbled for her handkerchief and blew her nose, self-consciously aware that Ben had stopped eating and was watching her with frowning intensity. "I'm—very unhappy," she whispered, and began to cry.

Once started it was difficult to stop. She jumped up from the table and crossed to the window. "Sorry," she managed in a muffled voice. "I'm not one for crying usually—"

"I'm sure you're not," Ben said quietly, "which makes me wonder why you're doing it now. Sit down, Kate. You don't want Mrs. Smith seeing you like this."

So Kate sat down again and struggled through her pudding, and was outwardly composed when Mrs. Smith brought the coffee in.

Ben broke the silence first. "Why are you so unhappy, Kate? Why should you care what Robert thinks about you?"

"Because—" she hesitated, then said sadly, "Because I'd like him at least to have a good opinion of me," and her voice wavered again, as she realized how unlikely that was.

Ben's nice face showed concern. "So you've changed your mind about him, Kate? Is that it?"

She nodded, her eyes filling up again, and Ben dropped his fork on to his plate with a little clatter. "I can't believe it! Oh, Kate, surely you can't have been so foolish?"

Kate didn't pretend to misunderstand him, and in a strange sort of way it was a relief to be honest. "Yes, Ben," she murmured, "I've been quite incredibly foolish. I've fallen in love with a man who never liked me and now positively despises me. But you don't choose to fall in love. It just happens, doesn't it?"

Ben's smile was rueful. "Too true. It's hard to know what to say."

She contrived a ghost of a smile. "Nothing to say, Ben dear. I've made a mess of things in every way, and the sooner I leave here the better."

Ben stirred his coffee before speaking. "Yes, I think it will be a good thing. There was a time when I'd hoped—" he halted abruptly and started again. "It's a pity really, because you fit in so well in the practice, and I think Dad's beginning to accept the fact that we need a third partner."

"You'll find someone easily enough," Kate said quickly, relieved to discuss something less personal. "More and more young doctors are anxious to get out of the rat race. City life isn't all it's cracked up to be."

She hadn't thought like this in the past. Glasgow had always been home to her. She still loved its noisy vitality, but no longer wanted to spend the whole of her working life there. For that matter her career, which had once seemed so important, was no longer enough to satisfy her.

She thought of Ben's last words as she drove back to Maggie's place for tea. If she changed her mind and asked to join the practice, would he have her? Would he want her, now that he knew she was in love with another man? How complicated life was, Kate thought tiredly, and drew up at Robert's front door, having left her visit to Lady Howard until the end of the afternoon.

The old lady was much better and received Kate in the small sitting-room which the family used for everyday living. "Stay and have some tea with me," she suggested while Kate was packing her medical equipment away. "Everybody's out and it's such a miserable day."

Kate stayed to cheer the old lady up, listening with genuine interest to her colourful stories of life in the colonies between the wars. She was so engrossed that she didn't hear the door open and was startled when Robert spoke behind them.

"Hallo, Aunt Margaret. Any tea left?"

Kate's whole body tensed and she sat very still, her eyes on the leaping flames of the log fire. When she turned round Robert had already taken a chair by his aunt, and was lifting the lid off the teapot.

"I'll ask for some more," said Lady Howard, but Kate jumped up. "Don't bother, I'll go."

When she came back the other two were discussing the date of Lady Howard's departure. Kate put the heavy Georgian teapot down carefully on the ornate silver tray, and returned to her place. She would excuse herself as quickly as possible, because being in the same room as Robert was more of an ordeal than she had expected. If he had shown even conventional friendliness she would have been content, but his eyes were hard and his voice cold, when he thanked her for fetching his tea. There was a disagreeable tightness in Kate's chest which seemed to get steadily worse.

"Don't you agree, Kate?" Robert asked suddenly, and she jumped and admitted that she hadn't been following their conversation.

"I was suggesting that my aunt stay for another week or two. Travelling up to London in this weather wouldn't be very pleasant."

"Rubbish! It's a two-hour drive, not a journey to the South Pole," Lady Howard said caustically.

"More than two hours' driving under these conditions. Wait a few more days at least." Robert's smile was full of affection. "Don't you agree, Kate?" he repeated abruptly.

She hesitated, surprised that he should bother to ask her opinion. "Perhaps it would be better," she agreed cautiously, "but it's up to your aunt, isn't it?"

Lady Howard smiled and patted her hand. "Good child! And I shall go if I want to, but as a matter of fact—" her eyes went from Kate to Robert—"there are a few problems that need sorting out, so perhaps I shall stay after all."

"Aunt Margaret," Robert said with grim amusement, "you're a very naughty old woman. What mischief are you planning now?"

She gave a throaty chuckle. "I want a few straight answers, young man. For a start, why are you being so disagreeable to this poor child?"

The poor child turned slowly scarlet, while Robert watched her sardonically. "Ask Kate," he said briefly.

Kate half rose, but Lady Howard made an imperious gesture and she subsided unwillingly in her seat. "I'd rather not talk about it," she stammered. She might have known that this answer was a waste of time, so with great reluctance and avoiding Robert's eyes, she did her best to explain.

"And please don't take it out on Linda," she ended. "The poor kid's had enough telling off already."

Lady Howard examined the magnificent diamond rings on her misshapen fingers. "And so she should have had, behaving like a village girl!"

"She is a village girl," Kate said hotly, but regretted the words when she saw Lady Howard's wrathful expression. "I—I mean, she belongs to Sherringdon village just like anyone else," she added lamely, and gave a small placating smile which did nothing to mollify the old tyrant's annoyance.

"Don't be obtuse, child!"

"Kate is never obtuse, Aunt Margaret," Robert said dryly. "Haven't you yet discovered that she disapproves of everything we stand for?"

"We're wandering off the point," Kate said quickly. "Please, Lady Howard, try to understand why Linda's been behaving like this. Robert tells her not to see this young man, but he doesn't give her a good enough reason."

"My reason was perfectly good," snapped the old lady.

"But not to Linda! Don't you see, she's young and

inexperienced, and Dave's an attractive lad in his way, and he's forbidden, so that makes him more exciting. Oh, surely you can understand?" In her agitation Kate jumped up and stretched out her hands to the old lady. Then she sat down again despondently. "If Robert won't understand why should you?" she sighed.

"Because I'm a woman," Lady Howard said unexpectedly. "And because I can remember my own girlhood so well. Robert, please go and find that tiresome niece of mine, and tell her to come here."

Kate she allowed to leave, after a not very severe scolding for her part in the affair. Kate let herself out of the front door just as Elizabeth Hannay drove up. Elizabeth got out quickly and called after her, "Miss Ferguson! Could I have a word with you?" Tall and slim, in a beautifully tailored car coat and neat dark trousers, she walked across to Kate. "How is Lady Howard?" she asked, and Kate said that the old lady was doing very well.

"Good." Elizabeth sounded quietly pleased. "Then she'll be going home in a day or so?"

Surprised, Kate could only stare. Elizabeth smiled faintly. "Don't tell me you'll be sorry. She must be an appalling patient."

Kate didn't return the smile. For some time she had been altering her mind about Elizabeth. When she had first met her she had admired her. Now she thought that the older woman was more than a little malicious.

"I never discuss my patients," she said coolly, and started to turn away.

"That sounds very priggish," Elizabeth said softly, and her expression was no longer pleasant. "I am, after all, a friend of the family. Robert tells me everything."

"Well, bully for you!" Kate exclaimed, and would have moved on, but Elizabeth continued, her voice low and controlled.

"Including Linda's little escapade and your part in it. I wouldn't care to be in your shoes if the girl turned out to be pregnant." The malice was open now, and the more distasteful for being accompanied by a smile.

Kate stared at the other woman in disgust, and Elizabeth looked back at her with that maddening smile still on her face. "What a beastly thing to say! I know Linda's a silly kid, but don't you feel any sympathy for her at all?"

"Absolutely none," Elizabeth said with devastating frankness. "She always was a cheeky little brat. She got what she asked for. Perhaps it will teach her a lesson." She narrowed her eyes, studying Kate's furious face. "I should keep out of Robert's way if I were you. After this you've even less chance than that stupid bitch Diana."

She uttered the last words with unexpected viciousness, then turned and walked into the house. The ladylike façade had most definitely slipped and her manner was openly hostile.

Shaken by this unpleasant incident, Kate let herself into Maggie's house, to find the other girl taking scones out of the oven. "I made them specially for you, Kate, so eat up. Isn't it a lovely day?" She rattled on cheerfully, more talkative than she had been lately, telling Kate that she and Ben had been skating that afternoon on the lake. It was Ben's half day, and he wanted to repeat the performance again at the weekend.

Kate was glad for Maggie's sake if Ben was showing an interest, but she found it hard to pay attention, a fact which Maggie noticed at last. "Anything wrong?" she asked. "You're looking a bit down."

So Kate recounted the scene with Elizabeth, omitting only the woman's last words, which she couldn't bring herself to repeat.

"Typical! The woman's as catty as they come. Don't let her upset you," advised Maggie.

"I can't help being upset," sighed Kate. "It was—nasty. Why does she dislike me so much?"

Maggie placed a comforting cup of tea in front of Kate. "Easy. Because she looks on any young and attractive woman as a potential rival."

Kate choked on her tea. "But Maggie, that's crazy! I suppose she's right to be jealous of Diana, but not of me." The last words came out a little wishfully and Maggie gave her a quick look. "I mean," Kate hurried on, "Robert's furious with me, because I—I covered up for Linda about something."

"I know about that," said Maggie disapprovingly, "and I think Robert had good reason to be furious. The odd thing is, though, that he seems more hurt than angry, especially about your part in it."

It appeared that Robert had unburdened himself to Maggie, asking her opinion as to what line he should take with his sister. He had also asked her if she felt that Kate's criticisms were justified. "Honestly, Kate!" Maggie sounded very indignant. "How could you have been so unkind? Robert tries terribly hard to be patient with those two."

"Oh, Maggie, don't you start now! I was only trying to see things from Linda's point of view. And anyway, I refuse to believe that Robert is capable of being hurt, at any rate by me."

"Everyone's capable of being hurt. Beneath that tough exterior Robert's as vulnerable as the next person, when his friends let him down."

"I didn't think he looked on me as a friend," Kate muttered, beginning to wish that she hadn't confided in Maggie.

"Of course he does! Or did. Only the other day he was saying what a splendid doctor you were, how kind to the old people, how good with the children. Come to think of it, Elizabeth was there, and probably wasn't pleased to hear how he admired you."

But not any longer, Kate thought unhappily. Now he must have reverted to his original opinion of her, and the hardest thing to bear was that it was entirely her own fault. Looked at in retrospect she had acted very culpably, blinded by her early prejudice against Robert. She should never have believed Linda, and she should never have ignored her original mistrust of Dave. What a mess she had made of things, and how awful if Linda *was* pregnant. This worrying possibility niggled away in the back of her mind all evening, so that she couldn't settle to anything, and in the end telephoned the girl and asked her to come over.

Maggie had gone round to Ben's place, so they were on their own. Linda seemed pleased to be invited, and anxious to let off steam. "Aunt Margaret wasn't nearly as horrid as Robert. In fact she was quite decent once she understood I hadn't—well, you know—" The girl coloured and looked out of the window. "I'm not as dumb as you all seem to think," she ended. "Give a boy like Dave what he wants and that's the last you'll see of him."

"That's a very cynical remark for a sixteen-year-old!" Kate exclaimed, and began to laugh helplessly, as she realized that her fears had been unfounded.

"But true." Linda kicked her shoes off and stretched out on the sofa. "You're not busy? I can stay for a bit?"

"Of course. Unless I get called out."

"You're being jolly decent, Kate. You might have been nasty, like Robert, because I—well, because I bent the truth a bit."

"That would have been the pot calling the kettle black," Kate said ruefully. "I wasn't honest with your brother either."

"What really gets me is finding out that Dave wasn't worth all the fuss," Linda went on. "He was still seeing Susan while he was going around with me, and he'd sworn that he wasn't." Linda punched a cushion irritably. "I'm off boys, actually. I think I'll stick to horses. They're nicer than humans!"

Kate looked at the young girl with amusement and

relief. The Dave episode didn't seem to have left any scars. It might even have helped her to grow up, and for that at least Robert ought to be grateful.

LADY HOWARD SEEMED to be in no hurry to leave, so Kate continued to visit her, though she was well satisfied with the old lady's medical progress. Elizabeth was apparently no longer staying at the Hall, but Kate gathered that she was still in Chartmouth. Diana, whose visits had been less frequent lately, had started coming round again, and meeting Kate one morning in the courtyard, stopped to chat.

She was full of the dance that her family were giving next Saturday, apparently an annual event well attended by local society. "I hope you're not on call that night?" she inquired.

"Well, I am, but anyway, I haven't been invited," said Kate.

"Gosh, haven't you? Mother does the invitations. She must have forgotten you're still here."

Remembering Mrs. Mitchell's patronizing manner, Kate thought the omission was more likely deliberate, but Diana insisted that she must come. "Maggie always does, and you should too."

"But if I'm on duty—"

"So what? You can be on call from our place. Do come." Diana turned to greet Robert, who had just emerged from the house. He agreed with the girl that everyone went to the Mitchells' dance, though whether Kate went or not quite plainly didn't interest him. He slid a hand through Diana's arm and they walked off in the direction of the stables.

That evening Mrs. Mitchell telephoned and confirmed Diana's invitation, but with considerably less enthusiasm than her daughter had shown. Kate consulted Ben, who offered to stand in for her while the dance was in progress. "I can visit a patient in evening dress, but it would look a little odd if you did!"

Kate laughed and agreed to go. "You are a dear, Ben. I don't think I'll get so much consideration when I join Angus's practice."

On the Saturday evening Ben telephoned at six o'clock to say he was taking over. "Give you plenty of time to titivate! See you at eight."

He arrived accompanied by the vicar's son, down from university for the Christmas vacation. Maggie and Kate got into the car carefully, anxious not to crush their dresses, and wearing overshoes to protect their evening slippers from the snow.

Every day there had been fresh falls so that driving was still difficult, but the Mitchells lived less than two miles from Sherringdon Hall, in a large modern house that looked as if it had come out of one of the glossy magazines. Colonel and Mrs. Mitchell greeted them in the hall, and the smile on Mrs. Mitchell's plump face faded a little when she looked at Kate.

They moved on and Diana showed them upstairs to the bedrooms, staying to chat while they removed their outdoor clothes.

"What a super dress, Kate! That creamy colour is fantastic with your red hair. And I like yours too, Maggie. Where did you get it?"

She chattered on excitedly, her always high colour more pronounced than usual, but when they went downstairs she became suddenly quiet. Robert had arrived with the party from the Hall. He stood beside his aunt, relaxed, smiling and handsomer than ever in evening dress. Diana gave a little sigh and whispered, "Doesn't he make every other man look sort of ordinary?"

A naïve remark, but none the less true. Robert did outshine the other men, and was the more endearing for appearing so unaware of it. Ben and Jack, the vicar's son, joined them and they all moved into the drawing-room, where people were already dancing. Jack seemed to regard Kate as his partner, and as he was a pleasant enough young man this suited Kate very well, because it left Ben to partner Maggie.

There were a good many older people present, watching the dancing or playing cards in an adjoining room. Colonel Mitchell, after a few duty dances, had retired to the billiard room with a few old cronies.

"The dear man hates entertaining," Lady Howard told Kate, when the girl sat bside her for a much needed rest.

"Then why does he do it?"

"To please his womenfolk." Lady Howard's eyes followed Robert and Diana, who were dancing together at this moment. "That girl grows more like her mother every day."

"In looks, maybe, but I think she's nicer." Kate lowered her voice discreetly, but the old lady didn't follow suit.

"Hum. Surely you don't like her? You must know she's after my nephew."

"Lady Howard, please! Someone will hear."

"Nonsense, there's too much noise," and indeed there was. The old lady bent towards Kate. "Well? Don't you mind if she marries him?" she asked sharply, and Kate shrugged unhappily.

"It makes no odds how I feel, does it? If he wants to marry her he will."

"You give up too easily, child," Lady Howard admonished her. "You're much prettier than Diana and ten times as intelligent. In fact I've come round to the view that you're just the girl for him!"

"Well, thanks," Kate said wryly, "I'm astonished that I pass muster. You do know I'm not an heiress?"

"I know very well, miss," Lady Howard said brusquely, not at all pleased by Kate's attempt at sarcasm. "Of course, it would have been nice if you'd had money too, but if Robert asks my opinion—"

"Oh, stop, stop!" Kate cried, half-way between tears

and laughter. "Robert doesn't even like me. He hasn't danced with me once this evening."

It was perhaps as well that Jack arrived then with two glasses of punch. "That old woman terrifies me," he admitted as he led Kate away to dance. "And her nephew's nearly as bad."

"Robert?" Kate asked, surprised that this nice but rather brash young man should admit to being intimidated by anyone.

Jack grinned. "He doesn't approve of me. Thinks I take advantage of Dad, which I suppose I do. And he's got an abrasive tongue when he cares to use it."

"Too true," Kate agreed fervently, thinking of the many times she had herself incurred Robert's displeasure. In an odd sort of way she wished that he was still annoyed with her. Annoyance was a positive emotion, and preferable to the studied indifference he had shown to her lately.

The dance went on until the small hours, but Kate thought that she had never enjoyed a social occasion less. She longed for it to end, but hid her longing behind a bright smile and vivacious manner. She ate supper with Jack, had a great many dances with him, and tried hard not to keep looking round for Robert, but she was only too aware that Robert's most frequent partner was Diana.

At the end of one dance the two couples found themselves side by side. Diana, flushed and happy, gave them a wide smile. "Come and have a drink. Let's sit down, Kate, and wait for the men."

Kate followed the other girl into the conservatory where chairs were scattered about invitingly. She sat down wearily, but Diana, exuberantly pleased with herself, moved around to the distant music, while she held forth on the great time she was having.

"I've changed my tactics," she giggled. "There *are* other men around who rate a second glance, don't you agree?"

Before Kate could reply the men joined them with drinks, and it soon became evident that Jack and Diana were old friends. "If friend's the right word," Diana laughed. "He pushed me into the village pond once. Do you remember, Jack? Mother was absolutely furious."

"I do remember," Jack grinned. "But you might mention that we were only ten at the time."

They reminisced on happily, while Kate sat and listened and avoided Robert's eyes. She was dismayed when they went off to dance together, leaving Robert and her quite alone, for there was no one else in the conservatory.

The music throbbed gently in the distance. Kate stared at the massed plants on their tiers and tried hard to concentrate on naming them. If only Robert would say something, anything, to break this horrible silence! She had just decided despairingly that she had better get up and go when he leant towards her.

"Shall we dance?" he asked. "Or would you rather sit it out?"

She jerked away from him, heart thumping uncomfortably. "You don't have to be polite. I don't expect it."

He raised his eyebrows and laughed. "What a funny girl you are! Why shouldn't I want to dance with you?"

Kate fingered a plant with hideous mauve flowers. "You know why. Besides, I'm tired. I wish you'd go away," but as soon as she had spoken she longed for him to stay.

He showed no inclination to do as she had suggested, and still appeared more amused than offended. "Trying to pick a quarrel, Kate?" He ran his fingers lightly down her bare arm. "You're looking very pretty tonight. I like that dress," and he moved his hand to her shoulder.

Kate stiffened, and he laughed again, and turned her towards him. "I'm not in the mood for arguments."

He put his mouth on hers, gently at first and then with increasing urgency. Her hands slid up to stroke his thick dark hair. She clung to him blindly, overwhelmed by a physical attraction that was frightening in its intensity.

Then he let go of her abruptly and leant back in his chair. "Wasn't that better than quarrelling?" he asked softly.

Kate had just become aware of other people entering the conservatory. She managed a smile and a nod in their direction, but didn't trust herself to look at Robert. Had she given herself away by returning his kisses so passionately? Was he laughing at her weakness?

"I—I think I'd like that dance after all," she stammered, and made to rise, but Robert caught her arm.

"Not worth it now. Besides, you said you were tired."

The other couples had seated themselves behind a bank of flowers and were engaged in noisy badinage. Kate risked a quick glance at Robert and found it impossible to interpret his expression. She was not sure what it was, but it was certainly not mockery.

"Why are you looking at me like that?" She brushed the hair back from her face with a quick nervous gesture.

He still had his hand on her other arm. "Do relax, Kate. Anyone would think you'd never been kissed before!"

"Not like that," Kate said unwisely, and drew in her breath sharply, as his expression changed.

"Not even by Bill? What an admission!" His grip tightened and she shut her eyes, because she was afraid they would betray her. She loved him so much and she longed to tell him so, but knew in her heart that he wouldn't want to hear it. He had amused himself for five minutes in breaking down her defences. All she could hope was that he would be decent and pretend to forget it.

"Open your eyes, little one," he said under his breath. "Here comes young Jack," and although his voice was light and amused he looked exasperated.

"Ben thinks it's time we broke it up!" said Jack, smiling down at them, and looking very pleased about something. "But I want one more dance." He caught hold of Kate's hand and swung her to her feet.

"Where's Diana?" Kate asked.

"Saying good-bye to people. Do you know something? I'd forgotten what fun she can be. Funny, you can live practically next door..."

He chattered on without expecting a reply, as they circled the drawing-room, and Kate saw Robert come out of the conservatory a minute or two later. He strolled over to where his aunt was sitting and leant against the wall by her side. Kate thought how wonderful it would have been if it had been Robert she was dancing with. She spun round in Jack's arms and had a momentary glimpse of Robert, staring in their direction, a frown on his face. Regretting that episode in the conservatory? Wondering how she would behave when they met next?

Then he bent to speak to his aunt and that was the last she saw of him, because Ben tapped Jack on the shoulder, and told him to break it up, there was work to do. Andy had telephoned with an urgent message.

On the way back to Maggie's place Kate and Ben bickered amiably over who should do the visiting. "It won't take me long to change. Of course I'll go, Ben." So they dropped Jack off at the rectory, and while Maggie made a cup of hot chocolate for them all, Kate changed into a thick sweater and slacks.

She left the other two sitting rather sleepily in front of the kitchen fire, Maggie with an air of contentment that she seldom wore. The emergency turned out to be a genuine one, which couldn't be said of all the night calls Kate had to make. Her only criticism was that she hadn't been called earlier, for the patient had been in pain for twenty-four hours, and his appendix had undoubtedly perforated. Strange how some people were so much more stoical than others, she thought, as she drove back to Sherringdon in the half light of early morning.

She had had to wait a long time for the ambulance and the man had been too ill to leave. She glanced at her watch, and decided that it was too late for bed. As she was getting out of her car Robert walked through the gateway. Lightheaded with lack of sleep and therefore less on guard, Kate smiled her delight at seeing him.

"Why aren't you in bed?" she asked.

"I was waiting for you." He took her black bag and the key of the door, which she had just produced, and opened up for her. "How was old Gooding? Ben told me you'd been called out."

"He'll need an urgent operation." Kate walked ahead of him, down the corridor and into the kitchen. To hide her confusion and uncertainty she occupied herself with filling the kettle and plugging it in, and dropping the bread into the electric toaster.

Robert seated himself at the table and watched her silently, while Kate wondered uneasily why he had come. She was clumsier than usual, dropping a piece of toast on the floor and muttering crossly to herself. She threw the toast at the waste bin, missed and glared at him when he laughed.

"Do you have to sit there with that superior look on your face?"

"Poor Kate," he said with unexpected gentleness. "You must be feeling very tired."

He had presumably not been to bed either, but he looked irritatingly fresh and well shaven. "That's right, I'm tired," she agreed. "And I wish you'd go away!"

"So you think attack's the best line of defence?" Robert queried softly, not a scrap put out by her rudeness. He rose and moved towards her, and Kate backed away quickly, until she was brought up short by the kitchen dresser.

He took the loaf of bread from her hands, his expression quizzical. "Do relax, my dear girl. It's a little early in the morning to take up where we left off last night. Right now I'm more interested in food than in making love."

She felt a complete fool, and fiercely resented the fact that he was so coolly in control of the situation. "You've got a nerve! What makes you think that I want you to—that I like you in that sort of way?"

The toast popped up and he removed it. "Come off it, Kate." He brought the butter over and busied himself with spreading it. "There you are. Eat up and perhaps your temper will improve!"

Fuming, Kate applied herself to the toast, but found herself unable to maintain a dignified silence. "You're very conceited. I suppose you think you're irresistible to women?"

There was a little silence, while Kate wished she hadn't spoken. "Conceit doesn't come into it," Robert said quietly. "I'm a realist, which you are not. You liked it when I kissed you, though you'd never admit it. For that matter I did too." He gave a sudden impatient jerk of his shoulders. "Why do you always make such an issue of things? We were both in the party mood last night or it would never have happened."

Kate took a long drink of tea and regained some of her outward composure, though inwardly she was torn by regret and despair. She had always known that she meant nothing to Robert, but it hurt to hear him state it. "My own feelings exactly," she said carefully. "And now if you'll excuse me I'm going to bed. With a bit of luck I might get an hour or two before the calls start coming in."

Robert rose politely, but detained her for a few moments while he asked for more details about Mr. Gooding. "He spent his entire working life as one of our cowmen. A grand old chap. Did his wife go to hospital with him?"

Kate told him that Mrs. Gooding had accompanied her husband in the ambulance, so Robert decided that he would defer his call until later. "I'll be off now," he added. "I can tell when I'm not wanted." At the door he paused again. "I wouldn't have bothered you if I hadn't been so concerned about old Gooding." He raised a hand in casual farewell and was gone.

Kate climbed the stairs slowly, wondering how she could have been such a fool as to imagine for even a few heady moments that Robert had called because he wanted to see her. Unhappiness, combined with the exhaustion of a sleepless night, had produced an overpowering lethargy. Too tired to undress, she pulled off her top clothes and crept into bed.

A hot water bottle, thoughtfully provided by Maggie, gave her a little comfort. It was unlikely that she would sleep, but at least she could rest unless she was called out again. She clutched the bottle to her, wondered if Robert had gone to bed, and sank unexpectedly into sleep.

CHAPTER TEN

THE SNOW LAY FOR SIX WEEKS, though driving was easier after the first few days. When the thaw came the Sussex lanes were inches deep in a disgusting grey brown slush. Kate wondered why she had ever thought country life attractive, and grumbled about it when she returned home after an evening surgery.

Maggie laughed and told her to brace up, there was worse to come. The roof was leaking badly and their bedrooms were in a terrible mess. The weight of the snow combined with the fierce January winds had caused many of the old tiles to slip.

"It only shows now that it's thawing," Maggie observed. "Robert's been saying for ages that our roof needs repairing, but it'll have to wait now until the weather improves."

Standing in her bedroom, Kate surveyed the bizarre collection of basins and saucepans, which were rapidly filling up with dirty water. "So what do we do?" she asked disgustedly. "We shan't get much sleep tonight unless we camp out downstairs."

"No need," Maggie smiled. "Robert says we must move in with him."

Kate was resistant to this idea, pointing out that the sitting-room sofa was quite adequate, and that there was a telephone right beside it. "If I sleep at Robert's it'll be awkward when I'm on call."

Maggie didn't argue, but set about emptying the pots and pans, which were filling up at an alarming rate.

"You need something larger," Robert said, when he came over later to survey the damage. "I'll send down some old tubs from the farm. Come over when you're ready, girls."

"Kate would rather stay here," said Maggie, and Kate blushed when Robert gave her an irritated look.

"Don't be silly, Kate. You'll be much more comfortable with us."

Her objections about the telephone he brushed aside, saying that there was an extension in one of the spare bedrooms. "Surely you can put up with us for a few days?" he asked impatiently, and because it would have been ungracious to refuse, Kate accepted his hospitality reluctantly.

She had done her best to avoid Robert since that morning after the dance. Lady Howard had left Sherringdon very soon after that event, so there had been no reason why Kate should visit the main house. She had applied herself to her work with a single-minded dedication, that had at least won her Miss Andrews' approval, and her comment that it would have been nice if Kate could have stayed on after Dr. Nicholson came back, at the beginning of April.

Ben did ask her if she would help out the first two weeks of his father's return, so that the old man could ease himself back into the practice gradually, but he hadn't suggested anything more long-term, so Kate had accustomed herself to the idea of leaving Sherringdon. She had also resigned herself to the imminent news of Robert's engagement to Diana. The girl was often at the Hall, either alone or accompanied by the vicar's son, Jack. It could only be a matter of time, Kate thought, and Maggie was inclined to agree with her.

"I wouldn't say they're ideally suited, but at least they have a good deal in common."

The superficial things like an interest in farming and horses, but what mental companionship could Diana offer to a man of Robert's intelligence? "None," Maggie agreed with a little sigh. "Once Elizabeth could have given him all that, but she made her choice and she's got to live with it."

"But has she? If she got a divorce wouldn't Robert marry her?"

"No." Maggie sounded very sure of that. "He's older and wiser now. He can see Elizabeth for what she is. That week when she stayed with him cured him for good and all."

"They seemed so close," Kate murmured. "I thought Robert was in love with her."

"So did Elizabeth. It gave her a nasty shock when she realized he was only being friendly, because he wanted to talk her into going back to her husband."

"Oh, Maggie, I'm so glad!" Kate exclaimed, then coloured under Maggie's surprised stare. "Elizabeth's not good enough for Robert," she added hastily. "She's... not a very kind person."

"In plain language a proper bitch," Maggie agreed. "At least Diana's a nice ordinary girl, though she'd better not overplay her hand in encouraging young Jack."

Nice, ordinary and rather dull, but Robert was a hard-headed farmer, not a romantic boy. He would consider it a good bargain if marrying Diana brought him the means to restore his estate to its former glory. And if he wanted the girl, Kate couldn't imagine that Jack's sudden interest in Diana would be allowed to stand in his way.

Lying in bed on that first night in Robert's house, Kate tried to convince herself that she couldn't possibly love a man with such a cold-blooded outlook on life. In the morning, coming down at seven-thirty to find Robert breakfasting alone, she knew the futility of this argument. She would love him whatever he did. She would even be grateful for these few days in his house, for it would be something to cherish when she was far away in Glasgow.

So she sat down opposite him and returned his "Good morning" composedly. There were daffodils on the table, and she stared at them while she waited for the cook to bring her breakfast.

"You're looking tired, Kate. Sleep badly in a strange bed?"

She raised her eyes from the daffodils to meet Robert's concerned gaze. "Yes, that's it. I've got used to Maggie's place."

"I expect you need a holiday. Andy tells me you've been working very hard."

"I expect I do." Kate applied herself to the bacon and eggs the cook had just put in front of her, and thought sadly that there wouldn't be much to remember if all their exchanges were on this level.

"Sorry you'll soon be leaving?"

"No, I'm glad!" Kate exclaimed, with an intensity that made him raise his eyebrows.

"Had enough of country life? Or is it the company that's getting you down?"

"Well...Sherringdon *is* beginning to pall. I miss the bright lights. Oh, you know, the stimulating atmosphere of a big city."

Robert's expression was hard to define, but it was certainly not one of approval. "I see, Kate. Silly of me, but I thought you were getting attached to this place."

"What an odd idea," Kate said brightly, and marvelled at her own ability for deception. Mercifully Maggie arrived then and took over the conversation. Kate sipped coffee and wondered if Robert really minded that she'd been disparaging about his beloved home. She longed to tell him that her idea of paradise would be to live with him here until she died, then she gave a little sigh and attracted the attention of the others.

"Penny for them?" asked Maggie, and Robert answered for her.

"She's worrying in case she's missed out on anything while she's been mouldering in the country. Young Kate's a dedicated career woman." There was an edge to his voice that seemed to surprise Maggie.

"What a funny thing to say! You know Kate's future is fixed up. She's going to work in her brother's practice."

"Until something better comes along. General practice isn't good enough for an ambitious girl like Kate, though it might make quite a useful stepping stone."

"That's not true!" Kate cried. "You're making too much of what I said. Why are you being so nasty?"

Dismayingly near to tears, she jumped quickly to her feet and rushed from the room, snatched up her bag from a table in the hall and made for the front door.

It hadn't been unbolted yet. Because her eyes were full of tears and her hands were shaking, she was clumsy in her attempts to open it. "Oh, damn, damn!" she muttered, and was put firmly on one side by Robert, who had come up behind her silently.

"Let me. It's inclined to stick." He shot the bolt and swung the heavy door wide. The grey weather of the last few days had given way to brilliant sunshine, and even at this early hour it was warm for February.

"Lovely day," Robert remarked, following her out on to the drive. Kate didn't feel up to answering him, but walked off to fetch her car. She was backing it out into the courtyard when Robert appeared in the gateway and waved at her to stop.

"Sorry, I'm in a hurry," she called through her open window, and moved the car slowly forward, assuming he would get out of the way.

He didn't move. He stood bang in the centre of the gateway, his face taut and unsmiling, so reluctantly she brought her foot down on the brake.

"Please, Robert, the surgery!"

"Oh, to hell with the surgery! And anyway, you're early, as you very well know." He strode up to the open window. "Look here, Kate, I'm sorry if I upset you." He frowned down at her, genuinely puzzled. "I was only teasing. No sense of humour, have you?"

"You weren't teasing," Kate retorted, allowing hurt

feelings to conquer her initial impulse to laugh things off. "You meant what you said, and you meant to be unpleasant."

He breathed out heavily in exasperation. "Why should you mind being called a career woman? Isn't that what you are?"

"If you call loving my work being a career woman then I suppose I am, but the way you say it you make it sound like an insult."

He shrugged. "You shouldn't be so touchy. Besides, when it came to the crunch—when you had to decide between marriage and a career—you chose your career, and I don't doubt you would again."

Kate's unhappiness changed to anger at this remark. "You know nothing about it. You've only heard Bill's side of the story—not that I'd bother to tell you mine. Get out of the way!" She trod hard on the accelerator, so that Robert had to jump quickly backwards.

She had cooled down by the time she reached the surgery, to the extent of feeling rather ashamed of herself. That night, before going to bed, she went along to Robert's office, to find him wrestling with the estate accounts. He sat, chin in hand, staring moodily at a pile of bills on his desk.

"Sorry to interrupt. I—I only wanted to say sorry." From his abstracted look his mind was still on his work. "For being rude, I mean. And—and for nearly running you down."

At that his gaze focussed and his expression sharpened. "Yes indeed, you'd have looked pretty silly if you'd had to give me first aid, wouldn't you?" He smiled suddenly with a charm that broke down all Kate's reserves, and she gave a shaky laugh.

"Oh, Robert, must we always quarrel? It would be so much nicer if we could be friends."

"Would it, Kate?" He shifted in his chair and rubbed his forehead wearily. "God, how I hate this job, but my accountant's been after me again."

She looked at him wistfully, wishing that there was something she could do to help. "Robert, I'm so sorry. I shouldn't have bothered you when you're busy."

"No. It was decent of you to come." He picked up the pile of bills and eyed them with a wry expression. "Maggie thinks I need a rich wife."

Kate felt as if she had been struck in the chest. "That'd be—one solution. I won't keep you any longer. Good night."

"No, stay and have a drink with me. I could do with a break."

"If you can really spare the time."

He poured her a sherry and waved her into a chair by the fire. Kate curled her legs up and watched the flames, too heavy-hearted to make light conversation. Robert sat down opposite and watched her thoughtfully.

"Why so solemn?" he queried.

In the flickering firelight he looked gentler and younger, and quite devastatingly handsome. "It's such a mistake—to marry for the wrong reasons," she murmured, hardly aware that she was speaking her thoughts out loud.

His eyes narrowed. "Is that a general observation, or aimed particularly at me?" he asked coldly, and she blushed uncomfortably.

"I—I was just thinking of what you said—about marrying a rich wife. I could never marry for money unless I loved the person too..." Her voice trailed off under his ironical look.

"Couldn't you, my dear? Then you're not as practical as I thought you were. Money is a more durable commodity than love—if it's handled wisely."

"That's horribly cynical!"

"But true. Look around you. How many happy marriages do you see?"

"Plenty," Kate said sturdily. "It's just that you notice the unhappy ones more."

"Maybe," but he shrugged his disbelief. "From al

accounts my parents were madly in love in the beginning, but it didn't last. They gave each other hell for years."

"I was luckier than you, because Mum and Dad were devoted to each other. His job as a geologist took him all over the world and whenever she could she went with him. That was why they were killed together in an air crash. If I loved a man that much I wouldn't want to outlive him either. Mum always said she hoped she would go first." Tears came into her eyes.

"Cheer up, little one," he said quite kindly. "I don't deny there are exceptions to every rule. But even your parents must have quarrelled sometimes."

"Of course they did, but if there's real affection and respect a marriage won't founder on the inevitable clash of personalities."

She spoke with the seriousness of deep conviction, and Robert listened thoughtfully. "It's nice to meet someone who still has ideals," he said unexpectedly. "Mine went a long time ago." He stared into his glass for a few moments and then looked straight at her. "Why did you break things off with my brother?" he asked abruptly.

All these months Kate had longed for the opportunity to try and explain. Now that she had it the right words seemed to elude her. Haltingly she did her best, but watching his impassive face turned towards the fire, she wasn't sure that she had succeeded.

"I haven't put it very well," she ended on a sigh. "And I would have liked so much to make you understand."

He turned to her then. "You don't credit me with much perception, do you? Bill is my brother and I'm very fond of him, but I know how selfish he can be. I had no idea that he expected you to give up medicine completely."

"You mean you think it was unreasonable?" Kate's eyes widened with surprise.

"Of course it was. It would have been a shocking waste of a good doctor—not to mention all that expensive training."

"Didn't Bill tell you why we broke up?" she asked.

"If he had I shouldn't have been so critical. Let's just say that his version was rather different."

"But you do believe mine?" she asked anxiously, and he nodded reassuringly.

"Yes, Kate, and I think you did the right thing in not marrying Bill. You would never have been happy together."

"You've been very understanding, Robert." She blinked away the foolish tears. "I won't keep you any longer. Don't work too late."

"No, doctor," he said solemnly, and she gave him a smile of such warmth that he looked surprised.

She slept that night as she hadn't slept for weeks, and regained so much of her old vivacity that Maggie commented on it one day. "I was getting worried about you, Kate. I don't want to pry, but you had something on your mind, didn't you?"

"Yes, I suppose I did," Kate admitted.

"And now things are better?"

Better, because Robert had been kinder and more understanding than usual. She couldn't hope for anything more, and at least she had the consolation of a rewarding job. On occasions when she felt depressed, Kate would remind herself of the millions of people with worse problems than her own. Surely a hopeless love affair faded into insignificance beside the great human tragedies?

THAT WEEK the builders repaired the roof and the girls moved back into their own wing. Kate hadn't much longer in the practice now, and the patients were just beginning to realize it.

"We'll miss you terribly," the mother of one of

Kate's problem families said. "Doctor Ben and his father are all right, but you understand things better, being a woman yourself."

She was only thirty, but looked ten years older, the result of having six children in quick succession, and a feckless husband who couldn't hold down a job.

Driving back from the surgery that morning, Kate thought how splendid it would have been to organize a local branch of the Family Planning Association. There were so many things she could have done if she'd been staying on, things that a woman doctor could handle more easily than a man. As she drove through the farm she saw Diana riding across the fields with Robert. They had been practising hard in the last week for the point-to-point races that were to be held at the end of March.

"You'll be expected to attend as our local doctor," Robert informed her one evening, and when Kate asked, "Why me? Wouldn't Ben be better?" he smiled and shook his head.

"Ben says he's done it for years and now it's your turn. Anyway, he and Maggie are going up to London that week-end."

Kate commented that they surely didn't need a doctor on the spot. Couldn't the ambulance men give adequate first aid?

"It's always been done," Linda cut in. "Some of the jumps are pretty tough and we've had one or two nasty accidents. It makes people feel better, knowing there's an M.O. present."

So on the last Saturday in March Kate arrived a few minutes after two at the entrance to the muddy field loaned by one of the local farmers. A large banner proclaimed that the Sherringdon and Sherbridge point-to-point was in aid of the local hospital group, and that the entrance fee was one pound for cars, twenty-five pence per person.

Kate leant out of her car to proffer a pound note, but

the man at the gate waved her on with a smile. "We don't charge the M.O. Have a good time, doctor."

Large though the field was, it was already tightly packed with cars, and Kate had trouble in finding a parking space. Gumboots were the thing, she decided, for the day, though fine, had been preceded by a night of heavy rain. She squelched back to the array of tents and stalls, which offered entertainment to those who weren't interested in the racing, spotted an ambulance and made her way over to it. The ambulance men greeted her as an old friend.

"Let's hope we won't be busy, doctor. At least the ground's soft if they fall off!"

Kate laughed and looked about her at the crowded noisy scene. Where was Robert? The first race was about to begin. The riders were lining up on the far side of the field, their horses restive and disinclined to wait for the starting pistol. A gust of wind blew Kate's red hair into her eyes, and she pushed it away impatiently, straining her eyes to see the faces of the riders.

"Like to borrow my glasses?" Robert asked from behind her, and she swung quickly round.

"I was trying to see if you were there. I mean, I thought I might as well back a rider I knew," she rushed on, not wanting him to jump to the wrong conclusion. No, the right conclusion, she thought confusedly. Why, oh, why did love have to have this demoralizing effect on one, making a well balanced sensible girl (or so she liked to think of herself) behave in this idiotic fashion?

"I'm too old for that race," Robert remarked with amusement. "It's for the under sixteens. But if you want a good tip back Johnny Palmer. He rides like a demon. Only hurry up or you'll be too late."

He piloted her through the crowd and pushed her up to the table where people were placing bets. Kate put down a pound note and he whistled. "Reckless little thing, aren't you?"

"It's in a good cause. I take it all the profits go to the hospitals?"

"Minus our expenses." She knew he was one of the organizers as well as one of the competitors. Indeed, the whole family were competing. She waved to Tim and Linda, who were over by the refreshment tent, and spotted Diana arm-in-arm with a tall young man who looked like the vicar's son.

"Isn't that Jack Simmons?" she said. "I thought he was back at university."

"The vacation must have started, but anyway he's been down most week-ends. He and Diana have become very thick lately.

She glanced at him, but his face was impassive. After placing her at what he considered an advantageous position to see as much as possible of the racing, he went off with another competitor.

Kate, who had half expected to be bored, found the novelty of the scene very entertaining. She knew nothing about horses, but listened with interest and amusement to the knowledgeable comments of the people around her. More than one of them recognized her and greeted her in a friendly way.

She watched several races, pleased that Robert had loaned her his field glasses, lost a couple of pounds, saw with a quickening of her pulse that Robert was riding in the next race, and was disgusted to be summoned by one of the ambulance men.

"Kid's fallen out of a tree, doctor. They will climb up to get a good view, though they're not supposed to."

Kate took a last quick look at Robert through the glasses, absorbing every detail of his loved and familiar face, then with a little sigh followed the ambulance man to the first aid post.

The child was a grubby ten-year-old, cheeky in spite of his pallor. Kate diagnosed a greenstick fracture of his forearm, applied a splint and bandage, and told his mother that if he sat quietly in the car it wouldn't do him any harm to watch the rest of the races. Then he would have to go to hospital for an X-ray.

"Cor! Will I have my arm in plaster? One of my mates did last term." Colour was already returning to the young face and Kate felt it was all right to leave him. She struggled back to her old place, trying to hear the commentator's voice, but the shouted remarks of the spectators and the distortion of the loudspeaker made it difficult.

"Who's winning?" she asked a local farmer's wife with whom she was on nodding terms.

The woman waved her programme excitedly. "Nothing in it. The first three are dead level. They'll be out of sight in a minute, round Bateman's wood."

"But who are they? Who's in the lead?" Kate was vainly trying to focus her glasses on the rapidly moving riders.

The farmer's wife said it was difficult to be sure, but she thought it was Robert Montgomery and two others, whose names Kate didn't know. "My money's on Mr. Montgomery," the woman said confidently. "He's won this race every year since he came back from Canada. My hubby thinks he's the best rider in the county, and he should know."

Her husband, a man of few words, grunted his assent, and Kate felt ridiculously proud and happy, like a mother whose adored child has been praised. And it was ridiculous, she told herself sternly. It was positively sickening to be so obsessed with another person. Obsessed she was, however, waiting with a rapidly beating heart, her glasses trained on the white gate that the farmer's wife pointed out to her.

"They should be jumping that any moment. They swing round the side of the wood and then they're at the gate. It's the last big jump and the worst—that's why only the best riders go in for this one. Here they are! What did I tell you? My man's in the lead!"

"Robert," Kate whispered. "Come on, Robert!"

She saw his horse rise to the formidable jump, closely followed by several others, then confusion. Two, maybe three horses down, the riders rolling clear, the rest of the field over and away. Anxiously she tried to focus on the fallen men, but a little crowd of spectators, who had been near the jump, were already surrounding them.

The farmer's wife, who was following the rest of the field, said disgustedly, "I've lost. Mr. Montgomery must have been one of those who fell at the gate."

Kate lowered her glasses, and cast a quick look at the riders who had crossed the finishing line. Robert's bright blue shirt wasn't among the motley collection of colours.

She raced through the crowd to her friends, the ambulance men. "I can't see what's happening," she gasped. "Can you?"

The senior man was already running a stretcher out from the back of the ambulance. "Jock thinks one of them is still on the ground. The other two are up. We'd better take a look. You'll come too, doctor?"

Kate stumbled after them, across a ploughed field still sticky from last night's rain. They splashed through a small stream, ran across another field under grass, and pushed through the group of anxious people gathered round the white gate.

Robert lay on his back, frighteningly still, and so covered with mud that it was impossible to tell what his colour was like. One of the other riders knelt beside him, groping for his pulse, but rose with relief when he saw who had come.

"Thank God you're here, doctor! I'm afraid he's pretty bad."

Afterwards Kate would always consider it the worst experience of her life, those terrible moments when she knelt beside Robert, not knowing how seriously injured he was. Her own heart was thumping with fear and exertion, but Robert's pulse was slow and strong.

She pushed the thick black hair off his forehead, touched a huge bruise on his temple, ran her hands down his arms and legs, and straightened up to speak to the ambulance men.

"He's concussed, but I don't think he's broken any bones. Let's get him back to the ambulance and I'll go over him more carefully."

They were sliding Robert on to the stretcher when Kate saw the third rider, sitting white-faced on the bank, nursing a grotesquely deformed wrist. He was a tough little man, who seemed more concerned about Robert than himself. Walking back with her to the ambulance, he told her how the accident had happened. A bird flying out of a thicket had caused his horse to swerve, so that it landed badly, cannoning into Robert's.

"He will be all right, doctor? Will you be sending him to hospital?"

"You'll both have to go," said Kate, her thoughts on Robert. Was he just concussed, or had he more serious brain damage? She longed to go with him to the Casualty Department, but she knew that it was her duty to stay here until the last race. The ambulance men were well trained and it was only a twenty-minute drive to the hospital.

Her legs felt unpleasantly shaky, so after she had seen the injured men off she sat in her car and stared at the horses lining up for the next race. Someone banged on the car window—Linda, with Tim close behind, both looking taut and anxious.

"We've only just heard. He's not badly hurt?"

"I hope not, but it's hard to be sure. They'll X-ray his skull. Examine him more thoroughly. And admit him, of course." Her voice wavered and Linda, leaning through the open window, gave her arm a friendly squeeze.

"It must be horrid having to examine people you know. Oh, Kate, you look quite white!"

"It was horrible, seeing him on the ground like that. I wish I'd never come." Kate got out of the car and shivered in the March wind. "How many more races?"

"Just two," Tim said consolingly. "Diana's in this one."

"Diana? How can she bear to go on, not knowing how Robert is?"

"She may not have heard about it. We were all down at the refreshment tent, trying to warm up with a cup of tea."

"Didn't you want to watch Robert's race?" asked Kate.

Tim shrugged and smiled. "No point watching. He wins every year."

"Not this time." Linda scowled and kicked at the turf with her riding boot. "Tim and I have been unlucky too. A rotten day! I've had enough."

They left for the hospital in Robert's car, while Kate stayed on reluctantly and coped with the well-meaning people who came up to inquire about Robert and the other man.

"Yes, I'm afraid he was unconscious."

"No, he didn't have a broken leg."

"Just unconscious? No other injuries?" That was Diana at last, pushing her way to the front of the crowd, accompanied by Jack Simmons, her faithful shadow. "He isn't badly hurt?"

"I don't think so, but it's hard to be sure," Kate told her. "Why don't you come to the hospital with me? I'm just leaving."

Diana bit her lip and shook her head vigorously. "I have an absolute horror of hospitals. Be a dear and ring when you've got some news. We should be back at the vicarage by five."

"If we're not, leave a message," Jack said carelessly. "Robert'll be all right. He's tough. Lots of people fall off horses."

"And some are killed," Kate muttered, stung by

their casual attitude, but they were already walking away arm-in-arm and she didn't think they heard. One had to make allowances, of course, for the fact that they had all ridden since early childhood. To them a tumble from a horse was all in a day's work, a calculated risk accepted by all riders. Even so, if Diana was still in love with Robert, Kate thought her lack of concern very strange. It made her wonder if the girl's show of interest in Jack Simmons had turned into the real thing. It was a possibility full of an irony that Robert might not appreciate, though he showed no outward sign of minding.

WHEN KATE ARRIVED at the hospital Robert had been through X-ray and was already in bed in the private wing. She introduced herself to the house surgeon on duty, and he brought her up to date on the medical findings.

"Nothing really," he announced cheerfully. "Skull and ribs O.K. No indication of intracranial bleeding, so we think it's a simple concussion."

"We?" she queried.

"Bodger and I. Our orthopaedic consultant, Mr. B. Hodgson." The H.S. was young and rather full of himself, so it amused Kate to see how deferential his manner became when his chief appeared.

She had never met Mr. Hodgson before, but his reputation was high, and she knew that Robert was in good hands. He came down the corridor from the private wing, accompanied by Tim and Linda, whom he appeared to know quite well. A quiet man, speaking with immense authority, he confirmed what his house surgeon had said.

"Robert's conscious now and wants to go home, but I've told him he must stay in for observation. Linda says you're a family friend, Dr. Ferguson, so try and persuade him to be sensible."

The idea that she had any influence over Robert

made Kate smile. "Does he need persuading?" she asked.

"I'm afraid so. Says it's a busy time on the farm and he'd prefer to stay in bed in his own house. You know what that would mean—he'd be up much too soon. So be a good girl and do your best." He patted her hand in a fatherly way, looked round for his house surgeon, and was off to see another new admission.

The staff nurse in charge on the private wing showed Kate the way to Robert's room, but asked to be excused because she was on duty alone at present. Robert lay flat on his back with his eyes shut, the mud washed away to expose multiple grazes and bruises down the left side of his face. As the door shut softly behind the nurse, Kate pulled a chair forward and sat down by the bed.

Was he sleeping, or had he relapsed into unconsciousness again? She felt for his pulse, was relieved to find it slow and full, and on a sudden impulse clasped his hand to her cheek. She held it tightly, overcome by the emotion she had been forced to suppress.

"Oh, Robert!" she whispered, and a tear rolled down her cheek and dropped on to his hand.

"Do you always cry over your patients?" Robert asked softly, and she let go of his hand precipitately.

She brushed the tears away and wouldn't look at him. "I thought you were asleep," she said gruffly. "Besides, I'm not crying over you, I'm crying because—oh, because I'm tired and I've—I've a headache."

"Then that makes two of us," Robert murmured. "I feel as if my skull's been split in two."

She looked up with quick concern. "Then don't you see? It would be madness to go home. Mr. Hodgson asked me to talk you out of it."

He gave a faint smile, winced and touched his bruised cheek. "I'm open to persuasion. How about holding my hand again?"

Her face flamed and she made to jump up, but he caught her by the arm, his grip surprisingly strong for a man who had been unconscious so recently. "No, Kate, don't go." He shut his eyes but kept his fingers round her wrist. "God, how my head aches!" he muttered, and drifted off to sleep, his grip relaxing as he did so.

Kate stayed where she was for a few minutes, possessed of a curious lethargy that was partly due to sheer exhaustion. Shock and suppressed emotion were more wearing than physical exertion, as any doctor could tell you. The body getting its own back on the mind, she thought tiredly, shut her eyes and tried vainly to relax.

In vain because she fell to worrying as to how much Robert would remember of her behaviour. She had held his hand to her cheek and wept over him, an idiotic thing to do. If he recalled what had happened it would mean embarrassment for them both. The post-concussion state often caused confusion and amnesia, so she could only hope that the incident would be obliterated from his mind by the time he woke up again.

CHAPTER ELEVEN

ROBERT WAS DISCHARGED from hospital on Monday. Ben had a telephone call from the orthopaedic consultant during morning surgery, and told Kate about it over coffee. "Mr. Hodgson wanted him to stay in longer, but he insists on going home. He'll have to take it quietly, though, and old Hodgson wants one of us to check on his condition every day. Any objection?" Ben looked at her doubtfully. "If you'd rather not I'll look in, but you are on the spot."

She had to face Robert some time and the longer she put it off the harder it would be. "It's all right Ben. I'll keep an eye on him. You've enough on your plate with your father back."

Old Dr. Nicholson had come home a few days ago and was to start work tomorrow, morning surgeries only for the first week, then a little visiting, but no night calls as long as Kate was still with them. When she got back from evening surgery it was nearly eight o'clock. Maggie had already been over to see Robert and reported that he was fine.

"His headache's gone. He looks rather tired, though he won't admit it."

"Then I won't disturb him tonight," Kate said quickly. "After all, he was seen by Mr. Hodgson only this morning."

On Tuesday, however, she nerved herself for what might be an awkward encounter. She left Robert's visit to last and when she arrived at the Hall it was nearly one o'clock. Maggie was with Robert, saying good-bye, for she was spending the school holidays on the Continent.

She stood up at once, but Kate told her not to rush off. "I shan't be two minutes. I just have to check Robert's pulse and blood pressure."

Briskly professional, she wrapped the cuff round his arm, asking meanwhile how he felt.

"Better," Robert murmured, watching her steadily as she pumped up the machine. She kept her eyes on the dial, recorded the result, flashed a torch in his pupils and pronounced herself satisfied.

"Good. I'll leave you in peace."

It was proving easier than she had expected. Robert's manner showed no trace of constraint, so probably he remembered nothing of their last encounter. Relieved, she flashed him a bright smile, which was received with a quizzical look.

"What's the rush?" he asked. "Stay and have a drink."

"You shouldn't drink after a head injury," she said severely, and he laughed.

"No, doctor, but I was offering you one! Let's drink to the success of Maggie's holiday."

It seemed ungracious to refuse and it ended up with quite a gathering in Robert's bedroom. Linda perched on the foot of his bed, and Tim lounged in the window embrasure. Kate found herself in the chair by Robert's bed, because there was nowhere else to sit, and tried hard for just the right degree of nonchalant behaviour.

Apparently she didn't succeed, because Robert gave her several sharp glances, and under cover of an exchange between Maggie and Linda, leant towards her. "Something wrong? You seem preoccupied." His brown hand rested lightly on hers, his handsome face, marred by his recent accident, was very close, so that she longed to stroke his bruised cheek.

"I'm... worried about a patient," she lied, and tried to pull her hand away.

"Man or woman?"

"I don't see—" She floundered to a halt.

He smiled with a touch of malice. "I just wondered, since you seem to get so involved with your patients." He lay back on his pillows and shut his eyes, the smile still there.

So he *had* remembered, but he wasn't going to be decent about it and pretend nothing had happened. Flushing, she tipped the remainder of her drink down. "I have to go—I've a surgery this afternoon." She avoided Robert's eyes and said a general good-bye.

That evening she telephoned Ben and asked him to take over Robert's case. She stumbled through some sort of excuse to be cut short in the middle.

"I understand, Kate. Don't worry, I'll be in to see him tomorrow." He sounded a little weary and she felt a pang of guilt. "I'll do some of your visits in return," she promised. "We'll sort it out in the morning."

The evening stretched ahead of her, solitary and unhappy, for Maggie had left to spend the night in London with Lady Howard, before she flew off to Italy in the morning. Kate regretted now that she wasn't leaving at the end of the month, which was in two days' time. Even if she no longer had to see Robert in a professional capacity she couldn't entirely avoid him.

She was staring unseeingly at a television play when the telephone rang. It was Lady Howard, who had heard the news of Robert's accident from Maggie, and wanted to know more details.

"Maggie's so vague, and it's useless asking Tim or Linda," she explained.

Kate did her best to reassure the old lady, but without success, because after firing a number of sharp questions Lady Howard pronounced herself dissatisfied, and said that she would come down tomorrow to see for herself. Thinking of the inevitable reaction from the young Montgomerys, Kate tried to dissuade her, to be brusquely told to mind her own business.

"And you're not to tell them I'm coming. They'll only try to put me off, even Robert."

Most of all Robert, Kate thought with wry amusement, and wondered if the old tyrant had any idea of the extra work her presence would create. Linda, it was true, seemed to have turned over a new leaf lately, and was doing much more to help in the house, so perhaps they would manage.

Next evening Tim took refuge with Kate after supper. "An evening of Aunt Margaret is such a drag. And she threatens to stay till the end of the week."

"Where's Linda?" asked Kate.

"Playing bezique with the old lady," Tim grinned. "I got away before my turn!"

Kate wanted to know how Robert was reacting.

"Looked a bit taken aback when she turned up, but you know Robert. His manners are a lot better than ours, so he kept his cool, unlike us. Linda was almost rude, mainly due to shock," and he grinned again.

"Is Robert feeling better?" Kate asked, and he nodded.

"Heaps better. Ben allowed him up today, but forbids him to do any work until the end of the week."

The next few days were less busy than usual, because Kate and Ben's father were sharing the work. After a hectic month she would have been grateful for the respite, except that it gave her more time to brood. However she looked at it the future was bleak. She wouldn't now be starting with her brother until the end of May, because his present locum wanted to stay on until then. So she would have a fortnight's holiday when she left Sherringdon, and no idea what to do with it.

She didn't want to go to her brother's home, because Angus and his wife would know at once that something was wrong. Families were like that. They couldn't be fooled, and she didn't feel up to answering questions. She would have to arrange a holiday somewhere—in the West Country, perhaps, a good place in the spring, with long walks on Dartmoor to tire herself out, so that at least she would sleep at night.

When she mentioned her plans to Ben he looked doubtful. "On your own? Not much fun, surely?"

"None of my friends are free just now. Besides, it'll be nice and quiet. Time to relax."

"Time to brood as well," Ben said gently, and put his large hand on her shoulder. "Kate, I know how you feel, and I don't like the idea of you going off on your own. Why not stay on at Maggie's place? At least you'd have friends around."

When she shook her head he didn't persist. Checking through the drugs in his black bag, he threw out the remark that he quite missed Maggie. "She's never gone away for a month before. Don't know what's got into her," he grumbled.

"She's gone with some of her colleagues, hasn't she? Perhaps one of them means something special."

Ben jerked his head up with a comical look of outrage. "You mean a man? Maggie's not like that."

"Oh, Ben!" Kate started to laugh, pleased with his reaction to her deliberate remark. "Maggie's an ordinary girl who'd like to get married. It's high time she found someone."

Just for a second she nearly told him the truth, but decided against it. If Ben's expression was anything to go by she had already set him thinking. Whether Maggie had gone off on purpose or not, her absence might produce results. Once she was no longer available Ben might begin to value her more.

As he turned to go out he remembered a message from Lady Howard. "She's quite put out that you haven't been over to see her. She leaves tomorrow, so she wants you to call this evening."

It was a royal command and not to be disobeyed, but even so Kate picked her time carefully. At six o'clock she saw Diana Mitchell drive up, accompanied by Jack

Simmons. Five minutes later she crossed the courtyard and was ushered into the drawing-room by Linda. Robert was dispensing drinks and talking horses with Jack and Diana. Beyond a brief smile in her direction he left her to Lady Howard's company, for which Kate was profoundly thankful.

They sat on a sofa near to the huge log fire, and Lady Howard quizzed Kate very thoroughly on the treatment of concussion. "When I had a fall from a horse I was kept flat on my back for three weeks in a darkened room," she commented.

Kate smiled. "That's no longer considered necessary. Times have changed, you know."

"Not for the better," came the sharp rejoinder. "Can you honestly say the boy looks well?"

Kate allowed herself a quick glance at Robert and admitted that he did look tired. Drawn was a better description, perhaps. Or worried? The ever-present problems of the estate?

At that moment Jack gave a loud guffaw at some remark of Diana's and flung a casual arm around her shoulders. Kate caught the quick flash of irritation on Robert's face before he turned away, and then she thought she understood. Robert didn't like the competition. Whether he loved Diana or not he had always looked on her as his for the asking.

"Jack seemed very smitten by Diana," she murmured, and Lady Howard gave a sour smile.

"I've a feeling it's mutual, and if so Robert has only himself to blame."

"Does he... mind?"

"Robert keeps his own counsel, but he doesn't look very happy about it, does he? They've just been telling us that they're going off to Ireland tomorrow, staying with Jack's relatives and competing in one or two horse shows."

Kate looked at the pair, who were bubbling over with high spirits and pleasure in each other's company.

"They really have much more in common than Robert and Diana do," she said thoughtfully.

"A silly girl and a silly young man," Lady Howard agreed caustically. "They bring out the worst in each other. And now tell me about yourself. When do you leave?"

Kate was spared a long inquisition by the arrival of Diana's parents. Mrs. Mitchell lowered her large frame on to the sofa and talked in a loud voice across Kate. After a minute or two of being squashed between these two formidable women she was rescued by Robert.

"I've a bone to pick with you, my girl." Hand on her arm, he led her to the far side of the room, away from everyone else. "You haven't been very friendly lately, have you?"

Kate stared out at the wide lawns that sloped down to the lake. "I've never seen so many daffodils," she murmured. "How beautiful they are!"

He gave an impatient glance through the window and turned her round to face him, so that she could no longer pretend an interest in his garden. "I know quite well why you've been avoiding me, Kate," he said quietly.

She drew in her breath sharply and backed away from him. "Then if you know," she managed, her voice almost inaudible, "it would be... kinder... wouldn't it, to leave me alone?"

He looked back at her in silence for what seemed a very long time. Kate was conscious of her heart thumping unpleasantly in her chest. She had only to put out a hand to touch Robert. She longed to do so, nearly did. Then he spoke, his voice cool, his face impassive.

"All right, Kate, if that's the way you want it. When do you leave?"

"On Saturday week." The lump in her throat made speech difficult.

His eyes appraised her. "Had a lot of night calls lately?"

"No," she said. "Why?"

"Because you look as if you've been short of sleep. Not nervous on your own, are you?"

"Why should I be?" But she spoke too quickly and without conviction, because he gave her a sceptical look. "Just that you're a city girl, and Maggie's wing is pretty isolated."

"Oh, I'm not scared of *intruders*." She stressed the last word unconsciously and his eyes narrowed.

"Of what, then?"

"I told you, I'm not scared of anything. Good heavens, this is the twentieth century!" Then she spoilt her case by adding, "I wish old houses didn't creak so much. And I swear there are mice." She glared at him fiercely. "And don't you dare laugh!"

"Far from laughing, my dear Kate, I was going to suggest lending you one of the labradors. I should have thought of it before. Some houses have an atmosphere that can affect sensitive people quite strongly, and Maggie's wing is the oldest part of the building. Bits of it date back to the fourteenth century." He gestured at her glass. "Drink up and I'll give you a refill. You're not on duty tonight, are you?"

She sat on the low windowsill and watched him cross the room, touched by his understanding, and relieved by the change in the conversation. What had those words of his meant? She must have misunderstood him, for Robert was not an insensitive or tactless man. It was unthinkable that he would humiliate her so cruelly.

When he came back she asked him which of the dogs she could have. "It's so silly," she apologized. "I've always prided myself on being rational and sensible. How can I be afraid of—nothing?"

"You're a doctor, my dear Kate. You should be able to answer that yourself." Puzzled, she could only stare and he made an impatient and angry gesture. "Don't the psychologists tell us we all have hidden fears? Of death or illness. Of failure or not being loved." His voice was ironical now. "It's not a dark and empty house that scares you, it's the emptiness in your life in spite of your fine career."

So he did know! She gave him one despairing and reproachful look, put down her drink with a shaking hand, and walked unsteadily away from him. No one noticed how upset she was. The young people were engaged in noisy badinage, and Lady Howard was writing a letter, all her concentration needed to hold the pen in her arthritic fingers.

Kate left a few minutes later, carefully avoiding even a glance in Robert's direction. At ten o'clock Tim arrived with Honey, who was the friendliest of the dogs.

"She'll sleep anywhere," the boy said, and indeed it was true. Honey, a little too fat and inclined to waddle, settled herself on the rug by the bed, and Kate turned off the light with the comforting feeling that even if she couldn't sleep she wouldn't be nervous. Each evening Tim or Linda brought Honey over, but of Robert Kate caught only glimpses, driving by in his Land-Rover, at the farm or in the fields with his men. In April work on the land started at dawn and went on until dusk, so that the crops could get off to a good start.

In Kate's last week at Sherringdon the Sussex countryside blossomed into its full beauty. Driving through the narrow, flower-studded lanes, she observed it all with a perception heightened by the knowledge that this was the place Robert loved. She had given up trying to understand why he should have spoken such unkind but perceptive words. Perhaps after all he was simply one of those men who resented career women, and lost no opportunity to jibe at them. It seemed out of character, for Robert was not small minded. It was a puzzle and likely to remain one, for Kate had no intention of risking further humiliation. She would make very sure that she was not alone with him again, in the few days she had left.

"WE SHALL MISS YOU, Dr. Ferguson," Miss Andrews said, at the end of Kate's last surgery. "A lot of the patients ring up now and ask to see the 'lady doctor.'"

Ben, whose office door was open, called to Kate to come in. He was sifting through his correspondence before he set out on his rounds. "I'm late and I've a lot of calls to make. If I don't get time to look in this evening, you won't leave without saying good-bye?"

"Of course not. I'll call in tomorrow morning. I'm not in any hurry to be off."

She had after all no special destination, having decided not to book up in advance, but to go where the fancy took her. In her restless and unhappy mood planning a holiday hadn't seemed worth the effort. She wouldn't be seeing any more patients before she left, but she had a certain amount of paperwork to do, so she spent the afternoon at the surgery, and didn't get back to Maggie's house until five o'clock.

She was sitting over a cup of tea when the telephone rang. Robert, sounding formal and remote, invited her over for a farewell meal.

"Supper tonight? Linda forgot to mention it yesterday." She was silent so long that he asked sharply, "You're doing something else?"

"No," Kate said bleakly, "but I'd rather not come. We—we might as well say good-bye now, don't you think?"

Her voice wavered and he cut in savagely, "God, Kate, do you think *I* want you to come? But Tim and Linda do, so can't we be civilized about it? Do the conventional thing?" When she didn't answer he made an exasperated sound. "Will you come, then? About seven?"

She felt too tired to argue. "All right," she agreed wearily, and he gave an unkind laugh.

"Cheer up. We shan't have to meet again after tonight," and he banged the receiver down.

She should never have given way, for the evening

was even harder to bear than she had anticipated. There were just the four of them, and neither Kate nor Robert contributed much to the conversation, which was kept going by the efforts of Tim and Linda. Robert maintained a face of cool politeness, behind which Kate sensed tension and something else. A desire to be rid of her as soon as possible? Anxiety in case she made a fool of herself?

Several times she caught him looking at her with an expression that was almost hostile. It seemed they were to part as they had met, and even friendship was impossible, between them. As soon as courtesy permitted Kate rose from her chair.

"Must you go?" Linda asked. "It's only ten."

"Do stay," Tim urged, but Robert got up with unflattering alacrity and opened the door.

"I expect she has a lot to do." He stood aside to let Kate pass, and she walked through into the hall on legs that were disagreeably shaky.

The young Montgomerys uttered cheerful good-byes. "Come and see us some time," Linda suggested. "We'd love to have you. Wouldn't we, Robert?"

Robert's reply was cold. "I doubt if she'd come. Kate finds country life boring."

"No, she doesn't!" Linda cried. "She loves it here, and anyone can see she doesn't want to go. If she did she wouldn't look so unhappy."

There was an electric silence. Tim, more sensitive than his sister, gave her a dig with his elbow. "Don't go on, Linda. Play you a game of table tennis?" and he hustled her away before she could commit any more blunders.

Robert opened the front door. "So it's good-bye, Kate." He held out his hand.

She was incapable of summoning a smile. It took every scrap of her self-control not to break down. His grip was firm, and when she tried to withdraw her hand he wouldn't let her.

"Linda's right, isn't she, Kate? You don't want to go, but you will because you put ambition before happiness."

His words made no sense. She gave him a look of bleak despair, wrenched her hand away and stumbled into the courtyard, blinded by the tears she could no longer control. The light burned above Maggie's porch. Kate had left it on because a dark house was so unwelcoming. With trembling fingers she tried to fit her key into the lock, aware that Robert's front door was still open.

He called to her, but she pretended not to hear. She brushed her sleeve across her eyes, slid the key in and pushed the door open, desperate to be alone. Footsteps crunched on the gravel and Robert called again, "Kate! Kate!" but she was through the door and had slammed it shut before he could reach her side.

She slumped against the wall, too exhausted to make any effort.

The doorbell rang, and when it stopped Robert's voice came, "Open up, Kate. You forgot to take Honey."

"I don't want the dog." Kate's voice rose and she struggled to control it. "Thank you, Robert, but I'm going to bed."

There was a little silence, then the bell rang again, longer and more insistently. The next time Robert spoke it sounded as if he was hanging on to his temper with difficulty. "Open this door! I shall keep my finger on the bell until you do."

The nerve-jangling noise began again, and there was only one way to stop it. Kate opened the door slowly and was put firmly to one side by Robert, as he stepped into the hall, followed by Honey. He flicked the inside light on and looked down at her, and now the hostility was open. "Tears, Kate? So you do have regrets, though you'd never admit it!"

"I don't know what you mean." Kate put a hand to

her aching eyes. "Please go, Robert. I'm so tired and I want to go to bed."

"When I've finished with you!" Robert said savagely, catching her by the shoulders and shaking her furiously. His fingers dug painfully into her arms. When he let her go at last she pushed her tumbled hair back and struggled to regain her breath.

"If you had any decency you'd go away," she whispered. "You must know how I feel about you! You must!"

He ignored her plea, grimly determined to have his say. "Yes, Kate, I've known since the day of my accident. If I'd had any doubts your staying away from me would have removed them. What a pity that you always allow your head to rule your heart! When you're a rich middle-aged doctor, maybe you'll have regrets, only it'll be too late then. Much too late."

She was so tired and unhappy that she could make no sense of his words, nor of his anger. When he took her in his arms she showed no reaction. He kissed her once, a hard punishing kiss, that bruised her lips. "That's to remember me by!" He shook her again. "I'm sure you'll be successful, but I doubt if you'll be happy."

She backed away from him and nearly fell over Honey. "Why are you so unkind? I didn't choose to fall in love with you. What's left but work, since I can't stay here?"

"You could stay if you wanted, and well you know it."

"Ben doesn't need me any longer."

There was a short silence while they stared at each other, then Robert said quietly, "I need you, Kate."

The words hung between them, astonishing, unbelievable. She was afraid she had misheard him, too confused to reply. Robert's face twisted into bitterness. "You don't have to say anything. We could have been happy together, but your career comes first, doesn't it?"

His hand was already on the latch when Kate reacted at last. "Robert, you can't mean it! You can't!"

"Of course I mean it, you little fool." He jerked the door open. "Though I wish to God I didn't!"

"Oh, Robert!" She took an uncertain step towards him, still not quite sure. "Medicine means a lot to me, but you mean more. I love you so much."

He still had his hand on the door. When he spoke his voice was harsh. "Don't say things you don't mean, Kate. I'm not like Bill, I'd never let you go. In my book marriage is for keeps, but you'd soon get tired of living in the country—you've made that very plain."

She gave a shaky laugh and started to explain. "I didn't mean it. I said all that because I didn't want you to guess how I really felt. I had no idea—none at all—that you felt the same way."

He studied her broodingly, unconvinced. "Didn't you, Kate? Do you think a man stays up all night waiting for a woman, unless he's crazy about her? After the dance," he added brusquely. "What a let-down that was!"

"But you could have *said* something," she protested.

"Could I, Kate? When you so obviously didn't want to hear? You were as prickly as a hedgehog that morning."

She gave a little sigh. "Because I was afraid of doing the wrong thing. You were so offhand and casual."

"Self-defence," he said dryly, and suddenly she blazed into anger.

"What fools we've been, wasting so much time! And even now you won't believe me. It's hopeless even trying!"

She drooped against the wall, worn out by that fierce spurt of emotion. A draught from the half-open door made her shiver. Then Robert spoke, very quietly. "I want to believe you, Kate. So come and convince me!"

She raised her head, and caught her breath with sudden hope. Robert, the proud and self-contained, looked at that moment as uncertain as a young boy and as vulnerable. With only one idea in her mind, to remove that look from his face, Kate reached up and very gently, kissed his bruised cheek. Robert, smiling for the first time that evening, half turned and kicked the door shut with his foot.

IT WAS THE EARLY HOURS of next morning before he left. Kate slept late and woke to the pealing of the doorbell. She rushed downstairs, Honey trundling after her, belting her dressing-gown as she went.

Linda stood on the doorstep, flushed and excited. "Sorry, Kate, did you think it was Robert? He's told us the news and we think it's great."

"Thank you, Linda. Were you very surprised?"

"Staggered," Linda said frankly. "I always thought it was Diana."

"So did I," Kate admitted, and the little niggle at the back of her mind threatened to cloud her happiness. Would Robert ever have admitted that he loved her if he had still had a chance with Diana?

"When Robert told us this morning, I asked him what made him change his mind about Diana. Because I think he would have married her, Kate, if you hadn't come along."

"And...what did he say?" She waited tensely for the answer.

"He said you made every other woman seem dull, even Elizabeth. That once he'd got to know you, he knew he could never marry anyone else. It's so unlike Robert," Linda said earnestly, "pouring his heart out in that way. Perhaps it's because he's so happy."

She rattled on for a minute or two, but Kate hardly heard her. The last unworthy doubt was banished for ever. She started when Linda shook her arm.

"How soon, Kate? How soon are you getting married?"

She came back to the present a little confusedly. "We haven't had time to make plans yet. Perhaps we'll talk things over this evening."

THEY DID JUST THAT, telephoning their news first of all to Angus and then to Lady Howard. Angus sounded pleased but surprised. With brotherly candour he dismissed Kate's apologies for letting him down.

"Think nothing of it. Our present locum's a splendid chap. We'll ask him to stay on."

Kate's feelings, a little ruffled by these remarks, were soothed by Lady Howard's outspoken approval. "An ideal match. Robert needs a girl who has something in her head."

"Lady Howard!" Kate teased, greatly daring. "How you've changed! I thought you didn't approve of educated women!"

"I like to think that I move with the times," Lady Howard stated with lofty disregard for the truth. "He'll have to teach you to ride, of course, so that you can keep your end up with the county."

"That sounds awful," Kate frowned, when she was repeating these words to Robert. She gave him an anxious look. "Perhaps I'm not really the right wife for a man in your position?"

"Don't be silly, Kate." There was a touch of impatience in his voice. "You fit in here perfectly. They're already working out how they can use a part-timer in the practice."

"Ben!" Kate exclaimed. "I forgot all about him!"

"I didn't. I rang him this morning, and he sends congratulations. I think they were sincere."

They were sitting by the dying embers of the fire in Maggie's sitting-room. Robert drew Kate's head down on to his shoulder.

"Could you get it through your head, my love, that

I'm just a hardworking farmer with an outsize overdraft? That all I have to offer is an inconvenient old house and an overgrown garden?"

But Kate was looking into the future, to a garden alive again with the shouts and laughter of children, to ponies in the stables and swimming in the lake.

"It's a lovely old house," she said contentedly, "and a beautiful wild garden. Our children will think it's paradise, and so shall I."

THE AUTHOR

Sheila Douglas is a British writer who has often written about the world of medicine and the people whose lives are caught up in it—doctors, nurses, hospital staff and patients. She brings a special warmth and understanding to her stories. This is clearly evident in such books as *Sherringdon Hall.*

South from Sounion

Anne Weale

Lucia knew instinctively that her sister's latest suitor, the wealthy, sophisticated Nicholas Curzon, was not at all the right sort of man for Cathy. And it was with many regrets that Lucia agreed to accompany the two of them on a holiday to Nicholas's Greek island home.

Gradually, Lucia came to realize that it had not been Nicholas's intentions toward her sister that had so troubled her from the beginning.

For no matter how hard she fought against it, Lucia knew she'd fallen in love with the man her sister planned to marry.

CHAPTER ONE

COMING OUT OF THE CINEMA into the bitter-cold February night, Lucia Gresham shivered, and turned up the collar of her shabby tweed coat. The coat was three winters old, and she had planned to buy a new one during the January sales. But then Cathy, her younger sister, had set her heart on a glittering, sequinned evening top to wear at New Year parties. So Lucia had agreed to postpone buying a new coat until next autumn.

Lucia was a teacher in the Infants' Department of the Alderman Evans Primary School in the unbeautiful north London suburb where she had spent the greater part of her life. She taught a class of nearly forty six-year-olds. On open day, her pupils' mothers often said they didn't know how she could cope with so many obstreperous youngsters. But, although she would have preferred a smaller class, in order to give each member more individual attention, Lucia found the children easy to manage. It was her wayward, twenty-year-old sister who taxed her patience, and caused her many restless nights.

As she walked briskly home to the large, ugly Victorian-Gothic villa built by Great-Grandfather Gresham, the problem of Cathy made her sigh and wrinkle her forehead.

If only Cathy would fall in love with some nice, steady boy, she thought longingly. But, at the moment, everything about her sister was calculated to put off nice, steady boys, and to attract quite the opposite kind. It was Lucia's nightmare that, if Cathy continued to pursue her present course, she might end up wrecking her life. Yet how was one to stop her? Any attempt to curb her only made her even more reckless.

It was not a long way from the local cinema to the quiet, tree-lined side road where the two girls lived. As Lucia reached the gates of "Montrose", she was alarmed to see a car parked in the driveway. Not an ordinary car, but a dashing dark blue Lancia Flaminia convertible.

For some years now, "Montrose" had been divided into two flats. The tenants of the top flat were a young married couple, Peter and Janet Sanders. Lucia often "sat" for them. They had a three-year-old son, and a second child on the way. She felt certain the car had nothing to do with them. Their friends, if they had cars, drove Minis. So the Lancia must belong to one of Cathy's escorts.

Her heart sank. The raffish young man with the scarlet Austin-Healey had been bad enough. But a man who drove a sleek, *de luxe* Lancia seemed likely to be even more of a menace.

Entering the house by way of the back door, she took off her coat and hung it up. Then, shivering, for it was almost as cold in the stone-flagged passage as it was out of doors, she went into the kitchen, and put on the kettle for coffee.

The kitchen had two doors; the one through which she had just passed, and another leading into the hall. When she had attended to the kettle, she opened the hall door, expecting to hear voices from the drawing-room.

All was silence. Puzzled, she walked down the hall to the foot of the wide, Turkey-carpeted staircase. A man's overcoat and dark silk scarf had been tossed carelessly over the rail against the thick newel post. On the table, near the drawing-room door, lay a pair of gloves—gloves of thin, supple leather with cut-out knuckles, the kind racing drivers wore.

There was still no sound of conversation, or music.

Usually, her sister's first act on coming home was to put on the radio, or her record-player.

Yet, even though it seemed odd that Cathy and her unknown companion were not talking, Lucia was unprepared for the scene which met her eyes when she opened the drawing-room door.

The only light in the room was that given out by the bars of a portable electric fire set down close to the brocaded settee which faced the empty fireplace. Cathy was sitting on the settee, but all that could be seen of her was a pair of long, slender legs, and a fashionably brief skirt. Her face, and the upper part of her body, were obscured by the dark head and broad back of the man leaning over her, kissing her.

Lucia's immediate reaction was that of anyone unwittingly intruding on two people locked in an ardent embrace. Her instinct was to retreat, if possible unseen.

But this reflex was swiftly displaced by a thrust of anger at Cathy's folly in letting the man make love to her. To the best of Lucia's knowledge, she could only have met him very recently. A fortnight ago, she had been gadding about with Roger, the Austin-Healey driver.

However, before she could think of anything to say, the man on the settee raised his head, and Cathy caught sight of her.

"*Lucia!*" With a squeak of mingled shock and dismay, she pushed free of his arms, and jumped up. "Oh—you gave me such a fright. I thought I was seeing things. What are you doing back so early? I thought you'd be out till eleven."

Lucia did not reply, but reached out her hand to switch on the overhead light. Briefly, she took in her sister's dishevelled blonde hair, and smudged lipstick. Then, hoping he would register the hostility in her eyes, she looked coldly and critically at the man.

By now, he also had risen. But he showed no sign of sharing Cathy's discomfiture. Casually straightening his tie, he returned Lucia's frosty stare as calmly as if she had found them discussing the weather.

His composure heightened her antagonism. For it seemed to her that any decent man would have the grace to look embarrassed. Not only was he unembarrassed, he had the audacity to walk towards her, hold out his hand, and say pleasantly, "I'm Nicholas Curzon. How d'you do?"

Lucia ignored his hand. "Good evening," she answered icily. Then, to Cathy, she said, "I've put the kettle on. Go and make some coffee, will you, please?"

In normal circumstances, Cathy would have resented this curt request, and told her sister to do it herself. But, for once, she did meekly as she was bidden. Lucia and Nicholas Curzon were left alone together.

"You look half frozen," he said, smiling at her. "Come to the fire and get warm. It's damned cold out tonight, isn't it?"

Much as she longed to toast her chilled hands and feet, she had no intention of allowing him to disarm her with affable small talk. "Yes," she said crisply, and sat down in a high-backed wing chair.

He moved the electric fire to where it would warm her. Then he straightened, and glanced round the room. Evidently it was the first time he had taken any notice of his surroundings.

The unflattering hard glare from the overhead light revealed a large, high-ceilinged room, which had not been redecorated or refurnished since before the war. Once a month, Lucia dusted, and vacuumed the huge faded carpet. And each spring she climbed to the top of the household step-ladder to dust the elaborate plaster cornice, and the tasselled lambrequins at the top of the heavy, interlined brocatelle curtains. But the two girls rarely sat in the drawing-room. Cathy was seldom at home and, when Lucia had time to relax, she did so in her great-grandfather's book-lined study across the hall. The dining and morning-rooms were now their bedrooms and the downstairs cloakroom had been converted into a bathroom.

"That's a fine piece you have over there." Nicholas Curzon crossed the room to examine a French, pilastered bureau-bookcase standing against the far wall.

It was the only really valuable piece of furniture in the house, and Lucia took particular care of it against the day when they might need to sell it. She was a good deal surprised that he had the discernment to recognize its worth.

While he was looking at the bureau, she scrutinized him. He was not a tall man, nor was he a good-looking one. Indeed, as she noted his lack of height, and his swarthiness, she was surprised that Cathy wished to be kissed by him. She would have expected her sister to find him rather repulsive. In spite of his surname, he obviously had a strong strain of foreign blood in him. No Englishman ever had such thick, black hair, and his nose was a big, bony beak jutting out between his high cheekbones. In profile, with that Punch-like nose, and an equally prominent chin, he looked quite ugly.

Then he turned, and strolled back towards her, smiling a little, as if her antipathy amused him. And, as she met his twinkling dark eyes, Lucia realized with dismay that there was something about him far more potent than mere handsomeness. She could not define it precisely, but she felt it like the warmth of the fire. Suddenly, she was afraid. For she knew then that, if he chose, this stranger with his money and his magnetism could be the instrument of Cathy's downfall.

He offered his cigarette case.

"I don't smoke," she informed him frigidly.

"Wise girl. Do you mind if I do?"

She shook her head, and watched him light up, and sit on the arm of the settee. She knew he must be got rid of, but how was she to go about it?

"You and your sister are not at all alike," he remarked, after some moments of silence.

"We are only half-sisters," she said. "My mother died when I was born. Cathy's mother was my father's second wife."

Why her father had married a shallow creature like Connie was something she would never fathom. It was hard to conceive of a more ill-assorted partnership and, from as far back as she could remember, they had made life misery for each other—or would have done, if her father had not been away from home for long periods.

"How long have you known my sister, Mr. Curzon?" she asked him.

"We met last week at the Maybury"—this was the West End hotel where Cathy worked as a florist. "I was waiting for someone in the lounge, and she was changing the flowers."

Lucia said blunty, "In other words, you picked her up."

The lines around his dark eyes crinkled. It was difficult to judge his age, but he was certainly well over thirty—much too old for a girl of twenty. "You could say so—yes," he agreed. "But life would be very dull if one never spoke to anyone without a formal introduction, don't you think?" And then, before she could reply, "How do you earn your living, Miss Gresham?"

"I'm a teacher," she said stiffly. "What do you do?" Besides preying on foolish, impressionable girls, she added mentally.

"I make containers—aerosols mainly. You probably have some in the house. Your hair spray, perhaps, or your furniture polish."

"I see." She wondered if he actually ran the business, or if he had inherited a directorship, and spent most of his time squandering the profits on high-powered cars, and wining and dining girls like Cathy.

Her sister came back with the coffee, and he got up to take the tray from her. While she had been out of the room, Cathy had tidied her hair, retouched her makeup and put on a short dance frock. She had also recovered her poise.

"We're going to an after-theatre party," she told Lucia, with a glance which defied the older girl to object.

Lucia bit her lip. She could not forbid Cathy to go with him, as a parent might have done. (Not Connie Gresham—she would have encouraged her. It was she who had given Cathy her misguided values.) Yet she felt as responsible as a parent.

Unexpectedly, Nicholas Curzon said, "Would you care to come with us, Miss Gresham?"

"Oh, Lucia loathes parties, and meeting people," Cathy put in. "Where is the worthy Bernard tonight?" she asked her sister.

"He's starting a cold, so he decided to go to bed early."

Cathy made a slight grimace. She despised Bernard Fisher, and could not understand Lucia's friendship with him. Secretly Lucia herself found him a little stolid and unimaginative. But they had some things in common—he was also a teacher—and it was really a case of half a loaf being better than no bread at all. Every Friday, they went to the cinema together, and had supper at the local Chinese restaurant.

"So that's why you're back early. I suppose you didn't dare go to the Soo Chow alone in case someone tried to pick you up," said Cathy, not without malice.

Lucia flushed, and ignored the remark. She knew it was ridiculously old-fashioned, but she did not like eating out at night without someone with her. What made her scruples even more absurd was that she was not the kind of girl men tried to pick up. Nevertheless, going to a restaurant alone would have been more of an ordeal than a pleasure to her.

"I wouldn't have thought you were a shy person, Miss Gresham," said Nicholas Curzon, as she handed him a cup of coffee. His dark eyes glinted with mockery. "You seem to me rather formidable."

"I'm not shy," she said looking away. "I'm merely old-fashioned. I believe in the conventions. Most of them are simple common sense. Where is this party you are going to? Are they your friends, Cathy? Or yours, Mr. Curzon?"

"For heaven's sake, Lucia, I'm not a child," Cathy said, with a flash of anger. And indeed, in her sophisticated dress, with her face rather heavily made up, she did look older than she was, and well able to take care of herself.

Nicholas Curzon laughed, and reached for her hand. "You didn't tell me you had a Guardian Sister, Cathy," He caressed her soft fingers. "I thought you lived on your own."

"The subject didn't come up," she said, with a shrug.

"No, it didn't, did it?" Again he laughed, his teeth very white against his gipsy-dark skin.

Cathy laughed with him, but a little uncertainly, as if she were not quite sure what the joke was.

He turned to Lucia. "The friends are mine, Miss Gresham, and you have my word that they are entirely respectable, and the party will not develop into an orgy. To allay any other doubts you may have, I am not married, and I never drink when I'm driving. You may rest assured that your sister will come home quite unscathed. If you still don't trust me, I can only suggest that you chaperone us."

For a moment, Lucia was tempted to call his bluff. She felt sure it was only a bluff. But then she realized that going to the party with them would probably only worsen matters. Cathy would be so furious that she might carry out her threat to leave "Montrose", and set up on her own. It was a threat she flung at Lucia every time they had a row. This time she might really do it.

Not that she would be able to maintain her independence for long. She was incurably extravagant, and had no idea of budgeting her wages. But if she did leave home, even for a few weeks, it might precipitate the ultimate act of folly which Lucia had always dreaded, and hoped to avert.

Aloud, she said, "I don't think that will be necessary, Mr. Curzon. But when you bring Cathy home, I'd be grateful if you'd be as quiet as possible. We have tenants living upstairs. Mrs. Sanders is expecting a baby, and she doesn't sleep well just now. It would be a pity if your car disturbed her unnecessarily."

"Don't worry. We shan't wake her." He glanced at his watch. "We'd better be on our way, Cathy." He helped her to put on her evening coat. "Goodnight, Miss Gresham. I expect we shall meet again." With a bow, and that annoying gleam of humour, he took his leave.

After the car had purred off into the night, Lucia collected the cups, and turned out the fire. As she crossed the hall to take the tray to the kitchen, Janet Sanders peered down from the landing.

"Are you just off to bed? Or do you feel like a natter?"

Lucia smiled up at her. "Hello, Janet. How goes it? I'll just dump this in the kitchen, and then I'll come up."

"Peter's gone to bed, but I stayed up to finish this jacket," said Janet, holding up a tiny white matinée coat, as Lucia came into her sitting-room. She grinned. "Also I'm dying to know about Cathy's latest. What a gorgeous car! What is its owner like? We looked out of the window when it drove up, thinking it must be someone coming to see us. Then we saw Cathy getting out. But I only glimpsed the top of her boy-friend's head."

Lucia sat down by the fire. "Oh, Janet, what am I to do with her?" she said, rather desperately. "She's just waltzed off to a party with a man who's got WOLF written all over him. When I came home, they were in the drawing-room, kissing each other. She only met him last week. He picked her up at the Maybury. She can't know anything about him."

It was Janet's private opinion that Cathy Gresham was a thoroughly spoilt little baggage, and that Lucia was much too soft with her. For instance, it was quite abominable the way Cathy never raised a finger to help keep their flat, or the large back garden, in order. She treated her home as if it were a hotel, and Lucia a willing drudge. Every cent she earned, she spent on herself. And when she had frittered through her wages, she sponged on her sister. Poor Lucia had hardly a decent rag to her back. Yet, to a discriminating eye, she was no less attractive than the younger girl. Her trouble was that she was nearly always tired and worried. But when she was relaxed, when her grey eyes lit up with pleasure and she showed her beautiful teeth in that rare, radiant smile of hers, she could look charming, thought Janet.

"You worry too much about her, my dear," she said. "After all, she's nearly twenty-one now. If she makes a hash of her life, it's her responsibility, not yours."

"Yes, I suppose so," Lucia agreed, with a sigh, "But she's so mixed up, Janet. She thinks clothes, and parties, and gadding about are the most important things in life."

"Maybe they are for her. Everyone is different, and it's hopeless to try and impose our ideas on other people," Janet said wisely. "Some people's idea of happiness is having a bigger and better washing machine. Other people want to climb mountains, or go to Australia. What *I* would like is a rambling old house in the country, and five or six children. But I'm afraid we won't be able to afford any more after this one is born"—patting the bulge under her house-smock. "You can't change Cathy's nature, Lucia. She'll never be like you—not in a million years."

"I don't want her to be like me. I only want her to be happy."

"What about your own happiness? Isn't that equally important?"

"But I am happy," Lucia said quickly.

Janet looked sceptical. "Are you?"

"Of course I am. Why shouldn't I be? I enjoy my work, and I think I'm reasonably good at it. I have quite a few friends. I expect I'll get married one day. What more could I want?"

Janet decided to speak plainly. She and Peter had lived at "Montrose" for two years now. During their first six months there, Mrs. Gresham had still been alive. So Janet knew how unfairly Connie had treated her stepdaughter. She had not been deliberately unkind. But she had made use of Lucia without ever giving her anything in return. All her affection and interest had been lavished on Cathy. Lucia, the ever-reliable maid of all work, had been treated with a kind of patronizing tolerance which must often have been more hurtful than actual ill usage.

Now, Cathy was battening on her sister's good nature even more ruthlessly than Mrs. Gresham had done. And since Cathy wasn't likely to change, it seemed to Janet that the only solution to the problem was for Lucia to alter.

"You may not be unhappy—but that isn't the same as being happy," she told her frankly. "Look, why don't you go abroad this year? You know you've always wanted to travel, and you're free for six weeks in the summer. You could go all over the place, and it wouldn't necessarily cost you a lot."

"Oh, Janet, how can I? I couldn't leave Cathy here alone. You know what a hopeless cook she is, and she'd never be able to cope with the cleaning and everything."

"Well, I daresay the place would be in a bit of a shambles by the time you came back. But would it matter? And as far as food goes, she could have her breakfasts and weekend meals with us. And we'd make sure she didn't throw any wild parties, or get up to any other mischief," said Janet persuasively. But even as she made the offer, she knew what Lucia's answer would be.

"It's very sweet of you, Janet," she said warmly. "But I couldn't possibly jaunt round Europe, leaving you with a new baby and Cathy on your hands. You'd end up a nervous wreck."

"Then why don't you both go?" Janet persisted. "Cathy hasn't made any plans for her fortnight, has she? You really should have a proper holiday this year, my dear. Day trips to the coast are all very well, but what you need is a complete break. It would do you the world of good."

"Cathy would only come if we went to some smart, expensive place, and she had a lot of new clothes to wear," Lucia said dryly. "She would hate staying at a cheap *pension*. Her idea of a foreign holiday would cost too much, and mine would bore her to tears."

"Well, it's high time she learnt to fit in with other people sometimes," Janet commented tartly. But she could see that a holiday abroad would be no fun for Lucia if Cathy was constantly griping because they could not afford to mingle with the smart set.

THE NEXT DAY was Saturday. As she had alternate Saturdays off, Cathy lazed in bed until eleven. By the time she got up, Lucia had been out for the weekend shopping, ironed a pile of clean laundry, polished the large hall floor, cleaned all the windows inside, and done the cooking.

She was having five minutes' rest when Cathy drifted into the kitchen, in a green silk peignoir trimmed with ostrich feathers.

"Did you have a good time at the party?" she asked, getting up to put on the kettle.

Cathy shrugged. "Not bad. It was a super house, and

there were some gorgeous clothes there. But the people were all rather old and dull."

"Mr. Curzon isn't exactly a youth."

Her sister went to the pantry to fetch the bottle of pure lemon juice which she drank every morning for the benefit of her complexion. Although she was so lazy in other ways, she never neglected her various beauty régimes.

"Oh, I don't mind older men," she said presently, wincing at the sourness of the juice. "It's older women who bore me. There was one woman there in *the* most super black dress. But she had a face like a bun, and great flabby arms, so it didn't do a thing for her. You can't wonder their husbands lose interest when they let their looks go. She must have been *eighty* round the beam."

"A good figure isn't everything," said Lucia. "Most people put on weight as they get older—men too."

"I think fat people are disgusting," said Cathy scornfully. "They ought to diet and exercise. I'm never going to lose my figure."

There were moments when her intolerance towards other people's imperfections exasperated Lucia so much that she wanted to shake her. But she said only, "You're lucky. You can eat what you like, and it doesn't make any difference to you."

Cathy perched on the edge of the kitchen table, and lit a cigarette. "Aren't you going to lecture me about Nico?" she enquired, with a challenging glance.

The kettle began to whistle. Lucia turned off the gas, and made two cups of instant coffee—black for Cathy, and with milk and sugar for herself. "Would it do any good?" she asked quietly, over her shoulder.

"No, it wouldn't!" Cathy said sharply. "And the next time you carry on the way you did last night, I'll walk out of this dump, and find somewhere decent to live. I'm sick of being treated like a kid!"

"So you've said before."

"This time I mean it. What gives you the right to dictate to me? You're only three years older than I am. You fuss and nag like some dreary old maiden aunt."

Lucia turned to face her. "Oh, Cathy that isn't true! I've never dictated to you. If I fuss a little, it's only because I don't want to see you get hurt."

"Don't worry—I won't be. I can take care of myself."

"That's what Margaret thought, and look what happened to her," said Lucia, reminding her of a girl who had used to live further along the road.

"Margaret was a fool," retorted Cathy. "She fell in love. I won't make that mistake."

"What do you mean?"

Her sister sipped her coffee. "Being in love never lasts. It may be fine while it does, but it always wears off sooner or later. One day you snap out of it, and find you've got to spend the rest of your life being an unpaid nanny and housekeeper. Well, that's not going to happen to me. I'm going to marry for the things which *do* last—a nice house, lots of clothes, a good time."

Lucia stared at her, appalled by the ring of conviction in her voice.

"What's more, I think Nico may be just the man I've been looking for," her sister continued reflectively. She glanced at the kitchen clock, and slid off the table. "By the way, I shan't be in to lunch. Nico's picking me up at twelve-fifteen, and we're driving out to the Hind's Head at Bray."

And she sauntered out of the room to go and get ready.

AFTER SHE HAD EATEN her solitary lunch, Lucia lit the fire in the study This was where she always spent Saturday afternoons during the winter. Sometimes she read, or sewed. Sometimes she curled up on the big black leather Chesterfield, and remembered other afternoons, long ago, when her father sat beside her, telling her about all the places he had seen since he was last at home.

Malcolm Gresham had been a journalist. He had made his name as a war correspondent and, after the war, had travelled the world from Kitimat to Kalgoorlie. In the course of these peregrinations, he had fallen under the spell of the Greek Islands. It had been his plan, when Lucia had finished her schooling, to give up being a newspaperman, and return to the islands for good. He had been tired of living out of a suitcase, and of the ephemeral nature of his work. He had wanted to settle down, perhaps to write books.

Providing he continued to support her financially, Connie Gresham had not cared if she never saw him again. It was only his love for Lucia, and her need of a settled home while she was growing up, which had prevented him from cutting adrift years before. Cathy was all Connie's child, and had nothing of her father in her.

Perhaps his plan would have been realized. Perhaps they would have lived on Hydra, or Mykonos, or one of the other islands in the Aegean. But, when Lucia was seventeen, Malcolm Gresham had been killed. It was ironic that, having come through wars, riots and various natural disasters without a scratch, he should have met his end in a car smash between London Airport and his home.

However, on this particular afternoon, it was not of her father, or of what-might-have-been, that Lucia thought as she sat gazing into the fire. The problem of Cathy had taken on a new urgency since her sister's extraordinary statement just before she went off to dress for her lunch date.

Had she meant what she said? Was it really her intention to marry not a man, but a way of life? Of one thing Lucia was sure. She had met Nicholas Curzon only once but, on the strength of that encounter, she would be prepared to stake a year's salary that there was no thought of marriage in *his* head. He was merely amusing himself.

About four o'clock, she put more coal on the fire, and made a pot of tea and some toast. It was already dusk, so she drew the velour curtains, and sat watching the firelight flicker over the rows of leather-bound volumes lining the walls. She had not slept well the night before, and presently she began to feel drowsy. Swinging her legs on to the Chesterfield, she decided to have a short nap.

She must have been asleep for some time. When she awoke, the fire was dying down again. She yawned, and sat up, rubbing her eyes.

"Good evening," said a voice from the shadows.

Lucia nearly jumped out of her skin.

"I'm sorry—I didn't mean to startle you." Nicholas Curzon switched on the table lamp beside the chair where he was sitting, and tossed the end of a cigarette into the fire.

For an instant, Lucia could hardly believe her eyes. "What are you doing here?" she exclaimed.

"Cathy came home to change her clothes. She told me to wait for her in here. You were sleeping so peacefully, it seemed a pity to disturb you," he explained, smiling at her. And then, as if he were an old friend of the family, entitled to make himself at home, he rose to replenish the fire.

In the moment while his back was turned, Lucia tugged down her skirt, and smoothed her rumpled hair. Glancing at her watch, she saw it was nearly seven o'clock. She had been sleeping for more than two hours. Not that it mattered. She had no plans for the evening. What did vex her was how long this man had been watching her sleep.

As if he knew what she thinking, he said, "Don't worry—your mouth wasn't open, and you weren't snoring. You did twitch once or twice. Were you dreaming?"

"I—I don't remember," she said brusquely. "What time did you and Cathy come in?"

"About twenty minutes ago. This is a very pleasant room. May I look at your books?"

"If you wish."

His mouth twitched slightly at the stiff formality of her tone, and he gave her a quizzical look, but did not say anything. As he turned to go to the bookshelves, he noticed a watercolour above the fireplace. "Hello... where did this come from?"

"It belonged to my father. It's a painting of the port at Hydra, one of the Greek Islands."

"Yes, I recognize the place."

"You've been to Hydra?" Unbidden, interest kindled in her.

"Several times. Have you?"

She shook her head. "I might have gone, if Father hadn't been killed. He liked the islands so much, he was planning to live there."

"Did he also like the Greeks?" he asked keenly.

"Yes, very much. Why?—Don't you?"

His dark eyes gleamed with amusement. "I am half Greek myself, Miss Gresham." He smiled, and touched his hooked nose. "I inherited this from my mother's father, Nico Tyropoulos. Don't tell me my fine Greek nose has escaped your notice."

"I did think you weren't entirely English," she admitted.

"I am almost entirely Greek," he replied, rather dryly. "I have been brought up as an Englishman, but I am still Greek in my instincts. Does that allay your qualms, or increase them?"

"I don't know what you mean," she said warily.

"You don't like me, do you?"

"I scarcely know you, Mr. Curzon."

"You don't like me," he repeated. This time it wasn't a question, but a flat statement.

Lucia began to simmer. Usually, it took a good deal

of provocation to bring her to boiling point. But this man's mere presence annoyed her. "Is there any reason why I should?"

He had taken a book from the shelves, and was about to open it. Without glancing at her, he said carelessly, "No—but I should be interested to know why you appear to have taken an immediate and powerful dislike to me."

She flushed. "You aren't obtuse, Mr. Curzon. It must be perfectly obvious to you."

He leafed briefly through the book he was holding, then replaced it on the shelf. Coming back to the fireside, he said, "You can't keep your sister on a leading rein for ever, you know. If she hasn't learnt sense by now, it's unlikely that she ever will."

Lucia lifted her chin, and gave him a sparkling look, "If you had a sister of twenty, would *you* approve of... of her association with someone of your age?"

"It would depend on the man," he replied. "But I should certainly not be so unwise as to show my disapproval, Miss Gresham. That would be asking for trouble."

"You would do something, I presume?" she said, with a snap.

"Not unless I had reason to believe that the man was a thorough scoundrel. Is that your reading of my character?" His mouth took on a wry twist. "I may not be an Adonis, but do I look such a deep-dyed villain to you?"

His teasing goaded her into saying, "You can hardly expect me to think you a thrustworthy person."

His eyebrows lifted. "Why not?"

"You told me yourself that you only met Cathy a week ago. Last night—" She broke off, hot colour suffusing her face.

"Last night I kissed her," he supplied. "Do you disapprove of kissing, Miss Gresham?"

Lucia's thin hands clenched. "Yes, I do—when it doesn't mean anything."

"What should it mean?" he asked mockingly.

She said, with anger and scorn, "I doubt if you'd understand if I told you, Mr. Curzon. I don't think we speak the same language."

"Possibly not. But I think Cathy and I have a pretty fair understanding," he answered negligently.

"Cathy pretends to be worldly—she isn't really. Why can't you leave her alone?" she exclaimed, exasperated.

"Wouldn't that be rather rude when I have already asked her to have dinner with me?" He took out his cigarette case, and made to offer it to her. But before she could wave it away, he forestalled her by saying, "Oh, no—I forgot. You have no vices, Miss Gresham."

Lucia felt then that, if she stayed with him a moment longer, her temper might run away with her. She had already mishandled the conversation. Instead of discouraging him, she had probably egged him on to pursue Cathy even more diligently.

Picking up the tea-pot, which she had left on the tiled hearth, she placed it on the tray. Nicholas Curzon moved to open the door for her. But while she intended to leave the room without speaking again, he had something more to say.

Holding the door-knob, so that she could not escape until he let her, he said, "You know, Miss Gresham, it's one of the curious quirks of human nature that the most censorious people are those with hidden weaknesses. You seem very anxious to protect your sister from the hazards which beset pretty girls. Is it possible, perhaps, that you envy her... opportunities? Naturally you'll deny it—but I can't help wondering if, under that strait-laced exterior, *you* would like to be soundly kissed by someone untrustworthy."

Afterwards, Lucia was sure that, if she hadn't been holding the tray, she would not have been able to stop herself slapping his face. As it was, she stood quivering with fury until, with that maddening half-smile, he opened the door.

She was still seething when, ten minutes later, Cathy came into the kitchen. "I don't know what time I'll be back, so don't wait up for me. I suppose you're going upstairs to watch TV with the Sanders'?"

"Possibly," Lucia said shortly.

"How do I look?" Cathy asked.

She was wearing the iridescent evening top, and a long, narrow silk-jersey skirt, with a slit at the back to allow her to walk in it. Her hair was piled high, and she had on her matched blonde hairpiece, and ear-rings from the Dior boutique in Conduit Street. Together, the switch and the ear-rings had cost more than her sister had spent on herself in a year.

Yet as she stood there, posed like a model girl, Lucia found it impossible to grudge her these expensive adornments. She was so enchantingly pretty, it gave one pleasure just to look at her.

"You look lovely, Cathy," she said, with sincere admiration.

"I wish I had a fur wrap instead of this thing," her sister said, putting on her evening coat. "We're going to Nico's flat, and then dining at the Hilton."

"To his flat? Oh, Cathy—" Lucia started.

The younger girl cut her short. "Don't flap. He has to change, hasn't he?"

"But you won't go in with him, will you? Surely you can wait in the car?"

"Oh, Lucia, don't be so old-fashioned," Cathy retorted impatiently. "Of course I shall go in with him. I want to see what it's like. But you needn't worry—I shan't let him take me back there, after we've dined. I'm not such a fool as to fall for the 'nightcap' routine."

"I don't think you ought to go in at all," said Lucia. "*He* may be planning to stay there."

"No, he isn't. He booked a table at the Hilton from

where we had lunch. Anyway, he has a housekeeper, so I can always scream for help if he does try to pounce," her sister added flippantly.

Lucia was not amused. "She may not live in. She may not be there in the evenings."

"Oh, for Pete's sake!" Cathy expostulated. "What an old Mrs. Grundy you are. Mummy never used to fuss like you do. She was much more broad-minded and modern. Anyway, I haven't time for an argument. Nico is waiting. See you tomorrow. 'Bye." She hurried out, leaving a faint fragrance of "Jolie Madame" behind her.

About eight, Peter Sanders came downstairs, and tapped on the study door. "Coming up to watch the box, Lucia?"

"I don't think so, thanks, Peter. Not tonight."

"You look fed up. Anything wrong?"

Lucia shook her head. "No, I'm just a bit tired, that's all. I think I'll have a bath, and go to bed early."

"Are you sure? There's a good show on later, and we've got some salami and pickled onions." He smiled at her. He was a big man, tall and broad, with a kind, easy-going personality, and endearingly sticking-out ears.

Lucia smiled back at him. But, for some unaccountable reason, she felt like bursting into tears.

"No, even pickled onions won't tempt me tonight," she said, with a shaky laugh.

"Well, see you tomorrow, I expect. Goodnight, Lucia."

"Goodnight."

After he had left her, she lay back on the Chesterfield and put her hands over her face. Once, when Janet had been upset by some minor catastrophe, she had seen Peter comfort her. He had put an arm round her, and gently rumpled her hair. "Never mind, love. It's not the end of the world."

Sitting alone in the study, and remembering that moment of tenderness, Lucia longed for someone who would comfort her like that when things went awry. She had never felt more lonely in her life.

NEXT MORNING, before she started to cook, Lucia went to Cathy's bedroom to ask if she would be at home for lunch.

"Yes, I'm not going anywhere today," her sister said, sitting up in bed. "In fact you'll be pleased to hear that I shan't be seeing Nico for a while. He's going to New York for a fortnight. So that's one weight off your mind for the time being, isn't it?"—this last on a note of sharp sarcasm.

It was indeed. But Lucia said only, "Oh, is he? Are you going to get up, or stay in bed?"

"I've nothing to do, so I may as well stay here." Cathy reached for her quilted bed-jacket. "You might bring me a cup of coffee, if you're not busy."

The day was cold, but dry. After lunch, Lucia decided to wrap up warmly, and go for a walk in the nearby park.

"Would you like to come?" she asked her sister.

Cathy looked out of the window at the sullen grey sky, and leafless trees. "Are you mad? It looks freezing out there. I'm going to stay in the warm and do my nails."

"Perhaps Roger will turn up," said Lucia. For now, in comparison with the obnoxious Nicholas Curzon, Roger seemed relatively innocuous.

Cathy shrugged. "If he does, I shan't ask him in. He was beginning to bore me before I met Nico."

During the following week, Cathy stayed in every evening. Lucia was not sure what to make of this unprecedented occurrence. She was glad of her sister's company, but at the same time, she had a disquieting feeling that this was the lull before the storm. Cathy made no further reference to "Nico", as she called him, but that in itself was suspicious. And she sat about with a slight, secretive smile on her face—like someone hatching a plot, thought Lucia uneasily.

The weekend passed, and Monday came round again. On Monday evening, Cathy came home in a fretful mood.

"Why can't we have a TV like everyone else?" she demanded, over supper.

"I don't particularly want one. I'd rather read. But you can get a set—if you're prepared to pay for it," Lucia said mildly. "Can you spare ten shillings a week, or whatever the rental is?"

"Why should I have to pay for it? I bet you'd watch it, if we had one," Cathy said petulantly. "I don't know why you always go on as if you can hardly make ends meet. I give you three pounds a week. There's the Sanders' rent, and your own salary. We can't be all that hard up. We don't have to pay any rent."

"You forget about the rates," said Lucia. "And this year we simply must have the outside of the house painted. Goodness knows how much that will cost. There are all sorts of expenses which you never think about."

"I don't know why we go on living here. Why can't we sell it, and live in a nice, modern flat? I loathe this ugly old place."

"You know I went into all that after Father died, and before we made the top floor into a flat," Lucia reminded her. "I'd like a modern place, too. But when you work it all out, we're better off staying here until one of us gets married."

"I'm surprised the worthy Bernard hasn't popped the question by now. Presumably that's what he has in mind," said Cathy mischievously.

"Don't be silly—of course it isn't. Bernard and I are just friends," Lucia said flatly.

"Well, in that case, don't you think it would be a good idea to get out and about rather more? You'll never get married if you never meet any men. Or are you still hoping that, any day now, some gorgeous male will stride into your life, and you'll take one look at each other and be happy-ever-after?" Cathy enquired derisively.

Lucia flushed. "I may be nearly twenty-four, but I don't think I need panic yet."

Nevertheless, as she sat up in bed that night, reading a book from the Public Library, her sister's jibe fretted at the back of her mind. Presently, unable to concentrate, she turned off her bedside lamp.

And as she lay awake in the dark, she realized that, while twenty-four was not old, it was perhaps rather late in the day to be cherishing dreams of the kind she held in her heart. For although Cathy had spoken in jest, she had come very close to the truth. Ever since she had been old enough to think about love and marriage, Lucia had believed that some day, somewhere, she would meet a man who would love and cherish her always. It was simply a matter of waiting for Fate to arrange it.

But lately, during the long, dismal months of this winter, small doubts had begun to erode her once rock-sure conviction. Now, suddenly, she wasn't sure any more. As Cathy had said, she never met any men—except other people's husbands and fiancés. Apart from her weekly outing with Bernard, the last time she had had a date was back in her training college days.

Naturally you'll deny it—but I can't help wondering if, under that strait-laced exterior, you would like to be soundly kissed by someone untrustworthy.

As Nicholas Curzon's mocking words echoed in her mind, Lucia buried her face in the pillow. "It isn't true!" she thought fiercely. "I don't envy Cathy...I don't. If I can't have my kind of love, I'd rather have nothing at all. I'll never want those empty kisses."

TUESDAY...WEDNESDAY...THURSDAY. As another week passed swiftly by, Lucia's apprehension mounted. Soon

Nicholas Curzon would return from his trip to the States—and then what? Perhaps, during his fortnight in New York, his interest in Cathy would have dissipated, she told herself hopefully.

On Friday morning, she woke up with a slightly sore throat, and vague aches in her joints. She took some aspirins, and wished it were Saturday so that she could stay at home and keep warm.

It was pouring with rain as she walked to school, and still drizzling at twenty to four. Shivering and sneezing, Lucia hurried home. She lit a fire in the study, and turned the oven on low to heat up the casserole she had prepared the previous afternoon. Then she swallowed some more aspirins, filled a hot water bottle, and went thankfully to bed.

At half past six, Cathy returned. Hoarsely, Lucia called out to her.

"No, don't come in. I think I've got 'flu," she explained, when Cathy appeared in the doorway. "Don't tell Janet, will you? She'll insist on coming down to look after me, and then she'll catch it, and so will Peter and Mark. I'll be all right. I just need a few days in bed."

By next morning, her head throbbed so that she could hardly bear to raise it. Cathy took her temperature and then, off her own bat, rang up the Maybury to say she would not be at work that day.

"Oh, you shouldn't have," Lucia said feebly, when she was told.

Cathy had also telephoned their doctor. He came round at midday, confirmed Lucia's own diagnosis, and scrawled a prescription for Cathy to take to the chemist.

"I'll look in again on Monday. You'll probably be feeling better by then. There's a lot of this about at the moment, and the worst of it is usually over in forty-eight hours," he said bracingly.

Surprisingly, because Lucia had thought she would

be terrified of catching the infection, Cathy spent the whole weekend doing what she could to ease her sister's discomfort. For part of the time, Lucia was feeling too ghastly to care what was going on around her. But as the fever and the piercing headache subsided she began to be touched by the younger girl's helpfulness and sympathy.

"You have been a brick this weekend," she said gratefully when, on Sunday evening, her sister washed her face and hands for her, and gently brushed her tousled hair.

"I'm not completely useless, you know," Cathy answered off-handedly.

Then she smiled, and it seemed to Lucia that a new rapport had sprung up between them, a more sisterly feeling than either of them had felt for a long time.

The 'flu had driven all thought of Nicholas Curzon out of Lucia's mind. But Cathy had not forgotten him. She was in her sister's room when, later that night, the telephone rang. Her indrawn breath and excited rush to the hall told Lucia all too clearly that she had been right in sensing that his absence had been no more than a hiatus in their relationship.

In her haste, Cathy left the bedroom door open. So Lucia could not avoid hearing her side of the conversation. Nor could she help a certain amusement at the way Cathy contrived to say their number without any trace of eagerness in her voice.

"Oh, Nico—you're back, are you? Did you have a good trip?" Lucia heard her say coolly.

But, presently, she asked him to hold on a moment, and came back to close the bedroom door. So her sister did not overhear the rest of what they said to each other.

The call lasted for about a quarter of an hour and, when Cathy came back, she made no reference to it. But there was a light in her eyes which made Lucia's spirits sink. Clearly, Nicholas Curzon had not lost interest. And Cathy's brief spell of fireside evenings was over.

ON MONDAY MORNING, Cathy went to work as usual. Lucia stayed in bed until ten. Then, as her temperature was back to normal, she got up and went to the study, and put a match to the fire Cathy had laid.

At mid-morning, Janet came down with hot milk and home-made scones.

"Oh, you're up. Is that wise? Cathy said you were better, but oughtn't you stay in bed a bit longer?" she said anxiously, when she discovered Lucia in the study.

"I'm practically well again. I expect I'll be back at school tomorrow or Wednesday."

Janet looked dubious. "I doubt if the doctor will let you go back this week. You look awfully washed out, my dear. And even this two-day 'flu leaves one very run down and depressed, you know."

It had certainly spoiled Lucia's appetite. She managed to swallow the milk, and eat one of the scones, so as not to hurt Janet's feelings. But they made her feel rather sick. The only thing she fancied was fruit and, as it was raining heavily, she could not ask her friend to go out and buy some more oranges for her.

Janet could not leave Mark alone upstairs for more than a few minutes, but she promised to pop down later. After she had gone, Lucia opened her bag, and peered at her reflection in the little mirror of her powder-case. "Washed out" was an understatement, she thought dismally. She looked as pale and pinched as if she had been laid up for weeks. A wave of post-influenza depression swept over her. Two large tears rolled down her cheeks, and dripped on her faded woolly dressing-gown.

It was at this moment, when she was on the brink of having an unrestrained howl, that someone tapped at the door. Thinking it was Janet back again, Lucia blinked away her tears and croaked, "Come in."

When Nicholas Curzon walked in, she wanted to die where she sat.

"Hello," he said with a smile. "I didn't ring the bell because I didn't want to drag you to the door. May I come in? How are you feeling today?"

And before she could collect her wits—which had never been so wildly scattered—he shut the door, dumped some parcels on the nearest chair, and began to shed his tweed overcoat.

"W-what are y-you doing here? Cathy's at work," Lucia stammered, flushing deep crimson.

"I know. I came to see you. I hear you've been laid low with 'flu. As a matter of fact, I expected to find you in bed. In which case, I was going to enlist the person upstairs to chaperone us," he added with a bland look. He bent to the discarded parcels, and tore off their rain-spattered wrappings. "Fruit... books... and some records. You have got a gramophone, haven't you?"

"Cathy has one," she said dazedly.

He brought a box of downy, golden peaches to the table beside the sofa, then the books, and the shiny-sleeved records.

"I had 'flu myself before Christmas. It makes one feel very low. Is a doctor keeping an eye on you?"

"Yes... yes, he's coming today," she said, still bewildered. She looked at the things he had brought her. "I—I really don't know what to say."

His dark face creased with amusement. "I can guess what you're thinking. *Timeo Danaos et dona ferentes.*"

She knew it was Latin, but not what it meant.

"It's from Virgil's *Aeneid.* 'I fear the Greeks, even though they offer gifts'," he translated. "Am I right? Was that what you were thinking?"

She mustered some slight self-possession. "It wasn't. It is now," she said.

He laughed, and sat down beside her. "I have no devious motive, Miss Gresham. I came because, last time we met, I was rather unkind to you. I'm sorry. Shall we forget it?"

It was not easy to be dignified in pyjamas and an ancient dressing-gown. And the fact that Nicholas Curzon was immaculately groomed from the crisp white edges of his cuffs to his black silk socks made Lucia even more conscious of her disarray.

But she said, as composedly as possible, "I had already forgotten it, Mr. Curzon."

Obviously, he knew too much about women to believe that this statement was true. But, whereas most men would have had the grace to accept the snub, he promptly capped it by saying, with an impudent twinkle, "A masterly set-down, Miss Gresham."

By now, it was dawning on Lucia that he had, by bringing presents, placed her in an awkward position. To be pointedly hostile would make her seem rude and ungracious. Yet to allow herself to be disarmed by his offerings would be equally galling. He had her in a cleft stick, damn him.

There was a pause. She fiddled with the tassels on the cord of her robe, and tried to appear unaware that he was taking in every detail from her carelessly-brushed hair and unpowdered nose to the scuffed velvet toes of her bedroom slippers.

It was really unpardonable of him to catch her in this state, she thought furiously. He must have known she would be looking and feeling a mess. Or perhaps the women of his mileau could afford to look elegant even when they were ill. *They* probably lay about in ravishing negligées, with every eyelash in place, and their hair tucked inside pretty, frilly boudoir caps. Cathy had one to hide her rollers. But Lucia could never set her own hair successfully, and it was her one extravagance to go to the hairdresser every Friday, after school. As the 'flu had made her miss last week's visit, her short brown hair had long since lost all style, and was curling in every direction.

When the pause had lasted much too long, and still she could think of nothing to say, she looked at the five or six books he had brought her. The one at the top of the pile was a collection of colour plates of Greece which she had seen and coveted in a bookshop some weeks earlier.

As she opened it at the title page, she saw, written on the fly-leaf—"To darling Nico, with love from Francesca."

"Do you often go to Greece, Mr. Curzon?" she asked, wondering who was Francesca.

"I'm hoping to spend Easter there." He leaned towards her, and turned the pages until he found the one he wanted—a picture of a small harbour, with fishing *caiques* moored at the quay, and a blue sea glittering in the sun. "A holiday there would do you good," he said, his face close to hers. "In summer it would be too hot. But in April the climate is perfect."

"Yes, I daresay it is," she said stiffly. She did not like being so near to him. It made her want to edge away.

To her relief, he rose to his feet. "I must go now. I have a luncheon appointment. No, don't get up." His mouth quirked slightly at the corners. "I've disturbed you enough as it is. I can see myself out. Goodbye."

And before she had time to phrase an aloof but civil expression of thanks, he had picked up his coat, and was gone.

A few minutes later, Janet reappeared. "Was that the doctor I heard? What did he—" She spotted the peaches and broke off. "Goodness, what luscious peaches! Who brought them? Not Bernard Fisher?"

Lucia explained.

"Well!" said Janet, wide-eyed. "What's the idea, d'you suppose?" She grinned. "Don't say he's after *you* now?"

"Oh, Janet, how can you laugh?" Lucia said crossly. "You wouldn't be amused if the wretched man had caught you looking like this."

"No, I suppose I wouldn't. Though you don't look as bad as all that." Janet paused. "I had the impression that he was rather a nasty piece of work. But whatever his morals may be, he *is* attractive, I gather?"

"Attractive? What do you mean?"

"Well, if he wasn't attractive, you wouldn't have cared what you looked like."

This remark made Lucia so annoyed that, for the first time since they had known each other, she looked at her friend with real anger.

"That had absolutely nothing to do with it. I couldn't care less what he thinks of me. I just don't like being barged in on by strangers, that's all."

Janet saw that she was genuinely upset by the man's unexpected visit, and made haste to change the subject.

"No, of course not," she answered soothingly. "Now, what about lunch? Could you fancy a nice poached egg?"

At four, the doctor looked in. He sounded Lucia's chest and back, and asked questions about her health before the attack of 'flu. Finally, he enquired how much she weighed.

When she told him, he said, "Hm... it might be a good idea to try and put on a few pounds. I fancy you were rather run down before this bug got hold of you. Made any plans for your holiday yet?"

She shook her head. "When can I go back to school, Doctor?"

"Not this week," he said firmly. "And if I were you, as soon as the term breaks up, I should try to get away for a bit. The weather should be better by then. A few days at the coast would do you a world of good. You teachers are lucky, you know. You may be run ragged in term time, but at least you get good long holidays."

After his visit, Lucia went back to bed. Although she had done nothing all day, she felt as exhausted as if she had been on her feet since breakfast time.

She was sleeping when her sister came home, and

did not wake up until eight o'clock in the evening. "Oh...I thought you'd be out tonight," she said, when she found she was back.

"No, I shan't go out until you're fit again. Where did the peaches come from?" Cathy enquired.

Lucia had left them in the study, untouched. The books and records she had put away in a cupboard.

"Mr. Curzon called this morning. He brought them."

"Nico?" Cathy looked startled. After a moment, she said, "That was nice of him. Did he stay long?"

"About ten minutes. When are you seeing him again?"

"I don't know yet. He asked me to ring him as soon as you were up and about."

Lucia sat up in bed. "Cathy, you didn't mean what you said one day about marrying for money, did you?"

"Oh, Lucia, don't let's go into all that again. I'm tired, and you're not well. This isn't the time for an argument."

"I don't want to argue. I just want to know if you meant it—or if you were only trying to shock me?"

Cathy gave her a long, thoughtful look. "Yes, I meant it," she answered, at last. "And I meant what I said about Nico. It's a pity he's so dark and foreign-looking. But he isn't actually repulsive, and one can't expect to have everything. So, if I can get him to marry me, I will. It won't be easy. He's not the marrying type. But I think I know how to handle him. Even clever men have their weak spots. And if I can bring it off, it should be just what I want."

Lucia said nothing, but slumped back on the pillows, with her eyes closed.

"I'm sorry, sweetie," her sister went on. "But after all, it is *my* life, and I am entitled to live it my way—not yours. I just don't want what you want. I don't believe in this love thing."

February passed. March began with a mild spell. Then the rain and cold winds returned, and the sky was grey again. For the first time in her teaching career, Lucia longed for the end of term. She could not throw off the after-effects of the 'flu. She went to bed early, but woke up tired and listless. She drank more milk, and ate lots of eggs and cheese. But she still flagged, and felt dreary. There seemed to be nothing to look forward to. Even when summer did come, it would probably be wet, she thought pessimistically.

By now, Cathy was seeing Nicholas Curzon once or twice a week. Whether it was he or her sister who was regulating the pace of their relationship, Lucia had no means of telling. It seemed that all she could do was resign herself to the situation.

Then, one morning, Cathy dropped a bombshell which jerked her out of her lethargy.

She should have realized something was afoot when she came into the kitchen to find her sister there ahead of her.

"You're early," she said, in surprise. For after a date with Nicholas, Cathy was usually late getting up the next morning.

"I know. But I couldn't sleep. I was too excited."

"Excited?" Lucia felt a thrust of alarm. "Surely he hasn't asked you—"

"To marry him? No—not yet," her sister cut in. "But he has made another suggestion." At the expression on Lucia's face, she burst into laughter. "*Not* an improper one, sweetie. I think by now he realizes *that* wouldn't wash."

"What then?" Lucia asked, puzzled.

"He wants me to go to Greece for Easter."

For some seconds, Lucia said nothing. Then, "Cathy, you can't!" she exclaimed. "For heaven's sake, Cathy—you can't."

Again, the younger girl laughed. "That's what Nico said you would say. So you are invited too, my pet. You're to come with me, as chaperone."

CHAPTER TWO

April in Greece! In the few seconds before Lucia's common sense reasserted itself, the pictures in the book Nicholas had lent her flashed temptingly past her mind's eye. She had a vision of herself lying on a beach in hot sunlight, with nothing to do but bask, and swim, and eat the delicious Greek dishes her father had told her about.

"It's out of the question," she said sharply. "I'm surprised at you even suggesting it."

"Why is it out of the question?" Cathy asked, frowning. "Oh, I knew you'd blow your top at the idea of my going alone. But if you come with me, it couldn't be more respectable. Give me one good reason why we can't go."

"I can give you half a dozen reasons. The most obvious is that we can't afford it."

"It would only cost us our fares, and some spending money. The night flight to Athens is seventy-six pounds return. That's one hundred and fifty-two pounds for the two of us. At most, we wouldn't spend more than a couple of hundred."

"Unfortunately, we don't happen to have two hundred pounds to spare just now," Lucia retorted crushingly. "And if we had, I'd think twice before blowing it all on a holiday."

"We've got more than two hundred. I've looked in the bank deposit book, and there's nearly three hundred."

It was on the tip of Lucia's tongue to say that she had had no right to look at the book. But as the deposit account was officially a joint one, she could not fairly accuse her sister of prying.

"All that money is earmarked for more important things," she said. "Having the house painted is bound to cost at least a hundred. It may even come to more than that. And we must have it done. The place is beginning to look derelict."

"I don't care if it falls apart," said Cathy. "I may not be living here much longer. But if it's the expense which worries you, why can't we sell that old bureau in the drawing-room? If it is a genuine antique, it should be worth more than enough to cover our fares."

"It's not the expense which worries me," Lucia said swiftly. "That's merely a practical objection. I'm much more concerned with the moral issues."

"What moral issues, for Pete's sake? I can't see anything *im*moral about being asked to make up a house party."

"How do you know it will be a house party? It may be just you and Nicholas."

"Considering how pure you are yourself, it's amazing how quickly you jump to nasty conclusions about other people," Cathy said acidly. "If Nico wanted to seduce me, he wouldn't bother to lure me all the way to Greece. He'd have made a pass at me weeks ago. The fact that he hasn't is one of the reasons why I think he's getting serious about me." She laughed. "He may not have begun with what you'd call 'honourable intentions'. But lately he's been quite exemplary. Well, perhaps not by *your* standards, sweetie. They're rather exacting. But, by mine, he's been positively saintly."

"I wish you wouldn't talk like that, Cathy. It sounds so... cheap," Lucia said, with a frown of distaste.

Cathy shrugged, but her face was flushed as she answered, "Well, whether you come or not, *I'm* going to Greece—and there's nothing you can do to stop me. I'll raise enough money somehow. I may even be able to pay the fare in instalments. One can do that now, I believe. I'll enquire about it today." And she marched off to her room, and presently left for work without saying goodbye.

WHEN LUCIA RETURNED from school that afternoon, she told Janet what had happened.

"Surely there must be some way I can stop her?" she concluded anxiously. "How old do you have to be to hold your own passport? Is it eighteen, or twenty-one?"

"I'm not sure. I think it's eighteen," Janet answered, looking thoughtful. Then, to Lucia's astonishment, she went on, "But I don't think you should try to stop her. I think you should both go."

"*What?* Oh, Janet, you can't be serious? Go to Greece as that hateful man's guest? I wouldn't dream of it."

"There's just a chance that 'that hateful man' may shortly be your brother-in-law, my dear. No, let me finish"—as Lucia began to protest. "Supposing he *is* beginning to take Cathy seriously? It's not beyond the bounds of possibility. She's extraordinarily pretty, you know, and men do fall for pretty faces, and lovely figures. Well, if he is thinking of marriage, have you any right to interfere?"

"But she doesn't love him," said Lucia. "And she's much too immature to marry anyone."

Janet shook her head. "I don't agree. Knowing Cathy, I think marriage to a well-off, indulgent older man might be the best thing for her. I doubt if she has the capacity to love anyone very deeply. Some people haven't. It's not their fault, it's the way they're made. I daresay it has some advantages. If they can't love intensely, they can't have their hearts broken either."

"No, I suppose not," Lucia answered, rather absently. Until now, it had never occurred to her that Cathy might achieve her cold-hearted ambition to become Mrs. Nicholas Curzon. Oddly, she found this new concept almost as repugnant as the other possible outcome of the affair.

"I certainly can't see Cathy as the wife of a poor man," Janet went on. "She simply isn't cut out for love in a cottage—or even in a semi-detached. Peter and I aren't hard up. But, if Cathy married someone like Peter, she'd either run him into debt, or nag him right round the bend."

Lucia had to admit there was a good deal of force in Janet's views. But Cathy was so very young. Surely it was possible that she might yet meet someone whose love would compensate for any material sacrifices she had to make?

When she said as much, the older girl looked sceptical. "Anything is possible. I think it's extremely unlikely," she commented frankly. "You must try to be realistic, Lucia. I don't want to offend you, but the fact is that Cathy's been hopelessly spoilt. Your stepmother never said, 'no' to her. And even you tend to let her slide out of most responsibilities. As I see it, the only solution is for her to marry someone who can afford to go on spoiling her."

She jumped up to comfort her son who, playing under the table, had banged the top of his head. "Oh, poor love—what a nasty old bump! Never mind, Mummy'll soon kiss it better."

"But, Janet, she isn't even attracted to him," said Lucia, remembering Cathy's remark that it was a pity Nicholas was so dark and foreign-looking. "How can she spend the rest of her life with someone whose only appeal is his money?"

Janet lifted her son on to what remained of her lap, and gave him a cuddle. "Physical attraction never lasts long anyway—not unless there's a mental attraction as well. Cathy must find him reasonably personable. I don't believe she's so hard-boiled that she'd marry a man who repelled her. What is it about him which you dislike so much, Lucia? It's not only because you're worried about Cathy, is it? I have the feeling that it goes deeper than that. You'd dislike him under any circumstances."

"Yes, I would," Lucia said crisply. "And so would you, if you met him. He's too darned sure of himself. He looks at women as if...as if he had only to smile, and they'd fall at his feet."

"Perhaps a lot of them do," Janet suggested.

"Possibly—but that's no reason to suppose that they *all* will."

"What you mean, I imagine, is that he appears to think he could charm *you*," said Janet shrewdly.

Lucia flushed. "He doesn't just think it—he's sure of it. He—" She paused to steady her voice. "He's even had the gall to accuse me of being jealous of Cathy."

"He said that? Good lord, what conceit! No wonder you don't like the man. So what did you say?"

"I just gave him a withering look, and left it at that. But I felt like hitting him."

"I should think so, too. Why didn't you tell me before?"

"Because every time I think of it, I get so angry I could throw things."

"Have you told Cathy this? It might put her off him."

"I doubt it. She would probably agree with him. Life is difficult enough as it is without her accusing me of sour grapes."

Mark clambered off his mother's knee, and returned to his play. He was a quiet, contented little boy, with Janet's chestnut-and-hazel colouring, and his father's sticking-out ears. Less adventurous than most three-year-olds, he would potter all day with a strange assortment of household cast-offs.

Watching him, Lucia said, "If I envy anyone, it's you."

"Do you?" Janet looked reflective. After a moment,

he said, "You know, Lucia, I've sometimes felt that ou made a mistake when you took up teaching as a areer."

"A mistake? But I love it. What do you mean?"

"Yes, I know you enjoy it now. And you obviously ave all the qualities a good teacher needs. But you adn't set your heart on being a schoolmistress before our father was killed, had you?"

"Well, no," Lucia conceded. "But I was only just eventeen when the accident happened. At that time, I adn't settled on any career. As soon as I'd taken my A evels, we were going to go abroad together."

"In other words, becoming a teacher was forced pon you by circumstances. It wasn't really your vocaion."

"I wouldn't put it quite like that. I had to start thinkng about a career. But I wasn't forced to take up teachng. I chose it."

"Yes, but would you have made the same choice if ou hadn't been left with your stepmother and Cathy n your hands? Or would you have gone in for omething... well, less safe and steady?"

"I don't know. Perhaps—why do you ask?"

"It's obvious from the photographs you've shown ne that you're very like your father to look at. I have he feeling you're like him in other ways, too."

Lucia looked puzzled. "I still don't see what you're etting at."

Janet hesitated, choosing her words. "You say you nvy me," she began. "But, apart from the fact that 'm happily married—and most women hope for that— don't think my kind of marriage would suit you at all. t's too placid for you, too predictable. Your father pent most of his life on the move. I think there's a lot f his restlessness in you, only you've had to repress it. 3ut no one can repress their nature for ever, and if you vere to marry someone as settled as Peter, you'd have o go on doing it. And however much a woman loves a man, she can't be completely happy if his way of life doesn't suit her."

"Well, I expect you're right," said Lucia. "But I may not have much choice in the matter. No one has proposed to me so far, and I can't see any prospect of it in the foreseeable future. I'm beginning to think I may never get married at all."

Her tone was light, and she smiled at her friend as she spoke. But Janet guessed that it cost her a pang to say it.

"Oh, rubbish!" she answered, at once. "You're much more attractive than you realize. If you spent a bit more on yourself, instead of subsidizing Cathy's extravagance, you could look quite stunning. Instead of letting her buy lots of new things for this Greek trip, you should buy yourself two or three outfits. You can't go in last summer's old things."

"I'm not going at all. I told you—I wouldn't think of it."

"Now you're being pig-headed," said Janet. "Look, however much you personally detest this Nicholas Curzon do try to look at the situation dispassionately. You can't stop Cathy going to Greece, any more than you can stop her marrying him, if that's what he has in mind. But if he has other ideas, he can't do much harm with you there. Besides, a couple of weeks in the sun is just what the doctor ordered. You *need* a holiday, Lucia. And don't you see? The best way to take the wind out of both their sails is to do what they least expect. Who knows? You may thoroughly enjoy it."

"What?—As the guest of a man I can't stand?"

"Sometimes life plays strange tricks," said Janet. "This could be a blessing in disguise. If you go to Greece, you may meet someone you *can* stand. If I hadn't done something which I didn't at all want to do, I would never have met Peter."

"I think it's highly unlikely that any of Nicholas Curzon's cronies will turn out to be *my* future husband,"

Lucia answered sardonically. "They're probably all as objectionable as he is."

She was already in bed when her sister came home that night. Next morning, Cathy left for work without a word about the Greek project. But, as she seemed quite cheerful and friendly, Lucia concluded that her enquiries about paying the air fare on the instalment plan must have been satisfactory.

It was Friday. After school, Lucia went to the hairdresser. Then she met Bernard Fisher at their regular rendezvous, and they went to the cinema together.

"You seem preoccupied this evening," he said afterwards, as they were on their way to the Soo Chow restaurant.

With a guilty start, Lucia realized that for the past five minutes he had been talking to her about the film, but she had no idea what he had said.

"Sorry, Bernard," she said contritely. "I'm afraid I was wool-gathering."

"You were rather absent-minded last week." He took her arm to steer her across the main road. "There's nothing wrong, is there, Lucia?"

"No, no—nothing's wrong." As they reached the opposite pavement she saw, in the window of a travel agency, a British European Airways poster of a hot landscape and, in the background, the Acropolis. Quickly, she averted her eyes.

At the Soo Chow, a Chinese waiter ushered them to their usual corner table, and presented them each with a menu. Lucia shut her mind to thoughts of Greece, and concentrated her attention on the question of what to eat.

Bernard was facing the entrance to the restaurant. A few moments after he had given their order to the waiter a look of surprise came over his face.

"Isn't that your sister?" he asked, with a nod in the direction of the door.

"Cathy—here? No, it can't be. She's gone to the

theatre tonight," said Lucia, without glancing round. As Bernard had met Cathy only once, and that a long time ago, he probably did not remember her very distinctly.

"I'm sure it is," he persisted. "There's a man with her—a dark, French-looking chap."

"What!" Lucia swivelled in her chair. "Oh, no!" she murmured aloud, as she saw the couple near the entrance.

Nicholas Curzon was helping Cathy out of her coat, and a waiter was hovering in readiness to hang it up for her. Lucia turned quickly away again.

"They've seen us. They're coming over here." Bernard pushed back his chair, and stood up, not noticing that Lucia's lips were tightly compressed, and her eyes had an angry sparkle in them.

"Hello, Bernard. How are you?" Cathy greeted him with a warmth which suggested that they were old, close friends.

While she was speaking to him, Nicholas Curzon bowed to Lucia.

"Good evening, Miss Gresham. I needn't ask if you have recovered from your bout of 'flu last month. I can see that you have." His dark eyes appraised her newly-set hair and plain dress. "You look very charming tonight."

The facile, meaningless compliment made her clench her hands under the table. But, as she was about to respond with a markedly chilly "Good evening," she remembered something Janet had said the previous afternoon.

Don't you see? The best way to take the wind out of their sails is to do what they least expect.

And, abruptly deciding to put this advice to the test, she made herself smile, and say pleasantly, "Thank you, Mr. Curzon. Yes, I'm quite recovered now, I'm glad to say. This is a nice surprise. What brings you two here?"

Before he could reply, Cathy touched his arm, and introduced Bernard to him. But Lucia had the satisfaction of knowing that her saccharine manner had momentarily shaken his urbanity. Not much, perhaps, but enough to make him lift that mobile left eyebrow.

As the two men shook hands, she noticed with surprise that Bernard appeared to wince. Although he had large hands, his clasp was rather a limp one. It was among several admittedly trivial reasons why Lucia knew she could never fall in love with him. Two others were that his nails were not always perfectly clean, and he kept his change in a purse.

One small point in Nicholas Curzon's favour was that, on the three previous occasions when they had met, his nails had always been spotless. But she would not have suspected, from looking at his thin, brown fingers, that his grip would make Bernard flinch.

Cathy smiled at her sister. "You don't mind if we join you, do you?"

"Not in the least," said Lucia amiably. "But I thought you didn't like Chinese food?"

For an instant, Cathy looked uncomfortable. Then she said, "Well, Nico does, and you've always said this place was particularly good."

"We think so—yes," said Lucia, glancing at Bernard. "But we're not connoisseurs, as Mr. Curzon may be." She gave him an innocent look. "I do hope you won't be disappointed, Mr. Curzon. It's a long way to come for a meal when there are several good Chinese restaurants in the West End."

Cathy sat down next to her sister, and Nicholas sat beside Bernard.

"Yes, there are indeed," he agreed smoothly. "But I have often found that the less pretentious restaurants in the suburbs serve better food than one gets at the better-known places. Now—" starting to study the menu, "what would you recommend?"

Lucia left it to Bernard to advise him on the Soo

Chow's specialities. She was in no doubt that he and Cathy had come here deliberately. The question was—why? And the answer seemed fairly obvious.

All through the meal she waited for Nicholas to bring up the subject of Greece. But even when Bernard happened to mention Easter, he did not take advantage of this opening.

It was Cathy who invited the men to come in for coffee, after Nicholas had driven them back to "Montrose" in his Lancia.

"Isn't it rather late?" Bernard demurred. Had they been alone, he and Lucia would have said goodnight by half past eleven. Now it was almost midnight.

"Oh, nonsense—it's barely twelve, and none of us has to work tomorrow." Cathy led the way into the house. "Shall I make the coffee, Lucia?"

"No, I'll do it," Lucia said hastily. "We'll have it in the study. Would you get the electric fire from the drawing-room, please, Bernard? I don't want to light the coal fire just for half an hour or so."

"Certainly." Bernard disappeared into the drawing-room, leaving Nicholas helping Cathy to take off her coat.

Alone in the kitchen, Lucia sagged for a moment. Putting on an act was easier than she had thought—for a short period. But a whole evening of pretence was a strain. In order to prolong her respite, she decided to make proper coffee instead of the instant kind. She had bought some fresh beans during the week and, although she had no cream in the house, there was a spare pint of Jersey milk in the pantry.

She was pouring the beans into the top of the wooden hand-grinder, when the door opened and Nicholas walked in.

"Can I help you with anything, Miss Gresham?"

She managed to mask her dismay. "I don't think so, thank you, Mr. Curzon." She began to turn the handle.

"That looks hard work. Let me do it for you." He

strolled round the scrubbed kitchen table, and held out his hand for the grinder.

Reluctantly, Lucia surrendered it. Now she wished she was making instant coffee.

"It's been a very pleasant evening. We must make up a foursome again some time," he said, in his blandest voice. The handle, so stiff for Lucia, went round with ease in his grip.

"Yes, it has been fun," she agreed, with smooth insincerity.

He would have to do better than that if he wanted to ruffle her.

"You aren't wearing a ring, I notice," he said. "But I gather it may not be long before you do announce your engagement."

This did shake her. "My engagement?" she repeated, staring at him. "What on earth gave you that idea?"

His black brows lifted a fraction. "Perhaps I have misread the matter—or perhaps you wish to keep it *sub rosa* for the present. In that case, I beg your pardon. It wasn't my intention to embarrass you."

"Not much!" thought Lucia succinctly. Aloud, she said, "Did Cathy tell you I might be getting engaged?"

"No, no—she hasn't been indiscreet. But she did mention that you and Fisher have been close friends for some time. It was entirely my own assumption that you had, as they say, an understanding with him."

"I see," said Lucia, thinking fast. Had he really made such an assumption? Or was this a new ploy?

"I daresay you don't believe in friendship between men and women," she went on lightly. "But that is all there is between Bernard and me. There's no question of an engagement."

"Perhaps not on your side, Miss Gresham. But can you be sure of Fisher's feelings? He must be an odd sort of chap if he doesn't find you attractive."

Lucia could control her voice and her expression.

She could not prevent herself blushing. However, in spite of her heightened colour, she managed to hold his regard.

"But I'm sure you would be the *first* to agree that being attracted to someone is not the same as wanting to spend one's whole life with them," she replied, in a level tone.

She could tell by the quirk of his mouth that he had not missed the delicate emphasis.

"How true," he agreed, with a twinkle. "Indeed it's even possible to be attracted to someone whom, in other respects, one dislikes."

Was he implying—again!—that she was attracted to him? Inwardly, Lucia bristled. But this time she did not allow her indignation to show.

"It may happen to very young, susceptible people," she said, rather pleased with her casualness. "But I doubt if superficial charm makes much impression on older ones. They see that it's superficial."

He removed the drawer from the grinder, and passed it across to her. "And you, I imagine, were never susceptible—not even in your salad days," he mocked gently.

Lucia tipped the ground coffee from the drawer. Was there nothing which would pierce his arrogance? Did he really believe that no woman alive could fail to respond to his magnetism?

"I wonder what he would do if I pretended to *be* charmed?" she thought. "Even he might turn tail if he thought we were both trying to catch him. No, I don't believe he would. It would only amuse him—confound him!"

"Then it's not because of Fisher that you don't wish to come to Greece for Easter?" he said, as she screwed the filter into the espresso pot.

"Aha?" she thought. "So we've finally come to the point, have we?"

Aloud, she replied, "Oh, no, it has nothing to do with Bernard."

"In that case, perhaps I can persuade you to change your mind. Cathy has told you, I believe, that you and she would not be my only guests?"

"Yes, she said it was to be a house party."

"Well, then what could be more *comme il faut*?" he asked, with a smile. "Even you will admit there is safety in numbers, Miss Gresham."

"That depends on the numbers," she said, with a touch of asperity.

He laughed. "And you suspect that my friends may be even more decadent than I am? You are quite wrong, I promise you. My other guests are all of unimpeachable probity. Cathy may find them rather dull. But you should like them very much." He paused to light a cigarette. "*I* may not speak your language," he added provokingly. "But my three other English guests will be right on your wavelength."

This deliberate reminder of their conversation in the study made Lucia's cheeks warm again. Turning away to fetch out the best china cups, she said, "Where exactly is your place in Greece?"

"It's on a small island called Marina. One gets there by steamer from Piraeus. If you decide to come, I'll meet you off the plane and take you there. Without a smattering of Greek, you might find yourselves at sea in both senses. A first journey abroad is always a little confusing."

He waited for her to say something and, when she did not, he went on, "I have a particular reason for wanting you to come, Miss Gresham."

Glancing at him, she saw that, for the first time in their acquaintance, his expression was wholly serious. He looked, she thought, almost stern.

"What reason, Mr. Curzon?" she asked.

A smile changed the set of his mouth, and lit up his eyes. "It would be premature to make a formal declaration of intent at this point," he said lightly. "But perhaps it would reassure you if I said that, since our first meeting, I have—let's say—changed my tune."

"You mean—" She stopped, her throat tight.

"I mean that, from now on, your sister's reputation will be as safe with me as it is with 'the worthy Bernard'," he said, quoting Cathy.

"I see," she murmured, in a low voice.

There was a pause. Nicholas smoked, and watched her. Lucia arranged the blue and white cups on a tray, and tried to put into order her conflicting reactions.

"Far from being reassured, you seem to be even more worried," he remarked ironically. "You don't believe me, I gather?"

"Yes...I think I believe you," she said, with a troubled glance at him. "It's just that I don't—"

"Well, we can't go into that now," he intervened quickly. "The coffee is about to boil over."

"Oh, goodness!" She hastened to turn off the gas.

When the tray was ready, he picked it up and took it to the door. But, as Lucia opened it for him, he did not at once pass through into the hall.

"Have I succeeded in changing your mind? Will you come to Marina next month?" he asked her.

She avoided his eyes. "It seems I must," she said hollowly. "Very well, Mr. Curzon, I'll come."

"In that case, you had better start calling me Nicholas. May I use your first name now?"

"If you wish."

"Good—that's settled." He took a pace forward, then halted again. "Oh, by the way, I think you are very wise to keep Fisher at arm's length. He may be an excellent friend, but as a lover—not your style at all."

IN THE FOLLOWING FORTNIGHT, Cathy's initial delight at her sister's capitulation was tempered by the gradual discovery that a change had come over the elder girl.

Lucia had given way on the most important issue, but she was not to be budged on the smaller ones—

such as how much Cathy could spend on clothes for their holiday.

By the time they came to grips on the subject, Lucia had had the French bureau expertly valued. The representatives of the two firms she consulted both assured her, that, if put up for auction, the bureau was certain to fetch at least four hundred guineas. This being so, it seemed to Cathy that they could afford to splurge a little.

Lucia, however, had other ideas. "No, we'll spend what we have in the bank, and perhaps it may not be necessary to sell the bureau after all," she said, very firmly. "When we come back, I'll see if I can get the bank manager to lend me the money for having the house painted. He probably won't, but I'll approach him."

"When we come back, I may be engaged," said Cathy. "Then money won't matter any more. I do think you're being mean, Lucia. You know everything depends on this holiday. I can't go to Greece in what I have. You can bet your life the other guests will look stunning. I want to look even more stunning."

But although she had usually been able to get what she wanted in the past, this time her sister was adamant.

"You can spend thirty pounds," she said decisively. "What you wear won't influence Nicholas. If he means to marry you, he will. If he doesn't, your clothes won't make any difference."

"Thirty pounds? That's nothing these days. What can I get for thirty pounds?"

"You already have plenty of pants and tops, and a couple of swimsuits."

"They're last year's styles. Everything is different this year," Cathy objected. "How much are you going to spend?"

"Fifty pounds," Lucia said calmly.

"What! Twenty pounds more than me? Why should you have the lion's share?"

"Because your wardrobe is packed with clothes, and you're pretty enough to look nice whatever you wear. I'm not pretty, and my cupboard is practically empty."

"But you wouldn't be going at all if it weren't for me. You've no right to spend more than I do. It isn't fair!"

"Oh, don't be so childish, Cathy," Lucia said sharply. "You don't think I *want* to go, do you? I'm sure to hate every minute of it. But if I've got to spend two weeks in an intolerable situation, I think I'm entitled to a few presentable clothes."

A few days before the end of term, she came home from school to find the telephone ringing. Rather breathlessly, for she had sprinted the last hundred yards to avoid being caught in a downpour, she lifted the receiver and gave their number.

"Lucia?"

"Yes—speaking. Who is that?" At first, she did not recognize the voice at the other end of the line.

"It's Nicholas here."

"Oh... hello." She sat down on the edge of the rug chest, and began to untie her headscarf.

"You don't sound very pleased to hear me. Am I calling at an inconvenient moment?"

"No, not particularly. I've just arrived home from school. What can I do for you?"

"I wondered if there was anything I could do for you? I gather from Cathy that you have all the arrangements in hand, but I thought I'd just check with you."

"There wasn't much to arrange. Everything is fixed, I think, thanks. When are you leaving for Greece?"

"Tomorrow," he told her. "All being well, I'll see you at Hellenikon Airport in the early hours of Thursday morning." She heard a low laugh. "Now that you've had time to get used to the idea, are you feeling a little more enthusiastic about it?"

"It will be nice to see a blue sky for a change," she said, in an expressionless voice.

"Is that all you're looking forward to?" It might have been a trick of the connection, but all at once, his voice sounded as close as if he were standing beside her in the hall. His tone was subtly different too—deeper, oddly disturbing.

She swallowed. "I shall enjoy swimming."

"Good weather and swimming? Surely you hope for more than that?"

"I don't think I follow you."

"Most girls go on holiday hoping to meet a man, don't they? Are you so different from the rest of your sex?"

Lucia did not answer. Since she could think of nothing crushing, it seemed best to keep silent.

"I don't think you know," his voice said, close to her ear. "I think, at Marina, you may find that the real Lucia is quite different from Miss Gresham, the rather prim schoolmistress."

"Well, if I do, it won't be through you," she retorted rashly. The moment the hasty words were out, she could not think what had possessed her to say such a thing. Her cheeks burned with mortification.

"Now that's a curious remark," he said, after a pause. "I have to ring off now, so you can explain it to me when we meet. See you in Athens. Goodbye."

THE SPRING TERM ENDED on the Wednesday before Easter, and Cathy had persuaded the Maybury Hotel management to let her start her holiday on that day, instead of the customary Saturday. Had they not agreed to this arrangement, she had intended to give in her notice.

"I can easily get another job," she had said confidently, when Lucia objected to her taking such a drastic step. "Anyway I probably shan't need one."

There seemed no doubt in her mind that she was going to return to London with a costly engagement ring on her finger.

By the time Cathy reached home on Wednesday evening, Lucia had done all but the last-moment packing for them both. The younger girl had only to have supper, and a bath, and find room for her toilet things.

The night flight to Athens took off at a quarter to eleven, and Peter was running them to the Air Terminal in his Mini. After Lucia had washed the supper dishes, and double-checked that all the ground floor windows were securely latched, she changed and went upstairs to spend the remaining time with Janet.

"Oh, you do look nice," her friend said warmly, when she saw her in her new clothes.

"You don't think this colour is too bright for me?" Lucia asked doubtfully.

For, in the past, she had always stuck to safe, serviceable colours like grey, and camel, and navy. But the lightweight coat and matching skirt in which she was going to travel were a vivid flamingo pink. Her turtle-necked silk-knit sweater was a lighter tone of the same colour.

"Certainly not! You look super," Janet assured her.

"Well, it's made of Courtelle, so it isn't too impractical. But I can't help feeling I ought to have had the navy version."

Peter came into the room, and stopped short in mock-stupefaction. But he wasn't teasing as he said, "My word! You look smashing, Lucia. I've never seen you so smart."

"Really?" Her face lit up. Peter was the type of man who seldom noticed what his wife wore, let alone the clothes of other women. Praise from him was praise indeed.

Presently, Cathy joined them. She had not seen Lucia's pink outfit, and her eyebrows went up at the sight of it.

"Goodness, what a bright colour," she remarked, with a critical look.

"Yes, and doesn't it suit her?" put in Janet.

"Mm...it's quite nice," Cathy said tepidly.

Janet could have slapped her. But Lucia knew that her sister was still sulking about not being able to spend as much as she had wished. So it was hardly to be expected that Cathy would enthuse about the things Lucia had bought with her larger allowance.

At last it was time to go.

"Goodbye. Have a lovely time," said Janet, giving Lucia a hug.

"Well, I'll try," said Lucia, with a wry expression.

Yet, in spite of many misgivings about the purpose and outcome of the holiday, she could not help feeling a thrill of excitement at the thought that, in a few hours, she would be in a foreign and beautiful country. To travel had been her dream for so long that she could hardly believe it was really happening at last.

CATHY DOZED for the greater part of the flight, as did most of the other passengers. But although she was physically tired, Lucia found it impossible to sleep with the knowledge that, thousands of feet beneath them, lay the towns and villages of Europe.

People accustomed to air travel might say it was boring and debilitating. For her, it was a magical experience. To fly through the night in a great, sealed cone of flight...to soar above the mighty Alps...to be heading south to the shores of the blue Mediterranean...how could anyone sleep at such a time?

About half an hour before they were due to arrive, Cathy roused, and went to the powder room. By the time she returned, other people were beginning to stir. Several heads craned to watch her pass along the aisle. For, in spite of the fact that Lucia's parsimony had forced her to travel in last summer's yellow wool suit she looked enchantingly pretty.

The aircraft touched down at a quarter past three in the morning and, after the close atmosphere in the plane, the outer air seemed almost as chilly as the cold April night they had left far behind in London.

"Where's Nico!" said Cathy anxiously, when they had passed through the Customs.

Although there were several people waiting to meet other passengers, there was no sign of Nicholas Curzon.

They stood looking about for some minutes. Then Lucia said, "There's an enquiry desk over there. If he's been delayed for some reason, he's sure to have telephoned through. They probably have a message for us."

But there was no message and, ten minutes later, they were still waiting for their host to put in an appearance.

"This is your fault," Cathy said fretfully. "It was absurd to expect him to meet us at this ungodly hour. For a measly twenty pounds more, we could have come by the day flight, and arrived at a reasonable time. He's probably keeping us waiting to pay you out for being so inconsiderate."

"Oh, don't be silly. It's far more likely that he's had a puncture on the way here," said Lucia. "Or an accident," she added, frowning.

Another ten minutes passed. The more she thought about the possibility of a car crash, the more disturbed she felt. She supposed it was because it reminded her of that terrible day when a policewoman had come to the house to break the news of her father's accident. Even though she had not been looking forward to meeting Nicholas again, it was common decency to feel some anxiety about him. One would not wish one's worst enemy to be involved in a road smash.

After they had been waiting for half an hour, and the man at the desk still had no news for them, she said, "There's no point in hanging about here. Let's go to the restaurant, and have some coffee."

"I want to spend a penny," said Cathy, in the restaurant.

She went off to the ladies' room, leaving Lucia wondering what was the best thing to do if Nicholas failed to turn up in the next thirty minutes.

"Miss Gresham?" asked a male voice.

"Yes." Eagerly, she looked up. But the man who had approached while she was pondering was not a member of the airport staff bringing news. He was a stranger in whipcord slacks and a dark blue sweater.

"I am Yannis Tyropoulos. Nico sent me to meet you. Unfortunately, there was a small accident on the way, and so I am late. I am *very* sorry. It is not pleasant to arrive in a strange city, and have no one to make you welcome. You have been distressed. I can see it in your face. Please accept my most humble apologies."

"Yes... of course," said Lucia, rather overwhelmed.

For, apart from the fact that he had seized both her hands, and delivered his speech very fast, and with a great deal of dramatic emphasis, Yannis Tyropoulos was the most handsome young man she had ever laid eyes on.

Still holding her hands, he sat down at the table, and beamed at her. "So you are the beautiful Cathy. But where is your sister... Lucia, is it?"

"I'm Lucia," she explained. "Cathy will be back in a moment."

"*You* are Lucia?" he said, puzzled. "But Nico said Cathy was the pretty sister, and Lucia was the clever sister."

"Or did he actually say the plain sister?" she thought dryly.

"That's right," she said, smiling. "Cathy is very pretty."

Still he looked puzzled. "How can this be? You are *lovely*." He pressed her fingers, and gave her such an enamoured look that, for one crazy moment, she almost believed he meant it. "If your sister is *more* lovely than you she must be a goddess."

"Well, see for yourself," said Lucia, as she spotted

Cathy coming back. Yannis turned to look, and she quickly withdrew her hands, and tucked them out of sight on her lap.

As Cathy approached, Yannis rose to his feet. But with his head turned away from her, Lucia could not see whether there was now an even more ardent look in his long-lashed black eyes.

Cathy was plainly as startled by his extraordinary looks as her sister had been.

Lucia said, "This is Mr. Tyropoulos, Cathy. Nicholas sent him to meet us, but he was delayed."

"How do you do?" Cathy murmured. It was the first time Lucia had ever seen her greet a man with a disconcerted stare on her face. Indeed, for a second or two, she looked almost shy of him.

Yannis shook hands. "Welcome to Greece, Miss Cathy. I am sorry your arrival in my country has been spoiled by the stupidity of the driver who hit my taxi."

"It's quite all right." Cathy sat down. "Why couldn't Nico come to meet us?"

Yannis also sat down. Now Lucia saw his eyes again. To her amazement, she realized that, far from gazing at her sister with rapt admiration, there was nothing in his expressioon but civil interest in a foreign visitor.

"Unfortunately there was another small accident at Marina this afternoon—that is, yesterday afternoon," he corrected. "It happened only a few minutes before Nico was to catch the steamer. So, as he must stay to bandage Ariadne, I am sent in his place."

"Who is Ariadne?" asked Cathy.

"She is the youngest child of my cousin Sofia. She is only six years old, so naturally she was very frightened when the scissors pierced her arm, and there was much blood."

Lucia remembered Nicholas mentioning that his grandfather's name was Tyropoulos. "Is Nicholas also your cousin?" she asked.

He turned to her so eagerly that, once more, she was

taken aback. "Yes, that is so," he confirmed, with his melting smile. "My father and Nico's mother were brother and sister. Now, you are tired, and must rest before the crossing to Marina. I will take you into Athens."

The drive from the airport to the centre of the city took about twenty minutes. Yannis sat in front with the driver, and chatted in rapid Greek. The two girls sat behind in silence, both of them rather dazed by the unexpected advent of this real-life Adonis into their lives.

When the taxi stopped, Lucia saw with dismay that they were at the entrance to a very *de luxe*-looking hotel.

"In ten minutes, you will be in a comfortable bed—fast asleep," said Yannis, helping her to step out.

"Oh, but is that necessary—to go to bed, I mean? What time does the steamer leave for Marina? Couldn't we just rest in the lounge?" she suggested anxiously.

Unwisely, perhaps, considering the hour of their arrival, she had not budgeted for spending what was left of the night in a hotel.

"The steamer departs from Piraeus at twelve o'clock," he told her. "So there is plenty of time for you and Miss Cathy to recover yourselves. Don't worry—everything is arranged. You will be called at nine, and we will have breakfast together, and perhaps a little walk round the city."

Lucia was too tired to argue. The problem of paying for these arrangements would have to wait until tomorrow. Without further objection, she let him shepherd her into the imposing foyer.

As soon as she had signed the register at the night porter's desk, they were taken upstairs by lift, and shown into a large, well-furnished double room, with a lobby and private bathroom.

Yannis tipped the baggage boy for bringing up their suitcases, and bade them goodnight.

As Lucia went with him to lock the outer door, he smiled down at her, and said softly, "Until tomorrow. Sleep well... *beautiful* Lucia." Then he passed into the corridor, and was gone.

WHEN LUCIA WOKE UP, chinks of light were showing through the curtains. Peering at the luminous hands of her watch, she found that it was seven o'clock. Yet, although she had been asleep for little more than two hours, she felt wide awake, and eager to begin her first day in Greece.

Quietly, so as not to disturb Cathy, she slid out of bed and crept to the window. As she poked her head between the curtains, she saw that already the city was bathed in brilliant sunlight. There was a good deal of traffic passing in the street below, but the sound of it was muted by the double-paned window. At present the hotel's central heating was still functioning, but no doubt this would shortly be replaced by the coolness of air-conditioning.

Deciding that she could not possibly lie in bed until nine, she padded to the bathroom, where she had a hot shower followed by a cold one. Then she made up her face, and dressed, and scribbled a note to Cathy, who was still deeply asleep.

There was no one about in the corridor as she made her way to the lift. But there were pairs of glossy-clean shoes outside most of the other bedroom doors.

"Kaliméra, Kyrie," she said experimentally, to the liftman, when the door slid open.

A broad smile split his face. *"Kaliméra, Thespoinís. Ti kánete?"* And then, in case she had not understood this last—"How are you?"

Ever since she had made the decision to come on this holiday, Lucia had been at pains to master the Greek alphabet, and to teach herself a little of the language.

So, instead of saying. "Very well, thank you", she

ventured to reply in his own tongue. *"Kalá—ké sis?"* she asked, hoping her pronunciation was correct.

Evidently it was not too bad. He laughed, and nodded approvingly. "Very good... very good."

He was still beaming at her when they stopped at another floor. As the door opened, Lucia was surprised to see Yannis waiting outside.

"Lucia, what are you doing up so early?" he exclaimed, equally surprised.

"Good morning. I was too excited to sleep, so I thought I'd have a stroll round on my own," she explained.

He stepped into the lift. "You certainly do not look as if you have been up here most of the night. What of your sister? Does she sleep still?"

"Yes, I shouldn't think she'll wake up for some time yet."

The lift reached the ground floor. Before she walked out of it, Lucia smiled at the liftman. *"Efharistó."*

He bowed. *"Parakaló."* Then, turning to Yannis, he said something which Lucia could not follow, but which was obviously about her.

"What did that mean?" she asked, when the lift door had closed upon him.

Yannis smiled, and slipped his hand under her elbow. "He said it is unusual for an English visitor to speak our language—particularly someone as young and lovely as yourself."

Lucia laughed. "I think you made the last bit up."

"No, I did not," he assured her. "You must understand that Greek men are not like English men. We are not stiff... afraid to show what we feel. We ask questions which, in England, would be 'bad form', as you say. While you are here, many men will show with their eyes that they would like to make love to you. You mustn't be annoyed. No harm is intended. It is our way."

By now they were at the entrance to the hotel restaurant. A waiter ushered them to a table, and Yannis ordered breakfast.

"How is it that you speak such excellent English, Mr. Tyropoulos?" Lucia asked.

"Not Mr. Tyropoulos... Yannis, please."

"All right—Yannis, then."

"I learnt English from Nico," he explained. "And also for one year I worked in England. It was useful experience, but I do not like your English climate. For me, there is one place to live—Marina. Thanks to Nico, it is possible for me to stay there now."

"Why 'thanks to Nico'?"

"The people of my island have always been very poor," he told her. "It is the same with most of the islands. Hydra and Mykonos have many summer visitors, but still there is much poverty elsewhere. For a man to make his way in the world, it has been necessary to leave home, and work in some richer country. England, perhaps, or as far away as America. First, Nico paid for me to have a good education. Now he has lent me the money to build a small hotel at Marina. This is not only a chance for me to be prosperous, but also it gives work to many others."

"I see," said Lucia thoughtfully. She should have been pleased to learn that Nicholas had a philanthropic side to his nature. Yet, obscurely, the discovery troubled her.

Their breakfast arrived—crisp French rolls, honey from Mount Hymettos, and coffee with hot milk added. This, Yannis explained, was known as *ghalikó kafé*, and was served only on request. But he had guessed that she would not enjoy Greek coffee, similar to the Turkish kind, so early in the day.

For Lucia, those first two hours of her first sunlit morning in Greece were an unforgettable, golden interval between her often unhappy past life, and the worrying uncertainties of the future.

As soon as they had finished breakfast, Yannis took

her out into the city. She did not need to fetch her coat for, even at this early hour, the air was gloriously warm. Indeed she would have been more comfortable in a cotton shirt than in her silky flamingo sweater.

By half past eight, all the shops were open, and the streets surging with traffic. To an experienced traveller, the heart of Athens might have seemed little different from that of any capital city. But, to Lucia's unjaded eyes, it was utterly different. For one thing, the sky above it was brilliantly blue—a sight which no English person could ever be blasé about.

And, even in the London street markets, she had never seen people chatting, and arguing, and gesticulating as animatedly as the citizens of Athens. Everywhere she looked, there were Greeks talking ten to the dozen. The sound of voices was almost as loud as the noise of the traffic.

"I suppose there isn't time to visit the Parthenon before we leave?" she said, strolling along with her hand in his.

He had possessed himself of it as they left the hotel, and was holding it too firmly for her to free it casually.

"No—but I think Nico has a plan to bring you to see the antiquities," said Yannis.

Lucia stopped dead. "Oh, look—what a lovely thing to see!" she exclaimed delightedly.

For trotting towards them, led by an old man with a grizzled moustache, was a donkey laden with baskets brimming with flowers.

Yannis let go of her hand and, before she realized his intention, went striding forward to intercept the flower-seller, and buy from him. A few moments later, her arms were full of carnations.

"Oh, Yannis, they're lovely—but how extravagant," she protested, torn between pleasure and dismay.

"*Éa penindári*—a few shillings," he replied, with a shrug. "It is worth much more to see you smile, beautiful Lucia."

She laughed, and blushed, and buried her nose in the flowers. She knew very well he was only flirting. He himself had warned her that his countrymen were uninhibitedly amorous. Nevertheless, she could not help feeling rather exalted at being treated with such delightful gallantry by this gay, and *so* good-looking, young Greek.

It was a few minutes after nine when they returned to the hotel. Hardly had they entered the foyer than Cathy came hurrying towards them, looking very put out indeed.

"Where have you been?" she demanded, staring at Lucia's bouquet.

"For a walk," her sister explained. "I woke up early and came downstairs, and met Yannis. Have you been up long?"

"Since eight," Cathy said tartly.

"Good morning, Miss Cathy. Did you sleep well?" Yannis asked politely.

For the second time, Lucia noticed that there was nothing in his manner to suggest he was addressing an exceptionally attractive girl. Cathy might have been a child or an elderly woman. His attitude was one of well-bred courtesy superimposed on indifference.

"Yes, thanks," said Cathy, rather huffily.

She had not yet had breakfast and, as the restaurant was now rather crowded, Yannis suggested that it would be best for her to have it in their room.

"I will see you later—when it is time for us to leave," he said to Lucia. "Excuse me now, if you please." And he went away to attend to some business of his own.

Cathy said nothing on the way upstairs, but Lucia sensed there would be an explosion as soon as they were alone.

There was. No sooner had Lucia closed the inner door than Cathy whirled round and said furiously, "Thanks *very* much! There's nothing I like better than hanging about in a strange hotel, being leered at by greasy little men!"

"I didn't notice anyone greasy downstairs," Lucia said mildly. "As far as I could see they were mostly middle-aged businessmen and American tourists. I'm sorry, Cathy," she added quickly, to avert another outburst. "I didn't think you'd wake up until you were called—and I did leave a note."

"You didn't say you were going out with Yannis."

"I didn't know it then. We met as I was going down in the lift."

"Why on earth did he give you all those flowers? You can't take them on the boat."

"No, I suppose not," Lucia agreed regretfully. "I'll give them to the chambermaid, and just keep one to pin on my coat. Aren't they lovely? Would you like one?"

"No, thanks," her sister said tersely.

"Don't be cross, Cathy. You've really no reason to be. Don't let's spoil our first day here by rowing."

"Oh, so you've changed your mind, have you? You're glad you've come—now you've met him."

Lucia ignored this. "Hadn't you better ring for breakfast?"

"I never thought you could be such a fool," Cathy said spitefully. "You've fallen for him, haven't you? You came in all flushed and starry-eyed. Well, well... who would have thought it? After all the lectures you've given me, about looks not being important and all that jazz, you've lost your heart to the first decent-looking man who's ever noticed you."

If she had hoped to make her sister angry, she did not succeed. For this outburst struck Lucia as being very much the kind of tantrum thrown by a spoilt little girl who had been left out of a treat. An over-indulged six-year-old would have stamped her feet, and yelled "I hate you". Cathy vented her feelings by saying the most hurtful thing she could think of.

"Well, what if I have?" Lucia said lightly. "You don't want me tagging round with you and Nicholas all the time, do you? I should have thought you'd be pleased that I've found someone to keep me company."

The younger girl's jaw dropped. It was true that Lucia had come into the hotel with a smile on her lips, and a pleased-with-life air about her. But Cathy had not really believed the accusation which she had just flung at her.

"You haven't really fallen for him, have you?" she asked, in undefined alarm.

Lucia repressed a smile. "Gracious, I only met him last night," she said cheerfully. "But he is rather fabulous, don't you think? And he does seem to like me."

She paused, and began to poke the stalks of the carnations into a vase of roses on the writing desk. "I might fall in love with him," she said reflectively. "Yes, I think it could happen quite easily.

CHAPTER THREE

CATHY WAS VISIBLY STUNNED. "Oh, you can't be serious. He's Greek."

"Well, what of it? Nicholas is half Greek."

"But he doesn't live here. He isn't Greek in his ways."

"Isn't he? He told me he was. He said, 'I've been brought up as an Englishman, but I'm still Greek in my bones'."

"What nonsense—of course he isn't," Cathy contradicted flatly. "He's not a bit like real Greeks."

"What's wrong with real Greeks?" asked Lucia.

This seemed to stump Cathy for some moments. At length, she said, "Well, they're not like us, are they? They've got some most peculiar habits. When I was waiting for you, some of the men in the foyer were playing with strings of brown beads."

"Oh, those were *komboloia*," Lucia told her. "Didn't you know about their 'worry' beads? They click them to soothe their nerves."

"There you are, then," Cathy said scathingly. "Englishmen don't need beads to soothe them."

"No—but they smoke cigarettes, and jingle loose change, and bite their nails," her sister pointed out.

"I think playing with beads is effeminate," Cathy said, with scorn. Then, illogically, she went on, "And I don't like the way they leer at people. I've never been ogled at the Maybury the way I was downstairs just now. It was horrid. I felt most embarrassed."

"Well, Yannis says it's one of the customs of the country, so we shall just have to brace ourselves," said

Lucia. "Actually, I think Englishmen leer just as much—only they're more furtive about it."

This frivolous response was so unlike her staid sister that it made Cathy blink.

"Can I ring for your breakfast? I want to practise my Greek," said Lucia. She went to the telephone on the table between the twin beds, and asked the switchboard for Room Service.

"Kaliméra. Boró ná páro tó próyevma stó thomatiómoo parakoló?"

This made Cathy even more amazed. "What on earth does all that mean? I didn't know you knew any Greek."

"Only very basic Greek," said Lucia. "If Nicholas asks you to marry him, he will probably expect you to learn to speak it really well. If he has a house at Marina, he must spend a good deal of time here."

Cathy looked alarmed. "I couldn't learn Greek. They don't even use our alphabet."

"Some of the letters are the same. It doesn't take long to master the others. With Nicholas to help you, you should pick it up in no time. The most difficult part is getting the pronunciation right."

Evidently she had expressed her request to Room Service correctly because, a few minutes later, a waiter arrived with Cathy's breakfast tray.

Lucia tipped him. *"Efharisto."*

"Parakaló." As he bowed, the man gave the two girls a smiling look of admiration.

"Even the waiters leer," Cathy said disapprovingly, when he had gone.

Lucia grinned, and said mischievously, "I think the first thing you ought to learn is *'Ftáni pyá. Fíyete!'*"

"What does that mean?"

Lucia assumed an expression of chilly hauteur. "That will do—go away!" she translated. Then she laughed, and went to the bathroom to collect her toilet things, and re-pack them.

PIRAEUS, THE PORT OF ATHENS, was about six miles from the centre of the capital. On the way there, by taxi, Yannis told the girls that it took four hours to reach Marina, which was not one of the islands served by the fast hydrofoil boats.

The island steamers embarked from the quays at Karaiskakis Square, and carried freight as well as passengers. To Cathy, the busy seaport scene was of little interest. But, for Lucia, everything she saw was enriched by her knowledge of the past.

She knew that, originally, the port of Athens had been at Phaleron, along the coast. Then a far-sighted Athenian politician called Themistocles had realized that, instead of strengthening the city's land defences, it would be better to establish a strong navy, and to build a fortified port at Piraeus.

In the face of strenuous opposition, he had managed to carry out his schemes and, a few years later, at Salamis, the Greek fleet of three hundred and fifty warships had routed a Persian Armada of more than a thousand ships.

In the fifth century, when Athens had been at the height of her glory and supremacy, the main harbour at Piraeus had been surrounded by a series of magnificent colonnades where the captains of ships could display cargoes brought back from far lands to the city's merchants.

But the splendid port with its four hundred limestone ship-sheds, and naval arsenal, had been partly destroyed by the Spartans, and completely laid waste by the Romans. They had rebuilt some of it for their own use, but after the collapse of the Roman Empire, Piraeus had ceased to exist, except as an insignificant seaside village.

Lord Byron had gone there to bathe. Lord Elgin had anchored his ship there while he was carrying off priceless classical marbles from the Acropolis.

Then, from about 1835, the port had been gradually

redeveloped until, today, it was once again the busiest harbour in the Levant, and one of the world's great sea-markets.

Not long after the steamer had cast off, Cathy began to turn pale.

"I feel ghastly," she muttered to Lucia.

On such a lovely day, with only a light wind blowing, it was hard to believe that anyone could be sea-sick. But obviously Cathy wasn't putting it on. Her face was grey-white, and she looked really ill.

Yannis said, "I will take her below. The sickness is not so bad when one is lying down. No, no, you stay here, Lucia." And he put his arm round Cathy's waist, and shepherded her away.

"I must go to her, Yannis. She can't be left alone feeling like that," said Lucia anxiously, when he returned.

"She is not alone. There is a stewardess to look after her. There is nothing you can do for her, Lucia, and I want you to see the Temple of Poseidon when we pass it," he said. "Also you must have some lunch." He indicated the wicker hamper he had brought on board with him. "We will have a picnic here on deck. That is, if you are not also indisposed?"

"No, I'm feeling fine," she assured him. "It never occurred to me that either of us might be ill, or I would have bought some of those anti-seasick tablets."

"It is unusual for someone to be ill on a day such as this," said Yannis. "In summer, when the *meltemi* is blowing, it is sometimes very rough among the islands. Myself, I am never sick, not even in a storm. But there are people for whom all sea journeys are an ordeal. Let us hope Cathy is not one of them. She is tired from last night, and excited. Perhaps that is why, today, she feels ill. It may not be so another time." He opened the lunch basket.

Lucia, who liked the gentle roll of the steamer and the salt breeze ruffling her hair, felt rather guilty about enjoying a picnic lunch with him while her sister was prostrate below.

But later, when the ship passed Cape Sounion, she was glad she had not missed seeing it. On the summit of the steep headland stood twelve gleaming-white Doric columns, all that remained of Poseidon's temple, built twenty-four centuries ago.

Several times during the crossing, she went below to find out how Cathy was. Fortunately, after a wretched hour at the beginning of the voyage, her sister fell asleep. She was still sleeping when, late in the afternoon, the outline of Marina came into view.

As the island drew nearer and nearer, Lucia's misgivings returned, and a knot of tension began to tighten inside her. She had not forgotten what she had said to Nicholas on the telephone, and she felt sure he would not have forgotten it either. At the first opportunity, he would delight in baiting her about it.

At first sight, Marina seemed to consist of a ridge of mountains, ringed by sheer limestone cliffs. But this was only the forbidding, northern aspect of the island. As the ferry steamed down the west coast, the cliffs gave place to rocky promontories protecting small, empty beaches. Behind them, the lower slopes of the hills were terraced for cultivation, and scattered villages could be seen.

The island's only town, also its port, was a huddle of whitewashed houses encircling a sheltered harbour at the southern end. The entire population of the place seemed to be waiting on the quay when the steamer put in. As Marina was not the end of its run, and it was only stopping there for half an hour, there was a rush to get the freight unloaded.

Supported by Lucia on one side, and Yannis on the other, Cathy tottered ashore. In spite of her long sleep, she still looked very wan. The noise and hurly-burly of the waterfront made her press her hands over her ears, and shrink closer to her sister.

Knowing what chagrin it would cause her to have to meet the other members of the house party with her yellow suit all creased, and her make-up awry, Lucia felt very sorry for her.

"You'll feel much better when you've had a bath and changed," she whispered encouragingly, as Yannis led them through the bustle.

"Ah, the jeep is over there," he said, indicating a Land Rover parked out of the way of the confusion.

For an instant, Lucia thought that the man standing by the jeep must be another of Nicholas's Greek relations. He was wearing a pink cotton shirt and sun-bleached blue jeans, and he looked as strong and tough as the men unloading the cargo.

Then he moved towards them, and took off his dark sun-glasses. It was Nicholas himself.

"Hello...how are you? Welcome to Marina. I'm sorry I couldn't come to meet you in Athens, but Yannis will have explained, no doubt."

Before either of the girls could speak, Yannis said, "Miss Cathy has not been well, Nico. She has been sea-sick."

"What—today?" Nicholas's eyebrows shot up. Then, observing Cathy's pale face, "Oh, poor child—how very unfortunate. What about you, Lucia?"

"I'm all right, thanks. But I think Cathy needs to rest for a while before she will feel herself again," she answered, hoping he would take the hint.

"Yes, certainly she must rest. We don't dine until nine. She'll feel much better by then. Are you coming up with us, Yannis?"

"No, I must return to the hotel, and see that everything goes as it should. I may come up later," said the younger man. He swung the girls' suitcases on to the front seat of the Rover. "Goodbye, Miss Cathy. Goodbye, Lucia. If I do not see you again today, we will meet tomorrow." And with a clap on the shoulder for Nicholas, and one of his ardent looks for Lucia, he left them.

Nicholas helped Cathy into the back of the Rover. "It's rather a rough ride to the house, I'm afraid. But it isn't far. Once we're there, you can relax. The others are all on the beach, and won't be back for some time yet."

Once they had left the town, the road became a rutted, stony cart track. Nicholas drove slowly and carefully, but even so they were bounced about a good deal, and Cathy looked as if she felt like bursting into tears.

After jolting uphill for some time, they came to a fork in the way. In one direction, the track continued upwards. In the other, it began to decline. Nicholas took the downward fork.

"We're nearly there now," he told them, over his shoulder.

Soon the sea came into view again. From this height, it looked even more blue than it had from the decks of the steamer. In the near distance were various small islets, some of them hardly more than rocks. In the far distance, Lucia could see the hazy silhouettes of islands comparable to Marina. They looked, somehow, as if they were all at anchor, and as if, should their moorings be loosed, they would float away to the almost imperceptible horizon where blue sea and blue sky merged.

The house, when it came into view, was as dazzlingly white as those in the town. Approaching it from above, they saw first the flat, balustraded roof, set out with tubbed plants and garden furniture.

Then the track turned a steep, hairpin bend which brought them level with the side of the building and its main entrance.

After the bright light out of doors, the interior of the house was cool and shadowy.

"I'll take you straight to your rooms," said Nicholas. And he led them down the long, wide passage which seemed to extend almost the whole length of the house. Near the far end of it, he opened a door, and showed them into a bedroom with white rough-cast walls, and a tiled floor.

"This is your room, Cathy. Yours is next door, Lucia. Which of these cases belongs to Cathy?"

Lucia told him, and he put the case on a chair near the bed. Then he took her through the bathroom which connected with another bedroom, and deposited her suitcase.

"When you've put Cathy to bed, come and have a drink with me," he said. "I'll be on the terrace. It's outside the big room across the hall."

After he had gone, Lucia returned to Cathy's room. She found her sister sitting on the edge of the bed, her eyes brimming with tears.

"My head is splitting. I feel dreadful," she said, in a quavery voice.

She looked so much like a sick child that Lucia sat down beside her, and put an arm round her. "Poor Cathy, it's been beastly for you. Never mind—you'll feel much better presently. Let me help you undress, and then I'll give you some aspirins. You heard what Nicholas said. They have dinner very late in Greece. You don't have to meet the others for hours yet."

By the time she had finished unpacking both cases, Cathy had fallen asleep again. Lucia washed, and changed her clothes. Her Courtelle coat and skirt showed hardly any traces of the journey. But it was refreshing to put on a plain, sleeveless dress of turquoise linen-like fabric. This, being made of another synthetic fibre, was also uncreased after hours in her suitcase.

Aware that she was putting off the moment when, alone, she must face her host, she spent some time brushing her hair. The house was not what she had expected. Although her bedroom was spacious and high-ceilinged, the white walls and bare, polished tiles made it seem like a room in a convent. The bedcover looked as if it had been woven on a hand-loom in a peasant's cottage. The only furniture, apart from the double bed, was a large, carved clothes cupboard, a chest of drawers which also served as a dressing-table, and an armchair covered in dark blue repp. The one ornament in the room was a rather beautiful mosaic ikon on the wall over the head of the bed.

When—unable to postpone the confrontation with Nicholas any longer—she crossed the hall to the big room he had mentioned, she found this also was furnished with functional simplicity. There was no trace of the luxurious, fashionable style of décor she had expected to find.

On the terrace outside, Nicholas was lounging in a garden chair, reading a Greek newspaper.

"Ah, there you are. How is Cathy now?" he asked, getting up, and casting the paper aside.

"She's asleep. If she doesn't feel better by dinner time, perhaps you wouldn't mind if she stayed in bed till tomorrow."

"Not in the least. I've never experienced sea-sickness myself, but I'm told it's a vile sensation. Poor Cathy—what a bad introduction to Marina."

"Yes," said Lucia. "Before we go back, I must get hold of some sea-sick pills, if it's possible to buy them here. If she was ill on a day like this, a choppy crossing would be agony for her."

"I'll go and get something to drink. I shan't be long." He disappeared into the house.

"What—no servants to fetch and carry for him?" thought Lucia. Then she remembered that, in Greece, as in most hot countries, the afternoon hours were idle hours. It was a little after five o'clock. Perhaps the staff were still off duty, and would reappear at six.

He was away about five minutes, and came back with two glasses in one hand, and a large jug of iced orange juice in the other.

"Will this suit you? Or would you prefer something with a kick in it?"

"No, thank you—that looks delicious."

Nicholas filled both glasses, and handed one of them to her. *"Ya sas!"* he said, raising his glass to her.

While she was sipping her drink, he asked one or two civil questions about the journey.

"How is the little girl's arm now?" Lucia enquired, remembering the reason why he had been unable to meet them himself.

"Oh, she's as right as a trivet today. She's playing down there on the beach," he said, nodding in the direction of a sloping pathway.

The beach was not visible from the terrace, but now and then the sound of voices and laughter drifted upwards.

"It was one of those accidents which make women shriek and wring their hands, but which aren't as bad as they seem once the bleeding has eased off," Nicholas went on. His dark eyes glinted. "I'm not implying that *all* women have hysterics in an emergency. I'm sure you would have dealt with it even more competently than I. You must be accustomed to minor injuries."

"Yes—fairly," Lucia agreed.

She had nearly finished her drink now. He picked up the jug, and came over to top up her glass. Looking down at her, he said, "Is that a new dress for the holiday?"

"Yes, it is, as a matter of fact."

"In Greece, when anyone wears something new we say—Wear it in good health."

His scrutiny made her uneasy, but she managed to smile, and reply, *"Efharistó, Kyrie."*

His eyebrow lifted. "So you've taken the trouble to learn some Greek?"

"My father said one should never visit another country without at least learning how to say Please and Thank you."

"Your father was right," said Nicholas. "But it's surprising how few people do. The British are some of the worst offenders. They expect all foreigners to speak some English, but they rarely bother to learn anyone else's language. Even people who consider themselves well-educated can generally only manage some stumbling French."

"I suppose you speak Greek like a Greek?" she said.

"Yes, it was my first language. Until I was six, I never spoke anything else. I was born on this island. If it hadn't been for the war, I would probably have spent my life here. But in 1938, when it was obviously only a matter of time before the holocaust, my father took us to England. He was killed in Crete in the summer of 1941. The following year, my mother died in an air raid."

"Oh... how terrible for you," Lucia said, in a shaken voice.

"It seemed so at the time. I was ten that year, and an English prep school was rather an alien environment," he said unemotionally. "Later, I realized it was the best thing—for her. She would have been wretched in England without my father, but she would have stayed for my benefit."

"Who looked after you after she died?"

"My father's eldest brother and his wife. They didn't approve of my mixed blood, so they spent a great deal of money on a public school education in the hope that it would knock the Greek out of me. Unfortunately—from their point of view—it had rather the reverse effect."

Lucia said, "If you feel yourself more Greek than English, why don't you live here all the time?"

His expression became sardonic. "I have expensive tastes. Here on Marina, a man who earns eight hundred drachmae a week is a Croesus. For me, it's the price of a pair of shoes—or dinner *à deux* at the White Tower," he tacked on, with a provoking glance.

Lucia—who, a few moments ago, had felt an upsurge of compassion for the loneliness and grief he must have felt when, still in short trousers, he was left both orphaned and exiled—had a swift revulsion of feeling.

Whatever pity he might have deserved at ten, Nicholas at thirty-six was the most insufferably cynical and self-centred person she had ever encountered.

However, she did not allow her animadversion to show, but said, quite impassively, "If your father was here for some years, how did he earn his living?"

"He was a sculptor, so he could work more or less where he pleased. It was—" He broke off, listening. The faint voices from the beach were closer now. "That sounds like the others coming up. I expect they're impatient to have a look at you. When I told them you were a teacher, they seemed to think you might cast rather a blight on us," he informed her, with a gleam of amusement.

Before they were fully within earshot, the voices died away. Probably the ascent was steep enough to make even young and vigorous people breathless.

Lucia wondered what they were like, and had little doubt that she would find them as incompatible as they her.

Nicholas must have divined that she was not exactly eager to meet them. He said, "Don't worry, they won't bite you."

And, as he spoke, they appeared. Three children. Three panting brown children, with sandy legs and wet hair.

They were so much out of breath he waited a little before introducing them. Then he said, "These are my sister's offspring, Lucia—Francesca, Stephen and Ariadne. This is Miss Gresham, children."

The eldest of them, Francesca, was a girl in her early teens. She was wearing a yellow bikini and, already, her figure was lovely. Stephen looked about twelve, and he too was tall and well-knit. The smallest one, Ariadne, still had the round cheeks and fat tummy of infancy.

"How do you do?" Francesca came forward to shake hands.

Lucia smiled. "How do you do."

Then Stephen approached and, after him, little Ariadne.

The formalities completed, Nicholas said, "I have to go to the village to fetch Aunt Katina. Look after Miss Gresham, will you, kids? Perhaps she'd like to see the beach." He smiled at Lucia. "You don't mind being left to their mercies *now*, do you? I shan't be more than half an hour." And without waiting for her reply, he disappeared into the house.

Francesca flopped into his chair. "What a disgusting fraud Nico is! He made you out to be a real old dragon who would keep us in order." She gasped, and turned very red.

"What's the matter?" Lucia asked, puzzled.

"You *are* the one who's a schoolmistress, aren't you?" Francesca enquired, in a chagrined voice.

"Yes, that's right."

"Oh, glory—thank goodness for that! I suddenly realized I might have dropped a colossal brick. I mean if you were the *other* one, he might have been telling the truth," she explained, rather confusedly. "Where is your sister, Miss Gresham?"

"She wasn't very well on the steamer, so she's lying down for a while."

"Oh, I see—poor thing. How rotten for her. I expect it's the olive oil. It often upsets English people."

"No, it wasn't anything she ate. She was sea-sick."

"Sea-sick? Today?" exclaimed Stephen, looking incredulous. "But the sea's as calm as a millpond."

"Try not to be a complete ass," his sister said crushingly, glaring at him. "Some people get sick if a boat rolls the least little bit. Don't they, Miss Gresham?"

"Yes, I'm afraid a few people do," Lucia confirmed.

Ariadne put in a remark. "I was sick in Harrods," she announced. "It was before I had measles. It went all over the carpet. Mummy said she could have sunk through the floor."

"I should think so too," said Francesca. "You should have told her while there was time to rush to the loo. You must have known you were going to be sick."

"No, I didn't," her sister protested. "It just whooshed up out of my tummy." She turned to Lucia and added, not without pride, "If you know where to look, you can still see the mark."

"Ugh! Horrible child!" said Francesca, pulling a face. "You'll make Miss Gresham sick in a minute. Shall we show you the beach now, Miss Gresham? Why don't you have a swim with us? The water's gorgeously warm."

"All right. I'll go and change," said Lucia. "And I think you had better call me Lucia," she added, as an afterthought.

It did not take her long to change into her new dark green swimsuit. Peeping into Cathy's room, she saw that her sister was still asleep.

The two younger children had already started down the beach path when she reappeared on the terrace.

"How lovely and brown you are," she said to Francesca, comparing the child's golden limbs with her own winter-pale arms and legs.

"Oh, you'll soon get a tan," said Francesca. "I was white too when we arrived. The thing is not to get burnt. Have you brought some Ambre Solaire? If not, we've got lashings we can lend you."

"I have some, thanks," said Lucia. "Are your parents here with you, Francesca?"

It might have been only her fancy, but it seemed to her that the girl's blue eyes clouded suddenly.

"No, Daddy's at home in London, and Mummy's in Paris," she said. "There's just us, and Nico, and Aunt Katina."

"But there are some other guests coming."

"No—no, I don't think so. At least, Nico hasn't mentioned it. Of course there's Yannis, and all Mummy's and Nico's hordes of relations. But they only pop in and out. They're not what you'd call guests."

"I see," said Lucia contemplatively.

The path turned, and she saw the beach—a crescent of sand lapped by crystalline shallows the colour of aquamarines. Stephen and Ariadne were already wading into the deeper turquoise-blue water.

"We're not allowed to swim unless there's a grown-up with us," Francesca explained. "Nico's a lamb. He lets us do things which would give Daddy and Mummy blue fits. But he's terribly strict about the sea. If we did break the rule, I think he'd pack us off home. You should see him swim," she added admiringly. "He could win a gold medal *easily*."

The sea was not, by adult standards, gorgeously warm. But it was at least five degrees warmer than any Lucia had ever bathed in.

The children all swam like fishes. Although they would probably have liked to stay in the water, they followed her out without protest when Lucia returned to the sand.

"I mustn't stay down here too long in case my sister wakes up and wants me," she told them, pulling off her cap. "Do you all have dinner at nine?"

"Stephen and I do sometimes," said Francesca. "Ariadne never does. She has supper at seven. To-night, we're all going to bed early."

Lucia followed them up the path. She had not brought a towel with her, and neither had the children.

"Shall I give you a heave?" Stephen asked, when they reached a steep stretch near the top.

"What nice manners they have," she thought, as he grasped her hand, and helped her to scramble up the awkward part.

When they reached the terrace, Nicholas was back. Sitting with him was an elderly woman, dressed in funereal black.

Nicholas rose, and his dark eyes swept Lucia's pale limbs and wet-suited figure in a way that made her wish she had on her beach coat.

He said, reversing the customary order of introduction, "This is my aunt, Lucia. She's lived all her life on the island, and speaks no English."

The two women looked at each other. Lucia found the Greek woman's gaze slightly intimidating. She had fine black eyes, but they did not reveal her thoughts. It was impossible to tell if she welcomed or disapproved of her nephew's foreign visitors.

When it seemed that she was expected to speak first, Lucia said shyly, *"Héro polí, Kyria."*

Immediately, a smile of the utmost cordiality creased the Greek woman's lined olive face. with both hands, she clasped Lucia's right hand. *"Kalos irthate, Thespoinis."*

Fortunately, Lucia knew the correct response to this formal expression of welcome. *"Kalos sas vrikame,"* she answered.

Aunt Katina turned to Nicholas, and said something which Lucia could not follow. First, he nodded and grinned. Then he shook his head, and said something too fast and idiomatic for her to catch even one word.

"I've explained to Aunt Katina that you only speak a little Greek, so it's no use her rattling away at you," he told Lucia.

"Oh, I see." She wondered what it was his aunt had said to make him grin and signify assent.

The Greek woman turned her attention to the children. It was clear from her gestures that she was telling them to go to their rooms and tidy themselves for their evening meal.

"I must go and change, too," said Lucia.

Leaving Nicholas on the terrace, she followed the others into the house.

She had left the bathroom's two doors open and, as

she entered her bedroom, Cathy called, "Is that you, Lucia?"

Lucia walked through to the other bedroom. "How are you feeling? Any better?"

"Yes—a bit." Cathy was lying with her back to the connecting door. Now she rolled over, and noticed her sister's swimsuit. "Oh, you've been swimming. How long have I been asleep?"

"Only about an hour and a half. There's still lots of time before dinner."

Cathy sat up. "Have you met the others? What are they like?"

"Yes, I've met them—they're charming."

"Well, tell me about them? Are the women terribly smart?"

"No... I wouldn't say smart. They're both very nice-looking," said Lucia, keeping a straight face.

"How many men are there?"

"Only one. He seems rather nice, too." She felt it was unfair to go on misleading her sister, and said, "They're children, Cathy. They're Nicholas's nephew and nieces."

Cathy gaped. "*Children?* I don't understand. Nico didn't tell me there were going to be children around. Where are the others? The grown-ups? The rest of the house party?"

"The children are the rest," Lucia explained. "Apart from Nicholas and ourselves, the only other adult here is his Aunt Katina who, I think, runs the house for him."

"What? Oh, there *must* be some others. Three kids and an aunt aren't a house-party. The rest of them must be out somewhere."

"Not according to Francesca. I asked her if there was anyone else here, or coming, and she said there wasn't."

"I call that the limit!" Cathy exclaimed, most indignantly. "He distinctly said it was going to be a house-party. I didn't come here to make sand pies with three grubby kids."

"I thought you came to be with Nicholas," Lucia observed, rather dryly. "Does it matter who else is around?"

"Well, of course it does. It's much more fun with a crowd of people. I assumed there would be at least ten of us."

"I doubt if there's room for a large party. There aren't enough bedrooms."

"That's another thing," Cathy said irritably. "I don't think much of *this* room. It's so bare—not a bit like his flat. And look at the sheets. They're like sacking!"

"They're unbleached linen. They wear for ever," said Lucia. She bent to sniff them. "Mm...what a lovely, fresh scent. They're probably dried on bushes, or stored with herbs in the folds."

"Well, *I* like smooth sheets, *and* a carpet on the floor, *and* a dressing-table," Cathy said, pouting. She slid out of bed and went to inspect the bathroom.

While she was having a bath—whatever other refinements it might lack, the house had excellent plumbing, and plenty of hot water on tap—Lucia dressed, and rinsed out her swimsuit. Then, putting it in a plastic bag so that it wouldn't drip on the floor, she went to find somewhere to hang it.

In the hall, she met Francesca, who showed her the way to a linen line. The house had no garden or boundary, but Lucia saw that a number of shrubs and trees had been added to the natural vegetation of the hillside immediately surrounding it.

"Come and see our room," Francesca invited, as they returned indoors. "Stephen's sharing with Nico this time, and Ariadne and I have the room next to Aunt Katina's."

The children's room was similar to Lucia's and Cathy's except that it had bunk beds, and two chests of drawers. Ariadne was already ensconced in the top bunk, and up there with her was Nicholas. He was reading from a paperback while she ate her supper.

He did not notice Lucia's entrance, and went on reading the story, which she recognized as one of Michael Bond's "Paddington" adventures. To her surprise, he read well, using voices appropriate to the characters, and holding Ariadne cuddled in the crook of his arm as, long ago, when he was at home, Malcolm Gresham had sat with Lucia at bedtime.

A few minutes after she entered the room, he came to the end of a chapter, and closed the book.

"Oh, just one more chapter—please, Nico," the little girl begged him.

"No, not tonight, chicken." He swung himself down to the floor. "Oh, hello, Lucia. Sorry, I didn't see you there." There was no self-consciousness in his manner. "How is Cathy now?"

"Much better, I think. She's having a bath. Is there anything I can do to help your aunt?"

"I shouldn't think so. Francesca gives her a hand when she needs one," he answered.

"Would you read some more to me, Lucia?" Ariadne asked hopefully. "She did say we could call her Lucia," she added, as her uncle shot up his eyebrows.

Lucia smiled. Ariadne looked very engaging in her blue pyjamas, with her hair brushed and tied in perky bunches. "Yes, I'll read to you."

"Are you sure you don't mind?" Nicholas asked.

"Not in the least. I like Paddington."

"Well, only one chapter," he said firmly, to Ariadne.

And then, before Lucia could start to climb the wooden bunk ladder, he put his hands on her waist, and lifted her up beside his niece.

He did it as swiftly and effortlessly as if she were no bigger than the child. Yet Lucia, although she was slender, stood five feet five in her sandals, and weighed a pound under nine stone. Bernard, a much taller man, could never have lifted her so easily.

"Oh!" she murmured, her cheeks suddenly hot.

The children laughed at her surprise.

"Isn't Nico strong?" said Ariadne. "He can lift me right up to the ceiling."

Nicholas rumpled her hair. "You're just a whipper-snapper. Finish your supper, there's a good girl."

He went out of the room—but not before he had given Lucia a rather mocking look, as if he knew it was not only surprise which had made her flush.

Cathy was putting the finishing touches to her makeup when Lucia returned to their quarters.

"Where have you been all this time?" she asked.

"I've been reading to the youngest of the children."

Cathy applied some pale lipstick. "So that's why Nico was so keen to get you to come. I didn't think it was the chaperone aspect which worried him. He obviously wanted you here to keep the kids out of his hair."

"He appears to be very fond of them," said Lucia. "And the two oldest ones are quite capable of looking after themselves most of the time."

"How old is the youngest?"

"She's six."

"Well, I'm sure he doesn't want her on his hands more than's necessary. He's not the paternal type, thank goodness," said Cathy.

"Perhaps you don't know him as well as you think," Lucia answered.

"Well, he's never mentioned them before, so he can't be all that fond of them. I suppose they were foisted on him to give the parents a break, and he realized that you would be the ideal person to cope with the little horrors."

When Francesca had said that Nicholas had described her as a dragon, Lucia had taken it as a joke. But now she began to wonder if he had meant it. Perhaps Cathy was right in suggesting that he had not volunteered to have the children at Marina with him, but had been asked to do so. The odd, rather unhappy look on

Francesca's face when Lucia had asked about her parents did seem to suggest that there might be a hidden reason for the children being in their uncle's care.

The possibility that Nicholas had not been sincere in what he had said in the kitchen at "Montrose", but had been deliberately gulling her, made Lucia so angry that she quickly returned to her own room, and closed the door.

It was not the first time she had had vengeful thoughts about Nicholas. Indeed *every* time she had met him, he had succeeded in rousing some ire in her. But tonight her suspicion and anger were mingled with hurt. And since that moment in the children's room, when he had lifted her on to the bunk, she could no longer deny to herself the cause of the hurt. When his hands had fastened on her waist, she had felt her heart flutter as wildly as a bird in a net. Every nerve in her body had quivered with shock and excitement. Even now, merely thinking about it, she felt hot and cold.

And the worst of it was that, deep down, she had felt the attraction from the beginning—from the night she had come home to find him kissing her sister.

AT ABOUT A QUARTER TO NINE, Yannis turned up. Kyria Katina was busy in the kitchen, and Nicholas was introducing the two girls to *ouzo*, the most popular Greek apéritif.

"Ah, you are better now, Miss Cathy," said Yannis, as he came into the large room known as the studio. But, although he looked courteously pleased to see her restored to normal, it was to Lucia that he gave his warmest smile. "And you, beautiful Lucia—what do you think of my island? Is it not delightful?"

"Yes, it seems a lovely place, Yannis." She flashed a swift glance at Nicholas to see his reaction to the younger man's flattering greeting. But he was lighting a cigarette, and she could not see the expression in his eyes.

"Tomorrow I will show you the hotel," said Yannis, helping himself to the savoury titbits called *mezés*.

"Tomorrow is Good Friday," she reminded him.

"The Orthodox Church doesn't always celebrate Easter at the same time as the Roman and Protestant Churches," put in Nicholas. "Sometimes the dates coincide, but this year Easter in Greece is later than in England."

Kyria Katina put her head round the door, and said something which Lucia guessed was a request for them to take their places at the table because dinner was nearly ready.

The studio was an all-purpose room, with two large sofas and several chairs grouped round the wide stone hearth at one end, and a dining area at the other end. Nicholas drew out the chair on which Cathy was to sit, and Yannis attended to Lucia.

"You'll find that Greek food is like English food," said Nicholas, as he took his own place at the head of the table. "When it's badly cooked, it's abominable. But well-cooked, it's very good. Tonight we're having *moussaka*, which is a kind of shepherd's pie. Would you care to try some *retsina*, Lucia? Or would you rather have ordinary wine?"

Lucia knew that resinated wine was an acquired taste, but she was curious to try it.

"I'd like some *retsina*, please," she said.

"I thought you would," he said, in a tone she could not interpret. To her sister, he added, "You had better have ordinary wine, Cathy. I'm sure you wouldn't like *retsina*. Most English people say it tastes like turpentine."

Kyria Katina's *moussaka* was delicious. The basis of the dish was minced meat, with aubergines, tomatoes, and onions. The topping was a rich sauce sprinkled with grated cheese. The only person who did not tuck in with relish was Cathy. But whether this was because she did not like the dish, or because her tummy was still unsettled, Lucia could not tell.

"Well, what do you think of it?" Nicholas asked, when she had taken her first sip of *retsina*.

Lucia drank a little more. The flavour was quite unlike anything she had tasted before. "I'm not sure yet," she said cautiously.

"You needn't be polite," he said dryly. "We shan't be offended if you don't like it. Very few non-Greeks do. Leave it, and have some of the other wine."

"No, I would rather have this, thank you." She turned to his aunt, and said, in Greek, "This is excellent, *Kyria*"—indicating the *moussaka*.

The Greek woman beamed and, as soon as Lucia had finished her first helping, urged her to have some more. The meal ended with fruit, and Greek coffee. Afterwards, Lucia asked, through Nicholas, if she could help his aunt to clear the table, and wash the dishes. But when this offer had been translated to her, Kyria Katina looked quite shocked, and replied that Lucia must rest after her long journey.

"Come—we will go up to the roof garden, and watch the sea by moonlight," said Yannis, taking her by the hand, and leading her from the room.

They reached the roof by way of an outside staircase.

"It is cooler now. Perhaps you should have a coat," he suggested, as they leaned against the parapet, and looked down at the glittering sea.

"I'm not cold. It's a lovely night," said Lucia, drawing in a deep breath of the clean, salty air.

He put his arm round her, and stroked her bare arm. "You feel warm. I like this scent you wear. What is it called?"

"It's *Blue Grass* toilet water." She tried to move casually away.

But his hand tightened on her arm, and held her still. He sniffed the nape of her neck. "Mm...it's very good," he murmured. And then he kissed her, behind her ear.

Somewhat to her surprise, Lucia was neither annoyed nor embarrassed. To be honest, she found it rather enjoyable. But when Yannis then turned her round, with the evident intention of kissing her on the mouth, she held him off, and said mildly, "No, Yannis—please don't."

"Why not?" he asked, looking perplexed. "You like me, don't you?"

"Yes, I like you," she began. "But—"

"And you are not betrothed?"

"No."

"Then why do you say I must not kiss you?"

"This time yesterday, we hadn't met," she reminded him.

"I wanted to kiss you last night," he said, smiling down at her. "If it would give us both pleasure, why must we wait?"

It was a question for which she had no ready answer, apart from the conventional one she had already given. To deny that she would enjoy being kissed would be pure hypocrisy, for even having his arms round her was a nice feeling. And although it was less than twenty-four hours since she had first set eyes on him, already she felt that she knew him quite well—and that there was much to like about him, quite apart from his physical magnificence.

Taking her hesitation for acquiescence, Yannis slid his right arm more firmly round her and, with his left hand, gently caressed her upturned face.

But, at the very moment when she would have to resist, or be kissed, she suddenly realized that they no longer had the roof to themselves. A few yards away, by the staircase, Nicholas was standing, watching them.

Her indrawn breath, and the pressure of her hands against his chest, made Yannis laugh and say softly, "Don't be shy, beautiful Lucia."

In spite of his low tone, Nicholas heard what he said.

"You're mistaken, Yannis," he remarked, strolling towards them. "Lucia isn't shy. It's merely that she doesn't approve of light-hearted kisses. Isn't that so, Lucia?"

She did not answer. But Yannis, entirely unabashed by his cousin's intrusion, kept his arm round her waist, and said good-humouredly, "I didn't hear you come up, Nico. Where is Miss Cathy?"

"She's still rather off colour, so I advised her to have an early night."

"I—I think I will, too, if you don't mind?" Lucia said quickly. "Goodnight, Yannis. Goodnight"—to Nicholas.

She had been in her room for only a few moments when the connecting door opened, and Cathy came in.

"A fine holiday this is going to be," she said petulantly. "There's nothing to do on this island. It's like the back of beyond."

"Well, it's no use complaining to me," Lucia said, rather tersely. "You're the one who wanted to come."

"There's no need to bite my head off. What are you ratty about?"

"Nothing. I'm tired, that's all. Go to bed, Cathy. We both need a good night's rest."

"Oh, all right... if that's the mood you're in." Huffily, Cathy withdrew.

Lucia bit her lip. She had not meant to snap at her sister. But after what had happened on the roof, her emotions were in too much confusion for her to bear the younger girl's grumbles with patience.

Cathy was not the only one for whom, in more senses than one, it had been an exacting day.

CHAPTER FOUR

VERY EARLY the next morning, before anyone else was astir, Lucia slipped out of the house to go for a walk.

In spite of her disturbed state of mind the previous night, she had fallen asleep within minutes of turning out the light, and had slept soundly until four o'clock. Then something had woken her, and she had been unable to doze off again.

She had not gone far from the house when she heard a whistle. Turning, she was annoyed to see Nicholas coming up the hillside after her.

Fortunately, he was too far away to see the vexation on her face, and by the time he caught up with her, she had masked it.

"Good morning. You're up early," he said, as he reached her. "You didn't find your bed uncomfortable, I hope?"

"No, quite the reverse," she said politely. "I don't know why I woke so early. But my father said this was the best time of day on the islands, so I thought I'd come out and explore. I didn't know anyone else was about yet."

"The others won't be up for an hour or so, but I always rise early at Marina. You don't mind if I join you, I hope? I want to have a talk with you." And with this somewhat daunting statement, he fell into step beside her.

Presently, when they had been walking in silence for about ten minutes, Lucia asked, "Are there any classical sites on Marina?"

"No, none," he told her. "But there are the remains

of a temple on one of the small islands you can see from the house. The place is uninhabited, but we sometimes go over for picnics. We might spend a day there next week. There's not much left of the temple—just some paving, and a couple of pillars. But we'll be spending the last two days of your holiday in Athens, so you'll have a chance to see the Parthenon."

"That reminds me—we owe you some money," said Lucia.

He raised his eyebrows. "What for?"

"For our room at the hotel in Athens the night before last. When I asked for the bill, they said it had already been paid."

"Certainly—you were there as my guests."

"Oh, but that isn't right. You must let us know what we owe you."

"Why?" he asked, with a glint of amusement. "If you can accept my hospitality here, why not in Athens?"

"Well...it's not the same," she objected awkwardly. "The hotel was obviously an expensive one. We can't possibly allow you to pay for it."

"Since I was responsible for your staying there, and I'm also rather better off than you are, it's proper that I should pay for it," he answered reasonably. Then he grinned, his dark eyes mocking her. "You're too punctilious, 'beautiful Lucia'."

When Yannis called her that, she could take it lightly. But when Nicholas echoed his cousin, even to tease her, a queer little tremor ran through her. Deciding to take the offensive, she said, with attempted nonchalance, "Is that what you want to talk about? To warn me not to take Yannis seriously?"

"I can't imagine that you would," he replied, with a shrug.

Instead of being appeased by this answer, Lucia found it rather annoying. "I don't know why not," she said airily. "I should think most women would be attracted to Yannis. He's not only very good-looking, but seems to be a nice person too."

"He's also a Greek," he said dryly.

"What has that to do with it?"

Nicholas looked amused again. "In Greece, love is one thing, and marriage is another. Greek men may be hot-blooded, but they aren't romantic in the English sense. Here, the girl with the best marriage prospects is the one with the largest dowry, not the one with the prettiest face. And Greeks very rarely marry foreigners. They believe in the proverb—'A homemade shoe, even if it's patched, is the best'."

Lucia made no comment on this but, a little further on, she said, "What *did* you want to talk about?"

"Let's sit down for ten minutes, shall we?"

They had reached a place, high on the headland, where the ground levelled out, and there was a stretch of rough grass and wild flowers, and two or three ancient olive trees.

"What do you think of the children?" he asked, when they had settled themselves.

Lucia was wearing a cornflower shirt, and paler blue trousers which allowed her to sit with her arms round her updrawn knees. "They seem charming," she said, looking towards the far headland on the other side of the bay.

Her father had told her about the extraordinary purity of the light in the Aegean, especially in the early hours of the day. This morning, she saw for herself what he had meant. It was as if, all her life, she had been seeing the world through a dusty window. Now the glass had been washed and polished, and the colours and shapes of the landscape were so rich and distinct that the expression "to feast the eyes" took on a new meaning for her.

"It was about the children that I wanted to talk," said Nicholas, lighting a cigarette. "I feel it's advisable for you to know the reason they're here without their parents—just in case they mention anything to you. They aren't supposed to know about it, of course, but I'm fairly certain Francesca does, and possibly Stephen too." He paused, his black brows contracted. "The fact is that my sister and her husband are on the brink of parting company."

"I see," said Lucia quietly. "Yes—I think Francesca does know." When he gave her an interrogative glance, she explained, "I asked her yesterday if her parents were here and I thought then there was a rather unhappy look on her face when she said her father was at home, and her mother was in Paris."

Nicholas drew on his cigarette. "My God, what fools people can be!" he exclaimed, with a rasp in his voice. "They've had a darned good marriage for fifteen years. Now, between them, they're going to wreck their own lives, and the children's as well."

The exasperation in his face and voice surprised Lucia. If she had ever considered the matter, she would have supposed that his attitude to the break-up of a marriage would be one of cynical indifference.

She said, "Well, if people can't get on together, it's sometimes better for the children if they do separate. I have a child in my class whose parents fight like cat and dog. The poor little boy has no security at all."

"Yes, that may be so in some instances," Nicholas agreed, rather impatiently. "But this is not a case of basic incompatibility. Until quite recently, Sofia and Richard were happy enough. They're making a mountain out of a mole-hill."

Naturally, Lucia was curious to know the cause of the rift. But she hesitated to ask in case he should think she was prying.

He fell silent for some minutes, and it was while he was in this state of frowning abstraction that she caught herself thinking what a well-cut, generous mouth he had, and how broad and strong his shoulders were. These were not the kind of thoughts she wanted to have about him, and it vexed her that she should so easily succumb to them when, in more important respects, she was inclined to dislike and mistrust him.

"The trouble with women is that they can never accept the defects of people's qualities," he said.

For once he was not trying to nettle her. Indeed, Lucia felt that he might have forgotten she was there, and was thinking aloud.

"What do you mean?" she asked.

He glanced at her then, but still with a rather absent expression. "Sofia was brought up by another branch of the family," he said. "She looks and thinks like an English woman. There's very little Greek blood in her. She's a capable, strong-minded girl, with a talent for organization. I wouldn't call her domineering. She's never had to fight to get her own way because Richard is an easy-going type who doesn't mind her managing things. But when a man lets his wife wear the trousers, she ought to realize that he's likely to be easily led by other people."

He paused, looking at a tiny, flying insect which had alighted on his darkly-tanned forearm. After a moment, he blew it away, and went on, "Unfortunately, Sofia's discovered that my brother-in-law has been involved with one of the secretaries in his office. It's over now, and it never amounted to much. But for one damn-fool lapse, she's seriously considering leaving him."

Lucia studied the toes of her gay scarlet denim holiday shoes. "What do you mean by 'it never amounted to much'?"

Nicholas crushed out his cigarette. "Richard was never serious about the girl. It was she who made all the running."

"How do you know?"

"Because I met her once, and she tried to entangle me," he said dryly. He gave her a sardonic smile. "There are predatory females too, you know."

"Perhaps that is what your sister can't forgive," suggested Lucia. "Perhaps she feels more humiliated because your brother-in-law didn't really care about the girl. I think, if I were married, I could forgive my husband for falling in love with someone else—but not for a casual affair."

"If you made him happy, he wouldn't need anyone else."

"You mean if a man goes off the rails, it's not his fault, it's his wife's," she said, rather acidly. "I suppose you think your sister ought to overlook the whole thing."

"No—but I think it would be a pity to disrupt five lives for the sake of pride," he answered mildly.

"Surely it's more than a matter of pride," she retorted, trying not to show her indignation. "How would you feel if you were married, and your wife was unfaithful to you? Would *you* swallow your pride, and forgive her for 'one foolish lapse'?"

"Certainly not!" he said promptly. "But that's an entirely different matter."

"I don't see why. It doesn't seem different to me."

The corners of his mouth twitched slightly. "How you do resent any suggestion that women are not men's equals!"

Her colour rose. "I happen to think they are. You don't, I gather?"

"I know they are not," he said blandly. "But that isn't to say I regard women as inferior."

"Well, that's handsome of you," she said, with a sting in her voice.

He grinned. "My dear girl, you may be inexperienced, but you're not ignorant. In theory, I daresay you're a good deal wiser than Cathy. You know as well as I do that a woman's emotional make-up is quite different from a man's. Equality doesn't come into it."

She said, with her face averted, "You mean a man

can make love to someone without it meaning anything special, but most women can't do that."

"Exactly," he said. "For a woman there is always some degree of commitment. For a man—very often none at all."

Lucia got to her feet, and dusted the seat of her pants. Then, digging her hands into her pockets, she said, "I'm not sure I believe in that premise. It's a very convenient one, of course."

With one lithe movement, he was on his feet beside her. "It's not a premise, it's an indisputable fact." His eyes narrowed and glinted. "I'll prove it to you, if you like."

She backed a pace, her heart thumping. "Prove it? What do you mean?"

He smiled. "If I kissed you, you wouldn't forget it. You'd remember it all your life."

His effrontery took her breath away. Then her chin came up, and she said, her voice not quite steady, "While you'd forget it in five minutes?"

"Ah, that I can't say till I've tried it. Perhaps... perhaps not. You might surprise me, 'beautiful Lucia'."

"It hasn't occurred to you, I suppose, that I might not want you to kiss me—that I might remember it as something unpleasant which once happened to me?"

His white teeth showed for an instant. "That's another thing about women. They're almost never honest with themselves. You'd enjoy being kissed as much as I'd enjoy kissing you. Why not be truthful, and admit it?"

"Because it doesn't happen to *be* true," she informed him hotly.

He lifted a sceptical eyebrow. "If it isn't, there must be something wrong with you. Any girl of your age who has never been made love to should be getting pretty impatient, I'd say."

Unwisely, she said, "What makes you so sure that no one has ever made love to me?"

"The fact that you're so agitated now."

"I wasn't agitated last night when Yannis wanted to kiss me," she reminded him.

"Yannis wouldn't kiss you against your will. You think I might, don't you?" he mocked her.

Lucia forgot she was a guest. "Frankly, I think you're capable of anything," she flung at him witheringly.

But of course it did not deflate him. He only laughed, and said, carelessly, "Well, don't worry, I'm not going to kiss you." And then he stretched out his arm, and lightly caressed her cheek with the back of his hand. "Even so, I think you'll remember this morning for some time."

Lucia went red, and then white. Without another word, she turned away, and hurried back the way they had come. She went down the hill track so fast that, several times where the ground was particularly rough, she very nearly sprained an ankle.

When they were in sight of the house, Nicholas caught her up, and grasped her elbow. "To return to the point we started from—if the children should say anything to you which is obviously connected with their parents, I leave it to you to deal with it as you think best. Now that you know the truth, you'll be prepared if Francesca should make some oblique reference to the situation."

Lucia resisted an impulse to shake off his hand. "I doubt if she'll confide her worries to a stranger," she replied, in a carefully level tone.

"It's often easier to talk to a sympathetic stranger than to someone close to you," he said, releasing her arm.

She made no comment on this, and they walked the rest of the way in silence, though she was aware that he was watching her, and could guess that there was a glimmer of rather sadistic amusement in his eyes.

Upon reaching the house, they found the three children waiting to go down to the beach for a pre-breakfast bathe. They had Nicholas's trunks and towel ready for him. But when they asked Lucia if she would join them, she shook her head, and said she had better go and see how Cathy was feeling this morning.

Judging by the singing coming from the little bathroom as she entered her room, her sister had woken up in a mood to match the bright, hot morning.

However, before she went to speak to the younger girl, Lucia sank down on the side of the bed, and wondered how she was going to endure two weeks of the cat-and-mouse game which Nicholas seemed to delight in playing with her.

"*Why* does he enjoy tormenting me?" she asked herself miserably. "Is it because I pretend to be indifferent to him? Dear heaven—if he only knew!"

Cathy came in, wearing flowery bell-bottomed trousers and a skinny white crochet top over an invisible bra. Yesterday, she had worn her hair-piece, but today she was showing off her new, sleek short-short cut, and a pair of giant puff-ball ear-rings. She made Lucia feel closer to thirty than twenty.

"Good morning," she said brightly. "What time do they have breakfast, d'you suppose?"

"When Nicholas and the children get back from their morning swim, I expect. They went down to the beach a few minutes ago."

"I hope they aren't long. I'm dying for a cup of coffee."

"Have you made your bed?" Lucia asked. She had stripped hers before she went out. Now she began to remake it.

"Oh, I shouldn't bother with that. There's bound to be a maid to do it. I expect they have someone from the village," her sister answered.

"Possibly—but I still think we should make our beds, and tidy up a bit."

"You can, if you like. I came here to take it easy."

And Cathy strolled out through Lucia's door, and disappeared.

They were all at the breakfast table when Yannis turned up again. He arrived in the Land Rover which Nicholas had evidently lent him to get back to the hotel the night before.

After he had said good morning to everyone, he asked his cousin, "You don't mind if Lucia spends the day with me, Nico?"

"If she has no objection, I have none," said Nicholas.

"We will have lunch at the hotel, and this afternoon we will swim," said Yannis. "We'll come back about six or seven. That is if you do not require the jeep today, Nico?"

"No—but shouldn't you first ask Lucia if she wishes to spend the whole day with you?" Nicholas suggested, rather snubbingly.

Yannis looked momentarily discomfited. "I am sorry," he said quickly, to Lucia. "Perhaps you would prefer to come another day?"

She gave him her brightest smile. "You know I'd love to come, Yannis," she said, with unnecessary warmth.

His black eyes glowed. "Then, if you have finished breakfast, we will leave as soon as you have fetched your bathing things."

Lucia pushed back her chair, and asked Kyria Katina to excuse her. She smiled at the children, and at Cathy. She did not even glance at Nicholas.

To reach the hotel, they had to pass through the town and drive a couple of miles beyond it. Like Nicholas's house, the hotel stood on the hillside above a bay. It had twenty guest-rooms, but only three were occupied at present.

"This year I am glad we do not have many early visitors," said Yannis, as they arrived. "If we were busy, I would not have time to be with you."

Taking her first to see the hotel's large kitchen, he introduced his mother and sisters, and several other female relatives who helped with the cleaning and cooking. His three sisters all spoke some English, but the other women made her welcome in their own tongue. To refresh her after the dusty drive, they gave her a glass of cold, sweet water, and a spoonful of some delicious fruit preserve.

Presently Yannis showed her over the rest of the hotel. It was a modest establishment, but though the bedrooms were neither large nor luxurious, they all had showers, and sea views, and the whole place was scrupulously clean.

"In the evening, if the guests wish to go to the *taverna*, my sisters look after the children," Yannis explained. "We are what you call a family hotel. There is nothing here for tourists who want excitement."

He left her in one of the bedrooms, so that she could change into her swimsuit. "When you are ready, you will find me on the beach," he said, as he went out.

Lucia unbuttoned her shirt, and hung it on the back of a chair. She should have felt relieved to be out of Nicholas's way for the day, but instead she found herself wondering what he and Cathy were doing now. Determined to shut him out of her mind, she quickly undressed and changed.

Yannis was already in the sea, when she arrived on the beach. He saw her crossing the sand, and waved a glistening brown arm. Lucia left her bag and wrap on a deck chair under one of several striped umbrellas, and strolled to the water's edge, fitting on her bathing cap.

"You swim well," he said, when she joined him alongside the diving raft moored about a hundred yards out in the centre of the bay.

Lucia turned on to her back, and kicked up a fountain of spray. "This is heavenly! You are lucky to live here."

He climbed on to the raft, and reached down a hand

to hoist her aboard. "It's not always like this, you know. In winter there are storms, and it is cold."

"Yes, but even then it must be beautiful." She settled herself on the edge of the raft, and dangled her legs in the water. "I wish I could bring my class here. Most of them have never seen the sea, or had a proper holiday. A day at Southend is their idea of the seaside. A fortnight here would make different children of them."

"Perhaps—but they have many advantages our children do not have," he reminded her. He studied her for some moments. "I find it very strange that you are not married. Surely you cannot intend to be a teacher all your life?"

"I might have to be," she said lightly.

Yannis looked puzzled. "Why is that?"

Since his perplexity seemed to be genuine, she said, with a smile. "I'd like to marry one day—but it's a matter of waiting to be asked."

"Ah, I see. You mean the offers you have had have not appealed to you?"

"I mean I haven't had any offers," Lucia said dryly.

"Now that I do *not* believe," he replied emphatically. "There must be a dozen men eager to marry you—particularly in England where there is no dowry to consider."

She laughed. "You're terribly good for my morale! If I spend too much time with you, I may start to believe that I'm a ravishing creature."

His black eyes sparkled. "It is my hope that you will spend all your time with me." He seized her hand, and pressed it to his bronzed chest. "If you do not believe what I say, feel how my heart beats when I am near you."

Lucia was not sure how to deal with this. "I can't feel it beating at all," she said, in some confusion. Then, quickly, "I don't think I ought to sit here any longer, Yannis. I may get sunburnt." And, freeing her hand, she slid off the raft and began to swim back to the shore.

Yannis reached the beach ahead of her, but he did not say anything as they walked to the umbrella where she had left her things. Lucia pulled off her cap, and they both lightly towelled themselves dry. Then she looked in her bag for her sun cream.

"I will do your back for you." He took the tube from her, and unscrewed the top.

"Oh, no—I can do it," she said hastily.

"You do not like me to touch you?" he asked, looking rather offended.

"No, of course not—I didn't mean that."

His expression changed. He looked pleased. "You are shy," he accused her, with a grin.

For an instant, there was something in his face which reminded her of Nicholas. And, as if it was Nicholas who was teasing her, she began to blush.

"Ah, I see how it is," he said mischievously. "You are afraid that I mean to make love to you. In England, it is not correct to make love before lunch, I believe."

At this, Lucia could not help laughing again. "Most people don't feel romantic first thing in the morning."

Yannis made a soft hissing sound. "The English are very inhibited. In Greece we are not so restrained."

She unclipped the straps of her swimsuit, so that her shoulders should tan evenly. "I was under the impression that Greek girls were much less free than English ones."

"Yes, that is true," he agreed.

"So it's only foreign girls whom you kiss whenever you feel like it?" she said, sitting down on a deck chair.

Yannis pulled his chair close to hers. "How can I help wanting to kiss you when you are so beautiful?"

Lucia's mouth curved. "Oh, Yannis, what an exaggeration! Compared with Cathy, I'm quite plain."

"Miss Cathy is pretty—yes, very pretty. But she is

not like you," he said warmly. "Her eyes do not shine like yours. Her voice is not soft. One does not burn to embrace her."

"Most men seem to," she said, with a smile. And she wondered if his lack of interest in her sister was because Nicholas had made it clear that Cathy was his girl. She would have liked to ask him straight out, but instead she said, "Does your cousin often invite his English friends to Marina?"

"No, it is not his custom. In the summer, Sofia and Richard come with the children. But in the spring only Nico comes. It was a surprise to us when we heard he was bringing the children, and also two English friends."

Lucia could not be certain, but she had the impression that Yannis knew nothing of the crisis between the children's parents. He began to smooth the sun cream over her back, and this time she did not object.

Presently, the people staying at the hotel came down to bathe. Later, two of Yannis's sisters brought jugs of iced lemonade, and dishes of sweet, sticky cakes, to sustain everyone until lunch time.

After lunch, the Greeks and their visitors rested. Lucia lay on the bed in the room where she had changed. Although she was not accustomed to sleeping during the day, she soon drifted into a doze, and did not wake until four. Then she and Yannis bathed again until it was time to return to his cousin's house.

On the way back, he asked, "It has been a happy day for you?"

She smiled, and nodded. "A lovely day, Yannis... thank you."

He took one hand off the steering wheel, and held it, palm upwards, in front of her. After a brief hesitation, she put her hand lightly on his. His fingers curled round it. Without taking his eyes off the bumpy track, he kissed the back of her wrist.

"The first of many days, beautiful Lucia."

BY THE TIME she had been at Marina for five days, Lucia was so full of vitality that she could climb the steep path from the beach and be less out of breath than the children. The heat, which exhausted Cathy, made her sister blossom. Cathy pecked on her food. Lucia felt so hungry that, if Kyria Katina had been a less generous provider, her appetite would have embarrassed her.

On Wednesday afternoon, as she was undressing for the siesta hours, Cathy came into her room.

"I can't stand much more of this," she announced, flinging herself down in the armchair.

"Much more of what?" enquired Lucia, although she did not really need to ask.

"This place! It's so boring, I feel like screaming."

Lucia lay on the bed, and clasped her hands under her neck. "Are you bored with Nicholas, too?"

"No...I'm not bored with him," Cathy said fretfully. "But we never have a minute to ourselves. Those darned kids are always hanging round us. And that's your fault," she added sharply. "You're supposed to be keeping an eye on them, not spending all your time with Yannis."

"If Nicholas expects me to entertain the children, he will have to say so," said Lucia. "And I don't think even he has the gall to do that."

Cathy inspected her fingernails. After a pause, she said, "Nicholas says that Yannis is a regular Casanova. He can't fool about with the local girls so he chases the visitors. You're the latest in a long line of conquests."

"That makes two of us," Lucia said cheerfully. "Though I doubt if Yannis's line is as long as Nicholas's."

Cathy sprang up, her mouth tight. "I don't know what's happened to you. Don't you care that you're making an ass of yourself?"

"Not in the least. I'm enjoying myself." Lucia yawned, and closed her eyes. "Do go and have your rest, Cathy. I'm too sleepy to have an argument."

"I don't want to rest. I'm sick of resting. I want some fun... some excitement," Cathy exploded.

"Then go and complain to Nicholas. Tell *him* you're bored. It's no use moaning to me," Lucia murmured, in a drowsy voice. She turned on her side, and nestled her head into the pillow.

After muttering something under her breath, her sister left the room, banging the door behind her. Lucia smiled to herself. Poor Cathy! It was rather cruel to be so indifferent to her troubles. There was no doubt that, from her point of view, the holiday was proving a most miserable let-down. But if it succeeded in making her realize that she and Nicholas were wholly incompatible, it would be a fortnight well spent. Two weeks of boredom was better than a lifetime of discontent.

"If she did but know it, I'm pretty bored myself," Lucia thought, with a sigh.

Being with Yannis was exhilarating for a day or two, but after that it began to pall, like a party which had gone on too long.

That evening, Cathy caused a sensation by appearing for dinner in a dress which would not have passed unremarked in a London discothèque. The top—what little there was of it—was a scattering of rainbow discs on a silver mesh base. The white crêpe skirt was so short that Kyria Katina gave an involuntary exclamation of horror. Even Yannis, who had arrived a few minutes earlier, looked rather flabbergasted. And Francesca and Stephen, who were dining with the grown-ups that night, goggled at Cathy as if she had walked in naked.

Lucia was equally startled. She had seen the dress when she had unpacked Cathy's suitcase for her. But she had never dreamed her sister would wear it at Marina, especially when the "house party" had turned out to be so different from her expectations.

The only person who seemed unmoved by the younger girl's appearance was Nicholas. He noticed the dress, but he showed no sign of surprise. Perhaps he realized at once that this was her way of showing that she was tired of quiet evenings on the terrace.

Lucia soon realized this too, but it did not lessen her mortification. For what Cathy had forgotten, or chosen to ignore, was that now, here in Greece, it was Great Week, a time of sadness and fasting. Although she continued to cook normal meals for the rest of the household, for the past few days Kyria Katina had been eating nothing but boiled vegetables. So for Cathy to put on such an immodest dress was more than a breach of good taste. It must give the gravest offence.

After dinner, while the children were helping their great-aunt to clear the table, Cathy said, "Why don't we go into town? There must be *some* night life, surely?"

"There would probably be a riot if we took you to a café in that dress," Nicholas said, in a dry tone. "We can run over to the hotel, if you like. They have a radio-gram so that the guests can dance if they wish to."

"All right, let's do that," said Cathy—making it clear that any diversion, however tame, was better than sitting about on the terrace till bedtime. "I can't think why you don't have a record-player here," she added ungraciously.

"Because I prefer not to have one," he answered mildly. And, as Cathy left the room to fetch a wrap, he watched her go with a look of secret amusement which Lucia could not understand.

When they reached the hotel, the radiogram was already in use. Several more guests had arrived since Lucia's first visit, and there were now about a dozen people, mostly foreigners, having a quiet party in the lounge.

It was about an hour later when Nicholas asked Lucia to dance with him. She had been dreading this ever since their arrival, and when at last the moment came, it was some relief to have the ordeal upon her, instead of being kept in suspense. She knew it was absurd to feel such apprehension because, for a few minutes, in the presence of other people, he would have his arm round her, but it was something she could not help. She could command her face and her voice, but she could not control the rapid, nervous beating of her heart. And what made her even more tense was the fear that, in spite of her outward calm, he might sense the turmoil inside her, and play upon it.

"Well, one week of your holiday is almost over. Have you enjoyed it? Are you glad I prevailed on you to come?" he asked, as they began to dance.

"Yes, I've had a very good time," she answered politely.

"I don't think Cathy has."

Lucia flashed a swift glance at him. "Cathy doesn't care for the sea, or the country. You must have known that before you asked her here."

"I did," he admitted.

"Then if you knew she wouldn't enjoy it, why did you invite her?"

A faint smile touched his mouth. "It won't do her any harm not to enjoy herself for a few days. It may even do her some good. She's a spoilt little baggage."

Lucia stiffened. "She may be rather thoughtless sometimes, but—"

His arm tightened, drawing her closer to him. "Loyalty is an admirable quality—but only when it's genuine, my dear Lucia. Forced loyalty does nobody any good."

She resisted an impulse to wrench herself free. "I don't know what you mean."

"Then I'll tell you—but not in here. Let's find somewhere private, shall we?" And without waiting for her assent, he danced her out of the lounge, through the open glass doors which gave on to the vine-shadowed terrace. There, releasing her waist but keeping a firm hold on her hand, he led her down to the beach.

To Lucia's relief, they were not the only people who

had left the party. Down by the water's edge, a young French couple were gazing out to sea, their arms round each other's waists.

Still holding her hand, Nicholas crossed the sand to one of the beach umbrellas. Then he let her go, and removed a couple of chairs from the pool of darkness into the moonlight.

"Too close?" he asked, on a mocking inflection. He moved the chairs further apart. "There—how's that? Will that make you feel safer?"

Lucia ignored this sally. She sat down, and crossed her legs, and made up her mind that, no matter what he said or did, she would not lose her self-possession.

Nicholas lit a cigarette. After some moments, he said, "You're a contrary creature, aren't you, Lucia? Most women are, of course, but you carry it to an extreme."

"Do I?" she said, without expression.

"You know you do," he said dryly. "You let Cathy upset and embarrass you, but if anyone dares to criticize her, you ruffle like an angry mother hen. You aren't blind to her faults. Why do you expect me to be?"

She did not reply—partly because she had no pat answer, and partly because she was watching the Frenchman and his wife strolling towards the far end of the beach. Perhaps they did not realize there were other people about, or perhaps they did not care. Suddenly, the girl broke away, and ran off. She did not get far, and when the man caught her, he pulled her into his arms and kissed her.

Lucia averted her eyes. The sight of them embracing filled her with pain and longing. She hoped Nicholas had not noticed them. She felt she could not bear it if he made some flippant comment about them.

Instead he said, "Do you think it's wise to spend so much time with Yannis?"

Again she stiffened slightly. "Wise?"

He gave her a sardonic glance, but made no attempt to explain himself.

If she had had any sense, she thought afterwards, she would have kept her own mouth shut. But after a pause, she could not resist saying, "Do you object to our friendship?"

"Is 'friendship' quite the right word?" he asked, with an uplifted eyebrow. "I think 'flirtation' would be more accurate."

"All right—flirtation," she said carelessly. "But I'm not in any danger of falling in love with him, if that's what you're hinting."

"Aren't you? How do you know?"

"Because I realize Yannis makes himself equally agreeable to lots of girls."

"You don't object to being the latest in a succession of romances?"

"No—why should I? He's amusing. He's very good-looking. I think he's an ideal holiday companion," Lucia answered nonchalantly.

He drew on his cigarette. "Your views have changed somewhat, haven't they? A short time ago you disapproved of that attitude."

She shrugged, and rose from her chair. "It depends on the people involved. Anyway, you said yourself that at Marina I might find myself being less 'prim'. It seems you were right." She began to stroll down to the sea. The French couple were climbing the path at the other end of the beach now.

Presently, Nicholas followed her. "Nevertheless, I think it would be advisable for you to spend less time with him," he said pleasantly.

It was Lucia's turn to raise her eyebrows. "Is that a suggestion or an order?"

"It's a piece of advice which you'd be foolish to ignore."

In spite of her resolve to stay calm, she had difficulty in keeping her voice smooth as she said, "Don't you think you're rather miscast as a mentor?"

He laughed. "On the contrary—my own peccadilloes

make me particularly well qualified to steer other people clear of similar follies."

"Possibly... but I happen to be both old enough, and sensible enough, to run my own life, thank you."

"You may be, but is Yannis?" Nicholas asked, coming closer.

Instinctively, Lucia stepped backwards. "What do you mean?"

"It would be rather unfortunate if he were to fall in love with you, don't you think?"

Was he serious? Oh, no, he couldn't be. This was just another ploy to confuse her.

"A few days ago you told me that Greek men were more concerned with dowries than with falling in love," she reminded him.

"A few days ago the situation was rather different." Again he took a step forward, and again she moved back a pace. "That was before you'd begun this determined flirtation, and before you had changed." He shot out a hand, and caught her wrist. "If you retreat any further, you'll spoil those pretty new sandals."

He was right. She had been so intent on edging away from him that she had almost backed into the shallows. Now, unless she broke from his grasp, she was caught between him and the water.

"Hadn't we better go back? They'll be wondering where we are," she said uneasily.

His fingers did not slacken. "We'll go back when I have your assurance that you'll stop this nonsense with Yannis." All at once his voice was quite different—clipped, decisive, and unmistakably in earnest.

Lucia clung to her self-control. "So Cathy was right—you did bring me here to look after the children. Why didn't you say so in the first place?"

"Cathy told you that? What rubbish! The children aren't babies. They don't need a watch-dog," he countered.

"You can hardly expect me to believe you're genuinely worried about Yannis. I should think the risk of his falling in love with me is as remote as...as your going into a monastery."

The sting in her voice made him grin. "I hope you are right—but no risk, however slight, can be discounted. The most inveterate philanderer usually meets his match in the end, you know. And for Yannis to think you were his would be a disaster."

"Thank you," she said, on an acid note.

He laughed. "Not the most tactful way of putting it, perhaps. But I think you know what I mean."

"No, I don't," she informed him frostily.

"Well, apart from the fact that you wouldn't suit each other, Yannis isn't in a position to take any girl seriously yet. He has to see his three sisters settled before he can think of marriage. It's a Greek tradition, and tradition dies hard in the islands."

"Oh, this is absurd!" she exclaimed. "You know perfectly well that marriage doesn't come into it. We are simply enjoying ourselves together. Why, Yannis hasn't even—" She stopped short, biting her lip.

"Hasn't kissed you?" Nicholas suggested.

Lucia flushed, and said nothing.

"I am sure he has tried," he went on. "If it hasn't happened yet, it soon will. You can't fend him off for ever, you know. And if you don't mean ever to let him kiss you, it's unfair to make him think you will."

"I haven't...he doesn't...oh, why can't you mind your own business?" Lucia flared, her eyes sparkling. She jerked her imprisoned wrist. "You're hurting—please let me go."

"There are moments when I'm severely tempted to wring your neck," he informed her softly. "Don't be a little fool, Lucia. Haven't you looked in your mirror lately?"

"W-what do you m-mean?" she stammered angrily.

"You underestimate yourself. You were always more attractive than you realized. Cathy thrives in the city.

You belong in the sun. Katina was saying this morning that she's never seen anyone change as much as you have since you arrived here. She's right. You're a different girl."

She swallowed, her throat oddly tight. "What has that to do with it?"

His hand slid up her arm to the curve of her bare, brown shoulder. He came very close, as close as if they were dancing. "This isn't England, and Yannis isn't like Bernard. But even sound, stolid Bernard might react unpredictably if he saw you as you are now. Any man might."

Lucia drew in her breath, and a queer kind of shudder ran through her. She wanted to run, but her legs seemed powerless to move. She wanted to speak, but her lips only quivered a little. If, in the moment of silence, he had taken her in his arms, she would have yielded as willingly as the French girl had to her husband, a short time earlier.

His hand dropped from her shoulder, and he moved away.

"Think it over. But I may as well warn you that, even if you choose to disregard my wishes, I can easily bring Yannis to heel."

And before she could master her voice, he walked off, and left her alone.

CHAPTER FIVE

NEXT MORNING Lucia woke to the sound of bells. It was Good Friday, a day of national mourning. All over the island bells were tolling as for a great funeral.

"This evening we'll go into town to see the *Epitaphios*," said Nicholas, at breakfast.

"What's that?" asked Cathy.

It was the children who told her. Although it was the first time they had been at Marina for Easter, they knew all about the ceremonies, and were eager to see them for themselves.

Yannis did not come to the house that day, but, as he had told Lucia he would not be able to see her, she was not perplexed by his absence. Indeed it was rather a relief, for it gave her more time to consider how to treat Nicholas's ultimatum.

After breakfast she went for a walk with the children. They wanted to show her a cave they had discovered during their holiday the previous year. They did not ask their uncle to go with them. Perhaps he had already said he had other matters to occupy him that morning. Cathy was invited, but she preferred to laze on the terrace, and do her nails.

"You and Cathy are not a bit alike, are you?" said Francesca, as they set out.

"No—but we are half-sisters," Lucia explained. "We had the same father, but different mothers."

"Oh, I see," was the girl's only comment. But later, on the return walk, when Stephen and Ariadne were some way ahead and out of earshot, she said suddenly, "Were your parents divorced?"

"No, my mother died," Lucia answered.

Francesca stopped to shake a stone out of her sandal. "How beastly for you—but in a way, not as bad as people divorcing, I should think."

Lucia watched her slip her thin brown foot into the sandal, and fasten the buckle. "Do you know anyone whose parents are divorced?" she asked casually.

"Yes, a girl at school—my best friend. She's a boarder, so she doesn't see much of either of them in term time. But she has to spend alternate holidays with them, and she comes back to school absolutely miserable. They hate each other now, you see. Her mother goes on and on about what a beast her father is, and he keeps saying it was all her mother's fault. They both want Annabel to be on *their* side, and if she doesn't pretend that she is, they're nasty to her as well."

It was very hot now. Lucia sat down on a rock, and blotted her temples with a handkerchief. What could she say to comfort Francesca?

"I don't think it's always as bad as that," she said, at length. "In fact I'm sure it's not. People who get divorced don't necessarily hate each other, you know. They might not want to go on living together, but that doesn't mean they have to be enemies. Often, they're on quite good terms—particularly if they have children whom they both love very much."

"But why do they stop wanting to be married?" Francesca's lower lip quivered. "I mean if they've been happy for years and years, why does everything suddenly change? Why do they start having rows and things?"

It was a question Lucia could not answer. All she could say—and she felt it was miserably inadequate—was, "Most people have rows from time to time. Often they lose their tempers, and say things they don't really mean—things which sound as if they couldn't stand the sight of each other. Haven't you ever quarrelled with your friend Annabel? Haven't you ever had rows with Stephen and Ariadne?"

"Oh, yes—but that's different. We're not grown up," said Francesca.

"Being grown up doesn't make life simpler," Lucia said on a wry note. "It tends to make it more complicated. You see—" But, before she could say any more, Ariadne came running back to them.

After what had happened the night before, the last thing Lucia wanted was to have another private talk with Nicholas. But her concern for Francesca outweighed her own feelings and so, after lunch, when the children and Cathy had dispersed to their rooms, she forced herself to follow him on to the terrace, and to say, "I'd like to talk to you—alone. Is there anywhere where we won't be interrupted for a few minutes?"

He lifted an eyebrow. "Won't this do?"

"No—the others may come back and overhear."

"In that case we had better retire to the store room. It's the only place where we can be sure of being undisturbed."

In the narrow, herb-scented store, Nicholas closed the door. "Shall I lock it?" he asked mockingly.

Lucia said briskly, "It's about Francesca."

He leaned his shoulders against the door, and thrust his hands into his pockets. "You disappoint me. When a girl wants to be alone with a man, it isn't usually in order to discuss a third person."

She flushed. "Please be serious."

The glint died out of his eyes. "Very well—what about Francesca?"

She told him what the girl had said to her on the way back from their walk that morning. "She was nearly in tears, poor child. Obviously she does know that her parents are on the brink of a separation, and she's terrified that it's going to result in the same sort of wretched tug-of-war that her friend Annabel is suffering."

"No doubt it would," he said grimly.

"Well, whatever happens, I don't think it's right that she should have to endure any more of this appalling suspense," said Lucia. "I know it's really none of my business, but if I were you, I should contact either your sister or your brother-in-law and tell them that she knows and that they'll have to do something about it."

"Yes, you're right," he agreed immediately. "I'll go into town right away, and try to get a call through to Paris. Perhaps this will bring Sofia to her senses. Thanks, Lucia. It was good of you to let me know at once."

"You asked me to tell you," she said, as he opened the door.

"Yes—but I am well aware that it must have cost you a certain amount of self-abnegation to approach me," he said, with a quizzical look.

Lucia ignored this, and walked past him into the passage. As she did so, Cathy emerged from her room. When she saw Nicholas following her sister out of the store, she looked puzzled and annoyed.

"My errand may take some time—possibly a couple of hours," he murmured to Lucia. Then, with a nod to Cathy, he left the house.

"What were you two doing in there?" Cathy enquired, when he had gone.

Unfortunately, Lucia could not think of any pat explanation.

"Just talking," she said off-handedly.

"About me?" Cathy asked suspiciously.

"No, not about you."

"About what, then?" her sister persisted. "What's going on between you two?"

"'Going on'?—What do you mean?"

"You know very well what I mean," Cathy said sharply. "Something is going on, and I want to know what it is. What have you been telling him about me?"

"Nothing," said Lucia truthfully. "What we were discussing just now had nothing to do with you."

"Then why were you skulking in that store place?" Cathy demanded. "And why won't you say what you were talking about?"

"Because it was something private—that's why," Lucia moved past her to go to her room.

Cathy followed. "It *was* about me—I know it was. What else could you have to say to him in secret? You've been telling him things about me, haven't you?—Trying to turn him against me?"

"Don't be silly, Cathy—of course I haven't." As her sister stepped into the bedroom, Lucia quickly closed the door in case the children should hear the younger girl's high, querulous voice.

"I don't believe you," said Cathy. "You've been up to something—I know it. Ever since we arrived here, Nico's been different towards me."

"Different? In what way?"

Cathy glowered at her in silence. Lucia could see that she longed to snap "Mind your own business", but at the same time, was bursting to pour out her pent-up feelings. She struggled with these conflicting impulses for some moments and then, reluctantly, but unable to govern her need to confide in someone, said, "I—I thought at first it was because those wretched kids are always hanging round us—but it isn't. It's Nico himself. Last night, when we were alone for a change—after you had gone to bed—he didn't even kiss me goodnight." She paused, her face flushed and indignant. "No doubt it will please you to know that he hasn't kissed me once since we've been here," she blurted, with unwilling frankness.

For a moment, this did please Lucia. Last night, when the three of them had returned from the hotel, she had gone directly to bed. But it had been some time before Cathy had followed suit. And until she had heard the younger girl's door opening and closing, Lucia's anger at Nicholas's behaviour on the beach had been exacerbated by the thought that, while she paced and fumed in her room he was doubtlessly making practised love to her sister.

"What I want to know is, why hasn't he?" Cathy went on, with a dark look. "What have you said to make him change? What have you done to come between us?"

Lucia sighed. "Nothing, Cathy."

"You can hardly expect me to believe that! You've been against him from the beginning."

"Only because he's so much older that you are... and because I thought he was playing with you." As she said this, Lucia remembered something Nicholas had promised on the night he had persuaded her to come to Greece.

From now on, your sister's reputation will be as safe with me as with Bernard.

"Hasn't it occurred to you that he may be treating you differently because he feels differently?" she said, with a queer, sinking feeling.

The significance of this escaped Cathy. "What do you mean?" she asked brusquely.

"I told you he was more Greek than English. Greek men may philander with foreign girls—but not with their own girls, or anyone they mean to marry. Where prospective wives are concerned they're as circumspect as the Victorians."

When, once before, Lucia had reminded her of Nicholas's Greek strain, Cathy had scoffed. This time she did not.

She said, "So you've changed your mind, have you? Now you do believe he is serious about me?"

"It seems so," Lucia replied.

"But you still don't approve, I gather?"

"No—because I don't think you love him."

Cathy shrugged. "That's his problem."

Lucia winced, and turned away. At that moment it seemed to her that her concern for Cathy was as wasted as water sprinkled on a desert. Since nothing she could do or say had any influence on the younger girl, she might as well give up the effort.

"Cathy may be a fool, but I am a bigger one," she thought bitterly. "I *am* in love with the man!"

It was the first time she had admitted to herself that what she felt for Nicholas was more than physical attraction. The sudden realization of how deeply she cared about him was a shock which made her heart pound. Perhaps she had not understood it before because love in actuality was so different, so painfully different, from love in abstract. She had always assumed that when at last she did fall in love it would be a mutual condition—not this hopeless, one-sided affair. She had thought, too, that love would be a gentle, gradual thing, a communion of thoughts and feelings developing slowly and harmoniously. Instead, it had been like a battle, each skirmish leaving her weaker and more vulnerable. Now, her defences in ruins, she did not know which prospect was the more intolerable—never to see him again, or to have to see him often because he was her half-sister's husband.

Cathy, her suspicions diverted by this unconsidered possibility which Lucia had just presented to her, said, "Perhaps you're right. How funny!"

"Funny?" Lucia queried blankly.

"Well, who would have thought that Nico might have a prim streak?" Cathy explained, with a laugh. "Still, men are peculiar creatures," she went on reflectively. "Look at the number of husbands who flirt with every girl in sight. But if their wives so much as look at another man, they go almost berserk with jealousy. I wonder if Nico is the jealous type?" she speculated, frowning slightly.

"It depends what you mean by jealousy," Lucia answered. "I shouldn't imagine he would be unreasonably jealous. He's too sure of himself. But I can't see him standing for any nonsense."

It was on the tip of her tongue to add, "Anyway, if a

woman was married to Nicholas, she wouldn't be interested in anyone else." Then she realized how revealing such a remark would be, and hastily checked herself. "I'm going down to the beach with the children. Are you coming?"

Cathy shook her head. "The glare down there makes my head ache. I'm sick of the beach. I'll rest until Nico comes back."

He came back sooner than he had anticipated. Not much more than an hour later, Lucia heard the drone of the Land Rover's engine. But she did not learn the outcome of his errand until the early evening, when they were all getting ready to go into town.

She had changed into a plain, dark blue dress, and was struggling with the zip fastener which had stuck in the small of her back, when someone tapped at her door. Thinking it was one of the children, she called, "Come in."

When Nicholas opened the door, his first glance was towards the other door. Having seen that it was closed, and that Lucia was alone, he then noticed that her hands were behind her back, and she was trying urgently to free the jammed fastener.

"Having trouble? Let me help you," he offered.

"No, thank you—I can do it," she said, backing away.

Nicholas looked amused. "If you wrench at it like that, you'll probably break it. Come on—turn round, and let me do it. I have seen your back before, you know." His eyes narrowed and glinted. "You have a birthmark at the base of your left shoulder blade."

Lucia flushed, and set her teeth. She knew it was absurd to be so flustered. If Yannis had offered to help her, she would have accepted quite calmly. But Nicholas was not Yannis, and the fact that he had studied her sufficiently closely to notice the small brown birthmark only added to her confusion.

"I came to tell you that I couldn't get through to my

sister," he said, leaving the door half open, and advancing towards her. "However, I dictated a message for them to give to her. Unless she has difficulty in getting on a plane, she should be on her way to Athens within the next twenty-four hours."

"What did you say? She won't think there's been an accident, or that the children are ill, will she?" Lucia asked, instantly visualizing how alarmed his sister would be at receiving a cryptic summons to come at once.

Nicholas took her by the shoulders, turned her round, and began to deal with the fastener. "No, no—I wouldn't frighten her. I simply said that Francesca knows about the breach, and is very unhappy, and that it's up to Sofia to come and handle the situation. I also talked to Richard in London, and told him the same thing."

"Did you tell him you had asked your sister to come?" said Lucia. Her voice sounded normal enough, but, inwardly, she was trembling at the touch of his fingers against her skin.

"When he asked that, I rang off," said Nicholas. "If he wants to know, he'll have to contact Sofia himself. If he has any sense, he'll nip over to Paris and ask her in person."

Lucia, who was wondering if Cathy could hear his voice and was likely to burst in upon them, said, "I think the teeth of the zip must be broken. You had better leave it. I'll put something else on."

"No, they aren't damaged. They're caught on a loose thread. Have you a pair of scissors with you?"

"Yes—here." As she stretched out her arm to reach the pair of nail scissors which were lying on top of the dressing chest, she saw his face reflected above hers in the looking glass. Their glances met for an instant. She looked swiftly away, afraid of what her eyes might reveal to him.

But when he had taken the scissors and returned his

attention to the zip, she could not resist stealing another glance at him. It was a temptation she would have to resist from now on. If he caught her watching him too often, he would surely guess her secret. He was not obtuse like Bernard. Nicholas understood women.

"There you are—that's fixed it, I think." He ran the zip up and down to make sure all the thread had been cleared.

"Thank you," Lucia said primly. Then she gasped, and her tanned face turned scarlet.

For as he drew the fastener up to the collar of her dress, Nicholas had bent and kissed her neck.

It was such an incredible thing for him to do that, if she had not seen it in the mirror, she would have thought she must be mistaken.

He met her outraged gaze, his own eyes amused. "I'm afraid I couldn't resist it," he said uncontritely.

With an effort, she kept her voice low. "Y-you seem to have no scruples at all."

"Very few," he agreed, with a twinkle, "But how was I to know it would annoy you? You didn't object when Yannis did it."

Her cheeks burned. "That was different." She turned, and faced him. With deliberate pointedness, she added, "I happen to *like* your cousin."

Nicholas's smile did not alter, yet, for a second, there was a flicker in the shrewd, dark eyes which made her wish she had not said that to him. But, whatever was passing through his mind, his tone was as smooth as usual as he said, "Do you still dislike me so much?"

She hesitated. "Not all the time."

"Only when I tease you... hm?"

"If that's what you call it," she said distantly.

He grinned, and strolled to the door. Before he went out, he said mockingly, "In that case, we're making progress. You used to detest me without reservations... remember?"

Some hours later after dark, Lucia stood in the thronged main square of the town, and watched the *Epitaphios* procession wind its way down the steep, narrow street from the church. First came the acolytes, youths in red and purple robes, some of them staggering under the weight of a great Cross, others bearing gilded banners. Then came the bier symbolizing the dead Christ. It was covered with wreaths of roses and fragrant lemon blossom and girls in white dresses were strewing it with handfuls of petals. As it passed the place where she stood, Lucia noticed that some of the people around her were weeping as if the bier carried a close and dear relative.

Immediately behind it came the richly-robed priests and local dignitaries, followed by a stream of unofficial mourners. In the flickering light of hundreds of candles, their faces looked drawn with genuine grief. As she watched them shuffle silently by, she realized that, to these unsophisticated Greek islanders, the horror and despair of the Crucifixion was as real and terrible as if they had seen it for themselves.

When it was time to go home, Cathy was nowhere to be seen.

"Where can she have got to?" said Lucia anxiously, as the rest of them made their way back to where Nicholas had parked the Land Rover.

"She'll turn up presently," he answered.

"Yes, she can't possibly get lost in a place as small as this," agreed Francesca.

But it was nearly half an hour later, and Ariadne had fallen asleep on her uncle's lap, before Cathy reappeared.

"Where have you been? What happened to you?" Lucia exclaimed, as her sister came hurrying up.

"I got separated from you in the crowd, and then I couldn't find my way back here," Cathy explained, rather breathlessly. She did not seem upset by her misadventure. Rather, she seemed excited, and oddly pleased with herself.

"Well, you had better pile in the back with the children and Lucia can come in front and take Ariadne," said Nicholas.

"I'll have her on my knee," said Cathy, climbing on to the seat beside him.

"She's quite heavy," he warned her.

"I don't mind. It isn't far." She settled herself comfortably, and helped him to transfer the sleeping child to her lap.

It was so unlike Cathy to want to have anything to do with the children that Lucia could not help feeling suspicious. Why was her sister suddenly in such a good mood? She had not been particularly cheerful on the drive down. What had happened while she was missing to raise her spirits?

Next day, she continued to be so unwontedly agreeable to everyone that Lucia's curiosity sharpened. However, she decided not to question the younger girl, but to wait until Cathy chose to enlighten her.

In the afternoon, Nicholas made the children go to bed for two hours, because they would be up until long past midnight. As she had done the day before, Kyria Katina travelled to town with some friends from the nearby village. The rest of the household drove down in the Land Rover. But this time Cathy did not volunteer to have Ariadne on her knee. She had spent a long time getting ready, and was wearing a pale pink crêpe shift with a smocked yoke, white mesh stockings, and pink patent shoes with silver heels. It was an outfit more suited to an evening at *Sibylla's* in London than to sightseeing among the crowds of Greek countryfolk.

From the moment they reached town, Lucia sensed an atmosphere entirely different from the funeral gloom of the previous evening. Tonight, the crowds were in the mood of suppressed excitement. Soon the days of fasting would be over, and the feasting and rejoicing would begin. Already, in the church, the bier and wreaths had been removed, and the new decorations of laurel and myrtle put up, and the aisle spread with rosemary.

It was while the children were buying their candles that Cathy disappeared again. One moment she was there beside them and, a moment later, she had vanished.

Lucia touched Nicholas's arm. "Where's Cathy? Can you see her anywhere?"

They both peered over the heads of the people around them. But of Cathy's bright, blonde head there was no sign.

"She seems to have lost herself again," said Nicholas unconcernedly. "Perhaps she prefers to look around on her own."

His indifference puzzled Lucia. "Will she be all right?" she asked, frowning. "I mean... that dress is so short, and Greek men are so..." She stopped short, somewhat embarrassed.

"Inflammable?" Nicholas suggested. He grinned. "They also have too much pride to risk a rebuff. She'll be stared at—perhaps even pinched. Nothing worse will happen to her."

His flippancy shocked her. "Don't you mind other men staring at her... touching her?"

"There's not much I can do about it, is there? If I go off and look for her, you'll be left unprotected."

"I can take care of myself," she informed him coldly.

"What makes you think Cathy can't?" Before she could answer, he turned away to speak to the candle-seller.

The candles were decorated with blue and white ribbons. Nicholas bought one for Lucia, and one for himself.

At twelve o'clock the church bells began to peal, and everyone cried out *Christos Anesti*—Christ is Risen. Within seconds, the sky was ablaze with coloured fireworks.

Nicholas lit the children's candles for them. Then he lit his own, and offered it to Lucia so that she could light hers from it.

"If your candle is still burning when you get home, it's a lucky omen," Francesca told her.

"It's also said that if a girl lights her candle from a man's, by the following Easter they'll be married," Nicholas added.

"Oh, really—how interesting," Lucia remarked composedly. But she did not feel composed. When he looked at her like that—his dark eyes glinting with devilment—it made her feel weak and breathless.

She had another bad moment, some time later. Boys were setting off squibs in the streets and, in the scuffle to get out of the way of one of them, she was pushed off balance. She might have fallen to the ground, but Nicholas was close by, and he caught her and held her close against him until the hissing, darting squib had burnt itself out.

"Are you all right?" he asked, relaxing his hold.

"Oh...yes." Quickly—perhaps too quickly—she freed herself from his arms. "Thank you," she added, as an afterthought.

"Don't mention it—*I* enjoyed it," he told her provokingly.

The children came back from further along the street. Ariadne looked nervous and tearful.

"Hello—what's the matter with you, mouse?" Nicholas asked, as she ran to him.

"She's scared of the squibs," said her brother.

"Up you come, then." Nicholas swung her expertly on to his shoulders. "The squibs can't hurt you there. Hold tight."

"Oh, Lucia—you've lost your candle," Francesca pointed out.

"So I have. I must have dropped it in the scramble just now."

"I can see it." Stephen darted off to retrieve the candle

from the cobbles. "I'm afraid it's been squashed," he said, as he picked it up.

It was at this point that Cathy reappeared. But she was not alone. There was a tall, fair man with her.

"Ah, here you are," she said brightly. "I've been looking everywhere for you." She smiled up at her lanky escort. "This is Grant Wallace. Grant, this is my sister Lucia...and Nico Curzon...and the children."

Even before he said he was happy to know her, Lucia had guessed that Grant was an American. She guessed too that Cathy had met him the night before, and arranged to meet him again tonight. But with what motive, Lucia could not imagine.

"Are you staying at the hotel?" Nicholas asked, when the two men had shaken hands, and Grant had said "Hello there" to the children.

"No, I'm here with a charter yacht party," the American explained. "We've been cruising around the Aegean for the past four weeks. This is our last stopover before we head back to Athens."

"Grant was filming the fireworks display," said Cathy. "I asked him if he'd noticed an English girl and three children in the crowd, and he very kindly offered to help me find you. I was rather nervous on my own, especially with all those beastly squibs going off."

She said this with such a convincing air of sweet defenceless femininity that most people would have believed her. But even if Lucia had not known her sister was acting, the tell-tale look of unease on Grant Wallace's face would have given her cause to suspect the truth of Cathy's statement.

Nicholas too seemed somewhat sceptical. "How come you got lost again, Cathy?" he asked, in his most bland voice.

"I don't know—I just did," she said innocently. "Never mind, I'm safe back now. Thank you so much for your help, Grant."

Since this was clearly his cue to leave, the American

said, "Well, I guess I'd better be getting back to my party." He took Cathy's outstretched hand and added, in the tone of a man who was not quite sure of his ground, "We're staying here a couple of days. Will I see you again?"

Cathy glanced at Nicholas. It was obvious that this was *his* cue to invite the American to the house. But, although he must have realized what was expected of him, he chose to ignore the opening.

There was an awkward pause until Grant, who was evidently not insensitive to atmosphere, went on with rather forced bonhomie, "Say, I have a great idea! Why don't all of you come to lunch on board *Cassandra* tomorrow? She's a real fine yacht. I'm sure the kids would like to look her over."

"Oh, what fun! We would love to, wouldn't we?" Cathy said eagerly, looking to the children to support her.

But before they could open their mouths, Nicholas said pleasantly, "It's very kind of you, Wallace, but not tomorrow, I'm afraid. Easter Sunday is very much a family occasion here, and it would upset my aunt, who is Greek, if we broke away from tradition."

"I see...I didn't know that," the American answered. "How about the day after tomorrow?"

"Sorry, that's booked up too," said Nicholas affably.

"Oh, too bad. Well, I guess this is goodbye, then," said Grant, with a disappointed face.

"Perhaps we'll see you in Athens. We're going to be there ourselves later in the week," Cathy told him.

He brightened. "Is that so? Well, look, if you're free any time, you must call me. I'll be at the Hilton."

"Naturally," Nicholas murmured dryly.

Grant detected the slight edge of sarcasm, and gave him a puzzled glance. It was plain that he had no idea he was trespassing on someone else's preserves.

He smiled down at Cathy. "In that case, I'll say 'au revoir'."

After he had taken his leave of them, Nicholas said briskly, "Come on, it's time you children were in bed."

"Already? But we haven't seen Aunt Hestia, or Yannis, or the girls yet," Francesca objected.

"And we aren't going to look for them now," he responded firmly. "We'll see them tomorrow."

Back at the house, he asked Lucia if she would see the children to bed while he drove to the village to wait for Kyria Katina's return with her friends.

Francesca was the only one of them who had managed to bring her candle home alight. "I wonder if it will bring me luck?" she said to Lucia, before she blew it out. "I suppose it's just a silly superstition really, isn't it?"

Lucia guessed where her thoughts lay. "I don't know," she said gently. "But even if it is, it's rather a nice one. I don't believe in any of the bad luck things—breaking mirrors, and spilling salt. But I don't see any harm in good luck omens. In fact, I think if you believe that everything is going to turn out well, it actually does help it to happen. It's always better to be optimistic rather than pessimistic, you know."

When the girls were settled for the night, she went along the passage to Nicholas's bedroom which Stephen was sharing with him. The boy was already in bed, reading a book.

"I'm not a bit tired. I can finish this chapter, can't I?" he asked her hopefully.

"What!—At this hour of night? Certainly not!" said Lucia, with mock severity.

"Nico reads half the night," Stephen grumbled.

"He's finished growing. You haven't. Come on—down you go. He'll be back pretty soon, and if you're not asleep he'll be annoyed."

"He seems annoyed already," said Stephen, putting the book away.

"Oh? What makes you think that?" She glanced at the other bed, the one in which Nicholas slept.

"I dunno exactly," the boy said vaguely. "But he's jolly ratty about something. Dad always shouts when he's angry, but Nico just gets a sort of look. It's nothing we've done. I expect it's the Government...or shares...or something like that. They're what makes Dad really riled." He remembered something, and grinned. "Once, he had a letter from the Income Tax people. It made him so furious he put salt on his cornflakes instead of sugar. We all sat waiting for him to take a spoonful and spit it out, but the funniest thing was that he ate the whole lot without noticing—or he would have, if Mum hadn't stopped him in case he was sick."

Lucia laughed. "Goodness, he must have been fuming." Absentmindedly—because, at twelve, he was probably past such attentions—she tucked him in. "Goodnight, Stephen."

"'Night." With a hippopotamus yawn, he turned on his side and snuggled down. In spite of being "not a bit tired", he was half asleep before she closed the door.

She found Cathy in the studio. She was lounging on one of the sofas, sipping a glass of *ouzo*.

"Now for the catechism, I suppose?" said her sister, pulling a face.

Lucia sat down. "I must admit I'm extremely curious to know what you're up to now."

Cathy studied her pearl-lacquered nails. "I thought it might be interesting to see how Nico reacted to some competition."

"You mean you wanted to make him jealous?"

"You could put it like that. You don't approve, I suppose?"

"I don't see why you had to tell lies," said Lucia.

Cathy made big, artless eyes at her. "Lies? I don't know what you mean."

"Oh, come off it, Cathy, don't act with me. You met Grant Wallace last night, and arranged to see him again this evening. You didn't get lost—you deliberately gave us the slip."

"Yes, I did as a matter of fact," her sister admitted. "But it wasn't until tonight that I decided to introduce him to the rest of you." She smiled, and sipped her drink. "It worked like a charm, didn't it? Nico pretended not to mind, but I could tell he was rattled by the way he squashed Grant's invitations."

"It seems a peculiar way to treat someone you want to marry."

"Ah, but then you don't understand men, sweetie," said Cathy wisely. "There's nothing, but nothing, like a sharp twinge of jealousy to bring a man up to scratch."

"Are you sure? If I were a man, and a girl tried those tactics on me, it would put me right off her."

Her sister shrugged. "If you were a man, you'd be like Bernard. Nico's very different, thank heavens. Ah, that sounds like the jeep coming now, so I'll disappear. Say goodnight for me, will you?"

"What's the matter? Are you afraid to face him?"

"Oh, no," said Cathy confidently. "Going to bed is strategy, my pet. If he's simmering now, by tomorrow he'll be at boiling point."

But when, shortly afterwards, Nicholas and his aunt came into the studio, and found Lucia there on her own, he did not appear to be under any kind of strain.

The two women talked for a while, with Nicholas translating for them. Then Kyria Katina said goodnight, and retired.

Lucia would have gone too, but when she was half way to the door, Nicholas called her back.

"I'm going for a swim," he said, as she turned towards him. "You don't look particularly tired. Why don't you come with me?"

"No, thank you, I don't think I will."

"It's a beautiful night. The sea is warmer at night."

"Yes, I daresay it is—but I'd rather not."

"Why? Are you afraid of being alone with me?"

She flushed. "No, of course not."

He smiled. "Much too vehement, Lucia. Denials are never convincing if they're too vehement."

Exasperation welled up inside her and overflowed. "Oh, you and Cathy—I don't understand either of you. You play with people like... skittles. What do you want me to say? That I *am* afraid of you? Very well, I am... if it gives you some weird satisfaction."

There was a tense silence which seemed to go on for ever, but probably only lasted for half a minute. Lucia wondered if anyone had heard her raised voice and would come to see what was the matter.

"Do you mean that?" Nichloas's voice was as quiet as hers had been loud. "Are you really afraid of me? What do you imagine I might do?"

Her mouth felt dry. "I d-don't know."

"Yes, you do—you think I'd make love to you, don't you? But that isn't what makes you nervous. What really scares you—if you're honest—is that you know you might enjoy it. For once in your life, your instincts might get out of hand. I might see the real Lucia Gresham, not the stiff-necked girl you pretend to be."

"How dare you!" she said, her voice shaking. "How dare you speak to me like that! What right have you to tell me what I'm like?"

"No right at all," he cut in, as she paused for breath. "But I'm getting a little tired of your touch-me-not attitude. I asked you to come for a swim because I thought you would enjoy it. You wanted to come, but you felt it was too big a risk. You couldn't trust me. You couldn't be sure I'd behave myself."

The sting in his voice made her flinch, but she stood her ground. "How can you expect me to trust you?" she flashed back at once.

He walked towards her, his hands in his trouser pockets. It took all her control to stand there until he stopped, at arm's length away.

"Have I ever given you cause not to trust me?" he asked.

"Yes, I think you have," she retorted, meeting his eyes.

"Well, go on... when and where?" he pressed.

Lucia clenched her hands till her nails dug into her palms. "Every time we've ever been alone. Yesterday, in my room, when you k-kissed the back of my neck. Tonight, in the street, when you said you'd enjoyed holding me. Right from the very beginning you've made me distrust you."

"I see," he said, after a moment. "So you can only trust a man if he appears to be entirely indifferent to the fact that you're a very attractive girl? That's a rather severe proscription, don't you think?—And one which certainly excludes Yannis."

"Yannis is different. Yannis is... free."

Nicholas lifted one eyebrow. "So am I," he said dryly.

Lucia gaped at him. "But I thought—" she began.

"Yes? What did you think?"

There was a muffled wail from somewhere along the corridor.

Nicholas stiffened. "What the devil... ?"

At the second cry, he brushed past her, and went to investigate.

CHAPTER SIX

IT WAS ARIADNE who had cried out. When, with Lucia close behind him, Nicholas entered the girls' room, and switched on the light, the child was sitting up in her bunk, having been uncontrollably sick all over the bedclothes. At the sight of the two grown-ups, she burst into tears.

"I want Mummy," she sobbed. "I want Mummy!"

"Oh, lord—poor kid. what a mess!" said Nicholas ruefully. "Don't cry, mouse. You couldn't help it." He began to unfasten his cuff links.

Lucia said briskly, "I'll see to her. I'm more used to this sort of thing."

Nicholas rolled up one shirt sleeve. "Look out—she's going to be sick again." With surprising presence of mind, he snatched up a plastic beach bucket, and narrowly managed to deal with the child's second spasm.

Francesca, only half awake, muttered, "What's the matter? What's happening?"

Lucia bent to reassure her. "Poor Ariadne's been sick," she explained. "You go back to sleep, dear. Your uncle and I will look after her."

"Ugh! How horrid. She is a pest," said Francesca, with sisterly callousness.

Having firmly quashed Lucia's insistence that she could cope much better than he could, Nicholas organized matters with an efficiency and total lack of squeamishness which could scarcely have been excelled by a trained children's nurse. Within a very short time Ariadne, in clean pyjamas, was ensconced in his own bed. He made Lucia stay with her while he removed the soiled bedding, and re-made the bunk with clean linen.

By the time he had finished these tasks, Ariadne had dropped off to sleep again.

"She doesn't seem to be running a temperature," he said, looking down at the little girl's round, peaceful face. "All the same, she had better stay where she is for the rest of the night. Then, if she should be ill again, I'll be on hand to attend to her."

Stephen had slept through all this coming and going. He did not wake when his uncle lifted him out of his bed, and carried him next door to sleep in Ariadne's bunk.

"That boy would sleep through an earthquake," said Nicholas, returning to his own room. He looked at Lucia. "I don't know about you, but after that I could do with some coffee."

She followed him to the kitchen. "What did you do with the dirty sheets?"

"Dumped them in a bucket of disinfectant, and put them outside. They can be washed in the morning."

Lucia sat down at the scrubbed kitchen table while he set about making the coffee. It seemed much more than thirty minutes since they had faced each other in the studio.

She could not help saying, "You're a very strange man, Nicholas."

He glanced at her over his shoulder. "Why? Because I know what to do when a child is sick? Nothing strange about that—it's simple horse sense. You have too many preconceived ideas about people, my girl. Nobody's all of a piece."

"You certainly aren't. You're the most confusing person I've ever met."

He made no comment on that. "Are you hungry? Would you like some bread and cheese?"

"No, thank you."

When the coffee was ready, he brought it to the table. Then he cut himself a hunk of bread, spread it with soft sheep's milk cheese, and sat down to eat it.

Lucia took a purple Calamata olive from the dish he had set out. She was itching to know what he had meant when, just before Ariadne's cries had interrupted them, he had said he was free. But she had not the courage to ask him point blank.

By now it was nearly three o'clock, and although she was still not tired, she did feel rather cold and devitalized.

Nicholas saw her shiver. "You'd better have a small brandy. It will warm you, and help you to sleep after all the excitement." There was a fugitive twinkle in his eyes which made her suspect that he was not referring to Ariadne's tummy upset, but to what had preceded it.

"Oh, no, really—I don't need brandy. The coffee will warm me."

"Brandy hits the spot more effectively." He fetched a bottle and glasses, and poured a small measure for her, and a stiffer one for himself. "It's a good thing you're not a Greek girl," he said with an enigmatic smile, as he pushed her glass across the table.

She gave him an enquiring look.

"If a Greek girl was found carousing with a man at this hour of the morning, she would have to marry him," he explained.

Her heart gave a queer little flutter. "I would hardly call this carousing," she said without expression.

"Not by English standards—no. But most of the older people here would see it in that light. To save your reputation, we should have to be married forthwith."

Lucia sipped a little brandy. "Then it's as well I'm not a Greek girl."

He watched her, his dark eyes unreadable. "Would marrying me be so repugnant to you?"

"I should think a forced marriage would be repugnant to both parties," she said evasively.

"That isn't what I asked you."

Her hands began to tremble. Quickly, she tucked them away on her lap. "I—I would never marry anyone unless I loved him," she said huskily. "If you don't mind I'll finish my coffee in my room." She pushed back her chair, and picked up the cup and saucer, leaving the glass of brandy where it was.

Nicholas opened the kitchen door for her.

"Thank you...goodnight," she said, without looking at him. Her hand was so unsteady that the coffee was spilling into the saucer.

"Goodnight, Lucia." He sounded amused.

He stayed at the kitchen door until she reached her room.

ON EASTER MONDAY, Nicholas received a telegram from the children's parents. They were in Athens, and would be coming to Marina on the steamer the following day. The two younger children were delighted by this news. Francesca's reaction was guarded.

Kyria Katina was concerned about where everyone was going to sleep. But Nicholas had already considered this problem.

"You won't mind spending your last night at the hotel, will you?" he asked, speaking to Cathy and Lucia.

Cathy brightened. "Our last night?"

"Yes—on Wednesday we three will be going back to Athens."

"What about the picnic, Uncle Nico?" Ariadne put in. "You promised us a picnic on the little island."

"We'll go there tomorrow," he told her. "The steamer won't arrive until four, possibly later, so there'll be plenty of time for a picnic before we meet it."

But the following morning, just before the picnic

party set out, Cathy announced that she had a headache, and would rather not go.

"Well, I'm afraid I can't disappoint the children," said Nicholas, not very sympathetically. "You'd better take some aspirins, and lie down."

"Shall I stay with you?" Lucia offered.

"No, no—you go and enjoy yourself," said her sister, with an injured glance at Nicholas.

The sea was flat calm that day, and it did not take long for him to row them across the glittering water to the little island. The children helped to pull the scarlet and blue boat on to the beach, and then they ran off to rediscover this favourite haunt, such a perfect setting for games of Explorers and Castaways.

"I'm going to swim," said Nicholas, when he had unloaded the two large baskets which Kyria Katina had packed with food and drinks.

Leaving Lucia free to join him or to follow the children, as she chose, he stripped off his shirt and shorts, and strolled into the sea.

After some indecision, she chose to swim. But when she entered the water, Nicholas was already out of sight beyond the rocks at the end of the island. By the time he reappeared, she was dry and dressed. As she saw him stand up in the shallows, his tanned skin glistening in the sun, she wondered if it would be wise to go after the children. But it seemed that Nicholas was not in the mood to tease her today.

When he came to get his towel, he said only, "Help yourself to the drinks if you're thirsty." Then he gave himself a quick rub down, lit a cigarette, and walked off.

She did not see him again until noon when he and the children came back, and they all had lunch. The children were ravenous, and fell upon the *dolmathes*—balls of savoury rice wrapped in vine leaves—as if they had not eaten for days. Kyria Katina had filled two vacuum flasks with *avgolémono*, a satisfying chicken and rice broth, enriched with eggs and flavoured with lemon. After this, Lucia could eat no more, but the children still had room for fruit, and sticky, honey-drenched *baklavas*.

"Hollow legs," said Nicholas, grinning at her, as he passed across a bottle of Fix beer.

She smiled and nodded and, for a moment, it seemed to her that there was a harmony between them which had never happened before. The feeling stayed with her when, presently, they all lay down to doze for a while.

She could have lain in the sun all afternoon, but it was not long before the children recovered their energies. Considerately, they crept off to play without disturbing the two grown-ups. Nicholas, when Lucia turned her head to look at him, seemed to have fallen asleep. He was lying on his back with one forearm shading his eyes, and his other arm lax on the sand.

But after she had been watching him for some minutes, he said, without moving but in a wideawake voice, "Would you like to see the remains of the temple?"

"Oh, yes, please. Where is it?"

He sat up, and stretched. "Near the top of the hill, on the other side. You can't see it from here. Not that there's much to see anyway. If you'd rather stay here and laze..." He let the sentence rest on a gesture.

"What about you? Perhaps you would rather be lazy?"

He stood up, and raked his fingers through his short, black hair. "It's our last day. We may as well make the most of it. Come on." He held out his hand to help her up.

Our last day... The words chilled Lucia's heart. As his hand locked with hers, and he pulled her to her feet, she felt a panicky sense of time running out...of London and loneliness waiting for her like a prison.

It had not been her wish to fall in love with him. It

had brought her no joy, only wretchedness. Would it be wrong, just for a few short hours, to forget that Cathy existed? To forget everything, past and future, and live only for this one afternoon?

It was quite a stiff climb up to the ruins. There was no path, and the hillside was rocky and overgrown with low, thorny scrub. By the time they reached the summit, Lucia was panting.

But now, below them, lay the seaward side of the island and, not far away on a grassy plateau, the two surviving pillars of the temple. When they came to it, Lucia stood for a time gazing at the worn, centuries-old columns, and the vivid blue vista they framed.

"Whose temple is it? Who built it here?" she asked, in a low voice.

"Apollo...Thetis...who knows? It has no history." Nicholas also spoke quietly. He touched her arm. "It's very hot. Come into the shade and rest, or you'll have a headache."

There were some cypresses nearby, casting black shadows on the turf. "What about the children? Will they be all right on their own?" she asked, as they sat down under the trees.

"They're down there—look!" Nicholas indicated the cove at the foot of the hill.

"Oh, yes, so they are. I didn't see them." She paused. "I do hope everything is going to turn out well."

"Between Richard and my sister? Well, we'll know that when we see them later on. The fact that they're arriving together seems promising, don't you think? Evidently Richard did what I hoped he would, and went to Paris to collect Sofia en route."

"Yes, it would seem so." Lucia watched some bees gathering pollen from a clump of bright yellow flowers growing out of a cleft between two rocks. Their intermittent buzzing, as they withdrew from one flower and hovered in the bright air before delving into another, was the only sound to be heard. The cove was too far below for the children's voices to carry up to the plateau.

Beside her, Nicholas lay down with his hands under his head. He said lazily, "The wind has shifted since this morning. I hope it doesn't mean a change in the weather."

She looked at the sky. "Surely not? There isn't a cloud in sight."

He did not reply to this and, after some minutes, she also lay back on the warm grass, and surrendered to the heat and the stillness.

At first, when he touched her, she thought it was unintentional. Then his hand closed on hers and she stiffened, wondering what was going to happen next.

Nothing happened. Minutes passed, but he did not move or speak. Perhaps he was waiting to see what she would do.

What she should have done—immediately, without thinking—was to free her hand, and open her eyes, and sit up. But, after the first few seconds of startled apprehension, she did not want to do what she ought to do. She knew it was folly, but she wanted him to hold her hand. And if, presently, he meant to kiss her, she wanted that too. For the first time in her life, she did not care what was right or wrong. All that mattered was that she loved him, and that she wanted desperately to have one memory to last her the rest of life; one moment, however illusory, of knowing what it would have been like to be loved by him.

"Lucia."

She felt him move, and opened her eyes to find him leaning over her, his dark head blocking out the sky.

"Yes?" she whispered, her heart pounding wildly.

And then, at the very last moment, with his lips only inches from hers, she was suddenly filled with shame and disgust at her weakness. Had she gone mad? How could she let him kiss her when he belonged to her sister? How could she bear to be yet another of his many conquests?

"No!" she burst out, turning her face away. "No—please don't. Let me go!" And thrusting him off, she twisted away and scrambled up.

She did not get far. She was scarcely on her feet before Nicholas had her by both wrists, holding her fast, gripping her painfully hard.

It was a moment out of a nightmare, for now, in his eyes, she could see something fierce and frightening. Too late, she knew that she should have accepted that first kiss, seconds ago. He had been only playing with her then. Now he looked angry and ruthless, capable of anything.

"Nicholas...*please*..." she begged, shrinking.

But although his bruising grip slackened, he did not release her.

He said in a harsh, mocking voice, "You should have remembered Pandora, sweetheart. She was warned not to open the box, but she couldn't control her curiosity. She had to know...and you had to know too, didn't you?"

He freed her wrists, and jerked her roughly against him. One hand in her hair, his other arm hard round her waist, he looked down at her flushed shocked face. Then slowly, taking his time about it, he kissed her.

When it was over, he said, "Well, now you do know."

Then he let her go, and went off down the hill towards the cove.

WHEN, ABOUT HALF AN HOUR LATER, Lucia started back the way they had come, she would rather have spent the night alone on the island than have to face Nicholas, after what had happened.

But, since face him she must, the only thing to do was to muster all her moral courage, and bear the ordeal as best she could. If he chose to make it as humiliating as possible, that too she must bear. She could not blame him. There was no one to blame but herself. She had asked for trouble, and she had got it. It was no use pretending that Nicholas had behaved badly. He had merely acted in character. You could not blame a tiger for being a tiger.

When she reached the beach, he and the children were already packing up the baskets. He glanced at her, bringing a rush of colour to her cheeks, but he did not say anything.

By the time they reached their own beach, it was clear that the weather was changing. The breeze had stiffened, and there was a bank of clouds along the horizon.

Kyria Katina was waiting for them on the terrace. She seemed upset about something, and spoke to Nicholas in a torrent of Greek which Lucia could not follow. He listened, then he patted her shoulder, and said something which sounded like the equivalent of "Don't worry." Then he told the children to go and tidy themselves as it would soon be time to meet the steamer.

Lucia would have gone with them, but he called her back.

"It seems that Cathy's headache was not as severe as she made out—or perhaps 'made up' would be more accurate."

She avoided looking at him. "What do you mean?"

"Shortly after we left, Cathy also went out. She hasn't come back."

She was forced to look at him then. "Where could she have gone? What could have happened to her?"

"I don't think there's any cause for alarm," Nicholas said coolly. "I imagine she decided to walk to town and find some diversion more to her taste than a picnic. Unfortunately, she has caused my aunt a good deal of anxiety. Katina couldn't understand whatever Cathy said to her before she went, and she assumed she was going for a walk, and would be back for lunch. She has spent the afternoon worrying in case Cathy has sprained her ankle, or some mishap."

"Perhaps she has," said Lucia, frowning. "What other explanation can there be? I'm sure she wouldn't walk all the way to town. It's several miles, and she hates walking."

"She would also hate spending the day alone with Katina," said Nicholas dryly.

"But what could she do there if she did walk all that way? There are no shops—at least, not her sort of shops."

He shrugged. "There's the yacht *Cassandra* with a susceptible American on board."

She had forgotten about Grant Wallace. "But is the yacht still here? I thought it would have left by now?"

"That remains to be seen. In the meantime, you had better attend to any last-minute packing you have to do. We shall be leaving in twenty minutes."

Lucia had packed most of her own and Cathy's belongings the night before. Now she had only to change her beach clothes for a dress, and fill her toilet bag, and her case was ready to be locked. Cathy had left various bits and pieces about in her room, but these were soon gathered up. After a final check to see that nothing had been overlooked, she carried both cases into the passage, and went to find Kyria Katina to say goodbye.

The Greek woman was in the kitchen, and so was Nicholas.

"Would you please tell your aunt how much I have enjoyed myself, and thank her for all her kindness," Lucia asked him stiffly.

He gave her a sardonic look, which she pretended not to notice. Then he translated what she had said.

Kyria Katina responded by embracing her warmly, and kissing her on both cheeks. Then she, in turn, said something for Nicholas to interpret.

"You are a nice, kind girl, and she looks forward to your next visit," he explained, with a glint in his eyes.

Lucia flushed, and was glad when the children rushed in, eager to go and meet their parents.

The steamer had not yet arrived when they reached the waterfront.

Nicholas gave the children some money to buy *caramellos* and pistachio nuts, and steered Lucia towards one of the *kafenions*. The local people were only just coming to life after the siesta hours, and a sleepy-looking waiter was flicking a cloth over the table tops.

"Oughtn't we to find out if Cathy is on the *Cassandra*?" she said, looking over her shoulder at the charter yacht which was anchored some way out in the bay.

"There's someone coming ashore from her now. I'll ask him," said Nicholas, indicating the dinghy which was coming into view round the yacht's bows. He ordered coffee and *kataifi*, another of the sweet, sticky confections to which Greeks of all ages were so partial, and sat down to wait for the dinghy to reach the quay.

Lucia marvelled that he could be so relaxed. Although it was more than two hours since the incident near the ruined temple, she could still feel the imprint of his mouth on hers. The memory of that long unsparing kiss made her tremble and turn hot and cold. Surely he could not already have dismissed it from his mind? Surely he must feel some discomfiture? Yet he did not appear to do so.

When the man in the dinghy climbed on to the quay, Nicholas whistled and beckoned to him. He was evidently one of the yacht stewards, as he was wearing a white drill tunic and black trousers. He had a large basket with him, and had probably come to buy provisions.

Lucia did not need Nicholas to translate the man's

answer to his question. The way the steward rolled his eyes, and his graphic gestures, made it clear that Cathy was aboard.

It was at this point that the steamer came in sight. Within minutes, the waterfront was as crowded as it had been on the day Lucia and Cathy arrived.

"There they are! There's Mummy!" Ariadne squeaked excitedly, when the steamer was near enough for those on land to distinguish those on deck.

Lucia kept in the background while the lively reunion took place, and it was Francesca, not Nicholas, who finally drew her into the family circle.

"Mummy... Daddy... this is Lucia."

"How do you do? I'm afraid you can't have had a very peaceful holiday with these three scallywags running wild," said Sofia, shaking hands.

As her brother had said, she did not look at all Greek. True, her hair was very dark. But she had blue eyes, and a fair, English complexion. She was very well dressed in an expensive grey jersey suit and silk shirt, with a red lizard bag and matching shoes.

"Where is your sister? There are two of you here, aren't there?" she enquired.

"You'll meet Cathy later," Nicholas intervened briskly.

And, as soon as Lucia had shaken hands with his brother-in-law, he marshalled them to the jeep for the drive to the hotel where they were all to have dinner.

Yannis had not seen Lucia since the night Nicholas had taken the two girls to the hotel to dance. He explained that he had been too busy looking after the visitors to be able to come to the house, and professed himself desolated that her stay was nearing its end. But Lucia was not in the mood to be amused by his melting looks and flattering speeches. Indeed she found his attentions rather tiresome, and was glad when he was called away, and she could be alone for a while. The children and their father had gone down to the beach. Sofia was having a bath and changing. Nicholas too had disappeared.

It was some time later, while she was sitting in a high-backed cane chair at one end of the terrace, that she overheard part of a conversation which plunged her into an even more profound state of unhappiness.

"So you have finally met your match. I can hardly believe it," she heard Sofia saying, in the nearby lounge. "Are you sure, Nico? It all seems to have happened very suddenly. Are you sure it will last? Are you positive you want to marry her?"

There was a pause in which Lucia waited tensely for Nicholas's reply.

"My dear girl, I was sure the second time I met her—and that was in February," he answered, in a voice quite different from his usual light, dry tone. "I think two and a half months is ample time for a man of my age to know his own mind."

"In that case, why aren't you engaged to her? It isn't like you to let the grass grow under your feet once you've definitely decided on something," his sister remarked, with a laugh.

It was then that Lucia realized she was eavesdropping. But, as it was impossible for her to leave that part of the terrace without passing the lounge doors and being seen, it seemed best to stay where she was, and hope that they would soon move out of earshot.

"Unfortunately, our relationship hasn't progressed as I hoped it would," Nicholas answered. "Bringing her to Marina was a brainwave which has misfired on me."

"I'll talk to her. I'll soon be able to tell how she feels about you," Sofia said confidently.

"You'll mind your own business, my dear. The situation is complex enough without you taking a hand in it."

"Why is it complex?"—on a puzzled note.

"Well, the sister is one fly in the ointment. In fact, if it were not for her, there would be no problem. You see..."

But, to Lucia's mingled relief and frustration, the rest of what he said was muffled by a distant roll of thunder. Without her noticing, the sky had clouded over, and the children and their father were hurrying back to the shelter of the hotel before the first slow drops of rain became a downpour.

Their return enabled her to slip away to her room. She was there, lying on the bed, when Cathy walked in.

"Hi," the younger girl said brightly. "Guess where I've been?"

"I know where you've been."

"Oh?" Cathy looked surprised. "How do you know?"

Lucia explained. But she felt too weary and dispirited to reproach her sister for her subterfuge, and for causing Kyria Katina unnecessary anxiety.

"I've had a marvellous day," Cathy told her. "The yacht is fabulous, and Grant is a sweetie. I told him I was dreading another trip in that horrid, ramshackle steamer—especially if the sea is going to be rough tomorrow—and he's offered to take us back on *Cassandra*. He has some tablets which should stop me being sea-sick again. But even if I am, at least I can be ill in comfort. We've got to be on board by ten o'clock."

"Shouldn't you have consulted Nicholas before you made these arrangements?" Lucia said dully.

"Why should he mind?"

"We are his guests. We are under some obligation to him."

"Oh, don't be so stuffy. You can't seriously expect me to travel on that awful steamer again. It's all right for you. You aren't sea-sick, and you don't seem to mind being surrounded by smelly peasants, and their even smellier goats and hens. I'll go and tell Nico now.

If he doesn't like it, he can jolly well lump it," Cathy declared.

About half past eight, when Lucia was tidying herself for dinner, Cathy came back to say that Nicholas had no objection to accepting Grant's offer.

"What are those marks on your arms?" she asked, noticing the discolorations which had begun to appear on her sister's wrists.

"Oh... nothing. I—I fell down when we were climbing about on the island," Lucia improvised hurriedly. "I didn't really hurt myself. You know how easily I bruise."

Cathy was not the only one to notice the marks. At dinner, Ariadne also spotted them, and caused Lucia intense mortification by pointing them out to the rest of the company. For the second time, she stammered her explanation about slipping among the rocks, and wished she had had the sense to put on a long-sleeved shirt.

By the time dinner was over, the rain had stopped. Nicholas thought it would probably start again before long, and suggested it would be as well for them to drive back to the house before the roads became any muddier than they were already.

When Sofia said goodnight to her, Lucia could not fail to notice a reserve in her manner which had not been there when they met.

"I suppose now she dislikes me for being 'the fly in the ointment'," she thought wryly.

After the others had gone, Yannis wanted her to stay up and dance with him. But she pleaded tiredness, and escaped to her room.

During the night there was a violent thunderstorm. Lucia, who had not been to sleep, stood at her window and watched the sea churning round the rocks in the flashes of lightning. She did not mind storms. But Cathy was terrified of them, and soon came scuttling into her room, begging her to draw the curtains and put the light on.

In the past, Lucia had always comforted her. But tonight she could not bring herself to put her arms round her. She sat in a chair, while Cathy huddled under the bedclothes, quaking each time a crash of thunder reverberated across the sky.

The storm lasted for nearly an hour. As, at last, it died down, Cathy fell asleep. Lucia opened the curtains, and took off her dressing-gown. She had been put in a double room, so it was not necessary to wake Cathy and send her back to her own bed. Before she switched off the lamp, she looked down at her sister for some minutes.

In sleep, Cathy's face had a sweetness which was often marred during her waking hours by expressions of boredom or petulance. As she lay there, her blonde hair lustrous in the lamp-glow, her lips slightly parted, her flimsy nightdress slipping off one smooth pretty shoulder, she looked extraordinarily appealing.

I was sure the second time I met her, Nicholas had said.

It was not hard to understand why he wanted her. It was for the same reason that, although he had lived to regret it, her father had wanted her stepmother.

Janet was right, thought Lucia sadly. I should have realized a long time ago that it never does any good to interfere in other people's lives. I should have let her go her own way. If I had, none of this would have happened. I should have known that, if either of us was going to make a hash of life, it would be me, not Cathy.

NEXT MORNING, the sun was shining. But there was still a good deal of cloud about, and a strong wind was making the sea very choppy.

Yannis came down to the waterfront to see them off. He said to Lucia, "I wish I could come with you, but I am needed here. Goodbye, beautiful Lucia"—and his black eyes danced, and he bent his handsome head to kiss her.

Cathy turned rather pale in the yacht's tender as it bobbed its way from the quay to *Cassandra's* moorings. But, once on board, she brightened again.

Grant was travelling with his parents, his sister and her husband, and another married couple who were friends of Mr. and Mrs. Grant Wallace Senior.

Mr. Wallace was the president of a large plant hire corporation. He had only recently recovered from an illness, and his doctors had advised him to take a long vacation. As he had two other sons, both vice-presidents, to run the business in his absence, his wife had persuaded him that it was high time they realized their life-long dream of touring Europe. The cruise among the islands of the Aegean was a leisurely preliminary to a programme of intensive sightseeing which would carry them through to the fall.

All this Lucia learnt from Mrs. Wallace, a small, trim, animated woman who seemed ready to pour out her life story if Lucia was willing to listen.

Everyone sat in the saloon, drinking and talking, till lunchtime. Lucia talked or, more accurately, was talked to by the three American women. Grant monopolized Cathy. And Nicholas chatted with Mr. Wallace and his son-in-law and the other man.

During lunch, the yacht began to roll. The sight of heaving grey waves and an apparently slanting horizon was too much for Mrs. Wallace.

"Oh, dear, you'll have to excuse me. I'm beginning to feel a little...you know. I guess I'll go to my cabin and lie down a while," she apologized, after the soup.

And, in spite of the tablets they had taken, Cathy and the other women were similarly affected.

After the main course Mr. Wallace, looking markedly less florid and cheerful, went to make sure his wife was all right. So did his son-in-law. Before the pudding arrived, both Grant and Mr. Hobart had gone. Only Nicholas and Lucia were left at the long, polished table.

Nicholas had some fruit tart. Lucia ate chocolate mousse. Then they both had cheese and biscuits, and coffee, and he asked her permission to smoke.

She watched him light a cigar. She had hoped for an opportunity to speak to him alone, and had prepared what she wanted to say. But now that the chance had come, it was difficult to begin.

"Let's go back to the main saloon, shall we?" Nicholas suggested. "Unless you would rather retire? It's going to get worse before it gets better, I fancy."

"Oh, I hope not—for the others' sakes," she said anxiously. "I don't mind it myself."

They removed to the larger saloon where a steward was putting away various objects which might be damaged if the roll became heavier.

Lucia waited until he had finished this task, and left them alone. Then she said briskly, "Nicholas, if you don't mind, I should like to go home tonight. Cathy can stay till Sunday, of course. But I should like to go at once."

For the first time since she had known him, she saw that she had startled him. He gave her a long, searching look which she met with studied composure.

"May I ask you why?" he said, at last.

She was ready for this. "As you know, I only came to Greece for Cathy's benefit," she began. "But it really isn't very convenient for me to go home on Sunday. School starts on Monday, you see, and there are various preparations to make. I could do with a couple of days to get back to normal."

"And you are prepared to leave Cathy here, alone with me?"

"Yes—now I am," she said calmly. "If she is staying at your cousin's house, instead of at a hotel, it will be perfectly in order."

"My cousin is expecting both of you."

"Well, I'm sure she won't mind my absence, if you explain the circumstances."

Nicholas smoked in silence for several minutes, his eyes on the spray-spattered ports. She wondered what he was thinking. She had expected him to accept her proposal, if not with enthusiasm, at least with only token objections.

He said, "This has nothing to do with term starting. It's because of what happened yesterday, isn't it?"

She made a mistake then. She pretended not to understand. "Yesterday?" she queried, looking blank.

He flicked the ash from his cigar, his mouth oddly grim. "Don't tell me you've forgotten already?"

She lifted her chin. "I would prefer to forget," she said, with a snap.

"You won't do so by making a drama out of it—by rushing back to England in a flurry of outraged virtue."

Her face flamed, but she managed to check her anger. "I am not in a flurry of any kind. I have been kissed before, you know. What happened yesterday was something which I should have thought you would want to forget as much as I do." She made her second mistake. "I think I understand why you did it, but that doesn't make it any less... discreditable."

"Oh, really? Why did I do it?" he asked, with one eyebrow arched.

"Need we discuss it?" she said stiffly. "It's over and done. I would rather pretend it never happened."

"Possibly—but it did happen, and I'm curious to know what motive you have ascribed to me. In fact, I insist," he said firmly.

Lucia wished she had not let her tongue run away with her.

Reluctantly, she said, "I—I can only suppose that you did it for the same reason that you've gaited me all along." She paused. "You aren't used to girls being indifferent to you. It was... a kind of challenge. You set out to prove that I was like all the others—that, sooner or later, I'd fall into your arms just like the rest of them."

His reaction to this was unexpected. "Good lord! Do you really take me for such a coxcomb?"

"I think you are very... sure of yourself."

"I certainly don't suffer from an inferiority complex," he agreed, looking rather amused now. "But I don't count myself irresistible."

Lucia said nothing to this, and after a moment, he went on, "I wonder why you assume that I'm such an inveterate Don Juan. That is your impression, I gather?"

"Well, aren't you?" she said, with a cold look.

"I wouldn't say so—not by most people's standards. Your low regard for my morals seems to be based on the fact that the first time we met I was kissing your sister. I agree I hadn't known her very long, but was it really such a blackguardly act? Even the sterling Bernard must have committed some indiscretions in his time. The only difference is that you don't know about them."

"I do know Bernard would never behave as you did yesterday," she said hotly. "But by your standards that was just a trifling indiscretion, I suppose?"

His expression changed to a look she could not interpret.

"No, that was a mistake," he said, in a flat tone. "But the only thing I regret is that I hurt you." He indicated her wrists which, today, were hidden by the sleeves of her lambswool sweater. "As for the rest—well, the blame wasn't all mine, was it? You did give me some encouragement."

"Oh!" Lucia sprang to her feet, all pretence of composure shattered.

Even if it was true—and to her shame, it was—she would not have believed he would taunt her with it. That was sheer cruelty.

Nicholas too was on his feet now, and perhaps her striken look caused him a fleeting compunction.

He said, "Don't fly off the handle—listen to me. I'm sorry if—"

But before he could say any more, the steward came in to ask if they wished for more coffee. And while Nicholas was irritably informing him that if they wished for anything, they would ring, Lucia walked out, and hurried away to find Cathy.

Her sister was lying on the bed in a small, single cabin. She looked rather wan, but not nearly as green and ghastly as she had on the outward voyage.

"No, I haven't been sick," she said, in answer to Lucia's enquiry. "The tablets have stopped that, thank goodness. But I do feel queer when I stand up, and I daren't look out of the window. Where is Grant? Is he in the saloon with you?"

"He disappeared too," Lucia told her. "Everyone did—except Nicholas." She parted the curtains which Cathy had drawn across the porthole. "But I think the weather is improving. It's not as rough as it was when we were having lunch."

Half an hour later, the sea had become so much calmer that Cathy ventured to sit up, and attend to her face and hair. While she was doing this, Mrs. Wallace looked in.

"My! That was a rough passage, wasn't it? I guess we've been lucky to have such good weather this far. I had no idea a yacht this size would roll that way. For a while there I was just flat out. How did you girls get along?"

She stayed talking for five or ten minutes, and then went off to see how her friend, Maisy Hobart, had fared.

"She's nice, isn't she?" said Cathy. "She must be fifty, I should think, but she's still very smart and with it. American women are less dull than Englishwomen of that age. I've noticed it at the Maybury. They don't give in to being old. They have better taste—more style."

"The Americans who stay at the Maybury can afford to have style," said Lucia. "Rich women are smarter than poor ones in any country."

"Don't you like Mrs. Wallace?" Cathy asked.

"Oh, yes, she seems very nice—though she does rather talk one's head off."

"That's better than saying nothing." Cathy retorted. "It's another thing I like about Americans. They're so enthusiastic about everything. They even shake hands with people differently—as if they really wanted to meet them, and wouldn't forget their names five minutes later."

If Lucia had been paying more attention to this conversation, instead of being preoccupied with other matters, it might have struck her that Cathy herself was being uncommonly enthusiastic about the Wallaces.

She said, "Cathy, listen—you wouldn't mind if I went back to England before you, would you?"

"Before me? What do you mean?"

Lucia explained, giving much the same reasons as those she had put to Nicholas.

To her astonishment, Cathy seemed horrified. "Oh, you mustn't—you can't!" she exclaimed, most vehemently.

"Why not? What difference will it make? You'll be staying with Nicholas's cousin. You'll still have a chaperone. As far as I am concerned, you can stay on after Sunday. Stay another week, if you wish—and if Nicholas asks you."

"But if you go it won't be the same," Cathy objected. "I want you with me—at least till Sunday. Please, Lucia."

And the more Lucia argued with her, the more obstinately she opposed the idea. In the end, nearly in tears, she said, "If you go home, I shall come with you. I won't stay in Athens without you. You're not being fair. You're spoiling everything!"

So, mystified by this sudden and unwonted dependence on her, but convinced that Cathy meant what she said, Lucia capitulated.

When, late in the afternoon, *Cassandra* put in to the yacht harbour at Piraeus, it was hard to believe that the early part of the day had been so squally. Now the sky was a bright, unclouded blue, and already the sun had dried out all signs of the recent downpours.

The Wallaces were staying in Athens for a further ten days before moving on to "take in" Italy.

"But Maisy and Donald are flying back to the States this weekend," Mrs. Wallace explained. "So why don't we all get together for a farewell party at the Hilton tomorrow night?" She turned to Nicholas. "You know Athens intimately, Mr. Curzon. Maybe, after we've dined, you could take us around the *bouzoukias*—do I have that correctly?—the ones off the tourist beat. You know what I mean—the really *authentic* places."

Lucia expected Nicholas to make some excuse. Instead he said, at his most charming, "It would be a pleasure, Mrs. Wallace—but only on condition that you will be my guests at the Vlachos. The Hilton is international. The Vlachos"—his mouth twitched slightly—"has a much more authentic atomosphere. If we dine there early, before sunset, you will see something unique to Athens."

"Is that so? How very interesting." Mrs. Wallace glanced round to gauge the reactions of the others. "Well, in that case, we'd be delighted, wouldn't we, honey?"—this to her husband.

"We would indeed. It sounds like quite an experience," Mr. Wallace Senior agreed heartily.

In the taxi, driving into Athens, Nicholas said to Lucia, "Are you still set on going home tonight? Do you want me to ring the airport?"

She bit her lip, wishing she could have said "yes".

But she had to answer, "No, not now. Cathy wants me to stay, so I've changed my mind."

"Good—it would be a pity not to see the Parthenon while you are here," he commented casually.

His cousin's house was in a narrow side-street in one of the older parts of the city. The taxi stopped at a gate in a high, whitewashed wall, and Nicholas got out and tugged an old-fashioned iron bell-pull. Almost immediately, the shutters at an upper window were flung open, and a woman leaned out and called down, "Come in—come in. The gate isn't locked."

Inside the gate was a small courtyard with a fig tree, and pots of geraniums of many colours. The house was built at right angles to the street, and a large black cat was sitting in the sun in the open doorway.

"Nico—my darling boy! What a pleasure to see you. It's much too long since your last visit. You know I never laugh as much as with you." The woman who stepped over the cat, and greeted Nicholas so warmly, was different from Lucia's expectations.

She had imagined his cousin being someone like Kyria Katina, or the women of Yannis's house. But Maria Sioris not only spoke fluent English, and dressed as elegantly as his sister. She also had one of the most beautiful faces Lucia had ever seen.

Nicholas kissed her hands, and murmured something in Greek which made her laugh and tap his cheek. Then he introduced her to her guests.

At first sight, she had seemed a young woman. But as they shook hands, Lucia saw that she was considerably older than Nicholas. There were lines round her great dark eyes, and threads of grey in her hair. Her throat and hands bore the tell-tale marks of maturity. But the beauty of her features was ageless. In ten, even twenty years' time, she would still have that marvellous profile, those wonderful eyes.

She led them inside to a large, cool room, and tinkled a handbell. Moments later, a plump maid came in and handed round the traditional offering to travellers of preserved fruit, water—ice-cold in engraved crystal glasses—and tiny cups of syrupy coffee. But while she chose to observe this particular custom of her country, their hostess was obviously a woman of cosmopolitan tastes. The room was furnished with lovely things from all parts of the world.

"Maria is a designer," Nicholas told them. "She has a dress shop in Boukourestiou Street. Tomorrow, you might like to go shopping for souvenirs. But not to Maria's place. Her prices are astronomical."

His cousin laughed. "Nico is so careful with his money. With him to guide you, you will be sure to find a bargain." She gave him a mischievous glance, and held out her arm so that the girls could admire an exquisite bracelet on her wrist. "This, for example, cost only a few *drachs* in the Flea Market. I wonder why I can never find such remarkable bargains."

Presently, she took the girls upstairs to their rooms, saying that they would be glad to bath, and rest for an hour, after spending most of the day on a crowded steamer.

Nicholas, following behind with the cases, told her about the Wallaces, and how he had arranged to take them to the Vlachos the following night. "You must come too, Maria."

"With pleasure—I am always happy to meet rich Americans. Perhaps I can sell them some clothes."

She had given the girls separate bedrooms, and apologized for not being able to put them up at the beginning of their holiday. At that time, she herself had been having a few days' break at Corfu before the high season gathered momentum.

"Holidays pass so quickly, don't they?" she said regretfully. "However, yours is not over yet, and we must see that your last few days are very gay."

When she was alone, Lucia sat down on the bed, and let her shoulders sag. Their last days in Greece would

CHAPTER SEVEN

THE FOLLOWING MORNING, at stalls in Pandrossou Street in the Plaka—the old city—Lucia bought presents for the Sanders. For Peter, she chose a pair of Tsarouchia leather slippers decorated with large pom-poms and, for Janet, gaily coloured, hand-woven *tagharia* bag. It was difficult to find anything typically Greek which would please three-year-old Mark, so she had to settle for a picture book for him. But for the new baby she found a beautiful embroidered infant's dress which would have cost four times as much in London, and for her class at the Alderman Evans Primary she bought two dolls—one a replica of an Evzone guardsman in his stiff white kilt and tasselled scarlet cap, and the other a girl doll in the national dress worn by the women of Rhodes on feast days.

The prices of all these purchases were settled by haggling between Maria and the stall-holders. As Maria explained, except in the very grandest shops, the customer was expected to bargain.

"Where are the best shops?" asked Cathy, who had no interest in souvenirs, and was impatient to discover the Athenian equivalent of Bond Street.

"They are in the Kolonaki quarter," Maria told her. "That's the expensive part of Athens. But first you must see Syntagma Square, which is the heart of the City."

In the sloping Square, dominated by Parliament House, once the royal palace, they had coffee and ices at one of the pavement cafés.

Nicholas pointed out the Grande Bretagne on the

corner of Venizelos Avenue. Built in the nineteenth century, and known as the G.B., it had long been one of the world's *grande luxe* hotels.

"I expect your father knew it well. It's a great meeting place for journalists and diplomats," he said to Lucia.

It was curious that he should have mentioned Malcolm Gresham then, at the very moment when she was thinking of her father and how, if only he had lived, they might have sat here together.

"Yes, I expect he did," she said huskily.

If Cathy had had unlimited funds, they would have needed a taxi to carry home all her shopping. Everything she saw, she coveted. When, on the way to Maria's shop, they passed *Katramopoulos*, the Court jewellers, she lingered so long gazing at costly rings that Lucia became embarrassed. Surely she did not expect Nicholas to buy one for her then and there?

"You do not care for jewels, Lucia?" Maria asked, sensing her impatience to move on.

"Oh, yes, they're magnificent—but rather beyond our means," Lucia answered, with a somewhat strained smile.

At Maria's shop, Nicholas left them and went off on some errand of his own. After the heat and noise of the streets, the interior of the shop was cool and quiet. The floor was laid with slabs of pale Pentelic marble which, in Greece, was cheaper than carpet. Fans stirred the foliage of plants growing in tall white jars.

Lucia sat down on a reproduction of a classical Greek dining couch, while Cathy darted about admiring the clothes and accessories on display. There were no customers in the shop, and Maria asked her assistant to bring cold drinks.

To Lucia's dismay, Cathy was not content with admiring the stock. Ignoring her sister's covert signals, she asked if she might try on some things.

"By all means," Maria assented. "I'll show you the fitting-room."

Lucia's heart sank. She felt certain that Cathy would not be satisfied with merely trying on the lovely clothes and, sure enough, it was not long before the younger girl reappeared in a white and gold evening dress.

"This is fabulous. I must have it," she exclaimed, parading about the showroom.

"But, Cathy, it looks frightfully expensive, and you already have several evening things," Lucia protested. "Besides, you can't afford it. You've already spent most of your money."

"You haven't spent all yours yet. You don't want anything else, do you?"

"I haven't enough for that dress," Lucia said, rather grimly.

"Then I'll borrow some from Nico, and pay him back later. How much is it?"—this to Maria.

The older woman glanced at the ticket attached to the zipper. She mentioned a price which made Cathy clap her hands. "That's marvellous! I'll have it, and wear it tonight."

The fact that she did—just—have enough money to pay for the dress was no comfort to Lucia because it was obvious to her that, out of misguided kindness, Maria had halved, if not quartered, the proper price of it. No dress of such fabric and cut could possibly be as cheap as she had said it was. She had not only sacrificed any profit, she was probably losing money on it.

The others had gone to the fitting-room, and she was alone in the shop, struggling with her chagrin, when Nicholas returned.

"You forgot to buy a memento for yourself, so I've found one for you." He took a small box from his pocket, opened it, and showed her what it contained.

It was a medallion on a fine gold chain. The face of the disc was made of azure enamel, rippled like the surface of the sea. Inlaid upon this shimmering ground was an intricate design in gold.

"Like it?" Nicholas asked.

"It's... beautiful," she said awkwardly.

"Put it on." He lifted it out of the box, and unfastened the clasp.

"No... please... I—I can't possibly accept it."

His eyebrows lifted. "Why not?"

She bit her lip. "I just can't, that's all."

"My dear girl, it's only a trinket," he said, with a gleam of amusement. "There are no 'strings' attached to it."

If he had not mocked her, if she had not been upset about Cathy's dress, she would never have answered as she did. The words were no sooner spoken than she regretted them.

"I should have thought you would realize that I wouldn't accept *any* present from you," she said coldly.

There was a moment of fraught silence. Lucia wanted to apologize, but her mouth and throat seemed paralysed. What Nicholas felt, she could not tell. His eyes were completely expressionless.

Cathy came back, too elated to sense the tension. But she noticed the blue and gold medallion still dangling from Nicholas's fingers.

"Oh, Nico, how pretty! For me?" she enquired delightedly, reaching out to take it.

His dark face reanimated. "Naturally," he said smoothly smiling down at her. "It matches your eyes."

CATHY HAD NEVER LOOKED lovelier than she did that night, in her new dress. In a different way, Maria was equally ravishing. She wore black, with a necklace of glowing crimson stones, and a chinchilla wrap.

Nicholas, when he saw them, bowed his admiration. "Mine eyes dazzle," he said gallantly, looking from one to the other.

Maria moved aside so that he could see Lucia, who had come down last and was behind them. But, although he smiled, and said, "Charming", there was no warmth or interest in his eyes. His appraisal was as brief as it could be short of discourtesy.

She knew then that never again would he look at her with that disturbing glint which had caused her so much unrest. Today, she had finally convinced him that she truly did detest and distrust him. From now on, the barrier between them would be of his making, not hers. That it was better so did not make it any less painful. She had not realized how much his indifference would hurt. In spite of her own becoming dress, and careful make-up, she felt suddenly plain and insipid—a girl no one would look at twice.

The Vlachos *taverna* was high up on the steeps of the Acropolis, with a splendid view across Athens to the church-crowned summit of the hill called Lykabettus and, further away, Mount Hymettus.

As soon as the party had settled themselves round a table on the terrace, they witnessed the unique spectacle which Nicholas had promised them—the reason why the ancient Greeks had called the city "violet-crowned".

As the sun set in a blaze of vermilion and gold, the distant slopes of Hymettus were bathed in a strange amethyst light. While it lasted, it was so breathtaking that even Mrs. Wallace kept silent.

She was seated next to Lucia, and presently, while they were eating *taramosalata*, a soft pâté made of smoked roe, she said, "Do you know, I don't believe I've ever seen a lovelier girl than your little sister, Miss Gresham. My son simply can't take his eyes off her, and I don't wonder at it. She's a real beauty, and such a sweet person, too."

Lucia smiled, and glanced along the table to where Cathy and Grant were laughing together.

"I think she likes Grant, don't you?" Mrs. Wallace murmured in her ear.

There was a meaning in her tone which made Lucia stiffen.

"Oh, I know all the wisecracks about American mothers and their sons," Mrs. Wallace went on, as if reading Lucia's mind, "But I've never been overly possessive with my three boys. I've seen the harm it can do. So far, I've been very lucky. My daughters-in-law are sweet girls, and I love them dearly. When Grant falls in love, I shall be the first to congratulate him."

"Isn't he rather young to settle down yet?" Lucia suggested cautiously.

"He's twenty-four," said his mother. "He's very mature for his age, and of course he has excellent prospects. I wouldn't say he's too young for marriage." She helped herself to some aubergine salad. "Tell me about your family, Miss Gresham. Cathy did mention that your parents had passed away. I guess that makes you feel a special responsibility toward her. Are you two quite alone in the world now? Or do you have many other relatives?"

Lucia answered her questions with a growing sense of consternation. It had not occurred to her that Grant might have fallen headlong in love with Cathy. And if it had, she would have expected his parents to be strenuously opposed to such a precipitate passion, especially with a girl of different nationality.

Instead, Mrs. Wallace seemed to feel that Cathy and her son were ideally matched, and that their engagement was practically a *fait accompli*—which indeed was what anyone would think, judging by the starry-eyed way Cathy was gazing into the young American's eyes.

From the head of the table, Nicholas was also observing her sister's behaviour. He was doing it discreetly so that neither Mrs. Hobart, on his right, or Grant's sister, on his left, was aware that he was only half attending to their conversation with him. But, every few minutes, he shot a swift glance at Cathy and, when he did, there was something about the set of his mouth which made Lucia wonder uneasily if, before the evening was over, there would be a scene.

He was after all partly Greek and, as she knew from experience, he could, when roused, be startlingly violent. Cathy had never seen that side of him. She had no idea how his eyes could blaze when he was angry. She had never felt the painful strength of those lean brown hands. But she might, if she went on ignoring him and playing up to poor, unsuspecting Grant.

It was three o'clock in the morning when Lucia collapsed into bed after the most gruelling evening of her life. But even though she felt exhausted, she could not sleep. She tried to make her mind a blank, but it was full of confused impressions... the Parthenon, golden in the floodlights, high above the haze of coloured neon which was Athens by night... the scent of honeysuckle and sweet basil, of French perfume and cigars... the mandolin-clanging of *bouzoukias* and the throbbing of *dumbeks*...

There had not, after all, been a crisis, as she had dreaded. From the Wallaces' point of view, the night had been a memorably gay and enjoyable one. After dinner, Nicholas had taken them to several *bouzoukias*, two of them well-known tourist places, but the last one a genuine workman's *taverna* where they had been lucky enough to see some of the regulars giving a spontaneous show of folk dancing.

Afterwards because, by Athenian hours, it was still early, they had gone to Zonar's for coffee and *ouzo*, and wound up the evening dancing at the Galaxy Roof Terrace of the Hilton.

Civility had obliged Nicholas to ask Lucia for one dance, though no doubt he would have preferred not to do so. But he had not talked to her. They had circled the floor in uncomfortable silence. She had looked fixedly over his shoulder, and he had probably been watching Cathy and Grant who were locked in a cheek-to-cheek embrace elsewhere on the floor.

WHEN SHE WOKE UP the next morning, Maria was standing by the bed, holding a breakfast tray.

"Oh, good heavens, have I overslept? I'm so sorry. What time is it?" Lucia asked, struggling into a sitting position.

"Don't worry. It's not so late, considering the hour we went to bed," Maria said, smiling, and setting the tray on the table beside the bed. "If I may, I will have my coffee with you. I have not been up long myself."

Lucia reached for her watch. "Goodness, it's nearly eleven. Is my sister still in bed?"

"No, she and Nico are more energetic than we are. They have gone out," said Maria. "I don't know where Nico has gone—only that he will return for lunch. Your sister is with the American boy. I did not see him myself, but Elli tells me that he called about an hour ago. I expect he has taken Cathy to see the Agora. They were talking about it last night."

"Oh, were they?" said Lucia, frowning. "I didn't hear."

"No, you were dancing then, I think." Maria sat down on the chair by the open window. She was wearing a green silk caftan, and her long hair was loose, held back by combs above her ears. "Do you mind if I smoke a cigarette? I do not eat in the morning."

"Not at all. Do you mind if I clean my teeth before I have breakfast?"

After she had done this, and brushed her hair, Lucia felt more alert. She climbed back into bed, plumped the pillows, and slowly sipped the glass of fresh orange juice which Maria had brought for her.

For a while, neither of them spoke. Then Maria said suddenly, "I wish I could go back to Marina. It's foolish of me, I suppose. There are other islands more beautiful... Corfu... Mykonos... Rhodes. But, for me, they are not like Marina. I do not love them."

"Is it a long time since you were last at Marina?" Lucia asked.

Maria shrugged. "Twenty years." She saw her guest looking puzzled. "Oh, you do not know about me? Nico hasn't told you?"

Lucia shook her head.

"In England, there would be nothing to tell," Maria said, gazing out of the window. "It would all be forgotten... an old scandal, no longer important. But at Marina such things are never forgotten—not in a hundred years. They do not speak of me, you know. To them, I am already dead."

She paused, and gave a faint sigh. "I don't mind that... I understand their feelings. What I did *was* wrong. But I don't regret it. I have never regretted one moment of it."

"What did you do?" Lucia asked.

Maria put out her cigarette, and clasped her thin, elegant hands. "When I was seventeen, my parents arranged a marriage for me," she began. "It was a good match because my father was poor, and could offer only a small dowry. I didn't love the man, but I didn't know about love then. My fiancé was good and kind, and I thought I was very fortunate."

She rose to refill her cup from the pot of French coffee. "About six weeks before our wedding, a boat came to the island. It belonged to a Frenchman... a writer. He spoke some Greek. Everyone liked him. He decided to stay for a time. He wasn't young—he was forty then. He wasn't handsome. His name was Raoul Vallet. We met in the street one morning, and we looked at each other, and it happened. One does not love at first sight, but there was something between us... it is hard to explain."

"I think I know what you mean," Lucia said quietly. It was what I felt the first time I looked at Nicholas, she thought.

"Ours was a very strange love affair," Maria went on. "We were never alone together. We scarcely spoke to each other. But, each day, the feeling between us grew stronger. I knew he wanted me, and I wanted him. It frightened me, yet I was happy, too. Oh, I was so confused—you can't imagine!"

Lucia said nothing.

"Four days before my wedding, I knew I could not marry Stephanos," Maria went on, after some moments. "That night, I crept from our house, and went to Raoul on his boat. I asked him to take me away with him."

She lit another cigarette, and her hand shook slightly as she held the match to its tip. "We had five years together—five years of heaven. He never married me. He already had a wife in Paris, but they hadn't lived together since before the war. He died very suddenly—a heart attack." She smiled, but there were tears in her eyes. "So you see I am a wicked woman. Nico is the only one who loves me in spite of my sins. He's a great comfort to me, and he brings me all the news from Marina."

After a little, Lucia said, "So you were only twenty-three when Raoul died? Have you never—" She stopped, afraid that what she had been about to ask would be impertinent.

"Have I never wanted to marry and become respectable?" Maria finished for her. "Oh, yes, I've wanted it very much. Unfortunately, I've never fallen in love again. I've been offered marriage...several times. Not here, in Athens, but in other countries. Sometimes I think it was stupid of me not to grasp those opportunities. When I'm lonely and tired, when I look at myself and see another line on my face, then I would marry anyone who would give me affection and companionship. But such moods pass. I'm not often depressed. And who knows? If I wait, and hope, perhaps one day there will be someone..."

The wistfulness left her face, and her black eyes twinkled. "To you, I am middle-aged—much too old to dream of a lover."

"Oh, no—I think you're beautiful," Lucia told her impulsively.

Maria smiled. "Thank you, my dear. But now let's talk about you. You are unhappy, I think—yes? This visit to Greece has been a difficult time for you?"

This caught Lucia unprepared. How much did Maria know? Obviously, since they were very close, Nicholas would have confided his feelings to her. But did she guess what Lucia felt? And what must she think of Cathy's behaviour last night?

"Sometimes, when one is deeply troubled, it is a relief to talk about it," Maria said gently. "You needn't fear that I will betray your confidence. I am very good at keeping secrets."

She looked so sympathetic, so understanding, that for an instant Lucia was tempted to tell her everything. But, on the very brink of confession, something held her back.

"Oh, please, don't be embarrassed. I didn't mean to press you," said Maria, seeing her discomfiture. "I shouldn't have spoken. It is not my business. Ah! Here is Demetrios"—this as her cat strolled into the room, and leapt on her lap.

From then on, they talked of cats, and clothes, and other things, until Maria rose, saying it was time she dressed and did her hair. But as she was leaving the room, she suddenly turned.

"Lucia, even if it is not my business, there is something I feel I must say to you. Nico is like a brother to me. I wish for his happiness as much as for my own. Will you let me speak?"

Lucia hesitated. "Very well."

Maria sat down on the bed. "Nico is not a boy. Naturally, there have been women in his life. But now, for the first time, it is serious with him. He hasn't told me this, but, knowing him as I do, I can sense it. For reasons which I don't understand, the girl he wants is pretending that she does not care for him. Forgive me for saying this so bluntly—she is being a fool."

Lucia pleated the edge of the sheet. "If he wants her, why doesn't he tell her? Why doesn't he propose to her?"

"Oh, my dear, you don't know much about men if you can ask that!" Maria replied dryly. "Do you think they are so different from women? That they have no pride? That their feelings can't be hurt as deeply as ours?"

"No, I don't think that. But surely it's up to the man to take the initiative?"

"Certainly—if he has reason to believe his love is returned. But you can't expect any man to offer himself to a girl who behaves as if she doesn't care that for him," said Maria, snapping her fingers. "That is asking too much."

Without looking at her, Lucia said, "Do you think she can make him happy? You know him so well. Do you really believe they are suited?"

Maria hesitated. "In this life, nothing is perfect," she said, on a wry note. "Even my happiness with Raoul was not quite perfect, because we could not have children." She paused. "Yes, I believe they are suited. They could be very happy together. But it's up to her to give him a sign...a word." She smiled. "Knowing Nico, I don't think he will need much encouragement. But all men need a little...just a little."

It was some time after she had gone away before Lucia got up. Was Maria right? Would her sister make Nicholas happy? Maria knew him, but what did she know of Cathy? She might be a very wise woman, but apparently she had not divined how Lucia felt about her cousin. If she had, she would never have appealed to her to check Cathy's foolishness.

If only I were *sure* that they would be happy, thought

Lucia, biting her knuckles. But I'm not sure... I'm not sure at all.

Shortly before one o'clock, Grant and Cathy returned. Maria offered him a drink and then, when he showed no sign of leaving, was virtually forced to ask him to stay to lunch. He would have remained at the house all afternoon if Nicholas had not said the girls must rest. At this, Grant asked what their plans for the evening were.

"We're going to see the Parthenon by moonlight. Why don't you come with us?" Cathy suggested.

"Yes, why don't you, Wallace?" agreed Nicholas, looking at him without a sign of the leashed exasperation which he must be feeling.

So, after arranging to come back at eight o'clock, Grant at last took his leave, and the others retired to their bedrooms.

When the house was silent, Lucia went softly down to Cathy's room on the floor below. It was very hot, and her sister was sitting at the dressing-table in her bra and briefs, creaming off her make-up.

"Whew! Isn't it stifling? It must be like an oven here in the summer," she said, as Lucia came in and closed the door.

"Yes, I expect it is. Can I borrow some of your nail varnish remover? I've used up my bottle."

"Help yourself." Cathy tossed some tissues into the waste basket, and began to peel off her false eyelashes. "What did you do this morning? Anything interesting?"

"No—I didn't wake up until late. Maria brought me breakfast in bed, and we talked for a while."

"I wonder why she isn't married?" Cathy murmured. "She's really quite glamorous for her age. A bit too bosomy and hippy, but her legs are still good, and I love her clothes."

There was a pause until, abruptly, Lucia said, "Do you still want to marry Nicholas?"

Her sister now had taken off both lashes and, with a pair of tweezers, was carefully removing shreds of adhesive from them. Without looking up from this task, she said, "Why do you ask?"

"Because, if you do, you must stop flirting with Grant. Nicholas loves you. I heard him say so to his sister at Marina. But he won't tell you if you go on making a fool of him."

Cathy looked at her then. "Well, well...you do surprise me. I thought your mission in life was to prove that he didn't want to marry me?"

"That was some time ago, when I didn't know much about him. Now I know for certain that he does care for you," Lucia answered, in a low voice.

Cathy swung round on the stool. "Then it's a pity he didn't say so before we left that dreary island. Because now it's too late. I'm afraid I shall have to disappoint him."

"*What?*" Lucia stared at her. "Cathy, you can't mean that? He loves you. He really loves you."

"He'll get over it," Cathy said carelessly. "I hate to admit it, but you were right in the first place. He is too old for me. We had a good time in London, but now he seems different somehow. Perhaps it's because he's in love with me. I liked him better when he wasn't. He was more exciting then. Now he's really quite dull—not half as much fun as Grant."

"Oh, God! You heartless little beast!" Lucia flared, with passionate contempt. "How can you dismiss him like that? He's worth ten of that silly boy."

Cathy rolled her eyes, and gave an exaggerated sigh. "Here we go again! Now it's Grant you're against. The trouble with you is you're jealous. You haven't a man in your life, so you don't want me to have one either. You've never approved of anyone—and you never will. You don't care about me. Sometimes I think you hate me. But you're scared of being left alone...of being an old dried-up spinster. Oh!"

She gave a cry of pain as her sister's palm struck her cheek.

For a moment, they stared at each other, equally shocked. Then, shaking, hardly knowing what she was doing, Lucia stumbled from the room.

She did not go back to her own room. She went downstairs, and left the house. And all that sultry afternoon, while the shops were shut, and the *kafenions* deserted, she walked and walked the narrow streets of the Plaka. Such few people as were about stared at her pale, set face. She passed them by without seeing them. She knew only that she must keep moving, she must not cry...

"LUCIA, WE'VE BEEN WORRIED about you," Maria exclaimed, jumping up, as Lucia pushed open the gate and walked into the courtyard. "Oh, my dear, how hot and tired you look!"

Nicholas's greeting was less kindly. "Where the devil have you been?" he demanded.

Lucia had not expected to find all three of them sitting in the courtyard. She had hoped to slip up to her room without anyone knowing she had been out.

"Don't bark at her, Nico," said Maria.

He ignored her. "Where have you been?" he repeated sharply.

"Only for a walk," Lucia answered.

"A walk—at this time of day? You must be mad. Nobody walks round Athens in the afternoon. You were supposed to be resting, not haring about on your own till you're fit to drop. Look at yourself, girl! You're exhausted."

"Nico is cross because he was worried," Maria intervened soothinly. "Do be quiet, Nico. There's no need to make such a fuss. Lucia is not a little girl who would run across the street without looking. I told you there was no cause for alarm."

"You were anxious. So was Cathy. We all were," he

reminded her curtly. Then, to Lucia, "You might have had the consideration to let someone know you were going out."

"I'm sorry," she said dully. "I didn't mean to worry you. I went further than I intended, and lost my bearings. Now, if you don't mind, I'll go up to change."

"Have a cool bath," Maria advised. "I'll send Elli up with a drink for you. Champagne, I think...we'll all have some. There is nothing like champagne for calming the nerves," she added, with a quizzical glance at Nicholas.

In her room, Lucia stared at her reflection in the mirror. Until that moment she had not realized what a sight she presented—her face and neck glistening with perspiration, her dress wilting, her hair all dusty and dishevelled. But at least she was in command of herself again. The blind, burning anger which had made her strike Cathy had died. She no longer wanted to fling herself down and weep. She felt only a profound tiredness.

She had had a bath, and drunk the champagne the maid had brought to her, and was slowly brushing her hair, when there was a tap at the door.

"I must talk to you. Please let me in," Cathy begged in a low, urgent voice.

Lucia laid down the brush. "The door isn't locked."

Cathy sidled into the room as warily as a timid child. She stood near the door, nervously fingering her watchband.

"Lucia, I'm sorry about what I said," she blurted. "I didn't mean it—truly I didn't."

"It doesn't matter."

"But it does...I feel terrible about it. When we found you weren't in the house, I was worried sick. I thought I might never see you again."

"Oh, don't be foolish," Lucia said wearily. "What did you imagine I might do?—Fling myself under a bus?"

"I don't know." Cathy hesitated. "I've never seen you so worked up before."

"Well, I think you've behaved despicably," Lucia answered, with cold calm. "But you'll never see things my way, so it's a waste of time talking to you. Just go away, and leave me in peace, will you?"

"Oh, dear, I've made such a mess of things," Cathy said, in a crushed voice. "Don't hate me, Lucia, please don't hate me. I never meant to get in this ghastly muddle. Until I met Grant, I honestly didn't realize love was important."

"Are you trying to convince me that you *love* him?" Lucia asked sceptically.

"Yes—because I do. I really do."

"The fact that his parents are even better off than Nicholas has nothing to do with it, I suppose?"

"No, nothing—I swear it. I'd feel the same if they were poor people. Oh, I know I haven't known him long, but the first time I met him I knew he was different...special. And he feels the same about me. He told me so this morning. We aren't properly engaged yet. We're going to wait till he comes to London in the autumn."

"Does he realize that, until you met him, you were all set to marry for money? Why does he think we've been staying with Nicholas?"

"Oh...I—I said Nico was an old friend of the family," Cathy said, flushing. Her blue eyes widened apprehensively. "You don't mean to tell him the truth, do you? You wouldn't do that to me?"

"I wouldn't—Nicholas might."

"Nico doesn't know about Grant and me. I mean he doesn't know we're in love."

"No, he thinks, as I did, that you're trying to make him jealous. If you go on flirting so blatantly, he may lose his temper and show that, as far as he's concerned, you belong to him. How will you explain that to Grant?"

"But I *don't* belong to him," Cathy objected. "He would have no right to say that."

"Wouldn't he? I think he would. You were his girl when we arrived here."

Cathy sank down on the end of the bed. "What am I going to do?" she asked helplessly. "If Nico made a fuss it would ruin everything!"

"Well, perhaps he won't—if you stop goading him. Whatever happens, you must think of his feelings, Cathy. Don't hurt him more than you have to."

Her sister was silent for some minutes. "*You* couldn't tell him...explain to him...?" she began tentatively.

"No, I couldn't," Lucia said shortly. "You're responsible for this situation. It's up to you to deal with it. We shall be going home the day after tomorrow. There isn't much time left. If Nicholas intends to settle the matter before we leave, you'll have to tell him the truth—that you've changed your mind. If I were you, I shouldn't bring Grant into it. You may change your mind about *him* before the autumn."

Cathy said, "You don't believe I do love him, do you? You don't think I'm capable of love?"

"I don't know. I don't think you've known him long enough to be certain of anything. Now we'd better finish dressing."

They dined at a small sea-food restaurant. Maria had invited a friend to join them. He was a commercial artist called Mikailis—his surname was unpronounceable to non-Greeks—and he was also a natural comedian, with a fund of humorous observations. He made the party seem very gay, and even Grant was convulsed by his hilarious but not unkind anecdotes about American tourists' reactions to the marvels of Greece.

Cathy was very subdued that night, though for a time this was not noticeable because of Mikailis's jokes, and the delicious red mullet which was the place's speciality. However, towards the end of the meal, Grant noticed that Cathy lacked her usual sparkle.

"Is anything wrong, honey?" he asked.

"No, no, of course not," she said hastily, flickering a troubled glance at Nicholas who, at that moment, was talking to his cousin.

Grant leaned closer to her, and murmured something in her ear. Instead of giggling and fanning her lashes, as she had the night before, Cathy shifted uncomfortably. When, unobtrusively, he slipped his arm round her waist, she wriggled and gave him a look which said clearly—"Don't!" Poor Grant was mystified, Lucia saw. But while she was sorry for him, she could not feel much sympathy for her sister's dilemma.

After dinner, they set out to see the Parthenon. The *Son et Lumière* performances did not start until May and, normally, the Acropolis was closed to sightseers at sunset. But on four nights each month when the moon was full, it was open from nine until midnight and, according to Nicholas and Maria, these were the best hours to visit it. During the day, it was always overrun with tourists, not to mention photographers, and touts selling postcards, sponges and tawdry souvenirs.

During their time in Athens, Lucia had become accustomed to the sight of the great limestone rock—a natural fortress—towering above the surrounding city. But as, squeezed in Maria's car, they drove up the winding way to the entrance below the Propylaea, she felt a mounting excitement at the thought that, presently, her feet would tread where, in the fifth century before Christ, Pericles had walked... and Socrates, Euripides and Hippocrates. Men whose names would live for ever, men who had changed the world.

To reach the "upper city", they had first to pass beneath the immense Doric columns of the Propylaea, where the stones were still marked by chariot wheels. Nicholas took them to the little temple Niké Apteros, where they could see right across the city to the sea, and the islands of the Saronic Gulf. Then they returned to the Propylaea from where the Sacred Way led up to the Parthenon.

As the party included three people who knew the Acropolis well, and three who had never seen it before, it was natural that they should separate into pairs. And it was by accident rather than design that Mikailis fell into step with Grant, and Maria with Cathy—leaving Nicholas to be Lucia's guide.

Long ago, the Sacred Way had been lined with statues. But now the slope to the summit of the plateau was scattered with slabs of rock and broken pillars. Nicholas took Lucia's arm to steer her among them. It was probably the last time he would ever touch her, she thought.

He said, "By the way, I had a letter from Sofia this morning. You will be glad to know that all is well in *that* quarter."

She did not miss the slight emphasis. She said, "Yes, I am—very glad."

Apart from pointing out the place where, when the Parthenon was new, Phidias's great ivory and gold statue of the virgin goddess Athena had stood, he did not spoil her wonder by priming her with facts and figures. She already knew about the subtleties of the architecture, but nothing she had read had prepared her for the eternal splendour of the tapering moon-silvered columns.

Yet, in a way, its atmosphere chilled her, for it gave her a crushing sense of insignificance and loneliness. It was a place full of nameless ghosts—people who had once been young and vital, but whom, like Helen, time had turned to dust. Lucia wanted to put out her hand and feel the reassuring warmth of living flesh. But only Nicholas was near, and he was deep in his own thoughts, and as unapproachable as a stranger.

ON THEIR LAST DAY in Greece, they picnicked under a plane tree somewhere among the foothills of Mount Hymettus.

"I fear it will not be many years before all this is built over," said Maria regretfully, looking at the spring carpet of anemones which surrounded them. "What a pity you must leave tomorrow. If you could have stayed another week, we could have taken you to Delphi. But that must wait until next time..." She yawned, and lay down to doze.

"I'm going for a stroll. Will anyone join me?" asked Nicholas.

"It's too hot to move," said Cathy. She disliked picnics, but was making some effort to hide her boredom, although she could not conceal her nervousness whenever one of the many bees flew near to her.

He glanced at Lucia, and raised an interrogative eyebrow.

She knew he was only being polite, and shook her head. "No, thanks. I'm going to have a nap, too."

"As you please." With a shrug, he walked off.

Maria made an odd, hissing sound.

"What's the matter?" asked Cathy.

"It is nothing...something has bitten me," said Maria, a trifle irritably.

When they returned to her house, Grant was waiting for them in the courtyard. At the sight of him Cathy brightened. Then she recollected her sister's warning, and hastily veiled her eagerness.

Maria chose to stay at home when the other four went out to dinner that night. Lucia, too, would have preferred a quiet supper at the house, but Cathy and Grant were eager to go out, and Nicholas also seemed in a restless mood.

It was not a convivial dinner party. Nicholas made no effort to be sociable, and to Lucia the food tasted like sawdust. Cathy was outwardly gay but, from time to time, she flickered a troubled glance at Nicholas. No doubt she was afraid that, before the evening was over, he would contrive a tête-à-tête with her.

While they were having coffee, and discussing where to go next, she left the table to go and powder her nose. The two men stood up and watched her walk away, Grant with admiration in his eyes, Nicholas with a look Lucia could not read.

Grant said, "Look, as this is our last night, why don't we split up for the rest of the evening? I'm sure you'd both be as glad of some time alone as we would." He grinned. "The English certainly are experts at hiding their feelings! I would never have guessed about you two if Cathy hadn't told me."

There was a moment of incredulous silence. Then, while Lucia was still aghast, Nicholas said, very quietly, "What did she tell you?"

"That you and Lucia feel the same way about each other as Cathy and I do," answered Grant, slightly puzzled. "Say, you aren't mad at her for telling me, are you? I know it isn't official yet, and she did say not to pass it on. But it was okay for her to tell me, wasn't it?"

Lucia did not know where to look. But it was not personal embarrassment which made her face burn. Her pain and anger were for Nicholas. If Grant's thunderbolt had shocked her, what must it have done to him? He might not be showing it—she did not dare even to glance at him—but, inwardly, he must be reeling.

It was at this point that Cathy reappeared. Unaware that anything was amiss, she sauntered back to the table, smiling at Grant as he sprang up to draw out her chair.

Nicholas also rose. "I think you're right, Wallace. We should split up. You have no objection, have you, Lucia?"

She looked up at him then, and marvelled at his self-control. Even she, knowing his state of mind, could not see any sign of stress in his expression. But his calm was not reassuring. It alarmed her more than if he had shown some reaction. She had a dreadful feeling that, at any second, his control might snap, and something appalling would happen.

"No...no," she said quickly, "I don't mind." And she picked up her bag and rose, anxious to leave with all speed.

"Where are you going? Why aren't we coming?" asked Cathy.

Nicholas moved round the table, and put his hand under her chin, tilting her face up to his.

"You're not very good at keeping secrets, are you?" he said softly.

"W-what do you mean?" Cathy stammered.

"You told Wallace about us...about Lucia and me."

Her pretty face drained of all colour. She looked guilty and frightened, and then appealing. Clearly, she was terrified that he was going to tell Grant the truth—that she was a liar and a cheat.

Beside them, Lucia held her breath. She felt no pity for Cathy. If he did, it was no less than her sister deserved. But, for his sake, she prayed he would not. If he vented his feelings now, in front of them all, it would intensify his humiliation later on.

To her infinite relief, Nicholas's command of himself was not yet strained to its limit. He released Cathy's chin and stepped back. "It doesn't matter," he said, shrugging. "Are you ready, Lucia? Shall we go?"

Her haste to get away made Lucia clumsy. As she walked out of the place ahead of him, she bumped against a chair and dropped her bag. He took a swift stride forward, and bent to retrieve it.

"Thank you," she murmured huskily.

He paid the bill, and had a brief exchange with the proprietor in Greek. Then, at last, they were safely outside in the darkness of the narrow street.

"Are those shoes comfortable? Can you walk a short distance?" he asked, in a level voice.

She nodded and, side by side, they began to walk

away from the restaurant. When they had gone a little way, he halted for a moment. In the brief flare of matchlight, she saw that his hand was so unsteady that he had difficulty in touching the flame to the tip of his cigarette.

CHAPTER EIGHT

HER HEART CONTRACTED with compassion for him. She would have given anything to be able to help him, to offer some comfort. But all she could do was to relieve him of her company as soon as possible.

So she said, in a brisk, flat tone, "I feel rather tired. If you could put me in a taxi, I'll go back to the house, and go to bed early."

Nicholas did not answer. But presently they came to one of the busy thoroughfares where it was not long before he was able to hail an empty cab.

Lucia expected him to say goodnight then and there. When he followed her into the taxi, she said, "Oh, please... it isn't necessary for you to come with me. If you'd just tell the man the address..."

"I want to come." He spoke to the driver, then settled back in his corner, and turned his face to the window.

It was some time before she realized that they were not on the way back to the house. She glanced at Nicholas, but he was still staring out of the window, and all she could see of his face was the line of his temple and cheek. She did not understand why he had not seized the chance to be rid of her, but she decided not to say anything.

When the taxi stopped, she saw that they were at the entrance to some public gardens. Nicholas helped her out of the car, and paid the driver. Then, his hand under her elbow, he led her into the park.

There were a number of people strolling about the main avenues, but he followed a path which led to a deserted part of the gardens, and to a fountain pool ringed by a paved walk. There, without speaking, he sat down on a marble bench, and lit another cigarette. This time his hand was steady, but she could tell by the way he smoked that his nerves were still taut.

It took her some minutes to brace herself to break the silence. In a low voice, she said diffidently, "Nicholas... I'm so sorry."

He was watching the falling water, and she thought he had not heard her, or was deliberately ignoring her.

Then he turned his head, and looked at her. "Are you, Lucia? I should have thought you would be delighted."

"Oh, no, how can you say that?" she protested distressfully. "I know I opposed you at the beginning, but that was a long time ago. I never would have wished for *this* to happen."

"I was afraid it wouldn't."

"*What?*" she could not believe she had heard him correctly.

"I was afraid it wouldn't happen," he repeated calmly. He dropped his cigarette and ground it under his heel. Then he took off his jacket. "Here—you'd better put this on, or you may get chilled." He draped it round her shoulders. "In my opinion, Cathy and young Wallace are very well suited," he went on. "I believe she is genuinely fond of him."

"But *you* love—*you* want her!"

"My dear girl, it wouldn't worry me if I never saw her again. Had it not been for the fact that I had to see her to see you, your sister and I would have parted company after a couple of dates."

"What?" she exclaimed, for the second time. "Oh, Nicholas, you don't mean that. You don't have to pretend to me. I know you love her. I heard you say so to Sofia."

"You heard..." he began, frowning at her. "What is all this? What d'you mean?"

She told him, and saw his frown clear. To her amazement, he laughed.

"Great Scott!" he said, grasping her hands. "This has been a tangled web, hasn't it? You little goose—it was you I was talking about. Cathy was "the fly in the ointment". Cathy was the maddening stumbling block. But for her, and your stubborn, misguided loyalty to her, I would have asked you to marry me long before this." His fingers tightened. "Don't you understand?—I love *you*, Lucia Gresham."

For an instant, it seemed to Lucia that she must be either mad or dreaming. Perhaps she had drunk too much wine, and the night air had made her intoxicated. Perhaps she was ill, and this was some kind of delirium.

"You do love me, don't you?" asked Nicholas.

And then, without waiting for her answer, he pulled her into his arms, and kissed her.

There was nothing dream-like about his kiss. It was even more shattering than that other one, on the day of the picnic on the island. And this time, when it was over, he did not thrust her away, but merely slackened his hold a little.

"Yes, you love me," he said, with a smile in his voice. "It's no use denying now, my darling. You've committed yourself. You can't say you don't like me now—not after the demonstration."

She said, in a small, breathless voice, "I've always liked you—well, almost always. I—I found I couldn't help myself."

"You did a good job of hiding it," said Nicholas dryly. "There were moments when you almost convinced me. I never had any doubts about attracting you—but love is another kettle of fish."

Lucia drew back and stared at him. "You never doubted that you attracted me? Oh, of all the arrogant—"

"Isn't it true?" he cut in.

"Certainly not," she retorted.

"I was always attracted to you," he replied imperturbably. "I wanted to do this"—kissing her neck—"the second time we met. If you're honest, you felt the same way. Oh, you would have pretended otherwise. I daresay you would have hit me, or kicked my shins. But, deep down, you would have enjoyed it as much as I would."

"In that case, I wonder you didn't try it, instead of only threatening to," said Lucia, recovering her spirit. "You told me often enough that I wanted you to kiss me, but you never actually tested your theory. At least, not until that day on the little island."

"Yes—and what a fiasco that was," he commented wryly. "The moment I touched you, you froze. You were as unresponsive as a statue."

"Well, for one thing, no one had ever kissed me like that, and it was rather overwhelming," she admitted frankly. "The second, more important reason was that I thought you belonged to Cathy. It was bad enough wanting you to kiss me. To...to enjoy it would have been worse."

"The trouble with you is that you have too many scruples," he told her. "If Cathy and I had been engaged, I could understand your feeling guilty. But Cathy's only interest in me was a mercenary one. You must have known that—I did."

"Yes, I did know that," she admitted. "But how was I to know what you felt? At first, I thought your intentions were strictly dishonourable. Then, when you invited us here, I concluded you must be serious. You did say, if you remember, that you had a particular reason for wanting us to come to Greece. You also said that you had changed your tune, and in future Cathy would be safe with you."

He touched her cheek with his knuckles. "If I had realized how obtuse you could be, I would have been more explicit. My 'particular reason' was that I wanted you to see my house, and the island. I wanted us to get to know each other. When I said that Cathy would be safe with me, I was trying to make it clear that there was no longer any emotional involvement between us."

After a pause, he added, "Not that we ever were as deeply involved as you assumed—or as she may have implied."

"You looked *very* involved the night we met," she reminded him.

"Yes, I suppose it must have seemed so to you, but actually it was the first and only time I ever kissed her. Do you believe me?"

Lucia slid her arm round his neck. "Darling Nicholas, I don't care how many girls you've kissed—as long as I'm the one you want to marry."

As a result of this statement, it was some time before either of them spoke again.

Eventually, he said huskily, "I think we had better not stay here, or I may forget that we aren't even formally engaged yet. You don't want a long engagement, do you? Can't we get married right away?"

Lucia came down to earth. "Oh, Nicholas, not right away. I must give at least one term's notice."

"That need not stop us getting married. There's no rule against it, is there? It would mean postponing a proper honeymoon, but I wouldn't mind that, would you? We've no problem about where to live. My flat will do for the time being. With a special licence, we could be married next weekend."

"Darling, that would be heavenly—but you must see it isn't possible. What about Cathy? I can't leave her alone in our house. She wouldn't be able to cope on her own."

"Confound Cathy!" he said impatiently. "She's caused enough trouble already. Why can't she move to a hostel for a few months?"

"Yes... that would be a solution," she agreed. "But even so it would take time to find somewhere suitable.

Then there's the question of what to do with the house and—oh, any number of things."

He held her face between his hands. "Do *you* want to wait?" he asked quietly. "Are there still some doubts in your mind? Do you want more time to be sure?"

The night was so bright that she could see his expression as if it were day. His eyes were narrowed and intent. The moonlight accentuated the strong bone structure of his face, and the lines of humour and experience engraved on his Greek-dark skin. In some ways, he was still a stranger. There were many things she had to learn about him. yet of one thing—the most important—she had no doubt. She loved him with the same passionate certainty that Maria had felt about Raoul.

"I'll marry you tomorrow, if you like," she said, in a whisper.

He gave her a quick, hard kiss, and drew her to her feet. "No, you're right. We'll wait until the summer. I'll arrange my affairs so that we can have the whole of August alone together. Not at Marina—the islands are too hot for most people in August. Come on, let's go and tell our news to Maria."

They walked back to the house and, although it was a considerable distance, it seemed only a short way to Lucia. With her hand in his, she could have walked the streets till daybreak.

As they were passing the windows of a jeweller's shop, he stopped to look at some rings. This reminded her of the blue medallion.

"Nicholas, I'm sorry I was so hateful to you that morning at your cousin's shop," she said contritely.

He grinned, and squeezed her hand. "You were hateful on several occasions. Fortunately, I have a magnanimous nature. Providing you promise to be a docile, submissive wife, I can overlook your past shrewishness. Do you want to choose your engagement ring, or would you like to be surprised?"

"I think we had better choose one together, or you may buy something wildly extravagant which I shall be terrified of losing. Anyway, my hands aren't elegant enough to show off anything too grand."

"Nonsense—your hands are charming," he said, raising the one he held, and kissing the back of it. "You know, your humility is almost as irritating as Cathy's vanity. She is not as irresistible as she imagines, and you are far too modest about yourself."

She said, with an innocent face, "I suppose I must have something special about me to have attracted *your* attention."

His mouth twitched. "Precisely."

"Oh—and you call Cathy vain!" she remonstrated, trying to sound shocked, but spoiling the effect by laughing.

How lovely it was to laugh *with* him, she thought, as they strolled on. How strange that, at the beginning, she should have disapproved of the wicked glint of amusement which seemed always to lurk in his dark eyes. She had thought him flippant, a man who mocked anything and everything. Yet now his teasing delighted her, and made her feel that it was she who had always taken life too seriously. How stiff and censorious she had been, judging him before she really knew him.

When they reached the house, they found Maria had gone to bed. But a light was still on in her room, and when Nicholas tapped on the door, she answered, "*Embrós*."

They found her sitting up in bed, reading. She took one look at their faces, and exclaimed, "Ah... *thávma!* At last all is well between you. I am very glad. *Brávo*, Nico!"

"You know?" he said, raising an eyebrow.

"One has only to look at you." She held out both hands to Lucia. "So! You took my advice? I was right, was I not? He needed very little encouragement?"

Before Lucia could answer, he said, "What advice? What are you talking about, woman?"

Maria told him, looking pleased with her part in the satisfactory conclusion of the affair. Then, smiling, Lucia explained to her that her well-meant intervention had actually made matters worse.

"You thought Nico loved your sister?" the Greek woman said incredulously. "Oh, how could you be so foolish? It was plain from the moment you arrived that his eyes were only for you."

"Plain to everyone but Lucia," said Nicholas dryly. "You should have been more direct, Maria." He looked at Lucia with a blend of tenderness and mockery. "Unfortunately, my betrothed is rather dense. It is no use giving her subtle hints. She has to be told in so many words. However, I think I have managed to convince her now."

Lucia blushed, and laughed. Catching sight of her reflection in the mirror on Maria's dressing-table, she was startled by the change in her appearance. A few hours ago, when she had been getting ready to go out, she had looked tired and strained. Now her eyes were shining, and her face glowed with the best cosmetic of all—happiness.

Nevertheless, she could not help tensing when, some minutes later, they heard a car drawing up in the street below, and she guessed that it was a taxi bringing Cathy home.

It was some time before the taxi departed, and her sister came slowly upstairs. Nicholas went to the door, and called her into his cousin's bedroom. Only then, as she saw the apprehensive look on the younger girl's face, did Lucia realize that Cathy, not knowing the consequence of Grant's blunder, was expecting Nicholas to upbraid her for her subterfuge.

"Come and join the party," he invited, as she hovered nervously on the threshold.

"The party?" she echoed.

"It will be a party when I've fetched a bottle and some food." He smiled across the room at Lucia. "I don't know about you, but I didn't enjoy my dinner much."

It was Maria who announced the reason for the celebration. "Nico and Lucia are to be married."

"*What?*" Cathy looked dumbfounded. "Oh... y-you can't be serious?"

"Never more so," said Nicholas, taking Lucia's hand in his.

The gesture seemed to convince Cathy that they were not playing an elaborate joke on her. "W-when did this happen?" she stuttered.

"It began a long time ago," he said.

For an instant Lucia was afraid that, when she realized he was lost to her, Cathy might want him back. But as her sister recovered from the first shock, her second reaction was a look of unmistakable relief. It was typical of Cathy to think first of herself, and to see at once that this astounding development absolved her from the recriminations she had been expecting.

During the weeks that followed their return to England Lucia sometimes thought how wretched the summer would have been for her if things had turned out differently. One day, perhaps, she would be able to take happiness for granted, but, for the present, it was still new and wonderful.

Several times a week, Nicholas took her out. They went to theatres, smart restaurants and dinner parties, and led such a gay life that, one night, she protested at his extravagance, and asked if he would not rather spend a quiet evening at his flat, listening to records and talking.

"I thought you did not approve of girls going to bachelors' flats?" he said quizzically, evidently recalling something her sister had told him.

"It's different when they are engaged."

"Yes—much more unwise," he said, kissing her.

"When we're alone, I don't want to listen to records. I want to make love to you. It's better for us to spend most of our time in public places. Besides, you have never had a gay time before, and it won't last long. I warn you—once we are married, all this gadding about will end. I shall spend my evenings relaxing at home, and you will be busy knitting for the first of our many children. You'll be lucky if I take you out a couple of times a year."

"I shan't mind," she said cheerfully.

If Nicholas had mooted a plan to live in South America it would not have perturbed her. Anywhere with him would be home.

It was only now, when already he had relieved her of most of her cares, that she realized how heavily they had weighed on her, and how deeply lonely she had been.

During June, they spent several weekends looking at houses in the country.

"I think Cathy really has changed," said Lucia, one hot Sunday afternoon, when they were driving out of London on one of these expeditions. "I asked her if she would like to come with us today, but she wants to answer a letter from Grant. She hasn't had a date since we came home, and he writes reams every week. So it looks as if they will get engaged when the Wallaces come to England in September."

As July passed, Lucia became as impatient as the children for the term to reach its end. On her last day at school, her colleagues presented her with a coffee service, and her class gave her a pretty tray. She was touched by their gifts and good wishes, but she felt not the smallest regret at giving up her career.

When, for the last time, she crossed the deserted asphalt playground, she saw Nicholas waiting for her outside the school gates.

"What are you doing here at this time of day?" she asked, in pleased surprise.

"I thought you might need cheering up," he said. "It must be a bit of a wrench, isn't it?"

For the first time that day, she felt a lump in her throat. "Oh, Nicholas, you are sweet to me. I hope I can make you happy."

He said casually, "You'd better, my girl. It's too late for either of us to back out now. In forty-eight hours, you'll be my wife." But the lightness of his tone was belied by the warmth in his eyes as he took her parcels.

Some children from the school were hovering nearby as he helped her into the car.

"Bye-bye, miss! Cheerio, miss!"

Lucia waved. "Goodbye...goodbye!"

The car drew away from the kerb, and she settled herself more comfortably, turning a little sideways so that she could look at the dark-skinned, Greek profile of the man whom, when she first saw him, she had instantly distrusted. Time had proved her wrong. Now, even forty-eight hours seemed a long time to wait to become Mrs. Nicholas Curzon. She remembered the bitter February night when, depressed and worried, she had walked home from the cinema, never guessing that, within a few months, her life would have changed course. But, whatever unpredictable vicissitudes the future might hold in store, she would never again have to face them alone.

THE AUTHOR

Anne Weale has built a devoted audience with her many fine novels. She vows "to continue to achieve a reputation for writing exciting love stories, always with something new in them." She certainly lives up to that reputation in the delightful book *South from Sounion*.